I0646717

The Runaway's RUIN

HELEN BRIGHT

VINCI
BOOKS

By Helen Bright

The Runaway Series

The Runaway & The Russian
The Runaway in Love
The Runaway's Ruin
The Runaway's Salvation

Vinci Books

vinci-books.com

Published by Vinci Books Ltd in 2025

1

A CIP catalogue record for this book is available from the British Library.

Paperback ISBN: 9781036707736

The EU GPSR authorised representative is Logos Europe, 9 rue Nicolas Poussion, 17000 La Rochelle, France
contact@logoseurope.eu

Chapter One

KOLYA

I'd had my warning. We all had. When we arrived home, we were to act suitably scared. Of course, I knew what I was about to see. My wife couldn't wait to send me photographs of my darling daughter all dressed up for Halloween. I have to say; she was the cutest little witch I'd ever seen. And it's not because I have a father's bias. Each of my guards agreed she was indeed the most beautiful little witch that ever wore a pointy hat.

Lily Ivana Barinov is a four-year-old replica of her mother, with the same copper-coloured curls, although she has my ice-blue eyes. She's a smart and tenacious little whirlwind who captures your attention with little effort. Oh, yes. It is safe to say my daughter is the star of our show. And I don't just mean for her mother and me. Lily is adored by everyone around her.

Ivan was smitten from the moment he knew Tess was pregnant. He's always had a lot of time and patience with children, but Lily is his world. They have a bond that even *I* am envious of.

I know that Yannis, too, is jealous of their bond. My friend is *all about* my daughter. The man is obsessed. He flew a designer in to decorate Lily's room in his villa to match her favourite book character, *Anna, The Little Princess*. He even had my tech guys install the same security system they designed for me to keep *his* little princess safe. I have seen more of Yannis in the four years since Lily was born than in all the years I've known him. Yannis says Lily brings joy to his life, along with a sense of peace within his heart, as if she could make everything right in his world.

Yannis had been close to my son. More like an uncle than a family friend. But James is now a very busy man: a twenty-five-year-old who barely has time to come home and see us from his base in America, never mind anyone else. He video calls Lily twice a week, and of course, I see him whenever we conference call for work purposes. Tess, Lily, and I fly over to stay with him two or three times a year, so it doesn't seem so bad for us.

Children become adults, and their need for you diminishes with the passing of time. I couldn't be prouder of the man my son has become, and KOLCAT US is thriving in his capable hands.

My father and elder brother, Yuri, dote on both Lily and James in a way I thought I would never see. Especially from my father. He calls Lily his *zolotse*, proclaiming she's precious to him. His greatest treasure.

Since we lost my brother, Aleksei, and his wife, Talia, in a light aircraft accident over the coast of Monaco, my father hasn't been the same man he once was. None of us has.

I will never forget the day I received the call that they were missing. The coastguard and another rescue team were combing the area below their last reported location for days.

Ivan had met with Aleksei whilst on holiday just hours before, so he was first on the scene. My father and I sent in our own teams, yet in the end, it was just a recovery mission. Although in our hearts, we'd known that from the start. We found some of the wreckage from their plane along with their luggage, but the sea had claimed their bodies, adding even more to our distress.

That was almost seventeen months ago, although it often seems like yesterday. As much as I distanced myself from my father in my younger years, since Aleksei's death, I've felt the need to be near both him and Yuri—despite them being so entrenched in the ugliness that is Bratva.

To that end, I have been pursuing a goal I once had with regard to operating a KOLCAT build site with the backing of the European Council for Business. Last month, I finally received the news that they fully supported my plans, so I purchased a large parcel of land I'd had my eye on in Estonia. With Ivan flying me to the airport, I can be in Moscow with my father within two hours. I'm hoping to convince Tess we need a holiday home there, though that won't be easy.

Sarah's Legacy, the charity we set up over four years ago, has gone from strength to strength. For a time, Tess, Jean, and Karen Foster—a former police officer who'd been involved in the investigation into Sarah's murder—were at the helm. However, due to the charity's success, we had to recruit two more regional managers after branching out into another two cities. Tess and Karen had been studying together on various courses to aid their managerial roles, so they hadn't spent enough time with Jean to notice those first subtle changes.

A member of staff in the Sheffield branch became concerned and alerted Tess to Jean's progressive forgetfulness and other strange behaviour. When we went to see her, she seemed fine.

Jean told us she'd been feeling a little under the weather due to lack of sleep. I wasn't so sure that was the only thing bothering her.

Sharon, the woman who'd been in contact with us, said she was concerned that Jean was acting the same as her aunt when she was in the early stages of dementia. So I left Lucas with Jean in the guise of him helping with deliveries and moving furniture around the office. After three days, he confirmed that Jean was certainly not herself. He said that minutes after she'd begun a task, she'd become confused and unsure of what she should be doing, although it wasn't happening all the time. Sometimes, she was just the same Jean we all knew and loved so dearly.

Tess and I went with her to see her doctor, and when he advised her to see a specialist, I was happy to pay to ensure that happened quickly. After numerous tests, they confirmed what we all feared: Jean had dementia.

Despite medication and help with retaining cognitive function, Jean's dementia was still progressing more rapidly than we expected. Understandably, Tess was devastated to hear this, and so was I. I felt as lost and as helpless regarding Jean's condition as I did with my mother's and aunt's cancer.

If there *is* a god up there in the heavens, he can fuck off as far as I'm concerned. He messes with and takes away the lives of good people. People who believe in him. My brother's wife was a believer; it hadn't saved her when their plane went down.

If God wants to target people, he should take aim at men like Mohammed Riass, the lying fucker who claimed to be a Turkish government minister of the same name. From what my sources tell me, along with other reliable information I have gathered, Riass is a prominent leader of a new breakaway ISIS terrorist group, who've been targeting Kurdish freedom fighters with some success. They've also been involved in terrorist activity along the Serbian border of Albania, and more worryingly for me and my team, Riass had links to a terrorist cell in the UK, which was discovered last year during several counter-terrorism raids. A friend who works for MI5 told me they'd found information on me and my family—photos and regular routines—as well as the main UK KOLCAT build site.

Riass was interested in a new weapon we sold to a Saudi buyer. The missile launcher has the usual long-range capabilities of our previous models. It's an exceptional weapon with changeable ground clearance and two target-width options, making it more adaptable for air and ground-based offensive manoeuvres. B26319-7 is hardly revolutionary in terms of what it can do, but it's easily transportable over most terrain due to its lean build and its trailer's adaptability. It can also be programmed both on the launcher and remotely. Again, that's not unique to this kind of weapon. What is somewhat unique is that the missiles fired can be detonated remotely with targeted precision at any point, which is rarely seen in anything other than nuclear weaponry. I designed the weapon myself, so my team and I will fly over to stay with the buyer, Prince Amir— the Deputy Defence Minister of Saudi Arabia—to give further demonstrations and all the relevant programmable codes. Codes that only one other technician and I have knowledge of.

The new weapon and the plans for the operations base in Estonia have kept me away from my family more than my wife and I are happy with.

Tess wants another child, which I'm more than thrilled about. When I was home last week, we talked about her stopping the Depo injection, but as she'd rightly pointed out, despite not taking contraceptive measures, we'd still need to have sex to make a baby, something we can't do if I'm away with KOLCAT.

I've promised my wife I'll cut my stay with the prince as short as possible, and then I'll take a full month off work. Of course, I'm off to Estonia first. Yet another trip away from my beloved.

I'm lucky to have her; I know this with everything I am. My beautiful Tess has just turned twenty-three. I'm almost twice her age, and it shows.

I shaved off my beard last year and keep my hair short now. I was sick of seeing all the grey creeping in and taking over my face and the sides of my head. It's still there, of course, but I'm not as conscious of it as I was. Tess says it doesn't bother her that I'm older; she remarked that she actually fancies me with grey hair. Be that as it may, I don't feel comfortable with it.

It doesn't help when I know there are younger men who want her. She turns heads wherever she goes, though she still doesn't see her appeal.

I suppose, in a way, we are one and the same, she and I. We both have our insecurities, though I never felt this way before Tess. I feel less confident. Vulnerable. Neither of those feelings sit well with me.

There's a young man working in the Manchester office of Sarah's Legacy who fawns over Tess and looks at her like she hung the moon. It's clear to see he wants her. I'd have said something about it if not for how much it pisses Franco off whenever he's near.

Oh, yes, I know *all* about Franco. I've known he's been

in love with her for the longest time. I knew when he offered to marry Tess to prevent her from going back into care. Some people would think I was crazy to employ a man who's in love with my wife, but to me, it serves a purpose. He's her bodyguard; it's his job to protect her. It's the same with all my guards. But due to how strongly Franco feels about Tess, his senses will be sharper, and his need to protect her much keener. When you love someone so deeply, you don't need to see or hear the danger coming their way; you have a knowing you feel in your very soul. There's no training available to give a bodyguard that same kind of edge. I keep him around because he'll keep Tess safe or die trying. If that makes me cruel, then so be it.

Too bad he's a good-looking bastard.

I trust my wife completely. She's a regular eye-roller when it comes to men flirting with her. It used to make her uncomfortable, but that's changed over the years. It's clear to see she has no interest in anyone else. She looks at me with such love and adoration and, lately, a little sadness, which is why, next month, I will make it up to her. We will take the yacht I bought her for her twenty-first birthday and sail around the Bahamas. We can spend our days together as a family, enjoying precious time with our daughter. But when the sun goes down, Tess will be all mine. I'll fill our nights with passionate encounters, the likes of which we will never forget.

Chapter Two

KOLYA

Two members of my new security team were at the gates of my home in Oxford as we approached. After speaking to Jonesy, they opened them and let us through. One of those guards at the gates today came from Yannis's security team.

Darius Anagnos had wanted to move to England for years. His aunt and uncle owned a cafe in Wimbledon, and he wanted to be nearer to them. His parents had passed away, and his aunt and uncle were the only family he had left. After three years of asking if I would take him, I finally gave in to Yannis's demands. I hired Darius around four months ago, though I still had my team bring him up to scratch. Although he'd served three years in the Greek military, he was nowhere near the level of my security detail.

Ivan and Franco don't get along with him. In fact, I'd go as far as saying Ivan detests him, though most of the other guards and I find Darius to be an unassuming man who follows orders well.

I added five new members to our close protection team when Lily was born, one of those being a female ex-army medic from the US. Her name is Lainey Palmer, and she's as tough as she is beautiful. All my team adore her, and although she's the only female member, she gets along well with every one of my guards.

I brought Lainey in as my daughter's personal guard, and as far as Tess was concerned, I couldn't have picked anyone better. Being both a trained soldier *and* a medic ticked the right boxes, and the fact that she's a natural with children was the icing on the cake.

Mark Rush and Greg Cassidy are another two close protection guards I brought on board. Both are ex-Marines who fit in seamlessly; it's almost as if they've been part of my team since day one. Mark's also an accomplished helicopter pilot, which has come in handy whenever Ivan's been away.

As we made our way up the long driveway, I keyed in Lily's date of birth on my phone, switching on the live camera feed to my home to find out where my darling wife and daughter were. I couldn't locate them anywhere in the extension—where we lived—so I transferred the feed to the old manor house where my guards resided. I found them making their way along the second floor, knocking on the doors of each of our guards' rooms. It was as close as Lily would get to the regular trick-or-treating other children do at Halloween. It's just not safe for a child of mine to do anything so public.

Tess insists Lily has as normal an upbringing as possible, although we had to make several compromises. She'd attended a local playgroup three half-days per week from her being two years old. Initially, the group seemed wary about the guards who had to accompany her. But after I gave them a sizeable monetary donation, which enabled them to purchase new books, toys, and other much-needed items, they readily accepted Lily's protective entourage. The women were particularly fond of Ivan, and I'm told he'd been propositioned by more than one of them. Being a six-foot-eight wall of muscle, his height and build usually intimidated people, but it seemed the mothers and nannies attending Happy Tots Playgroup in Oxford were up to the challenge of taming my Russian behemoth cousin.

Tess said they loved Ivan because he took an interest in the women *and* their children, remembering their names and asking how their weekend went. They liked that he paid attention. Of course, he did have an ulterior motive when doing so.

Each parent/caregiver of Happy Tots was investigated thoroughly by my team, as well as the parents and teachers at the infant school she is now attending. Lainey is allowed to stay in the classroom with Lily in the guise of a classroom assistant/helper. Ivan, too, if he's not guarding Tess.

Andy, another new guard, stays outside the classroom, with Dave guarding the school gates. It's a lot of organisation, but seeing my daughter's smiling face and the constant chatter about her school day makes it worthwhile. I would do anything to make my wife and daughter happy. Anything at all.

Once the car stopped outside my home, my guards and I got out as quietly as possible and made our way to the kitchen, filling our pockets with various sweets and chocolate bars from a bowl Nan had filled in readiness. She had a huge smile, telling me how excited my daughter had been all day. They'd trimmed up most of the house with various *scary* Halloween decorations, and Lily had been wearing her witch outfit since breakfast.

Last month, my father had sent Lily a gift after she'd complained that there were no dolls with the same curly red hair as she had. The doll was the spitting image of Lily, with copper-coloured curls the same size as both her and her mother's and uncannily realistic eyes. I thought it a little creepy if I'm honest, and as it was the same height as my daughter, it wasn't so easy to avoid looking at it. Lily calls the doll Anna, after the princess in her favourite stories. She insists on dressing Anna in her princess gown, which still sheds glitter months after she received it, although, from the photographs in the messages I'd just opened, Anna was also dressed as a witch for Halloween.

My phone buzzed again, this time with a message from Kevin telling me that Lily and Tess were approaching, so everyone went quiet to listen for a knock at the door.

"Trick or treat, a penny or a sweet!" my little darling proclaimed with an excited giggle before knocking loudly.

We all gathered at the door, and right on cue, everyone feigned being shocked and scared as I opened it.

Lily laughed out loud before leaping into my open arms. "It's only me, Daddy. I'm not really a witch. Look—I'm just Lily!"

She took off her black pointy hat and held up her basket full of treats.

"Trick or treat, everybody?"

After giving her the treats I'd pocketed, I gave her a quick kiss, then let her go so my guards could spoil her. Tess stepped into my line of vision, grinning widely.

"Trick or treat, Kolya?"

I tugged my beautiful wife against me, whispering "Treat" before kissing her soft, candy-flavoured lips.

"Later," she replied. "I promise a night full of Halloween treats after the party."

Her amber eyes shone with mirth and a wicked glint that excited my travel-weary body. She pulled away from me and walked towards Lily. Her basket was overflowing with the sweeties she'd been given, so Tess began the task of convincing her to save some of her haul for another day.

Glancing back at the doorway, I found Yannis filming everything on his phone.

"I thought I would capture a few special moments from today so you can look at them when you aren't busy working," he said somewhat testily.

Why did he always feel the need to have a dig at me? He knew my meeting was important. If it weren't, I wouldn't have taken it.

Yannis had been pissing me off lately with his sarcastic remarks and endless visits. Nearly every time I came back home, he was here, giving me grief for being away from my family. Tess didn't like him turning up out of the blue, either. He was supposed to meet us in London so we could all go to the party together, yet here he was again, invading my home life. I would have enjoyed spending time with my wife and daughter before we left.

No wonder his business was doing so poorly. He was never there to do anything about it.

Yannis hadn't told me about the company's problems; I found out from his cousin, who is one of the shareholders. For the past six years, the shipbuilding and hotel empire his father and grandfather created had been losing money fast. It was probably the reason he was so angry with me when I didn't buy one of his shipyards. Although, I did purchase his yacht for Tess's twenty-first birthday a little over two years ago. I paid him ninety-five million euros, an amount that Tess couldn't get her head around. It was already five years old when I bought it, but I knew it was an absolute steal for the spec on that vessel. The yacht was named Princess Annis, but neither Tess nor I referred to it by anything other than *the yacht*. I asked her if she wanted to change the name, but she didn't feel the need.

We'd already sailed to the Cayman Islands, as well as the Bahamas, which Tess adored. She also preferred to stay on the yacht than with Yannis whenever we visited his island, although we did spend the occasional night in his home to appease him.

Like me, Tess values our private time as a family, which Yannis should appreciate. After all, as he so often makes a point of telling me, I should not be missing out on all the precious moments with my wife and daughter.

Before I could give Yannis a clever comeback, Ivan walked into the kitchen from the tech room and told us we'd been granted a 5 p.m. flight time, which gave me just over an hour to spend with my daughter.

Chapter Three

TESS

Nan was busy in the kitchen serving us hot roast pork sandwiches, although Lily and Danny had cheese. Bess hung around the table, begging for scraps again. I swear that dog should have been twice the size for the amount she ate. It didn't help that everyone kept feeding her. She was a master at the *"I'm so hungry because nobody ever feeds me"* eyes. I once saw Ivan cook a twenty-two-ounce sirloin steak just for her.

Lily sat on Kolya's knee, telling him about the new game Lainey and I had been teaching her.

"You have to have lots of squares with numbers in them. It's called scopscotch," she said before taking a bite out of her sandwich. She kept trying to speak with her mouth full until Kolya told her to wait until she'd swallowed all of it. She opened her mouth to show him the bite was all gone before telling him how to play.

"Sometimes there's one square, and sometimes it's two, but you're only allowed to put one foot in each square. And you have to hop—that's when you jump on one foot. Oh, and you have to throw a stone into the square, and then you hop to it and pick it up when you come back," she informed him.

"I remember playing that on the street when I was a little girl," Nan told her. "It's called hopscotch."

"That's what I said, Nan. Scopscotch," Lily replied.

Kolya stifled a laugh before asking, "Do you like the game, Lily?"

She took a moment to consider his question.

"Well, I'm not very good at hopping and balancing. Not like Mummy and Lainey. But I'm better than Ivan because his feet are too big for the squares, and Mummy says if your feet go over the lines of the square, it's cheating."

Kolya looked at Ivan and burst out laughing.

"I wasn't cheating," Ivan protested. He pointed at Lainey and declared, "It's her fault for making the squares too small."

"If I'd made them any bigger, Lily would've needed to do more than one hop to get to the next square," Lainey replied.

"Please tell me someone filmed Ivan attempting to play hopscotch?" Kolya begged, still laughing at the thought of his cousin hopping around.

Franco held up his phone. "I did, boss. Sorry it's jumpy. It's difficult to film when you're laughing so hard."

Everyone around the table scrambled for Franco's phone while the man this was all about grabbed another sandwich.

The thing about Ivan is he couldn't care less what anyone thinks about him. He'll do anything Lily asks without a single complaint. Lily's happiness is more impor-tant to him than anyone thinking he looks foolish or unmanly. And, let's face it, I doubt Ivan could ever look unmanly. With his height, frame, and the plethora of tattoos he's accumulated, Ivan has that stereotypical image of being mean and dangerous, something I know he plays upon when the situation requires it. But Ivan has a softness that he reserves for those he loves. His stunning blue eyes light up whenever Lily's around, and when he smiles, he melts your heart. Of course, I've also seen Ivan's flirty side. When he gives the ladies his *sexy-eyed come-on*, then follows it with that half smile and raised brow... No wonder all the women at playgroup used to fawn all over him. One woman even had the cheek to ask me if I'd ever seen him naked, and if so, was he as big all over as she'd been imagining?

Lily slid down from her father's knee and walked around the table to Ivan. When he lifted her into his arms, she hugged him tightly, saying, "We'll chalk you some bigger squares next time, Ivan. I'll just do more hops."

Ivan smiled, then kissed her forehead. "Thank you, my little Lilypot. You know I love you very much, don't you?"

"I love you more, Ivan," she replied.

My heart always seems to do a little flip whenever Lily and Ivan have one of their adoringly sweet moments. Knowing that someone loves her as much as Kolya and I do is so reassuring. I know if ever anything happens to her father and me, she'll be well taken care of. Lily will never have the same childhood experiences I had. She'll never know what it's like to go without food, warmth, and love.

Of course, there's not only Ivan who adores our little girl. Nan, Jack, Yannis, and each of our guards have a soft spot for her, especially Lainey, Danny, Jonesy, Nate, Kevin, and Franco—the man who helped me deliver her safely into the world. Since that most special time, I've become so much closer to Ivan and Franco. We shared an experience none of us will ever forget. They were my strength that day in so many ways. I love them both dearly and can't imagine my life without them in it.

While everyone else was trying to get a look at the video of Ivan hopscotching, Yannis and Darius—our guard who used to work for him—began speaking to each other in Greek, their voices low. I wasn't having that. It's just plain rude. And to be honest, Yannis had pissed me off all day with his snide comments in front of Lily about Kolya rarely being around, so that was the last straw for me.

"Yannis, Darius, I'll have none of that here. You know the rules. If you want to go off somewhere and speak in your own language, that's fine, but while you're in our company, it's not acceptable. It's almost like you're whispering behind your hands about us. I don't allow it from Kolya and Ivan, so I won't have it from you two, either."

I'd made that rule within the first six months of living here. If Kolya and Ivan switch to Russian, it usually means they're arguing. If they have a blazing row in English, at least I can intervene and calm them down.

Darius apologised quickly, though he looked less than sorry. Yannis smirked at me before saying, "I'm sorry, Mother."

I pushed my chair back from the table and stood as tall as possible.

"I wasn't joking, Yannis. This is my house, and those are my rules. If you don't like it, you know where the door is, which also applies to Darius. Both of you speak good English, so there's no need to revert to Greek while you are in our company. Doing so shows a level of disrespect I find particularly repugnant."

Since having Lily, I've tried to cut back on my swearing, at least in her presence. It helps when dealing with the business side of the charity, too. Karen Foster taught me to take a deep breath and find a word or phrase that's more socially acceptable when dealing with people you'd rather tell to fuck off. Jonesy says I sound like I've swallowed a dictionary, but my husband definitely approves.

Ivan handed Lily back to Kolya and came to stand behind me, resting his hands on my shoulders while Franco moved to my left. The room became unnervingly quiet, apart from the odd rustling of sweet wrappers from Lily, who seemed oblivious to all but her Halloween treats.

"Kolya, I think you should pass your wife some of Lily's chocolate. She appears to be in a mood," Yannis declared with an eye roll. Darius snickered like a schoolboy at his response.

Kolya's pale blue eyes fixed on Yannis and Darius; that icy glare stopped any further snide remarks from his long-time friend.

"I suggest you think carefully before you open your mouth to speak again, Yannis. Aggravating my wife any further would not be a wise move on your part."

"Kolya, you know I didn't mean any harm." Yannis appeared surprised at Kolya's words. He held his hand over his heart. "Tess, my darling, you know me and my sense of humour. I swear I meant no offence."

"Then I suggest you think about some of the offhand comments you've been making today and consider the fact they lacked anything but sarcasm." I rolled the sleeves of my sweater up to my elbows and placed my hands on the table, holding his uncertain gaze.

"I might be a wife and mother now and live a life much different from the one I did as a young child and teenager, but I'm still no pushover. I don't need the man I married or the men at my back to fight my corner. So if you want to take me on, Yannis, go ahead. I guarantee you won't come out of it smiling."

I glanced over at Kolya, who was staring at me, his eyes hooded and filled with lust. Typical! Whenever he sees me get angry over something, it makes him want his wicked way with me. As much as I wanted that to happen, I knew we had to leave soon.

Yannis came around the table and stood before me with a genuine look of regret on his handsome face.

"Tess, please forgive me. I know I've upset you, and I am deeply sorry for doing so. Your friendship means the world to me, and I'd be lost without you in my life. Please… I'll do anything to make it up to you." He took my hands in his before kissing the back of them.

"Anything?" I asked innocently.

"Anything at all."

Chapter Four

KOLYA

"Did you know about this?" Yannis hissed as the makeup artists continued painting our faces.

"I knew she was arranging our outfits, but she never said anything about makeup," I admitted.

Yannis and I had been attending Benedict Grayson's Halloween parties for at least twenty years. My first wife, Catherine, knew his family well; Benedict's father had been their family doctor.

Benedict Grayson was the surgeon who'd operated on Tess when she'd been shot while saving my life. For that reason alone, I will always feel I owe the man.

The Graysons' Halloween parties were legendary; the couple sparing no expense on their Surrey mansion to create a *hauntingly spooktacular event* every October the thirty-first. Well, at least that's what it said on this year's invitation.

Many of those who attended were in competition with one another over their outfits, especially Grayson himself. It was truly a sight to see.

Tess never really seemed to enjoy it that much, even

though she loves dressing Lily up for Halloween, so I told her we didn't have to go this year. Imagine my surprise when she told me she was looking forward to it and had organised outfits for me and Yannis.

We each wore a pair of black dress trousers and a white shirt open to the navel. The artists had worked on our faces first, painting them in a black and white skull design before moving to our exposed chests, on which they painted the word *SOUL* in red and black lettering. Why Tess had wanted us to look the same, I had no idea.

"I've got to get a photo of all this, boss. Kevin will go apeshit if I don't," Franco declared. He took out his phone and snapped away before sending them to Kevin, who would indeed be amused. My tech guy regularly attends those Comic-Con events, where children and adults alike dress up as various comic book characters, and he often sports a whacky outfit, although his partner, Nate, is yet to follow suit. He persuaded Jonesy to go as Batman a couple of years ago and has been working on getting Ivan to attend as Aquaman this year.

"That reminds me, Kolya, you must see the photographs Adrianna took of Lily the last time you came to stay with me. I've already selected a few for the villa, but I'm sure you and Tess will want some, too," Yannis informed me.

"Is she still visiting the island?" I asked.

Adrianna was the only grandchild of Yannis's old housekeeper, Galena, who sadly passed away after suffering a heart attack six months ago.

"Whenever she's not in class, she is there. She asked about moving into her grandmother's home permanently, although I cannot understand why she would want to do so," Yannis replied with a shake of his head, which earned him yet another admonishment from the makeup artist.

"You are neither blind nor stupid, Yannis. Surely you know by now that Adrianna has a crush on you. She's been that way for years. Perhaps she thinks that her being on the island will bring you two closer. She's grown into such a beautiful young woman, as I'm sure you must have noticed."

"Don't be ridiculous, Kolya. I've known the girl since she was a baby, and I grew up with her father. She's just comfortable around me because I was close to her grand-mother, and I do like to spoil her. I've been buying her cameras and photography equipment since she was thirteen years old, after I learned she was interested in the subject, and my guards and I helped create a darkroom in Galena's home for when she visited. Now I pay for her university fees, just as my father paid for her father's."

"How old is she now?" I questioned.

"She just turned nineteen. I took her to the opera in Athens to celebrate her birthday, and we dined at Meltemi afterwards."

"So you took her on a date…"

"It was hardly a date, Kolya. She's studying in Athens, so I collected her after I left the office. The poor girl's been distraught since her grandmother's passing. Besides, I think I will take a leaf out of your book and stick with British women when it comes to dating."

Both Franco and I rolled our eyes at Yannis's attempts to flirt with the pretty young makeup artist, who did nothing but smile and tell him to be quiet and still.

I wasn't sure whether the person making me up was male or female. The artist sported an androgynous look amongst their many piercings and tattoos, and the sound and tone of their voice was neither masculine nor feminine. They'd introduced themself as T, so that didn't help either. I knew Kevin would have researched them thoroughly before they came here, so I wasn't worried about any threats, but I prided myself on being able to read people, and I couldn't get a handle on the mysterious yet talented artist.

I wondered who was with Tess, other than Ivan and Rashid, and if she was having a similar makeover. Finding out I wouldn't get the chance to make love to my wife before the party was frustrating. In my mind, I'd had us ditching Yannis for an hour or so and hitting our bedroom at the hotel for some serious reconnecting time, but as soon as our helicopter had landed, Tess told me I would be getting ready with Yannis and wouldn't be able to see her until just before we left.

Although I was disappointed not to spend more time with her, I had to admit I was intrigued. She'd gone to so much effort to get Yannis and I to look the same, so what on earth was she going as?

When Tess eventually walked into the room, I nearly fell over in shock, and I wasn't the only one. The sight struck me completely dumb.

"Holy fuck! You look so damn hot—in a disturbingly freaky way," Franco exclaimed as he took in Tess's almost terrifyingly sexual appearance. "Sorry, boss, I didn't mean to cross a line, but jeez, what the fuck?"

Franco pinched the bridge of his nose and shook his head. I knew what he meant, so I let his inappropriate appraisal of my wife slide.

Tess stood before us in a floor-length bottle-green satin

gown. It had two splits in the front that almost reached her panties and clearly showed she was wearing black stockings and suspenders. It had a high, wide collar and long sleeves, which tapered to a point and hooked over both her middle fingers. The dress itself was very *"Dracula's bride"*, but that wasn't what drew you the most. They had coloured some of her delightful copper curls black, with small thin snakes and bats winding around them. The makeup on Tess's face was so pale it appeared almost white, and thin black veins surrounded her heavily made-up eyes. Her lips were the colour of a fine Merlot, the dark red such a striking contrast against her pale skin.

Franco was right. Tess did look disturbingly hot.

I'd wanted to spend some time alone with my wife and make love to her before we went to the party, but now, after seeing her appear so sinfully sexual, the need to make love had been replaced with a need to fuck. Hard. Preferably with her looking like the freakishly sensual vision every man in the room couldn't tear his eyes away from. Being near her without being intimate would be pure torture.

Tess sashayed towards me and Yannis with a hint of mischief in her scarily sexy eyes. She held out her hand to Ivan, who followed dutifully by her side. He handed her two black leather leashes with cuffs on the end.

"Tonight, I am the Goddess of Darkness, and you are my soul demons. Kolya, hold out your right hand, and, Yannis, hold out your left. When we enter the party tonight, everyone will know that you are mine to command. I will lead you until we arrive at our destination, then I'll unleash you unto the unsuspecting masses so you can steal their souls and offer them to your goddess," Tess informed us in a powerfully seductive voice.

We'd never attempted role play in the bedroom. It

wasn't really my thing, but after Tess's performance tonight, that might have to change. My cock was as hard as steel, and the urge to touch her sinful body and fuck her senseless was almost unbearable.

"Kolya, your wife is like a walking, talking Viagra." Yannis shifted slightly and winced as he did so. I could sympathise with him on the erection front, but I did not like the fact he was so aroused by my wife.

Tess raised one darkened eyebrow, then declared, "You would be wise not to displease me, Soul Demon, or I will have to bring out my whip."

Yannis groaned loudly, causing the makeup artist to chastise him once again.

"Come here," I demanded, holding out my hand. Instead of letting me pull her towards me, Tess slapped the leather cuff over my wrist. She dropped the leash it was attached to, then stepped out of the way so that T could finish the last of my makeup.

After they sprayed our faces with something to set the makeup, T gave us two bottles of an oil-based cleanser and told us to use throwaway cotton makeup pads or a dark washcloth to remove it. I didn't expect it would come off easily, especially the dark around our eyes.

Tess and Ivan had moved towards Franco. She posed and twirled so he could take photographs of her in the guise of sending them to Kevin, but I knew most of the images would be for Franco's eyes only.

"Tell me, T, will this makeup stay on when I kiss my wife?" I asked.

"It should, but I'd play it safe with just a quick peck on the lips if you must."

"Oh, I must," I insisted in a low, gravelly voice. I walked over to where Tess and my guards stood, then lowered my face to hers. Our lips had barely touched before she pushed me away.

"Behave yourself, Kolya," she ordered. "Everyone looks great tonight and I want to keep it that way."

"I have to hand it to you, Tess. You've made sure we look the part. We'll make quite the entrance at the party, though Grayson will throw a fit if we outdo him," Yannis remarked while trying to fasten the leather cuff around his wrist.

"If you're ready to leave, I'll go and do my pre-flight checks," Ivan informed us. As he passed by me, he snapped a photo with his phone. "I'm sending this to your father and Yuri. They thought Tess looked disturbing, so I can't wait to hear what they say about you."

Chapter Five

Within minutes of the helicopter landing on the grounds of the Graysons' home in Surrey, I had a sudden attack of nerves. Making such a showy entrance didn't seem like such a great idea after all.

Where was Lainey when I needed her?

Both she and Kevin, the Comic-Con king, had helped me pick out the makeup designs and outfits after I'd told them how much I hated attending these Halloween parties. When I told them the reason why, they decided I should bow out of the events in style.

From the first time I attended with Kolya, I'd been treated like some young, stupid bimbo—a token bit of skirt they assumed was only after Kolya's money.

Nearly everyone who went along had known Kolya for years, having been friends with his previous wife before him. Most of them were old money, so a young ex-foster kid from a Yorkshire pit village was a fly in the ointment in their stuck-up social circle. Every time we attended, they did little more than say a polite hello before turning their noses up at me. They'd constantly mentioned Catherine when speaking to me.

Catherine would have loved this party.

Kolya and Catherine made such a wonderful couple.

We always looked forward to seeing what Catherine was dressed as.

I remember the year that Kolya and Catherine came as…

And the list goes on and on and on. The women were so much worse than the men. Surprisingly, the only female I have a half-decent conversation with is my old foe, Caroline Dawson. I'm not saying she and I are friends, but the woman has earned my gratitude and respect over the last few years.

Three years ago, Caroline married Evan Alderly of Alderly Gin. Within weeks of their marriage, she'd contacted me regarding Sarah's Legacy. She'd persuaded Evan to have his company donate some of their profits to the charity. They'd also offered a work placement combined with a funded college course to a teenager in the process of leaving care. I was extremely grateful, yet stunned nonetheless, and asked why she'd wanted to do it. Caroline told me the Dawson family had adopted her when she was six years old. Her birth mother had abandoned her when she'd taken up with a new boyfriend who didn't want kids. Caroline spent two years with different foster families while waiting to be adopted and considers herself lucky to have been part of such a loving family, instead of the life she could have had in the care system.

From that day forward, Caroline and I have been on speaking terms, neither of us mentioning the night we nearly came to blows. Even though she's married, she still flirts with other men, though never with Kolya. She knows I wouldn't tolerate that.

Kolya helped me out of the helicopter and shielded me while I adjusted my dress. I couldn't believe I agreed to the splits in the front going so high. Showing off my body like this just wasn't me. It might be okay for Lainey; she has a dark and even African American skin tone that glows beautifully when it catches the light, and her figure is the perfect mix of strength and femininity—whereas mine is freakishly pale and not as firm lately.

In between taking care of Lily and working on Sarah's Legacy, the gym sessions I'd been doing with Franco and Jonesy had fallen by the wayside, and I'd been so fed up with Kolya being away I'd been tucking into all the goodies Nan baked more often than was healthy. Comfort eating isn't the best idea when you have to wear such a revealing outfit.

While we were waiting for Yannis to exit the helicopter, Kolya slipped his hand through the left split at the front of my dress and twanged the back strap on my suspenders.

"Stop it, Kolya," I protested. "I don't want it to come undone."

"I can't help it. You are my wife, and you're way too sexy for me to resist. I've been hard since you walked into the room looking so temptingly scary. If it was up to me, we'd have never left the hotel, and I'd be getting busy between your legs right now."

I glanced at Franco, who was standing to my right. Even with the loud, incessant whir of the rotor blades, I was sure he'd heard what Kolya had said.

"Keep your voice down, Kolya. People can hear what you're saying," I scolded.

"I don't care who hears me. You are my wife! I've every right to say these things."

Kolya had a wicked gleam in his icy blue eyes. He raised

his eyebrows as if he welcomed me to challenge him over what he'd said. I wasn't sure what had got into him tonight, but I also wasn't about to stand here and argue, especially with the cold October air and the chilly draft from the rotor blades freezing my tits off. Besides, his naughty words and predatory gaze had given me a much-needed boost of confidence. My husband still found me sexy, so I could work with that.

When we entered their home, Benedict Grayson and his stuck-up, bitchy wife, Eleanor, greeted us with enthusiasm, as they always did. The leashes ensured I had both Kolya and Yannis by my side the whole time, instead of the usual separation that occurred whenever Benedict spoke about their squash games. Kolya used to play regularly whenever he was working in London, but due to his increasingly busy schedule, he hadn't had a chance to do so.

I held on tightly to the leather leashes attached to my soul demons; the occasional tug reminding them they had to stay by my side.

"You have to let me know who did your makeup. I might have to book them for next year's party. You all look amazing, don't they, Eleanor?" Grayson gushed.

"Mmm, I suppose they do," she replied, running her eyes over both Yannis's and Kolya's exposed chests appreciatively. "Catherine would have loved how you look, Kolya. You know how much she adored our parties. I remember when she—"

Yannis held up his hand. "Excuse us, Eleanor. I know how much you like to remind his wife that her husband was previously married to your friend, but we'll have to keep moving or Kolya will try to get his hands under Tess's dress again. And while I don't mind being a voyeur in their teasingly sensual show, I would much rather find my own willing partner to indulge in some depraved Halloween-style fornication."

As soon as Yannis finished speaking, he tugged sharply on the leash and led us over to a set of double doors that opened up to a large room with a makeshift dance floor and bar area. The Surrey mansion had been in Eleanor Grayson's family for generations, from what I could gather, and as much as I couldn't stand the woman, she had a beautiful home. I glanced across at the snarky witch, who looked like she was being berated by her glowering husband.

"Who wants a drink?" Yannis asked, gesturing towards the bar.

"I want to talk about what happened with Eleanor," Kolya said. His expression was unreadable because of the makeup, though his posture was stiff and unyielding.

"What is there to talk about, Kolya? Benedict married a royal bitch who was friends with Catherine. She doesn't appreciate the fact that you've moved on and are happy with Tess, so she takes great pleasure in bringing up Catherine's name whenever she finds herself in your current wife's presence. I overheard her at last year's Halloween party and was tempted to say something then. She said that Catherine *never* would have worn such a dress as Tess was wearing, and she knew you must feel her loss keenly when you came to these events, remembering how much she loved them."

Kolya turned my way and asked, "Is this true?"

"Yes. Whenever we come here and you go off chatting with someone, she approaches me, either on her own or with more of Catherine's old friends, and proceeds to tell me how wonderful you and she were as a couple, and how irreplaceable she is."

"Why didn't you tell me?" Kolya questioned. "I would

have said something to her. No wonder you never wanted to come here. I'm so sorry, Tess, let's go home. I didn't want to come here tonight, anyway."

"No!" Yannis said firmly. "Why not stay and watch her suffer? As you can see, due to all the secret planning our beautiful Tess did, we have the best Halloween costumes here. Let's stay and make the rest of the guests jealous. It will give them something to talk about other than inheritance tax and afternoon tea at The Ivy."

I let go of the leash and threw my arms around Yannis.

"Thank you, Yannis. I know Catherine was your friend, too, so you didn't need to stick up for me, but I'm grateful that you did," I told him.

"You do not need to thank me, Tess. I'll always have your back. Just tell me I'm forgiven for earlier. After all, no one wants to piss off a goddess of darkness, not even a soul demon," he said with a wink. The wink looked so odd with his skeletal makeup that I couldn't hold back a giggle.

"I forgive you, Soul Demon." I gave him a kiss on the cheek, then went to unfasten the leather cuff around his wrist.

"What are you doing, Tess? I want to keep the cuff and leash. It might make for an interesting night if I find a woman who is willing to play." Yannis winked at me again, then made his way to the bar.

Chapter Six

KOLYA

I needed a drink, and luckily Yannis had the foresight to bring me a double. The amber liquid warmed my throat yet didn't ease my fury. I never thought I could raise a hand to a woman in anger, but I wanted to cross the room and slap Eleanor Grayson.

"Calm down, Kolya. She's not worth it." Tess placed her wineglass on a table and took my left hand in hers.

"Come on, my soul demon husband. Show your goddess you've still got the moves."

I quickly drained my whiskey and set my glass beside hers. Tess let go of my hand and tugged me onto the makeshift dance floor using the leather leash, then wrapped her arms around my neck. I placed a hand on her upper back and one over her shapely bottom, pulling her tight against me while we found our rhythm to Nina Simone's "I Put a Spell on You".

"Why didn't you tell me, Tess? We've been here every year since we married; you've had ample time to let me know what she was doing."

"Truthfully, the first time she did it, I just thought it was her reaction to seeing you with your new wife. She was Catherine's friend, so it must have been a bit of a shock to her. But when it carried on and she involved her other friends, I knew it was more about me than Catherine. I thought about saying something but decided against it. You've been friends with these people for a long time, though I know it's more so with their husbands. I didn't think a few bitchy comments from their wives should spoil the rare time you get to spend with them in social settings. And let's face it, you put up with Gary from the Manchester office of Sarah's Legacy, even though you've taken a dislike to him for some reason."

"I've told you before; I don't like the way he looks at you. He follows you around, staring at your ass in those sexy-as-fuck pencil skirts you wear," I grumbled.

"He doesn't look at my arse, Kolya. And I rarely wear skirts to work. I've probably only done it once," she protested.

"That's all it needed to reel him in, my darling. I bet he was imagining the tights you wore were stocking and suspenders, like these." I trailed my right hand from her ass to the front of her dress, slipping it through one of the splits until I could feel the lacy top of her stocking. My cock pulsed back to life; our slow, sensual movements encouraging its solidity. I pulled her tighter against me, then turned us around, shielding us from prying eyes, though not from the ever-vigilant Franco.

"Kolya, stop it. People are looking," she hissed.

Nuzzling her neck and ear, I breathed in the delicious, heady perfume she wore, then ran my fingers gently up the inside of her thigh to her silky underwear.

"If I slip my fingers inside, will I find you wet for me?" I whispered in her ear.

"I don't know what's up with you tonight, Kolya; it's not like you to give everyone a show."

I could feel Tess's embarrassment on the side of my face through the heat from her cheek, yet I could also feel her panties growing damp with arousal as I stroked her covered sex with my fingers.

"No one can see us, my darling," I lied, while staring into Franco's watchful eyes.

"Kolya," she groaned, half objection, half longing. I wasn't the only one who needed sexual release.

I slipped two fingers under the elastic of her panties and ran them up the already slick lips of her sex. When she tried to voice a breathy protest, I took her mouth in a savage kiss, silencing her. Fuelling the fiery passion that lapped at my reasoning. Without a care for who could see, I nudged her legs a little further apart and thrust both fingers inside her, pressing hard against her clit with the heel of my hand each time I entered her tight, wet heat. In less than five seconds, Tess was moaning into my mouth, trying to pull away so she could catch her breath.

"Please, Kolya, not here. I don't want anyone else to see me come. Only you."

My eyes left her wanton gaze for a moment and fixed on a glaring Franco, bringing me back to my senses with a sharp stab of possessiveness.

Tess was right! No other man should get to see the look of ecstasy on her face when she comes.

Only me.

Only EVER me!

From the day I took her virginity until the day I breathe my last.

As much as he wants her, Franco will never see my wife in the throes of passion. Didn't mean he couldn't hear her come for me.

On me.

With me.

With that thought tearing its way through my last shred of control, I removed my fingers from the heaven that awaited me between Tess's legs and brought them to my mouth, tasting the addictive ambrosia my touch had created.

When the taste of her hit my tongue, my cock throbbed almost painfully.

"I have to fuck you, Tess. Now!"

She nodded and licked her lips; her chest rising and falling rapidly. I grabbed her hand and led her past all the other couples on the crowded dance floor. I was aware the song had changed but I was too far gone to notice the music or lyrics. We hurried out of the main room towards a small hallway, where we bumped into a most apologetic Eleanor.

"Kolya, Tess, I'm sorry if I upset y—"

"Fuck off!"

She seemed shocked by my swearing. But really, what did she expect from me? In any case, I didn't have the time or patience to deal with her unwelcome and no doubt insincere apology.

Undeterred, she followed us down the hall until we arrived at a small bathroom. I turned on the light, pulled Tess inside, then slammed the door behind me, leaving a startled Eleanor outside.

I locked the door and leaned back against it for a moment, waiting to see what Tess would do now that we were alone. Had meeting Eleanor killed her ardour? It had done nothing to diminish mine.

She licked her lipstick-smudged lips nervously.

"So…?" The word came out breathy, almost a whisper, and most definitely a question. She was wondering whether I'd changed my mind. My raging hard-on and the lust in my eyes seemed to answer that question for her without me uttering a single word.

After a few seconds, her whole demeanour began to change. Tess pulled up her dress, took off her panties, and held them out towards me with the tip of her index finger. My dark goddess smiled seductively, then threw her panties at me. I caught them with one hand and brought them to my nose, inhaling the damp centre of the silky material.

"The scent of your arousal calls to me in the most primal way. It makes me want to drop to my knees and bury my face between your thighs, but the need to fuck you is overriding the need to taste you, Tess. So turn around and hold on to the sink. This might be quick, but it certainly won't be gentle."

I stalked towards her, predator to prey, and like a meek little lamb, Tess complied with my request. But when I came up behind her and looked in her eyes through the mirror, I saw confidence and strength staring back at me. Just like the goddess she had professed to be.

Dark. Sensual. Eager to take what I had to give.

I pulled up her dress till it was bunched around her waist, then ran my hands over the pale skin of her ass cheeks, nudging her legs a little further apart as I did so; then I freed my erection and ran the head between her folds, gathering enough slickness around my cock so I could slide home with relative ease.

My eyes closed unbidden while I savoured the blissful, euphoric feeling I experience every single time my hard flesh invades her willing body. I opened my eyes to see Tess staring back at me through the mirror expectantly. The dark, cleverly made-up veins around her amber eyes didn't detract from the heavy-lidded lustful need I saw so clearly. My wanton wife was anticipating the rough I'd promised, of that, I had no doubt.

Even though she still wore heels, I had to bend at the knee as I built up an almost punishing rhythm, fucking her harder with each thrust. Tess lowered her face to her arm, muffling her sounds of pleasure. I didn't want that.

I wound her hair around my fist and pulled slightly, lifting her head a little so I could clearly see her reflection in the mirror above the sink. The makeup we wore and the fact that people might hear us added a kinkier edge to our passionate encounter, and in no time at all, I felt the familiar build to climax. I stopped abruptly, causing Tess to moan with frustration.

"Why did you stop?" she questioned breathlessly.

"I want more," I replied, pulling out of her body and then turning her around to face me. Her dress began making its way down her hips, so I urged her to keep hold of it while I lifted her slightly, setting her on the black marble countertop beside the sink. Then I parted her legs and sank my cock inside her once again, kissing her hungrily, messing up our makeup in the process.

I fucked her slow, yet hard. My knees knocking against the cupboard door underneath the counter with each slam of my hips. A ceramic soap dispenser fell into the sink and smashed when my movements became more frantic. The noise caused me to slow down again for a moment. I pulled away from her slightly and glanced down at my cock as it left the wet heat of her glorious sex.

"Look at us, Tess," I commanded. She watched my glistening, well-lubricated length slide in and out of her body with ease and groaned in pleasure.

"Please, Kolya, don't tease me. Make me come. I need it," she begged.

I kissed her again, thrusting my tongue in and out of her mouth, mimicking the same forceful rhythm happening below while rubbing my thumb around her swollen clit. Tess pulled away from our kiss as her orgasm hit, crying out as her sex clenched around my throbbing cock as I came with her.

"I love you," I whispered, resting my forehead against hers while we both came down from our climactic high.

"I love you, too, Kolya, more than ever. And I miss you so much."

"I know. I miss you and Lily, too. And I promise to take a month away from work when I'm back from Saudi."

Once our breathing had normalised, I heard raised voices outside the bathroom door.

"That sounds like Franco!" Tess stated.

"And Eleanor," I added. I pulled out of her and handed over her panties.

Once we'd cleaned up, Tess looked in the mirror and sighed. Her lipstick had already smudged before we came in here, and the black from my mouth paint had imprinted onto her cheeks, nose and neck. I fared little better, with both red lipstick and black paint bleeding into the white in a most macabre way.

I opened the door to witness an argument between Franco and Eleanor. Ivan looked on with mild amusement —if the smirk he wore was any indication. Dave stood behind Franco with his arms folded, his expression unreadable.

Eleanor turned towards us, giving Tess a disgusted look.

"How could you?" she yelled.

"How could we what, Eleanor? Fuck like rabbits in your bathroom?" I leaned in as if to whisper in her ear, yet spoke loudly enough to be heard by those nearby. "You might want to clean up in there. Sex that good can often get a little messy."

"I want you off my property, immediately!" Eleanor declared. If looks could kill, I wouldn't be breathing; such was the rage and pure hatred in her eyes.

"With pleasure," I replied, chuckling at the way her cheeks turned a mottled red as she tried to control her fury.

I signalled to my guards it was time to leave, taking my wife's hand in mine as we walked away. When we got to the door of the hallway, I glanced back at a visibly shaking Eleanor.

"By the way, you'll be pleased to note your precious Catherine never did that," I told her, nodding towards the bathroom.

Chapter Seven

TESS

Instead of flying back to the hotel—which meant us waiting around on Eleanor Grayson's lawn while our earlier-than-scheduled flight back to London was approved—Ivan suggested we fly back home to Oxford. Yannis and his guard would have to make their own way back to the hotel, though we weren't sure he still intended to go. According to Kolya, his best friend was onto a sure thing, so he probably wouldn't have been coming back with us, anyway.

I was happy to be going home. It meant we'd get to be with Lily first thing in the morning. Kolya felt as though he'd missed out on spending quality time with our daughter lately, so it would be good for him to be there with her when she woke up.

Lily seems to be growing up so quickly. She changes so much from week to week. And it's not just her height and baby-faced appearance I'm talking about; her speech and her behaviour have changed, too. She's a proper little girl now, one who rules the Barinov household with a sweet smile and a sassy yet loveable personality.

It seems like only yesterday when she said her first words and learned to sit unaided. The years are flying by, and as much as I love each and every new milestone she achieves, I do miss baby Lily. She's so independent already; God knows what she'll be like two years from now.

I worried I wouldn't be ready for a baby when I found out I was pregnant, but I've loved every minute of being a mum. I couldn't wait to do it all again.

My Depo injection was due on Monday, but I'd decided not to go for it. We wanted to try for another baby and, fingers crossed, I hoped to be pregnant within the next few months. I couldn't wait until Kolya was finally back from Saudi; we were going to spend a full month together. No work for either of us. Perfect!

Kolya held my hand in his and kissed the back of it. I leaned into his shoulder and closed my eyes, letting the warmth of his body and the gentle swooping of the helicopter soothe me. He'd been kissing me like he was ready to go at it again as I'd adjusted my seat belt, but I think he made our guards a little uncomfortable, especially Franco, who'd exchanged seats with Dave before we left. He sat up front with Ivan, and I couldn't help feeling sorry for him. Franco had borne the brunt of Eleanor Grayson's anger while Kolya and I were oblivious to all but each other.

Ivan seemed to think the whole thing was incredibly funny, laughing in Eleanor's face while blocking her from running after us, yet Dave was as impassive as always. Franco, on the other hand, seemed both angry and upset. I made a mental note to speak to him about it on Monday while we were on our way to Yorkshire. He and Ivan would be accompanying me to the Sheffield office of Sarah's Legacy before heading to visit Jean. I'd have loved to have taken Lily, but her class was having a party for one of the classroom assistants and she didn't want to miss it. Besides, it was so hard to keep explaining who Lily is to Jean. Luckily, she still remembers who I am, though she often forgets my age and the fact that I don't live with her anymore.

When our helicopter came in to land, I had to suppress a yawn. I felt so tired, but I didn't want the night to end. Kolya was due to leave for Estonia the day after tomorrow, so I wanted to make the most of our limited time together.

Kolya unbuckled my seat belt and took my hand in his as he helped me disembark. I hitched up my dress in the other hand, then we ran towards the house, which wasn't an easy task with the high heels I wore. Once inside the kitchen, I kicked them off and graciously accepted the cup of tea Danny handed me. Lainey came out of the hallway and quietly closed the door behind her.

"I was checking on Lily, making sure she hadn't woken up when you landed. She's sound asleep, despite her protesting she wasn't tired earlier."

"Thanks, Lainey. What time did she go to bed?" I asked.

"We finally got her down about eight, after Jonesy read her *Room on the Broom* again," Danny replied.

I have to admit, I loved listening to Jonesy reading all those rhyming stories. I found his Welsh accent and the tone of his reading voice to be quite soothing.

"Thanks for watching her tonight," Kolya said before taking a sip of his tea.

"No problem, boss. Though we didn't expect you'd be back this early." Lainey gestured at our faces. "Your make-up's smudged a bit."

"It appears it wasn't kiss-proof after all," Kolya replied with a smirk.

"Ahh, right. Well, as long as you looked good at the party."

"I can assure you, Lainey, Tess looked amazing," Kolya stated. He placed our cups on the kitchen counter and gifted my lips a soft, sensual kiss.

"I think that's our cue to leave," I heard Danny say.

I pulled away from Kolya and wished them both good-night before they left, thanking them once again for looking after Lily.

Kolya kissed me more forcefully this time, pinning me back against the cupboard as he pressed his body into mine.

"I want you again," he murmured in between kisses. "I can never get enough of you. You're like a drug to me; an addiction I just can't fight. I hope you're ready for our holiday, Tess. I plan on getting my fix morning, noon and night."

"Good luck with the daytime fix. Lily won't want to be away from you. You know what she's like, Kolya. Besides, it should be enough for you just to be near me. We don't have to have sex three times a day," I told him.

"Three times? Is that all you think I meant? Really, Tess, I thought you knew me better than that. I think three times might be enough for a night-time fix, but I'll need more than that to get me through the day."

Kolya smiled in that devilishly handsome way that made my heart skip a beat and my tummy quiver. My husband never needed to use fancy words to turn me on. His sex appeal was inbuilt into his whole demeanour. The way he looked at me, the way he moved; everything about him was just so bloody sexy. To have him as my husband made me the luckiest woman ever.

"You have a silver tongue," I mused.

"I can show you where I'd like to use it," he said, cupping me gently between my legs.

"As wonderful as that sounds, we both need to get this makeup off, and I need a shower. I'll have to wash these black streaks out of my hair, too. I have some makeup remover oil for our faces, but we might need a couple of goes to remove it. I've left the stuff the makeup artists gave us at the hotel," I told him.

"Tess, as long as we're naked and in touching distance, I don't care how long it takes to remove it."

To make sure we'd get the makeup off before we did anything else, I wrapped myself in a towel after I'd undressed. Kolya, however, stood there stark naked and blatantly aroused while he poured makeup remover on a cotton wool pad and swiped it over my face. After every swipe, he kissed me. Sometimes just a tiny peck, though it was mostly soft and sensual. He did the same when I removed *his* facial makeup, but it wasn't until I began removing the words from his chest that things got a little heated.

His kisses consumed me, and I had to pull away to catch my breath. Kolya didn't want to let me go, keeping us chest to chest as he manoeuvred us into the shower, pausing briefly to discard my towel. Once inside the shower, I had no reprieve from the passion and need my husband continued to emanate. It appeared Kolya missed me as much as I missed him.

He placed his hands under my bottom and lifted me while his mouth was worshipping my breasts, his cock teasing my slick opening. Kolya nipped and sucked on my nipples roughly, making me gasp when the sharp bite of pain quickly turned to pleasure. Without warning, he thrust inside me to the hilt. I cried out from the shock of it, along with the blissful thrill of being taken, owned, and loved by the man who held my heart.

Chapter Eight

KOLYA

Lily and I brought Tess breakfast in bed. My poor wife was exhausted after the events of last night. I couldn't keep my hands off her, and we'd been making love for hours before we finally succumbed to sleep.

I awoke early to find my darling daughter climbing into bed beside me. She was holding Anna, that damned doll my father bought her. She loves it because it's the same height as her and its eyes and hair are exactly the same colour. I hate to look at it. To me, its eyes are so uncannily realistic they seem peculiar for a doll. I feel like it's staring at me, and it makes me uncomfortable. Of course, my daughter adores it. She says Anna is her best friend, and I'd had to pretend to give the doll the same breakfast as Lily this morning.

Jonesy knows I dislike the doll and once left it in the car, along with a recording of an evil, freaky laugh playing on a loop. I'm still waiting to pay him back for that.

"Good morning, my darling." I brushed tousled copper

curls away from my wife's face before placing a chaste kiss on her full, pouty lips.

"Wake up, Mummy. Me and Daddy and Anna have made you some breakfast, but I wasn't allowed to make you a cup of tea. Daddy says I'm not big enough yet. When will I be big enough, Mummy? Ivan says I'm growing bigger every day, so I'm sure I could make one now. Do you think—"

"No, Lily. I've told you before about what happens if you spill hot drinks on yourself. When you're big enough, I'll let you know," Tess admonished in a croaky voice.

"Well, I'm good at making pretend tea in my fairy tea set," Lily replied haughtily.

"That you are, *milaya moya*. My sweet girl makes the best fairy tea ever," I told her.

"I'll go and make some for you now, Daddy," Lily replied before dashing off to her room with a beaming smile.

"Has she had her breakfast?" Tess asked before taking a bite of toast.

"She had porridge, and she tried to get me to give the doll a bowl, too."

My wife tried hard not to laugh but couldn't hold it in.

"You do realise she'll be taking Anna on holiday with us, don't you?" she questioned.

"We could tell her the doll has to stay home to keep Nan company, so she won't miss us and get sad?" I suggested.

"Do you honestly think that will work?" Tess rolled her eyes at my pitiful attempt at subterfuge.

"No. But I really don't want her to bring it along. I think it has staring eyes."

"Kolya, it's just a doll; of course it has staring eyes. It's when it starts to blink you should worry," Tess joked. "And

48

if you make her leave it behind, as soon as your dad finds out, he'll probably have another one made and sent to her."

"Then we'll definitely take it with us. There's no way I'm having two of them in my home," I declared.

My phone vibrated in my pocket, and because I was sitting beside Tess on the bed, she felt it. Before she could say anything, I held up my hand to stop her.

"Don't worry, my darling, this isn't about work. Everyone knows I'm spending the day at home with you and Lily." I took out the phone and opened the message, which was from Kevin. I showed Tess what it said.

"Another walkthrough?" she questioned. "Do I have to do it? It's hard enough knowing we have weapons hidden in Lily's room, never mind having to check they're accessible and ready to use."

Tess hates the fact we have weapons readily available throughout our home, and especially in Lily's room. This was something I'd grown up with, so it didn't bother me in the slightest.

We'd always had guns hidden away in the guards' accommodation, and in selected places around our part of the property, but after Lily came along, my team and I decided to have a panel of hidden weapons storage built into her bedroom furniture. We'd continued to implement this in every room in our home over the last twelve months, along with other fail-safe security measures. At the push of a button, I could make the entire extension into a kind of panic room, by sealing it off from the outside with blast-resistant, bulletproof shutters. The technology for this was built into my phone. Not even Kevin could override my command, though he oversaw the design and setup of this amazing tailor-made technology. It even had Yannis's approval. And where Lily's safety was concerned, that was hard to come by.

The only people who know the whereabouts and have access to the hidden weapons cache in the extension are those who spend a significant amount of time here. This includes most of my guards and, of course, James. I did not feel the need to include Yannis. I fear he, like Tess, would disapprove of those in Lily's room and in areas where she plays.

"So what did you promise Lily we'd do today?" Tess asked before taking a sip of her tea.

"We made a list over breakfast," I informed her. "First, we are going to make a card for someone at school, then we have to watch the princess cartoon *again*," I said with a groan. "And after lunch, we are going swimming."

"I suppose I'd better get dressed, then," Tess muttered.

"No need, my darling. Lily has decreed that today is a pyjama day. So, slip on your robe and prepare to be covered in glitter. Our little princess wants the card to sparkle."

About an hour after our Sunday lunch, Kevin, Franco, and Ivan did the weapons walkthrough with Nan, Jack, Lainey, and Danny, while Tess and I went to the indoor pool with Lily.

At four years old, my daughter can swim the width of the pool unaided. She's an exceptionally determined child and quite forward when it comes to learning something new. She's so very precious to me. No wonder my father calls her his treasure.

With so many adults around to give in to her every whim, Lily could have been an overly demanding, badly behaved child, or, in other words, a spoiled little brat. Yet she's nothing of the sort. Lily is a pleasant, caring child who loves and values her extended family more than anything.

Tess makes sure Lily appreciates the things in life that matter, and I'm grateful to my wife for doing so. Yes, Lily does have more toys than most children, but she's aware they're just material things and could easily be replaced, should the need arise. My wife taught her that it's more important to love and value what can never be replaced. A lesson for us all, I feel.

"Daddy, watch me!" Lily yelled as she jumped from the side of the pool into a pink blow-up dinghy. Unfortunately, she clipped the side of it with her leg when she landed, so it flipped over before she could grab the handles on the side, causing her to sink into the water underneath it. With my heart in my mouth, I dove under rapidly, reaching her within seconds, but my clever daughter's head had already broken the surface by the time I got there.

From under the water, I grabbed her legs and held them to my shoulders before rising above the surface.

My wife's laughter rang out through the indoor pool room as I waded towards her with Lily sitting on my shoulders, yelling, "Look, Mummy, I'm the Loch Nest Monster."

Lily never said the name right, no matter how many times we corrected her.

John, the head gamekeeper at Glengarran, had been telling Lily tales of the Loch Ness Monster, which fascinated her. I wasn't happy about it at first because I thought it would scare her, but that wasn't the case at all. Since then, she's insisted she's seen Nessie in the Loch at Glengarran several times. When I pointed out that couldn't happen because the monster lives in Loch Ness, Lily rolled her eyes and said, "Daddy, everyone needs to take a holiday. Even Loch Nest Monsters."

Tess swam away from us, heading towards Lily's upturned dinghy.

"Hurry, Daddy, she's getting away," Lily bellowed before getting me to let go of her legs so she could leap off my shoulders and swim towards her mother.

When she reached Tess, she put her arms around her and gave her a kiss. I watched as they rubbed noses and giggled. It was a heart-warming sight. My beautiful wife and daughter...so happy and full of love.

I swam towards them and joined in with their loving embrace, kisses and nose rubs, vowing to make more time for my family once the next two business trips were out of the way.

Chapter Nine

KOLYA

After our swim, I told Tess I'd bathe Lily and wash her hair while she took a shower. Due to Tess and Lily having the same hair type, I know the work that goes into keeping it tame and manageable. Tess says it's best to deep condition their hair for about thirty minutes at least once a week, and especially after being in the pool for two hours. The things a man learns when living with curly-haired women...

I always enjoy the time I spend bathing Lily. She becomes even chattier when it's just her and me, and she doesn't protest about having her hair washed half as much as she used to.

She told me about a new girl at school who had brown skin like Lainey and Nate but *"doesn't talk like them because she doesn't come from America."* I knew about the girl Lily mentioned, of course. The school had given me her details so my security team could check out their family. I know that goes against data protection, but they understand why I have to know, and the security measures my team needs to take to ensure Lily's safety. I'm sure the regular monetary donations I make to the school ease the headmistress's conscience.

The new girl and her family have moved to the area from South Africa. Her father is a sculptor who works with different metals to create dragons and other mythical creatures. Looking at his past creations in the dossier I received, the man is extremely talented, and his work commands high prices.

Lily also told me that her school was going to practice Christmas songs soon, so we spoke about which were our favourites. I sang one from my childhood in Moscow and told her I would teach her a few to sing as a surprise for her grandfather.

In her playschool's nativity last year, Lily played the part of the Christmas star, guiding the three kings to the baby Jesus. She wore a silver star-shaped outfit that had battery-powered twinkling lights around its outer edges. She was so young, and yet she memorised the words to most of the carols they sang. We were all so proud of her. Tess and Nan had tears in their eyes, and surprisingly, when my father video-called us after we sent him the recording, his eyes were glassy, too.

He told us he felt my mother's presence beside him when he and Yuri had watched it. He still feels her loss so keenly, even after all these years. As much as he encouraged me to remarry, my father wouldn't even consider it. I know he's been with other women since my mother's passing, yet he's never felt the need to make another lifelong commitment. For his sake, I hope he finds someone who can love him, despite his position in Moscow's criminal underworld.

Yuri doesn't have a significant other, either. But then again, his choice of significant other wouldn't be acceptable to my father and many others in Russian society.

My father thinks Yuri's one true love was the ballerina, Nadia Pushkina, who died when a sniper's bullet went straight through her father's back and hit her in the heart, killing her instantly. I knew differently.

Nadia had been Yuri's best friend. She was the same age as him, and they'd been friends since childhood. Nadia's father, Konstantin Pushkin, had been my father's lawyer, as well as a good friend. Nadia knew my brother was gay, yet they went along with the engagement my father and Konstantin steered them into. When Nadia was killed just two weeks after their engagement party, Yuri was devastated. He'd lost the one friend who truly understood him.

My father took Yuri's grief to be the mourning of someone who'd lost his future wife, and he left him alone for a long time. When Yuri hit thirty, however, my father began again with the marriage demands. But even though Yuri went on dates and was often seen with women, they weren't the gender he wanted to be in a long-term relationship with.

He came out to Ivan, Aleksei and me after Lily was born, but he made us swear we would never reveal the truth about his preferred partner to anyone other than our wives.

I would like nothing more than for my brother to find a man he can share his life with, but I fear that will never happen. Not publicly, anyway. Not while my father is alive, and not while Yuri is so fully entrenched in the Bratva.

Lainey came to take Lily to the guards' quarters in the old manor next door, while Kevin and Nate did weapons checks with us in each of the rooms.

In our newly refurbished kitchen, the breakfast bar rises, and the end cupboard panel is a secret door that opens outwards, revealing steps down to a cellar/panic room. We have more weapons down there than in any other room in the house. I've had plans drawn up to link the cellar in this part of the property to the old below-stairs servers' quarters in the manor. The work would mean we'd lose the patio beside the pool while they dug down and created a passageway, but at this time of year, we wouldn't miss it. Tess didn't think it was necessary, and, until recently, neither did I. However, after my run-in with Mohammed Riass, I felt the need to be more vigilant, especially regarding those I care about the most. My wife and children are at the top of that list.

Chapter Ten

TESS

I hate doing the hidden weapons checks. I understand Kolya wants us to be as safe as possible. We all want that. But with all the security we have in our home, I don't see the need to have guns hidden everywhere.

It's not so bad in the kitchen. I think the way the entrance to the cellar is hidden away as part of the kitchen units is amazing. It kind of reminds me of the hideaways at Glengarran. I love pressing certain points in the panelling and decorations to reveal all the hidden doors and passageways. There aren't many rooms at Glengarran that don't have secret passages. It's easy for us to hide weapons there. But here, in our main home, we have to have lockable security measures built into the furniture.

The hidden area in our lounge is under the sound system. The wooden shelf under the speakers lifts to reveal a fingerprint scanner. Once scanned, the wooden unit below opens up, giving us access to two handguns, two semi-automatic rifles, and three magazines of ammunition for each. The same is repeated throughout each room. Kolya made sure one of the rifles in each hideaway was a lightweight Ruger. I've favoured that particular gun since learning how to shoot.

When we got to Lily's bedroom, I voiced my displeasure about having weapons in the place where our daughter sleeps, and once again, Kolya, Nate, and Kevin brushed off my concerns.

"Tess, this is just a precaution. We will probably never need to use them, but I'm sure you'd rather be safe than sorry," Kolya remarked as he opened up a drawer just below the cupboard we keep Lily's spare bedding in. Underneath the drawer is a switch which needs to be pressed and held in for three seconds. That activates the fingerprint scanner. When it recognises your print, the decorative panel below it falls outward, giving you access to the guns and ammo. Kolya took out the handguns and Sig rifle, then closed it back up again so I'd have to re-open it. Kevin made sure everyone who needed access to the weapons in our home did a walk-through and check at least once a month. He did it to check the fingerprint scanner still worked for everyone, as well as to inspect the guns.

So there I was, standing in my daughter's bedroom, wearing my cute Bambi nightshirt while loading a magazine full of ammo into a semi-automatic rifle. Not something I ever envisaged having to do to keep my husband happy.

Since having Lily, being around guns feels wrong. Especially when they're in our home. But with Kolya being an arms developer—who also sells the weapons his company produces—that leaves us open to all kinds of threats and danger.

The face of the man who shot me during the failed assassination attempt on Kolya would be imprinted on my mind forever. As would the face of the getaway driver, Eitan Harel.

Whenever I heard Kolya or one of the guards mention someone they had concerns about, I made sure I researched them thoroughly and committed their faces to memory, just in case. Mohammed Riass was the latest one to have me worried. He was heavily involved with ISIS, and the break-away group he leads claimed responsibility for several recent terrorist attacks. I know the areas and people he attacked are nowhere near the places Kolya does business, but still; he had information on my family and KOLCAT, so I couldn't help feeling worried, and I made sure I memorised *his* face.

As soon as we finished the weapons check, Kolya went to get Lily from Lainey and Danny. He was going to put her to bed and read to her, which I knew would take at least an hour. Lily likes to keep him talking and always gets an extra story.

Kolya's a great dad. James and Lily are lucky to have him.

I never met my dad. I doubt my mum could have been one hundred per cent certain who he was, anyway. When I was a child, I used to dream about a man knocking on our door and declaring he was my father. I imagined him saying he never knew I existed until recently, and as soon as he found out he had a daughter, he'd set out to find me and take care of me. But that never happened. If someone tried to claim they were my father now, I'd wonder if they were doing it because of who I'm married to. After all, being Kolya's wife makes me a very rich woman.

After I showered, I went to Lily's room, kissed her goodnight, and then left her in Kolya's capable hands. Stifling a yawn, I made a cup of hot chocolate and relaxed on the sofa with my Kindle. I was halfway through a paranormal/urban fantasy romance series and couldn't wait to see who the heroine chose to be with out of the two men who were in love with her. One was a vampire, the other a fey prince. Personally, I hoped she'd choose both. I'd fallen in love with both male characters for different reasons, and I couldn't pick one above the other.

I love to read paranormal and fantasy novels. They let me escape from things that upset me in real life—like the fact we hide guns in our home and Kolya having to go away again.

"What are you reading, my darling?" Kolya whispered. He'd sneaked into the room so quietly that I'd jumped when I felt his breath at my ear. He laughed when I leapt up from the sofa and dropped my Kindle.

"Not cool, Kolya," I admonished. "My heart's racing now."

"But was it shock that caused it to race, or are you reading something kinky again?" he taunted. He grabbed my Kindle off the floor and began reading. After a few seconds, Kolya glanced my way, his eyebrows raised.

"You're reading about a threesome," he remarked. "Is that something that arouses you, Tess?" His words were delivered as a question, but his tone was accusing.

"It's not like that, Kolya. She was in a relationship with the first guy, but he pushed her away when he became a vampire, even though he was still in her life. Then she met and fell for the second guy, who is actually a fey prince. But she still loves the vampire, and he loves her, too. The vampire was going to let her be with the prince because he couldn't give her the life he thought she deserved," I explained.

Kolya moved to sit on the sofa, so I sat beside him. I could feel how tense he was, but I couldn't figure out why.

"Then the vampire does not love her. I wouldn't ever let you go, Tess. Not for any reason. If I knew you'd even looked at a man that way, I'd kill him!" he stated. He sounded angry, as if he thought the story was personal.

"Tone it down a bit, Kolya. It's only a story. Don't worry; I'm hardly likely to leave you for a fey prince."

"Death will be the only way we'll part, my love, be it mine or yours. And know this… If you should ever leave this earth, then I will follow. Losing you would crush me."

"Then it's a good job I'm not going anywhere, isn't it?" I put my arms around him and kissed his stubbly cheek. He got like this whenever he was going to be away from me for a few days. Unreasonably possessive. Insecure in our relationship. I've no idea why. It's not like I have the urge or even the opportunity to have an affair. Not with Franco and Ivan guarding me.

"I love you, Kolya. I always have and always will. Nothing will change that. You are my first love, and you'll be my last. Just because I'm reading a story where there's a love triangle and the heroine has a threesome, it doesn't mean I'm secretly fantasising about one. I read a few shifter stories last week, but I won't demand that you howl at the moon."

"I'm glad to hear it," he replied haughtily, though I felt his cheek lift with a smile.

"But if you were up for it, I could let you in on my *Kolya's a vampire* fantasy. I can think of quite a few places I'd like you to bite me," I told him.

"Now *that* sounds like a fantasy I could get on board with," he replied.

Quick as a flash, he twisted around, pinning me underneath him, kneeing my legs apart forcefully. I laughed and tried to push him off, but Kolya was having none of it. He grabbed my hair and closed his fist tight, pulling my head over to the left, exposing my neck and throat.

"You'd bite my neck?" I questioned. "I thought you'd have gone for the femoral artery. I know how much you love being down there."

"But when I bite you here, the whole world will see."

Before I could ask what he meant by that, he began kissing down my neck, licking at my pulse point before grazing it gently with his teeth.

"Mmm, that feels good," I told him. His mouth moved lower to the base of my neck, just above my collarbone. He knew what it did to me whenever he kissed me there. I felt him shift slightly, his hand moving up the inside of my thigh.

"Kolya, not here," I told him breathlessly. He ignored me, uncaring of the security cameras in the room.

"It's okay. Lily was fast asleep when I left her. She won't disturb us."

"I meant the cameras, Kolya. Anyone could see us."

"You know they won't watch. Relax, Tess. Let it happen."

Just as he finished speaking, he slipped his hand down my knickers and began stroking me with his fingers.

"You aren't playing fair," I murmured. His kisses turned to gentle sucking, then he clamped his teeth on my neck and sucked harder.

"Kolya!" I said the word as a warning, but he didn't stop. I felt his fingers breach my folds with knowing precision. He wasted no time down there; he didn't need to. I was already wet and extremely turned on. He began rubbing his fingers around my clit with enough pressure to have me writhing against them, pleasure building with each second that passed.

The orgasm slammed into me and took my breath, leaving me dazed and weak. Kolya let go of my neck and groaned loudly. Even though he wore jeans, I could feel how thick and hard his erection was against my bare thigh. I unbuttoned the offending denim and was pleased to find he'd gone commando. I'd barely touched him before he pushed my hand away and tugged my underwear down, tossing them on the floor. I used my feet to push down his jeans before wrapping my legs around his waist, crying out when he thrust his hips forward, burying his hard length inside me to the hilt.

Our lovemaking was rough, passionate, almost desperate—both of us vocalising our pleasure and love for each other. The leather of the sofa hindered my movements somewhat, leaving me vulnerable, unprotected against my husband's punishing rhythm, which perversely turned me on even more. We came together, hot, sweating, and thoroughly exhausted.

Even though we knew we had to go and get cleaned up, neither of us wanted to move, and when he kissed my lips and told me he loved me more than ever, I was so utterly overwhelmed with emotion I began to cry.

Chapter Eleven

The downdraft from the helicopter rotor blades felt especially chilly in the damp November air. Ivan flew me to Heathrow Airport early so I could check everything was in order before they loaded the missile launcher onto its flight. I had other people who could do this, but there was something so satisfying about witnessing one of your own creations heading off on its *maiden voyage*, so to speak.

The launcher and three missiles were being flown from Heathrow to Turkey, where the ex-military aircraft would refuel before continuing on its journey to Saudi Arabia. The missile's guidance system was being flown directly to Saudi from Frankfurt—the airport closest to its build site in Germany—later this evening. As always, the original guidance system prototype would remain at KOLCAT's principal base here in the UK.

Only I and one other knew the codes for the new guidance system and would pass them on to the prince after he witnessed the first missile strike its target. Prince Amir had decided to use the missile to begin demolition work on one of his many unused palaces. A little extreme, perhaps, but it would be an excellent demonstration, nonetheless. We already had the target ordinance and distance needed regarding programming and missile detonation. I had the plans ready and waiting; they would be my first order of business on my flight from Estonia to Saudi. Three members of my design and build team were flying out from Germany with the guidance system to install and connect the device, making sure everything was ready for the prince's first live demo.

Ivan bid me a safe journey before heading back to Oxford so he could fly Tess up to Yorkshire.

Thinking about my wife brought a smile to my face. I couldn't help but recall the vision of her naked upper body when I kissed her goodbye before I left. She'd slept on her belly, her face turned to the side. I could see the love bites I'd left on her neck, shoulders and back. When I moved the hair from her face and kissed her cheek, she'd mumbled something unintelligible and rolled over onto her back. The quilt had barely covered her breasts, both of which bore love bites, although they weren't as noticeable as those I saw when I adjusted the quilt. Those below her hip bones and on the inside of her thighs stood out in stark contrast to her pale Celtic skin.

Yes, I think it would be fair to say I'd gone a little overboard with the love bites. I knew my wife would have something to say to me after she viewed them in the harsh light of day.

I'd looked in on Lily before I left. She was sound asleep with that damn doll beside her and, thankfully, hadn't heard the creaking sound the hinges on her door had made as I slowly eased it open. I made a note to add a little oil to them when I came home.

After checking all relevant paperwork and watching the plane carrying the launcher and missiles taxi down the runway, my security team and I drove over to where one of my private jets was waiting. Lucas, Jonesy, and Darius would accompany me to Estonia. Mark and Greg flew out last night so they could secure the town hall—the venue in which I'd be meeting the local mayor and an EU council member. As soon as we arrived at our meeting, Mark and Greg would check in with Jonesy, and then they'd make the twenty-minute journey to the new KOLCAT build site, ensuring it met the security measures that Gustav and his team put in place. There would be two armed guards arriving at the site within the hour who would stay to patrol the perimeter until just after I left.

We had a bullet-resistant Toyota Land Cruiser waiting for us at the airport, which I'd had shipped out last week. The vehicle would remain in Estonia for the duration of the build. It wasn't my usual choice to use when there was the possibility of the press being involved when we broke ground, but Lucas had gone over the terrain surrounding the build site and suggested we had a tough, unstoppable four-wheel drive.

As soon as we were airborne, I reclined my seat and closed my eyes, hoping to get an hour's rest.

"Are you okay?" I heard Lucas ask. I opened my eyes and glanced his way. He was watching Darius, who was rubbing his temples.

"I have a headache," he replied without looking up.

"I bet it's a tension headache. You've been jumpy since we left Oxford. What's up? Did you get knocked back by that woman you've been seeing on your days off? Didn't she want to play a game of *hide little Darius* yesterday?" Jonesy taunted. His blue eyes lit up as the grin spread across his face. He was a wind-up merchant of the highest calibre, yet never maliciously so.

"At least he's getting more than you, Jonesy," Lucas laughed.

"You're not wrong there, mate. When we get back from Saudi, we'll have to have a few nights out on the pull. Maybe head somewhere different this time. There used to be a few bars in the capital where you were almost guaranteed to find a good shag at the end of the night, but most of them have closed now."

"Maybe we should head up north? Newcastle is a good night out and there are some fit birds up there," Lucas suggested.

"Don't try to tell me that you two have been through all the single women in London. I won't believe it," I interjected. Jonesy and Lucas shrugged their shoulders.

"It's not the same anymore. Most of the single women are out with dates they've met on Tinder or... some other dating app," Jonesy replied with a dismissive flick of his hand.

"So why not add yourself to Tinder?" I countered.

"You must be joking, boss. Jonesy on Tinder? No one would swipe right for him." Lucas chuckled at Jonesy's shocked expression.

"Lucas, how do you know what to do on Tinder? Are you on it?" Jonesy questioned.

"Why would I be on Tinder? It's for dating, or for those wanting a serious relationship. Been there, done that, and got the fucking T-shirt. I'm not setting myself up to get shafted again. I don't mind having a good time with a woman, but I'm not bothered about making it a permanent thing."

Lucas had married a woman he'd been seeing before he

went into the army. She'd been pregnant with twins, and he'd been thrilled at the prospect of becoming a father. When he got back from his second tour of duty in Afghanistan, he'd found it hard to be part of a family. At first, PTSD played a factor in his inability to settle into civilian and family life. But as time went on, the unhappy couple realised that whatever love they'd had for each other before they married had long since faded.

As soon as he moved out, she became involved with Charlie, his childhood friend. It was something Lucas found hard to deal with, especially on the weekends he collected his daughters.

Two years ago, when the girls were eight, one of them became seriously ill. After medical testing, it emerged that Lucas wasn't their biological father. Obviously, he was distraught. He was also angry to the point of wanting to hurt his ex, but being the man he was, he could never hurt a woman. He'd been paying maintenance for his daughters above and beyond the recommended amount since he and his ex-wife had split, and as far as the girls were aware, he was their father.

He overcame his anger and bitterness with his ex and sat with the little one in hospital until she recovered. Neither Lucas nor his ex-wife wanted to give her the news while she was so ill. Lucas even asked if they could keep the revelation from the girls. He'd been a part of their lives for so long, and he loved being their father. Their mother denied his request, so he went to a solicitor to fight for them legally. That's when he got the news about their biological father also denying him access. His ex-wife had been having an affair with Charlie—the man she'd since married—when she and Lucas had first begun dating. So after being the father of twin daughters for so long, Lucas was told he could no longer be in their lives.

His legal team informed him he could claim back the child maintenance payments he'd made over the years, but Lucas didn't want that. All he asked was to be allowed to send them Christmas and birthday gifts. This was also denied. So, he set up a trust fund in their names to be given to the girls when they reached eighteen, along with letters he'd written them. The girls would be classed as adults by then, so their mother and biological father wouldn't have a say legally.

No wonder he didn't want to be in a serious relationship. It would be hard to give your love and trust to a woman after the experience he'd had.

"Darius, there are headache pills in the first aid box in the galley. Just tell the flight attendant what you need," I told him. "Jonesy, Lucas, I'm going to get some sleep, and I suggest you do the same. We have a long day ahead of us."

Chapter Twelve

TESS

I can't believe you left all these marks on me!

I threw my phone on the bed after sending Kolya the text. I was still tired when I awoke and hadn't noticed them until I had a shower. Being so fair-skinned, I tend to mark easily, but this was overkill. He'd left them everywhere. I knew I'd have to get creative with my clothing choices to hide the love bites on my neck and chest.

After glancing through the clothes I regularly wore to work, I realised none of my usual shirts or blouses would be any good; not even with a pretty scarf. So I took out a cream polo-neck jumper I'd had for a couple of years but had never worn and paired it with coffee-coloured tapered trousers. As I searched for suitable matching footwear, I heard my phone ring.

"Kolya, you are in big trouble when I see you."

I heard him laugh before he said, *"Good morning to you, too, my darling."*

"I'm having to wear a polo-necked jumper to cover them up," I groaned.

"You don't have to cover them, Tess. There's nothing wrong with a few love bites," he replied with a chuckle.

"You know how unprofessional I'd look if I turned up at work today looking like a reject from a vampire movie, yet you still marked me."

"You could have stopped me at any time, Tess, but as I recall, all you kept saying was 'Yes! Oh, God, yes.'" I could hear the sultry smile in his voice.

"I didn't realise I would look so bad, Kolya. You've never marked me like this before."

"I looked you over this morning before I left. All over. You were beautiful, as always. Love bites and all."

"I know why you did it, Kolya, and it pisses me off to think you'd feel the need to do so. You might as well have written *'Property of Kolya Barinov'* across my forehead with a black Sharpie."

"I think you are overreacting," he remarked with an audible sigh.

"Well, it's a good job I've been able to cover them up because I'd hate to see Lily's reaction."

He was quiet for a few seconds, and if it wasn't for hearing him sigh again, I'd have thought he'd hung up.

"I'm sorry, Tess," he said, a measure of contriteness to his voice. *"I never thought about that. I just… I'm sorry."* I could tell he meant it, too.

"I love you, Kolya, and I hate arguing with you. Especially while you're away. Let's forget about it for now; just remember you have to make it up to me when you come home."

"Anything you want, my darling, it's yours."

"I have to finish getting dressed before I get Lily up for school," I told him. "Are you going to call back and speak to Lily before she leaves?"

"Of course. We have another two hours before we reach Estonia, and I'm missing you both already. I wish I could turn the plane around and fly home."

"I wish you could, too."

"It was so cold at Heathrow this morning. Make sure Lily has her hat, scarf and gloves on for school. We don't want her to catch a chill before our holiday."

"Okay. Call us in about an hour, then you'll see her wrapped up warm, ready for school. Love you, Kolya."

"Love you too."

I finished dressing, then went to put the kettle on before I woke Lily. If I don't get two cups of tea in the morning, I tend not to like the world or anything in it, and Lily is the same with her porridge and honey. She's like Goldilocks: it has to be just right. She never used to be so picky with her food, but in the last few months, she's become a bit of a diva.

"Good morning, Lily." I kissed her cheek and then opened the curtains. The sky was a dull grey, and mist filled the air. Lily mumbled, then turned over, hooking her arm over Anna the doll.

"Come on, Lilypot, it's time to get up."

She mumbled again but didn't open her eyes.

"Isn't it party day today? You made such a pretty glittery card and—"

"Can I wear my pink party dress and sparkly shoes?" Lily asked as she threw back the covers, all tiredness forgotten.

"Sorry, my lovely, it's uniform only. But you can wear a sparkly bow in your hair if you want."

Lily carried on talking while she went to the bathroom.

"Wash your hands after you've used the toilet," I reminded her.

"I know, Mummy, you don't have to remind me every time," she yelled.

I picked out her school uniform and made my way back to the kitchen. Ivan had arrived and was in the process of making a large pan of porridge.

"Do you want some?" he asked. It looked as though he'd emptied all the porridge oats into the pan. It was almost overflowing.

"No, thanks. I'm going to have some toast."

"I will have toast, too," Ivan said before crossing to the fridge. "And eggs." He took out four eggs and grabbed another pan.

"What time did you get back from the airport?" He'd been up early to take Kolya to catch his flight, so I had no doubt he'd had breakfast earlier. This was all just a snack for him. Ivan's appetite knew no bounds.

"About six a.m., so I went for a swim to pass the time," Ivan replied.

Franco came into the kitchen just as we all sat down for breakfast.

"The kettle's just boiled," I gestured towards the counter where we'd left him a cup.

"Good morning, Franco," Lily said through a mouthful of porridge.

"Good morning, princess. Are you gonna draw me another picture today?"

"Yep. It's party day today, but Mummy says I have to wear my uniform." Lily rolled her eyes, then continued eating her breakfast.

"Did you go out last night?" Ivan asked as he handed Franco a sheet with today's itinerary.

"Yeah," was all Franco said.

"Why so secretive? Is it that you don't want to kiss and tell?" Ivan queried.

"Something like that," Franco mumbled. He glanced at me for a second before he looked away.

"I've decided to visit Jean before we go to the Sheffield office," I told him. "I thought she might be a bit more with it if we see her earlier."

"It's probably a good idea. She was sleepy the last time we visited," Ivan remarked. He'd been quite upset when he had to keep reminding Jean who he was. As she'd kept yawning, he blamed it on her being tired as opposed to her dementia. None of us had corrected him, though we all knew the truth. Ivan did, deep down. He just didn't want to face it.

"Finished!" Lily stated. She placed her spoon back in the bowl and clambered down from the chair.

"You need your hat, scarf, and gloves today. Your dad says it's really cold outside," I told her.

"That's because it's going to be Christmas soon, and that means it's winter," she explained in a very matter-of-fact tone.

"Have you written to Santa to let him know what you'd like for Christmas?" asked Ivan.

Lily's mouth fell open, and she looked at me with panic on her face. "No, I haven't. I better do it quick," she said before racing off to her room.

"We haven't got time to do it before school, Lily," I shouted after her.

"But he won't know what to bring me," she yelled back. Moments later, she ran back into the kitchen with pencils and paper. "You'll have to help me write it," she announced.

Glancing at the clock, I shook my head. "We haven't got

time, love. Lainey, Dave and Danny will be here any minute to take you to school."

"But, Mum—"

"We can do it after school. Then you can take your time and do your best writing." I shot Ivan a look that told him he was in trouble for mentioning it.

"But—"

"And after you've done your best writing, you can add some glue and make it pretty with glitter. I'm sure Santa Claus would like that," Ivan prompted.

Lily glanced at the glittery card she'd made for the teaching assistant, then nodded reluctantly.

"Okay, but you'll have to help me," she told him.

"Of course I'll help you. Now, let's get your coat on, or you'll be late for school."

"Good save," I whispered when Ivan looked at me with a smug grin.

Nate walked into the kitchen carrying a small black bag. "Kevin put some more of the photographs from Jean's photo albums onto discs. He's made sure there are names on each photo to remind her of who they are."

We all agreed what a good idea it was to list the names. Even though Jean's memory had diminished, her ability to read didn't appear to have been affected yet, though I was never sure she was making sense of what she was reading. It seemed like she could read the words perfectly, but they didn't always compute with her brain. For a woman that loved to read and enjoyed books as much as Jean did, the whole thing was just so sad.

My phone rang, alerting me to an incoming video call, so I left Franco in charge of helping Lily put on her coat while I answered.

"Hi, you almost missed us. Lily's just putting her coat on."

"Daddy," Lily squealed. "Guess what? I'm going to write a letter to Santa after school, and I'm going to make it pretty and sparkly with glitter. Mummy and Ivan are going to help me."

"What a good idea. Then Santa will know what to bring you on Christmas Eve."

"Yep. I'm going to tell him how good I've been and ask him if I can have another doll like Anna," Lily replied with a beaming smile, which Kolya clearly struggled to return. Ivan, Nate, and Franco hid their chuckles well, but we all heard Lucas and Jonesy howling with laughter behind Kolya.

Lainey entered the kitchen ready to take Lily to school, so Kolya said goodbye and told us he'd call before his flight to Saudi.

Grabbing my coat, I walked outside with Lainey and Danny to where Dave was waiting in the car. Lily always went to school in the same vehicle, which was a bullet-resistant Range Rover, and had to be lifted into her car seat. Andy—one of the new bodyguards Kolya hired after Lily was born—was waiting at school for her to arrive. He checked the premises every morning, and Lily wasn't allowed anywhere near the school until Lainey had received his all clear.

Chapter Thirteen

TESS

I'd wanted to speak to Franco about the whole Halloween party debacle at the Graysons', but he'd sat up front with Ivan during our helicopter flight to Doncaster airport. He did the same as soon as we got in the car when Nate drove, leaving me to sit with Ivan in the back. It seemed like Franco was avoiding me, which I could fully understand. It was pretty obvious what Kolya and I had been up to in the Graysons' bathroom, and the more I thought about it, the more embarrassed I became. At the time, I'd been so into what we were doing, I just didn't care.

Traffic flowed freely from the airport to Jean's house, and within twenty minutes, Nate was parking the car. He volunteered to wait in the vehicle, as per protocol, while Ivan, Franco, and I went inside. Jane, her carer for the day, came to greet us, telling us that Jean had a good sleep last night and had wanted to do some baking.

When we entered the kitchen, there were seriously tempting muffins and scones on cooling racks.

That was another thing with Jean. If you held up an egg

and asked her what it was called, she more than likely wouldn't remember, yet she could quote the ingredients needed for buns and cakes as if she were reading them from her old recipe book.

When we entered the dining area, Jean looked up from her chair by the table and broke into a smile.

"Tess, what are you doing home at this time?" she asked.

Home… It had been years since I lived with Jean, but I didn't want to remind her of that.

"I wanted to call and see you a bit earlier today. It looks like you and Jane have been busy baking." I gestured towards the goodies on the kitchen counter.

"We've made scones," Jean acknowledged.

"And muffins, too," Jane reminded her. She placed a tray with Jean's best teapot and cups in front of us. "I'll grab us all a plate and we can tuck in. Would anyone like jam and cream with their scones?"

Ivan's face lit up like Christmas. "I'd love jam and cream on mine," he told her. "Would you like some help?"

Jean looked from Ivan to Franco and back to me again. She opened her mouth as if to say something but stared at us instead.

"You remember Ivan and Franco," I prompted.

"Of course," she replied with a smile. "How could anyone forget these two handsome young men?"

She blushed when both Franco and Ivan kissed her on the cheek.

We sat and chatted about her baking, the weather, and the flowers Ivan sent her every other week. I glanced around the room at all the photos of the various foster children she'd looked after over the years. There was one of Sarah and I getting ready for the Halloween disco at school, which reminded me of the ones I'd brought to show Jean, so I delved into my bag and took out some photographs of Lily in her Halloween outfit. Kevin printed them off for me yesterday and had written her name and age on the back. Jean loved Lily's outfit and mentioned how pretty she was, and how she had my hair. I told her how well Lily was doing at school and how much she missed her.

Seeing Jean so happy and cognisant made my day. I couldn't wait to tell Kolya about my visit.

It wasn't until we were about to leave and Jean was seeing us out of the door that her memory lapsed. She asked me if I knew whether Sarah had detention again. I looked at Jane, who was standing a few steps behind Jean. She gave a slight nod, acknowledging Jean's memory slip. Before I could answer, Ivan said, "You look tired, Jean. It's no wonder when you've been up so early. And doing all that baking, too! It was very much appreciated, by the way."

"You're welcome to call here any time. Just because you're all grown up now and don't live here anymore, it doesn't mean you can't come back and visit your old foster mum."

Ivan looked confused for a moment, then he schooled his expression into a beaming smile. He kissed her on the cheek and told her we'd visit again soon. After Franco and I hugged her, we set off down the path to the car, turning around and waving back at Jean as we opened the doors.

"How was she?" Nate asked as he drove us away from the house. Ivan sat beside him, leaving Franco to join me in the back of the car.

"She was great today, Nate. It was only when we were about to leave that she got a little confused," I replied.

"She thought Ivan was one of her old foster kids," Franco added.

"She was tired, that's all. And she remembers me from when we stayed with her before Sarah's funeral. So it's only natural that she would get confused."

Franco glanced my way and shook his head at Ivan's *"because she's tired"* excuse again. He didn't say anything, though. None of us wanted to face how rapidly Jean's illness was progressing.

When we first found out she had dementia, I'd asked her to come and live with us, but she wanted to stay in familiar surroundings. Her doctor agreed that familiarity would be beneficial, but we knew she'd need help at home, and it wasn't possible for us to be with her daily. Kolya hired a team of twenty-four-hour carers, so she'd never be on her own. Jean often introduces them as her foster children, which I think is lovely. Several of her past foster children come and visit her regularly, too. I've met quite a few of them over the last four years, and though some of them were strangers before that, I kind of feel an affinity with them.

I hate it when Jean mentions Sarah, though. When she was first diagnosed with dementia, the staff at the clinic we took her to said we should correct her with a gentle reminder whenever she got something wrong or asked about someone who was no longer with us. But I hate to be the one reminding her that both her husband and Sarah are dead. I doubt there could be a gentle way to tell a person that someone they loved dearly had passed away. And at the stage she's at now, we'd probably have to do it every single day. I didn't want Jean to be dealing with grief on a daily basis, so along with her carers, we decided to change the subject or tell her a lie rather than hurt her with the truth.

Though traffic had been good from the airport to Jean's house, it wasn't that way on our journey to Sheffield. It gave me ample time to go through my emails and checklist for the day.

Karen had sent me the details of two more companies offering apprenticeships to teenagers about to leave the care system. We'd need to look into each company and make sure they weren't just looking for cheap labour. While that didn't happen often, it sadly wasn't unknown. Some of our care leavers had been exploited enough without experiencing it in the workplace, too.

As always, Franco was a good sounding board regarding Sarah's Legacy and the work we did there. Though he hadn't been through the care system, he'd lived in a pretty rough area and had a tough upbringing. According to Franco, teenage boys in his old neighbourhood ended up as foot soldiers for a crime family or actual soldiers in the US Army—risking their lives either way.

The office for Sarah's Legacy was based just outside Sheffield City Centre, in a large Victorian house that had been converted into a doctor's surgery many years ago. We originally chose the building because it had a driveway and garden, which we altered to give us ample parking space once the building works were finished. Kolya and I kept as many of the property's original features as possible, although we'd added a top-of-the-range, energy-efficient central heating system, along with ultra-modern kitchen and bathroom facilities. Altogether there were five offices, two meeting rooms, a kitchen, a dining room, three bathrooms, plus a large homely reception area. The décor was bright and welcoming, and the whole building had a positive vibe about it. It was a great place to bring those ready to leave care or vulnerable teens looking for work, a home, or further education. We did our best to provide a brighter future for those who had no one else to help. Of course, the teenagers who came to us had to be willing to work hard and behave appropriately. We had strict rules that our service users had to adhere to.

If someone was struggling emotionally, we offered counselling and whatever assistance they needed. If their struggles were related to addiction, they had to enter a rehab programme to receive our help. But if our service users were taking advantage or generally being little shits, they would receive no further help from Sarah's Legacy. This would also mean eviction if they were living in one of our properties. It may seem harsh, but it had to be done. It wouldn't look good for our service users or the charity itself if we were seen to condone inappropriate behaviour.

As we pulled up outside the building, one of our liaison officers, Amina Khan, was just about to get in her car. When she spotted us, she waved, then waited until we all got out of our vehicle before giving us her usual cheerful greeting.

"Good morning, all. I hope you've had a great weekend. I'm just about to do some shopping, so if you want me to bring anything back for you, let me know and I'll add it to my list."

"Hi, Amina, as long as we've got tea and milk so I can have a cuppa, I'm good," I replied. Of course, Ivan added a dozen more items, all food-based, to Amina's already long list.

Amina was one of Sarah's Legacy's first service users. She'd been one of three sixteen-year-old Asian girls with a British-Pakistani background who'd been victims of a similar child grooming gang to the charity's namesake. Amina had rebelled against her strict Muslim family and had been sneaking off to the youth club with her non-Muslim friends, changing out of her traditional clothing in favour of skinny jeans and a low-cut top. The gang, which was made up of mostly British-Pakistani men, had seen Amina and her friends as fair game. All three girls had suffered physical and sexual abuse. Unfortunately for Amina, when her parents found out what had happened, they laid the blame on her, disowning her completely after saying she'd brought shame on the family. So Sarah's Legacy stepped in and helped provide Amina with suitable accommodation in one of our properties, which had an on-site residential team member.

As Amina hadn't previously been made a ward of the court, we didn't have any legal loopholes to jump through—not like I did when I ran away from the care home I'd been living in. As she was going on seventeen and had plenty of experience helping out at home, Amina could look after herself in her small studio flat, but she received training from us on how to manage the allowance we gave her. Amina took a year-long college course in health and social care before signing on to do an apprenticeship with Sarah's Legacy. She'd been so grateful for the help and support she'd received from everyone here and said she wanted to give something back.

Amina completed her apprenticeship with us and was now a regular full-time employee. She's one of a number of great success stories at Sarah's Legacy, and we are all extremely proud of each and every one of them.

I consider Amina to be a great addition to the team. She's smart, hardworking, gets on with everyone she meets, and has a great sense of humour.

I know she has her down days. It's understandable after everything she went through. But she refuses to let what happened in her past take anything away from the person she is now or her goals for the future. In short, she doesn't want to live her life as a victim, because that would mean the groomers still had a hold over her.

I adore Amina, and if I were her family, I'd be incredibly proud of the young woman she has become. Yet they still refuse to have anything to do with her. I can't understand how anyone can hold their status in society in higher regard than their own child—someone they should love unconditionally.

I'll always fight for my daughter's safety and well-being, and will love and cherish her always. Lily and Kolya are my everything. I couldn't imagine living in a world without them.

Chapter Fourteen

KOLYA

After the meeting ended, we posed for the obligatory handshake photograph and answered a few questions from the press. The interpreter, a tall, stern-looking woman who appeared to be in her late fifties, was certainly earning her pay today. I could tell she didn't appreciate the barrage of questions from the insistent journalists determined to bag a headline scoop.

A short while later, Jonesy, Lucas, and I made our way out of the town hall, along with Artjom Kask, the local mayor. The EU representative, Michel Arman, had been milking the occasion, making out as if it was the EU's idea to approach *me* about locating my latest venture here in Estonia, in order to bring employment and prosperity to the region. I let him have his moment in front of the cameras, neither confirming nor denying his claims.

I could have told them how I'd been planning this for years, only to have my last attempt at a KOLCAT base in Eastern Europe thwarted by an EU council member, who did not like my wife's reaction to Caroline Dawson. I made sure the judgemental bastard suffered for looking down on my wife. The private investigator—whom I have on retainer —can dig up a shady business deal no matter how deep it's buried.

Darius nodded our way when he saw us approach the doorway, letting us know all was well. He'd been standing guard in front of the town hall—his position helping him monitor the entrance to the building and our vehicle outside. I checked my phone, which had been on silent both during the meeting and when taking questions from the press. Tess had sent me a couple of texts, informing me that Jean was well and had been more like her usual self until just before they left. I relayed the information to Jonesy and Lucas, who smiled and told me they were glad she was okay. Both men were fond of Jean and always enquired about her welfare.

I dread to think of how Tess will react as Jean's dementia progresses. She was the only positive influence Tess had from her childhood.

I sent her a quick text back, telling her I was glad she had a good visit, and that I loved and missed her, always.

Just as I put my phone back in my pocket, I was jostled to my left by Darius. Jonesy, who'd been by my other side, jumped in front of me quickly, thinking there was a threat.

"Sorry, boss. You can stand down, Jonesy. I was dizzy, and I..." Darius murmured.

"Jesus, Darius, get with it, man. If you were feeling that ill, you should have told us sooner. We could have swapped you out with either Mark or Greg," Jonesy stated.

"Do you still have a headache?" I asked with concern.

Darius looked a little anxious. His shoulders were hunched, and when I glanced down at his hands, I noticed a slight tremor.

"I will be okay. I just need a glass of water." His eyes flicked from me to Jonesy, then back again. We'd gained an audience, though thankfully, none of them were press.

"Can you make the journey to the build site?" I asked. Darius nodded and stood up straight. "Good. Then let's get in the vehicle and discuss it there."

Sunlight had broken through the clouds, and I appreciated the slight warmth it gave us. They'd forecast showers throughout the morning, but so far, the weather had been quite pleasant. It had been pouring with rain the last time I'd taken hold of a spade and broken ground on a new KOLCAT build site, and even though we'd had umbrellas, everyone involved had been drenched by the time I'd said a few words and the press finished photographing us.

Jonesy took the lead, then switched to my left when we got to the Land Cruiser. Darius waited until Jonesy and I were in the back before getting in the front passenger seat beside Lucas. I handed him a bottle of water, which he accepted gratefully.

The mayor's car was due to lead us off from the town hall; we would follow him, and then Michel Arman's car was supposed to follow us, but he was still in the building.

"Boss, the mayor's pulling away. What do you want us to do?" Lucas asked.

"Follow him. Arman is getting on my last nerve. Jonesy, tell Greg we are without our tail car and ask him if there's any press hanging around the build site. If there are, let's get this thing over with and leave the EU representative and his over-inflated ego out of it. He will learn the hard way that I don't appreciate being kept waiting."

I tapped Darius on the shoulder. "It's up to you whether you stay in Estonia until you feel up to travelling home or take a flight back today. If you need to see a doctor, call Gustav and have him recommend someone."

"Thank you, boss." Darius didn't look my way when he replied. He was staring out of the window, taking in the impressive scenery.

The drive from the town hall to the build site took us through twelve miles of varying terrain, though the roads we travelled were well maintained. Once we'd left town, we encountered five miles of dense forest on either side of the road. The trees, which were mainly pine and spruce, were tall and impressive, though they blocked the sun from the midday sky, making it seem much later than it actually was.

We'd been travelling a little over six minutes when Darius announced, "I'm going to be sick. Pull over."

"Grab a bag from under the dash, for fuck's sake," Jonesy yelled.

"No bag," Darius declared. He was retching while unbuckling his seat belt, then he tried to wind his window down. Being reinforced by bullet-resistant glass, it would only come down three inches.

It wasn't protocol to stop without the protection of guards following us in another vehicle, but I didn't want to make the journey back to the airport in a car reeking of vomit.

"Lucas, pull over," I commanded. His eyes met mine in the rear-view mirror as he did so, silently questioning my command. The car in which the mayor travelled carried on ahead of us, disappearing from our view as our vehicle slowed.

"Boss, I'm calling in this unscheduled stop." Jonesy took out his phone as the Toyota pulled over to the grass verge at the side of the road. Darius leapt out and carried on retching as he held on to the door.

"Yes, warn Greg that we might be—" My words ceased, and I felt a cold chill down my spine when Darius suddenly stopped retching and ran off towards the trees. Within seconds, a Jeep sped out from the forest on the opposite side of the road, while men with guns came out from where Darius had fled.

"What the fuck? Lucas, drive," Jonesy yelled before unbuckling my seat belt. He pulled me down flat against the leather seat, covering my body with his. I felt him move above me, trying to close the passenger door while I searched my pockets for my phone. I couldn't find it, nor could I see it on the floor. Then I remembered Darius knocking into me as I'd put it away. Fuck! He'd played us all.

Lucas had already put his foot down, but the passenger side door and window were still open, leaving him unprotected from the sudden, relentless onslaught of bullets. I heard Greg's voice come through the speakers as Lucas began telling him we'd been ambushed. I raised my head and shoulders so I could make my voice heard over the sound of rapid gunfire, but as I opened my mouth to speak, I only managed to say the name Darius before being hit in the face with something warm and wet, the metallic-tasting liquid gathering around my lips. The Toyota began losing acceleration, and a glance in the rear-view mirror told me what I already knew. Lucas had been shot several times. A bullet to the temple ending my loyal guard's life.

I could no longer hear Greg's voice through the speaker system, just a steady stream of white noise accompanying the sound of heavy footsteps approaching the vehicle as we slowed to a stop.

"I can't get a signal on my phone," Jonesy raged. "The bastards must have a scrambler."

We searched below the seat for our hidden guns and ammo, but we both came up empty. Darius again! He must have moved the guns while we were in the meeting.

"Stay down, boss," Jonesy commanded. His voice was deceptively calm, despite the hopelessness of the situation. He knew as well as I did that this could go one of two ways: kidnapping or assassination. Jonesy would die either way.

I grabbed his hand and pulled it towards my heart.

"Regardless of whether I meet my death today, I swear I will find Darius and make him suffer before I kill him," I vowed. "Even from the afterlife."

"Not if I find him first, boss," he replied. He, too, wore my fallen guard's blood about his face, and the pristine white shirt under his open grey blazer bore a claret-coloured spray.

When the footsteps came to a halt beside our vehicle, I took my first clear look at our attackers. At a guess, they appeared Middle Eastern, though it wasn't until I heard a familiar voice that I could confirm it. What sounded like a command was given. Guns were pointed at our heads while someone reached over Lucas and flicked a switch to unlock our doors. Jonesy and I were pulled from the vehicle and forced to kneel.

"Mr Barinov, I told you we would meet." Mohammed Riass strolled up to the Toyota, the half-dozen men surrounding us stepping back to let him through.

"The fucking arsehole's trying to sound like a Bond villain," Jonesy hissed. I smirked at Riass, despite my fear.

"Do you think this will get you the weapon?" I questioned. I tried to sound as calm as Jonesy had earlier, but I didn't have a hope in hell of achieving that.

Riass grinned. "I already have it, and the missiles. My people in Turkey took possession of them fifteen minutes ago. They will be loaded onto a shipping container bound for Albania within the hour."

He obviously wasn't aware the weapon was missing its guidance system. Or that without it, and the relevant codes, the missiles were useless.

"You won't get the codes from me," I told him adamantly.

Riass looked from me to Jonesy, as if contemplating something. He stepped away from us and signalled for someone. Two of his goons came up from behind us and pulled off our jackets, then I felt the press of cold metal between my shoulder blades. From the corner of my eye, I tried to see what kind of guns they would use to kill us. Why I did that, I couldn't say. I knew the practice moves I'd done with Franco and Jonesy as a means to escape from this position wouldn't help at all. The armed men in front of us would end us within seconds.

I quickly discarded any more thoughts of escape and instead pictured my wife as she lay sleeping this morning. I remembered the feel of her lips on mine when she'd kissed me so passionately last night, and the sound of her voice as she told me she loved me. If I was going to die today, I'd do so with thoughts of the woman I loved etched on my mind.

"Boss, after we've killed Darius, I reckon we should take these fuckers down," Jonesy stated with a nervous laugh. He knew this was it for us. Our death was imminent.

I saw Riass signal to the men behind us as I took a deep breath and replied, "It's a deal, Jo—"

Chapter Fifteen

TESS

Karen and Amina presented their findings and information about the workplace offering apprenticeships, and to my relief, they appeared to be a genuine upstanding company. The next step would be to set up a meeting with the managing director and get a feel for the working environment. We had four candidates we felt would be suitable, but we needed to make sure they had funding for smart interview clothing, along with the means to get there. Amina had several bus and train timetables on hand and had already printed off directions and bus routes for each interviewee.

"Now that we have the first order of business out of the way, spill the beans about the swanky Halloween party. The photos you sent were stunning," Amina demanded while she took out her phone. "I particularly liked this one of you, Tess, but I have to say, I think Kolya and his friend looked amazing."

I could feel the heat in my cheeks as I recalled the wickedly sexual experience I'd shared with Kolya in Eleanor Grayson's bathroom.

"You're blushing, Tess. I'm guessing your outfit had the desired effect on Kolya," Karen added.

"Definitely," I replied. "I wasn't really sure how Kolya and Yannis would react to having to wear all that makeup. And it took a lot longer than I thought, but it was worth it. The photos don't really do their work justice, but believe me, they totally transformed us."

I showed them the rest of the Halloween photos I had on my phone. They knew what I'd been planning for the party, and I'd already sent them a few of the best ones, as well as some of Lily in her witch outfit.

Karen spent Halloween night in her local pub, where they'd held a themed quiz followed by a disco. She'd gone dressed up as the wicked witch from The Wizard of Oz— green face and everything. She looked amazing, as did her friends. I laughed out loud while swiping through the photos on her phone. Her younger brother, Andrew, hated dressing up and hadn't bought an outfit, so Karen and his girlfriend decided to improvise in spectacular fashion. Using her abundance of leftover green face paint, along with a torn-up T-shirt and cropped jeans, they transformed him into the Hulk. The seriously unimpressed look on his face in most of the photos was priceless. She said it took four pints of beer for Andrew to start smiling. I would much rather have been with them on Halloween night than at the Graysons'.

Amina bemoaned the fact she hadn't done anything special for Halloween, other than have a horror movie marathon with two of her friends, which would have been great if she actually *liked* horror films.

Just as we began to list the scariest horror movies we'd ever seen, Franco entered the room without knocking and headed straight for me, his face solemn.

"Tess, there's been an incident. We need to leave immediately."

"An incident? Franco, what is it? What's happening?" I pushed my chair away from the table and stood on shaking legs. Grabbing his forearms, I begged, "It's not Lily, is it? Please, Franco, tell me it's not Lily?"

"No, Tess, it's not Lily. She's safe and already on her way home." He looked me in the eyes, unmoving. Barely even breathing, it seemed. And then I knew.

"Oh, God. It's Kolya, isn't it? Has he been injured? Is he alive?"

Franco shook his head. "We don't know for sure. His car was attacked en route to the new build site."

Amina let out a distraught whining noise, then covered her mouth with her hand. Her eyes darted to Karen, who made her way over to the coat rack in the corner. She unhooked my jacket and brought it over to me.

"Come on, Tess, let's get you down to the car so you can start your journey home. Lily needs you." She helped me put on my jacket as if I was a child incapable of managing it myself. There were questions racing through my head. Important questions. Necessary questions. But try as I might, I couldn't get them out. The shock had left me voiceless.

Karen placed a reassuring hand on my shoulder before turning to Franco. "I'll go down and provide assistance at the door. I assume Nate or Ivan has the car ready to go?"

"Nate's driving; Ivan's waiting by the door. We've no reason to believe there's a threat to Tess, but—"

"We follow protocol anyway. That's understandable in the circumstances. Amina, grab Tess's bag from under the table and let's get going," Karen ordered.

Amina handed me my bag before throwing her arms

around me. "I know you have all these people around you, but if you need me, I promise I'll be there."

I nodded in acknowledgement, and as soon as she released me, I took hold of Franco's outstretched hand.

I don't know how I made it down the stairs. Not while all those questions were slamming through my head. Every few seconds, my vision would waver from the sheer ferocity of them. *What exactly happened? When did it happen? How did they get to him? Who were they? Did they kill him?*

If not for Franco's steadying hand, I would have fallen for sure. It wasn't until I reached the doorway and saw Ivan's grim expression and red-rimmed eyes that my legs gave way and I finally found my voice.

"He's dead, isn't he? Ivan, please, I need to know what happened. Has he been shot? Do you know who attacked him? What about the others? Jonesy, Lucas, Darius?"

Franco swept me up in his arms and carried me out of the building, placing me on the backseat of the car before climbing in beside me. Ivan climbed in the other side and took me in his arms before he spoke—the timbre of his deep voice as comforting as his bear-like hug.

"Kolya and Lucas tried calling to alert the team that they were being ambushed. We think Darius had been hit because they heard Kolya saying his name through the noise of the shots. By the time the team reached their vehicle, it was empty, but there were bullets embedded in the front seats. There was a significant amount of blood around the driver's seat and a little over the back, as well as outside the vehicle. The car that should have been directly behind them when they left the town hall was delayed and arrived at the site of the attack just after Mark and Greg got there."

"So we don't know for certain if anyone's been killed.

They might just be injured," I stated. It was clutching at straws, I know, but I didn't want to face the alternative.

"We know at least one of them is dead. Mark and Greg believe it's Lucas because he was driving," Franco said, his voice cracking at the end of his reply.

"How do they know? He might just have been hit in the arm or something. When you see a lot of blood, it's easy to mistake—"

"There was evidence of grey matter in with the blood on the headrest, Tess. There's no mistaking that." Franco leaned forward, his elbows resting on his thighs, his head in his hands. I ran my shaking hand through his short black hair, trying to offer him comfort. Lucas was his friend, a fellow bodyguard. If it was true…if he was dead, it would hit all the guards hard.

Lucas was a good man. We were all fond of him, but at that moment all I could think of was, *"at least they're not saying it's Kolya".*

If that makes me a bad person, so be it.

Despite the devastating news pointing to the contrary, I desperately hoped that my husband and the rest of his guards were still alive.

Chapter Sixteen

TESS

We had Kevin on speakerphone throughout our journey to the airport, yet he could tell us nothing more than we'd previously heard, other than the police in Estonia were putting up roadblocks on all major routes out of the area. There were also police checks and roadblocks around the nearest port and airport. While we appreciated their help, this looked like an organised attack, so they'd probably planned their escape route with police presence in mind.

James had video-called me from his office at KOLCAT US and assured me he would find his father as soon as possible. He'd already made arrangements with Gustav to have a team of trained operatives flown out to Estonia from Berlin. He'd informed his uncle and grandfather of the attack, and they, too, were sending a team out to search for Kolya and his men. Although obviously distressed, James immediately took charge of the situation from his end.

I was grateful that I didn't have to inform my father-in-law what had happened. Roman Barinov was devastated when he lost his son and daughter-in-law in a plane crash about seventeen months ago. It was heartbreaking to see him so distressed, and I don't think he's ever really come to terms with it.

Roman hadn't always been the best father to Aleksei, from what I could gather. Aleksei and his wife, Talia, had fertility problems and were unable to conceive, despite taking every route medically for that to happen. Roman laid the blame at Talia's feet, even though the couple's fertility issues were mainly to do with Aleksei's low sperm count. Talia wanted to adopt a child, but Roman wouldn't allow it. He'd said that a child's blood means everything within the Bratva, and only those who shared Barinov blood could ever be considered family.

On one of our few visits to Roman's home in Moscow, he'd casually suggested over dinner that Aleksei should let one of his brothers father a child with Talia. As you can imagine, that wasn't the best conversation to have while dining with the whole family present. Aleksei had reprimanded his father for discussing such a sensitive issue in front of everyone, and he was warned by Roman that he should remember who he was speaking to. Talia announced she'd lost her appetite and got up to leave, clearly upset by his suggestion. I pushed my chair away from the table and stood, wanting to offer her comfort. Roman commanded I sit and eat, but I ignored him and followed Talia from the room and into the garden. Ivan joined us but said nothing, nodding his head towards the ever-present guards. We each put an arm around Talia while she cried tears of both anger and frustration.

Once the guard had moved out of earshot, Talia told us she feared Roman more than ever, but felt trapped within the powerful walls of the Barinov Bratva. I suggested that she and Aleksei should come and stay with us for a while, and maybe think about moving to England permanently. Talia gave a tearful laugh before saying that death was the only way she and Aleksei could leave the Bratva life.

Aleksei and Kolya joined us a few minutes later, both apologising to Talia for their father's behaviour. Talia thanked Kolya but told him his apology wasn't necessary. We left them with Ivan in the garden while we went to check on Lily, who was in bed sleeping, thankfully, and that was the last time I saw Aleksei and Talia.

Despite Roman's despicable treatment of Talia, he was always so pleasant and generous with me. Probably because I'd given him another grandchild to spoil, something he wanted me to repeat as soon as possible.

Please, God, let that happen, I prayed. *Let my husband and his team be found safe and well.*

Another video call came through as we were about to exit the car and head inside the airport. It was James, and he looked even more distressed than I'd seen him earlier.

"Tess, where are you?"

"We're about to go into the airport," I informed him before asking, "Do you have an update? Have they found everyone?"

"Don't leave the vehicle. Get back on the road and head home via the M1. Tell Kevin to let you know if there are any roadworks or accidents you should be aware of that could slow you down, and have him send an armed team to meet and follow your car when you exit the motorway."

Nate reversed out of our designated parking space and drove as quickly as possible to the exit barrier.

"James, wha—" Before I could finish speaking, Franco snatched the phone out of my hand.

"We're heading to the exit now. What do we need to know? Do you have a confirmed threat?"

"No official confirmation of a specific threat to Tess, but I'm not willing to take any chances. We've just received news that the weapon and missiles we were transporting to Saudi were stolen from the aircraft when it landed in Turkey. All crew members and guards on board were killed, along with five airport employees. The plane carrying the guidance system was still in the air, so as a precaution, we had it turn back. Though Prince Amir was overseeing security in Saudi, I wasn't willing to risk the thieves getting their hands on that or the crew. Without the guidance system and codes, the missiles are nothing but ornaments. At this point, I think we can all guess who's behind this. It also makes me think they've kidnapped my father as a bargaining chip in exchange for the guidance system and codes."

My heart sank, though the word kidnapped was far more welcome to my ear than killed.

"So this is all just a precaution because of the lapse in security at the airport in Turkey?" Franco confirmed.

"Yes. I want you to avoid all airports until we can confirm they haven't been compromised. By the time it takes you to get to Oxford, I have no doubt there'll be press outside the gates. Kevin will have whoever's guarding them explain to the press that we cannot guarantee their safety if they hang around. The local police will be informed and should be able to issue them with warnings. You have the other helicopter at home if you need to make any other journeys, which will give you freedom from the press. But with all the security installed at home, I'd prefer it if you stayed there until we garner more information."

"What about you, James? You have to keep yourself safe." I needed to hear him tell me they couldn't get to him, too.

"Don't worry about me, Tess. All KOLCAT US sites are on lockdown. I have my security around me, and I won't leave this building until I know it's safe to do so. I'll fly back to England as soon as I can, though I won't be taking the company jet until I can confirm that both

it and the airport are secure. I have the use of a friend's plane if I need it."

"When it's safe, get the pilot to fly the KOLCAT jet to another airport and board it there. Send one of your regular security team along to verify all is well, then you can meet the plane when it lands. Do not use a small airport. It needs to be one with adequate security," Ivan ordered.

"I'd already thought of that, but it will take time, and I might have to leave immediately. I need to figure out what I'm going to say to the secretary of defence in both the US and the UK. They'll assume the worst when they know someone previously associated with ISIS has their hands on a new surface-to-air missile launcher." James closed his eyes and pinched the bridge of his nose. Signs of worry and fatigue clearly evident on his handsome face. He looked so much like Kolya. Those same ice-blue eyes, same hair. He had the same commanding presence as his father, too. Just looking at him made me want to cry, so I heard little of what he'd been saying.

"—then I'll get a statement ready for the press. If you are contacted by anyone outside the family or our security team, say nothing, Tess."

"Say nothing. Yes, okay." I wiped my eyes and the fresh trail of salty tears from my cheeks.

"Don't cry, Tess. I'm having a hard time keeping it together as it is. I need you to stay focused. Keep the faith. We WILL get him back. Even though the stolen weapon is a fucking media and political catastrophe, it means we have something to barter with. They need the guidance system and codes, and we need my dad back unharmed."

"I can't be without him, James. I need him. Lily needs him."

"As do I, Tess. As do I."

Chapter Seventeen

TESS

Thankfully, there were no press outside the gates when we finally made it home. I'd tried contacting James again, but I couldn't get through. Kevin kept up the open communication with us until about fifteen minutes before we drove up our long driveway. Andy and Dave came out to greet us from the car; both were armed and ready for action. Danny was by the door, waiting to usher me inside. His face looked almost grey with worry, but that wasn't what caused the fear to grip my throat in a tight hold. It was the tears streaming down Jack's face as he held his sobbing wife in his arms while she cried, *"No, no, no."*

I ran into the tech room, closely followed by Franco, Ivan, and Nate. Kevin switched off a screen as I entered before turning to face me. He stood quickly and was about to say something when I raised my hand to stop him.

"Switch the monitor back on, Kevin," I commanded in a shaky yet determined voice.

"Tess, maybe you'd like to sit down first. You need to—"

"What I *need* is to know exactly what happened. I know

he's gone. The reactions from everyone here told me that. Please, Kevin. I'm his wife. Don't keep anything from me, no matter how bad it is."

"I wasn't going to keep this from you, but you are right. I'm so sorry, Tess. Riass captured and killed Kolya and his guards. So I need you to sit down and take a breath, love. This is something that no one here ever wanted to see. Ivan, you too. James wanted to break the news to you himself, but he's had to take what we assume will be a lengthy call from the Pentagon, even though he's in bits over the loss of his father. So take a seat, both of you. Please."

Kevin gestured towards the chairs to his right, in front of the blank monitor. Ivan took my left hand in his and tugged me onto his lap as he sat. I could hardly move. It felt like every muscle in my body had seized.

Kolya had been killed. My husband, the father of my child. My soul mate. Gone. Dead. Murdered.

Tears filled my eyes and ran down my cheeks, but I couldn't lift my hand to wipe them away.

I became vaguely aware of movement by the side of us, my eyes fixing on Kevin when he tapped a few keys and switched on the monitor. Both Ivan and I held our breath as the video began to play.

Mohammed Riass rambled on in a language I didn't understand. He stood in front of a roaring bonfire, which appeared to be in a wooded area. Tall trees surrounded him and his heavily armed men. Riass's sidekick, Najaf Bashir—also known as the executioner—held an AR-15 rifle above his head with both hands while repeating some of the same words as Riass.

"What are they saying?" Ivan asked.

"From what I've been able to interpret, they're saying that people in power have been quick to dismiss them and what their group stands for, but they will realise now that was a mistake. Their reach is far and wide, and to deny their importance is to wage war with an army more powerful than you can ever imagine. Riass says that today he captured and killed an important man who sold weapons to his enemy. He also says he has taken Kolya Barinov's latest creation and will use it to strike out at those who wish to bring him down."

The camera panned left to where a pile of bodies lay sprawled one atop the other at various angles. It took a few seconds and the camera zooming in before I realised what, and who, I was seeing. The body on top of the pile was Lucas. His chest was peppered with bloody holes, and there was a bullet wound that had taken out the side of his head, though his eyes were open, staring lifelessly at the grey sky. Underneath him was Jonesy, his face bloody and battered, eyes closed. Kolya lay underneath Jonesy. I let out a high-pitched cry as I reached out to touch his bloody face on the monitor. Both he and Jonesy had been beaten badly, and from the look of all the blood on their shirts, had been shot in the torso, though from the angle of their bodies on the pile and the tears streaming down my cheeks, I couldn't quite see where.

Ivan's arms tightened around me as his head fell to my shoulder; the fabric of my winter coat soaking up his tears. I needed its comforting warmth more than ever.

"Are you sure they're dead?" Franco's voice sounded gruff and low, so he cleared his throat before adding, "I mean, there's no doubt about Lucas, and I know there's blood on their shirts, but I can't see any bullet or stab wounds. And where the fuck is Darius?"

As if answering Franco, the camera swept back towards Riass. He stepped to the side and gestured towards the large bonfire, shouting something and laughing along with his men.

"He's saying that burning the infidels will keep his soldiers warm, so we can assume Darius is underneath all that burning wood," Kevin replied.

We'd been told that Kolya had shouted Darius when the call Lucas made connected with Greg and Mark, so they'd surmised that he'd been shot first. Though I was thankful we'd been spared the torture of seeing any fatal wounds and his face in death, the sight of those despicable men laughing while his body burned made me feel ill.

"Tess, you don't want to see the next bit, trust me," Kevin stated.

"I'm staying," I told him. Then immediately regretted it when the camera panned back to the pile of bodies. A group of Riass's men began kicking them and shouting something.

"They are saying praise Allah and death to the infidels. I recognise that much, at least," Franco commented before slamming his clenched fist against the desk.

I placed my hand against the screen again, as if doing so could somehow stop the violence against my husband and our beloved guards. Even though the camera only stayed on them for mere seconds before the screen went blank, it was enough to break whatever composure I had miraculously retained.

"I'm going to be sick," I cried, scrambling away from Ivan's lap. Nate passed me a waste paper bin a second before I lost the contents of my stomach, which seemed never-ending, and was made so much worse by my constant sobbing. I felt as if I couldn't take a full breath and began to panic. Ivan held my hair away from my face while someone rubbed my back and muttered soothing words. But I couldn't be soothed. Not by anyone ever again, or so I thought.

The door to the tech room swung open, and a little voice said, "Mummy, don't cry. Why is Mummy crying, Ivan? Is it because she's missing the party at school?"

"No, Lily. Mummy's very sad today. We all are," Ivan told her in a croaky voice, doing his best to hide his tears.

"Don't be sad, Mummy. I can hug you and make you feel better."

I felt my beautiful daughter wrap her arms tightly around my leg, so I looked down at her and forced a smile. Lily let go of me and headed over to Ivan. After giving him a squeeze, she turned to Kevin and hugged him, too, before asking, "Who else needs a hug?"

Franco stepped forward. "Come here, sweetheart. I could do with one of your special hugs, then I think we'll go and make your mommy a cup of tea, okay?"

"Okay, Franco. But Mummy says I'm not allowed to make real tea, so I'll have to do a pretend one with my tea set," Lily said. She squealed in delight when Franco lifted her up and carried her out of the room.

Lainey handed me a box of tissues so I could wipe my mouth and blow my nose. "I'm so sorry, Tess. I was keeping her away, but Lily heard you crying from her bedroom."

She placed a hand on my shoulder before grabbing another tissue to wipe away my tears.

I nodded my response and let her pull me into her arms. My tears continued, heavy and full of grief, but Lainey didn't suggest I try to stop them. If anything, she encouraged me to cry. She told me to let it all out, that I had people here who loved me, who would take care of me and Lily. People I could rely on to keep me safe.

"We couldn't keep Kolya safe, though. What makes you

think Riass will stop at him? What if he comes after us? We have to be ready for him, Lainey," I told her through my sobbing. Then I looked around the tech room at Ivan and the remaining guards, holding their tortured gaze with my own. "We have to be prepared. All of us."

"We will be, Tess. Mark my words, that *ublyudok* will pay for what he's done," Ivan muttered. He turned to Kevin. "What about my uncle and Yuri? Do they know? Have they seen the video?"

"James rang his grandfather to break the news to him before he sent it. He was waiting until you came home before letting you know. He didn't want you and Tess to find out what had happened while you were still in the car. I haven't heard from him since. It was Brad who called to let me know that James was speaking with someone from the Pentagon and would be in touch as soon as the call was over."

Ivan made a huffing noise, then took out his phone. "I'm going to call Yuri. I want to see what they are doing to find them. Maybe they can use their... connections." He tapped a few keys on his phone and walked towards the door of the office. Before he could leave, I called out to him.

"Ivan, whatever you discuss, I want to know. Whether you think I need to hear it or not."

Ivan nodded, then turned away. He only took one more step, then stopped, his body stiffening. He said my name but didn't turn back to face me.

Taking a deep breath, I asked, "What is it?"

"I want to be there, Tess. When you tell Lily, I want to be there. I need to be there for both of you."

My heart, which had already broken, seemed to shatter into tiny pieces on hearing his words, and my stomach twisted so violently I thought I might throw up again.

How could I tell my daughter, who was only four years old, that her father was dead? I'm her mother. I'm supposed to protect her from anything that could upset her and make her cry.

"I don't know if I can do it," I answered honestly. "I... I wouldn't know what to say. She thinks her dad is invincible. She wouldn't understand."

Lainey's hands cupped my face, her thumbs wiping the rolling tears from my cheeks. "Don't think about it now, Tess. Take as much time as you need to process this yourself before broaching the subject with Lily. You don't have to be the one to tell her. As long as you're there to hold her and wipe away her tears, it won't matter who breaks the news. We just need to figure out the best way to go about it, using words she'll understand.

"When her aunt and uncle died in the plane crash, you told her they went to heaven to be with Jesus and the angels. We could tell her that something happened on Kolya's trip, and now he, Jonesy, Lucas and Darius have gone to heaven. She doesn't need specifics, but if she asks, you could tell her that sometimes bad people do things that hurt others, and a very bad man hurt her daddy and his guards. But that's *only* if she asks. The thing is, no matter how much we try to shield her from this, the press will hound you, and she might pick up certain things from them. Like I said, you take as much time as you need until you feel ready to do so. I don't want you to push yourself to do it now."

"That's just it though, Lainey. I don't think I'll ever be ready to tell her. I'm not even ready to hear the words myself. I know what I saw, and I should just accept that he's dead, but the thing is... I don't feel it. It feels like we're still connected. In here." I banged my fist against my chest.

"You mean you still feel him with you, in your heart?"

I let out a strange sound comprising a half laugh/half sob.

"No, Lainey, my heart is too broken. I feel Kolya where I've always felt him, even before our hearts connected. I feel him right here: in my soul."

Lainey's calm, comforting composure broke. She threw her arms around me and held me tight to her chest while her tears flowed. After a few moments, she replied, "And that's where you'll always feel him. Because love—I mean that genuine, all-consuming love—can never die, even when we do. It's too powerful for that. You and Kolya shared a love so true it transcends life, death, and anything in between. You'll always feel him with you, Tess. Take comfort from that."

But I couldn't take comfort from it. There was too much hurt and anger waging war in my head to let me find comfort in anything. Too much sorrow; too much pain. And way too many questions to even think about explaining my loss to someone else, let alone my own child.

Chapter Eighteen

TESS

Lainey guided me out of the tech room and through to the kitchen where Nan sat cuddling Lily.

Yet another adult taking comfort from my child.

I could hear Lily repeatedly question, "Why are you crying, Nan? What's made you and Mummy sad?" She sounded confused and upset. It wasn't fair to keep this from her, no matter how hurt she would be. Witnessing our heartbreak without understanding the reason was hurting her anyway. I had to tell her.

Just the thought of doing so made me stumble, causing Lainey to turn and grab me. "Don't move; just breathe, Tess. Deep breaths in... and out, nice and slow, just like that."

I followed Lainey's lead, watching her take those breaths with me. After six deep breaths, I could finally move. Franco pulled out a chair, and as soon as I sat, he handed me a cup of tea.

After taking a small sip, I asked, "Can someone go and fetch Ivan?"

"I'll bring him," Danny replied.

Lainey crouched down beside the chair. "Are you sure you want to do this now? I can distract her—maybe watch a video or two?"

"I think it's best we do it now, but thank you, Lainey. For everything. She'll need your support more than ever after this. We both will."

"And you will have it, Tess. Whatever you need, just ask. You're not just my employer; you're my friend, too. I'll always be here for you."

Her words touched a piece of my broken heart. I tried to say thank you, but I couldn't speak due to the thick lump of sorrow lodged in my throat.

"Deep breaths," Lainey reminded me.

I breathed as deep as I could—in through my semi-blocked-up nose, then out through my mouth—at least a dozen times, and the lump in my throat lessened enough for me to chance another sip of my tea.

Lily stared at me. I knew that look. It was one that held a thousand questions. She was a naturally inquisitive little girl. Kolya said it was a sign of high intelligence and thought she'd make an excellent scientist. He loved the idea of it and told me he was just as inquisitive when he was a child, excelling in almost every subject. The physics and chemistry he'd studied helped him understand the science behind weaponry and ammunition—knowledge he expanded upon to create a lucrative, world-renowned business. He said that one day she'd take KOLCAT to even greater success than it had now. But after all this, I knew I couldn't let that happen. If she did have an aptitude for science, I'd encourage her to choose another path in life. I'd keep Lily as far away from KOLCAT as I could.

She scrambled down from Nan's knee and made her

way around the kitchen table to me. Lily's ice-blue eyes—so much like her father's—bore into mine as I lifted her onto my knee.

"I can do some breathing with you, Mummy. I'm good at it. Watch."

Lily proceeded to show me how good she was at breathing, with loud, exaggerated sounds backing up her claim. Franco, Danny and Lainey clapped and remarked how good she was. She grinned widely and accepted their praise, and I smiled despite my sadness.

Ivan came into the room looking dishevelled. He'd discarded his tie, and his shirt had the top three buttons undone. He made his way to the sink and splashed cold water on his face, drying it on the sleeve of his shirt before coming to sit beside us.

I placed my free hand in his, took another deep breath, held it for a few seconds, and then exhaled slowly. He squeezed my hand a little, letting me know he was ready to do this.

"Lily, I need to tell you why everyone is so sad today."

She looked from me to Ivan, then over to Nan, who'd begun crying again the moment I spoke.

"Something happened on your daddy's trip and…" I couldn't tell her he'd died; the words wouldn't form in my mouth. So instead, I added, "I'm so sorry, sweetheart, but he's gone to heaven to be with your aunt Tali and uncle Leksi."

Lily didn't respond, though her features creased in confusion.

"Jonesy, Lucas, and Darius have gone to heaven, too," Ivan told her in a croaky, tear-filled voice. He cleared his throat and wiped his eyes.

"Have *they* gone to see Auntie Tali and Uncle Leksi?" Lily questioned. She still sounded confused.

"Of course," Ivan replied.

"Well, when Daddy gets back from seeing Auntie Tali and Uncle Leksi in heaven, we are all going on holiday, and then it will be time to put our Christmas tree up. He's going to teach me to sing some more Christmas carols in Russian." Lily smiled brightly. She obviously didn't understand, and though it broke me a little more inside, I had to speak the words I found so hard to say.

"Lily, when you go to heaven, you can't ever come home again. Your daddy died today, sweetheart, so the angels came and took him to heaven. That's why we are all so sad."

Lily's lower lip began to quiver, so I gathered her in my arms and hugged her tightly. I heard several sniffles around the room, but I daren't raise my eyes to see who cried. Ivan pulled my chair closer and wrapped his arms around us. His breaths were ragged, and he sniffled so loudly I almost didn't hear Lily's tear-filled whisper.

"My daddy *will* come home, Mummy. He promised."

After a minute or two, Lily wriggled free of my arms. "I need to go to the toilet," she announced. "And I want you to take me."

She planted her feet firmly on the floor, waited for me to stand, and then held out her hand. As soon as I slipped my hand in hers, she led me out of the room. While she was doing her business, she chatted to me about school and the party she was missing. Not once did she mention her father or the others. It was like the last few minutes hadn't happened.

Although it was still daytime, I wanted to go to bed. I felt a level of exhaustion comparable to severe jet lag—

where you know you should be awake and alert but your mind and body tell you otherwise.

Lily wasn't interested in having an afternoon nap, but when I said she could watch films with Lainey instead, she shook her head and told me she wanted to stay with me. Summoning up what little strength I could find, I removed my coat and shoes, and then we lay on her bed while she flicked through the pages of a storybook. I awoke around an hour later to Lily tugging at my jumper.

"Mummy, I'm hungry, and I need a drink." Her tummy rumbled loudly to back up her claims.

For a few blissful moments, I forgot about the devastating news we'd received today. Then my new reality came crashing down, trapping me in feelings of loss and grief. They weighed so heavily on my chest I could barely move.

"Why don't you pop out to the kitchen and see who's around? Mummy will be there in a bit, I promise."

Lily frowned. "No! I want you to come with me."

"I can't, sweety. I'm still so tired."

"I'll wait until you're not tired, then," she said, though she didn't let go of my jumper.

She looked troubled—like she had something else she wanted to say but didn't know how to phrase it. I tucked her wayward copper curls behind her ears and placed my hands on her cheeks.

"What is it, Lily? What do you want to say? You can talk to me about anything, love. Anything at all."

"But I can't." She sniffed and wiped away the tears appearing in her eyes. "Because if I do, I'll make you sad. And I don't want to make you sad because you'll cry, and then I'll get sad and cry."

My earlier exhaustion seemed to melt away with every tear she shed. She was my priority, no matter how drained and mired in grief I felt. I had to find strength from some-where so I could be the mother she needed me to be.

"We've had some terrible news today, Lily, so feeling sad and crying is okay. It's normal. Healthy, even. And everyone around us will be unhappy for a long time, so if you cry in front of them while you are eating your lunch, they'll understand."

She nodded and placed her hand over mine.

"I don't want you to leave me, Mummy."

"Oh, sweetheart, I could never leave you. You're my little girl, and I love you more than anything in the world."

"But we love Daddy, and now he's in heaven, and you said people that go to heaven never come back. I don't want you to go to heaven, Mummy."

"Oh, Lily." I pulled her onto the bed with me and held her close, whispering soothing words through silent tears. "Don't worry, love, I'm not leaving you. I'm going to stay wherever you are. Always. I plan on being an old lady when I eventually go to heaven, and you'll be all grown up and have a family of your own then."

Her tummy grumbled again, and though it took a lot of effort, I got out of bed and carried Lily into the kitchen.

Lainey, Danny, Ivan and Franco sat at the table discussing the day's tragic events, but they stopped talking as soon as we entered the room. Nan was busy stirring some-thing in a pan while staring out of the window.

"Lily's hungry," I announced. Ivan stood and held his arms out for my daughter, but she shook her head and clung even tighter to me. Everyone looked confused, espe-cially Ivan. They all knew how close the bond between them was.

"She wants some Mummy cuddles for a bit, that's all," I informed him, though I hoped the look in my eyes told him more than my words. He nodded his understanding and went to the cupboard to get us some plates.

"Nan's made beef stew," he informed us, placing two bowls on the table.

Lily lifted her head from my shoulder.

"I don't want stew; I want pizza," she said in a small voice.

Ivan smiled and winked at her. "Do you know what, Lily? I think that's a good idea. Who else wants pizza?"

Danny raised his hand.

"So me, Lily and Danny for pizza, though I wouldn't object if Nan saved me some stew for later. Especially if she made dumplings, too," he told her while repeatedly raising his eyebrows. Lily giggled and told him he was funny. It was the sweetest and most welcome sound I'd ever heard.

Nan took two large pizzas out of the fridge and turned the oven on. She glanced over at me and tried to smile, but it wasn't happening for her. I saw her eyes fill with tears before she quickly turned back to the window.

"Nan, sit down. Ivan will sort out the food." She looked as exhausted as I felt. I'd lost my husband, as well as three guards, and two of those guards were dear friends. But to Nan—who'd already gone through the experience of losing her only child—Kolya, Jonesy, and Lucas were like her sons. Darius hadn't been with us long enough for her to form a close bond with him, but she'd mothered him all the same.

"I can't, Tess. I need to keep busy. If I don't, I'll..." She glanced my way and shook her head, biting her lower lip to keep the tears in her eyes from falling.

"Just know that we don't expect it. And you don't have to be strong for us." After kissing Lily's cheek, I carried on. "We've talked about this, and Lily knows it's okay to cry and be sad. We don't have to hide it from her. She understands."

Nan nodded in acknowledgement, then turned back towards the window without saying another word.

I thought Lily would remain on my knee while eating her pizza, so it surprised me when she moved out of my arms and into the seat that Ivan held out beside me. She knelt up on the chair and tucked into a large slice of margarita. I felt vulnerable without her warmth and weight on my knee. More exposed to other people's feelings. I bit my lip and dug my nails into my thighs, trying to keep the crippling grief at bay for a little while longer.

"We are going to get everyone together for a serious discussion about everything that happened in Estonia and Turkey. Roman, Yuri, and Gustav will all be present via video call," Ivan informed me.

Before I could reply, Lily announced with her mouth half full of pizza, "I want to have a serious discussion with everyone, too."

"Is that so?" Franco remarked. "What about?"

"I'll tell you if you go and fetch Jack and Nate and Kevin. Oh, you'll need to bring Andy and Dave, too."

"I think Andy, Jack, and Dave are out walking the grounds, so they'll be gone another half hour, at least," Franco informed her.

Lily thought about it for a moment, and after seeming to come to a decision, she nodded.

"Okay, you can fetch Kevin and Nate. I'll tell the others later." She dismissed Franco with a wave of her hand.

Grinning widely, Franco replied, "Yes, ma'am." He saluted her, then went to collect Kevin and Nate.

Lily stuffed a huge bite of pizza in her mouth, oblivious to the curious stares coming her way from the rest of the adults in the room. A few minutes later, Franco, Nate and Kevin entered the kitchen.

"You wanted to see us, Lily," Nate prompted.

"Yes, sit down, all of you. This is very serious." The words she was using made her sound so grown up, but they lost their effect when she wiped the pizza base from around her mouth using her sleeve.

"I've talked about it with Mummy, and she says she's not going to heaven until she's an old lady. So I want everyone here to promise me that you won't go to heaven either. And, Nan, I know you're already an old lady, but—"

"Oh, charming. I'm not that old, missy." Nan tried to sound peeved by Lily's words, but the smile on her face gave her away. Most of us around the table hid our smirks behind our hands, though Ivan and Danny actually laughed. It sounded hollow to my ears, but not to Lily's. She gave them a menacing stare until they apologised and looked down at their plates in disgrace.

She continued speaking, trying to get her point across to the adults in front of her.

"Like I was saying, I don't want anyone else to go to heaven. Mummy says you can't ever come back when you go there, and even though the angels and baby Jesus live there, I don't think heaven is as nice as my teachers said. Not for grown-ups, anyway."

"What makes you say that, Lily?" Nate asked.

"Because the other Jesus—I mean, the big one who's on the cross—he never looks happy. He always looks really sad."

"But the big Jesus on the cross is the baby Jesus when he's all grown up. I thought you knew that, Lily. Can't you remember what the priest said when your class went to church at Easter?" Lainey asked while looking at me for direction regarding this odd conversation.

"Nope. I remember we did some Easter bunny cards,

and Ivan wore my headband with fluffy rabbit ears and was mad at Daddy when he took a photo and sent it to Uncle Yuri and—"

"I think we should forget about religion for now and focus on the real reason Lily wants this discussion today," I quickly interjected. "She just wants assurances from us that we won't lose anyone else. And while that's almost impossible to do because none of us knows what's around the corner, we can all promise to do our very best to keep safe. For Lily's sake, if nothing else. Isn't that right, sweetheart? Is that what you wanted to say?"

"Yes," she said solemnly. "So please don't die and go to heaven, okay? Because me and Mummy will be even sadder if you do."

Chapter Nineteen

TESS

I thought I'd have Lily glued to my side once she'd finished eating, but it only took Lainey suggesting they build a playhouse in Lily's room—which they could sleep in—for my darling daughter to abandon me. Our conversation over dinner reassured her. We'd all promised to keep safe and away from heaven, and she trusted us to keep our promise.

I was grateful to be on my own. I wanted to lie on my bed with my eyes closed, blocking out the horrors of the day. I needed to be in a room that reminded me of Kolya. Of us as a couple. A place where we were free to be intimate, and not just sexually. Intimacy with a life partner comprises so much more than that. And due to us always being surrounded by guards, staff and family, we learned to value those times and places where we could just be... us. Kolya and Tess. Husband and wife. Friends, lovers, and so much more.

To know I would never experience that again was something I wanted to block out for as long as possible.

I couldn't wait to lie on our bed and cuddle Kolya's

pillow, taking in the scent of him and me together, yet when I closed our bedroom door behind me, I noticed Nan had been in and changed our bed linen. She always washed towels and bedding on Monday mornings, and in my grief, I'd forgotten about that. Now the pillowcase held a spring-fresh fragrance instead of the sexy, musky scent of my husband.

I opened up his wardrobes, searching for something that still held *his* scent, not just the cologne he wore, and I came across the grey blazer he'd worn when he arrived home on Saturday. I took it off the hanger and draped it over my shoulders. Closing my eyes, I tried to imagine he was with me, that the jacket around my arms and shoulders was his tender caress, but it didn't work.

My tears ran freely, accompanied by great heaving sobs that turned into loud, wailing cries. I fell to my knees, and my hands beat hard against the carpeted floor.

Why had this happened? Why had God, the universe, or whoever the hell was in charge up there taken him away from me after only five and a half years? Was I being punished for something? Why, when I'd finally found another family, did the world see fit to take away my happiness once again?

I sat up and grabbed the box of tissues from the chest of drawers. The bedroom suddenly seemed too big and too empty, despite the furniture it contained. I wanted to hide away from it and the feeling of being all alone in this vast, ugly world. So I slipped my arms inside Kolya's blazer and climbed inside one of his wardrobes, closing the door behind me.

Only the feel of his clothes and utter darkness surrounded me, which suited my mood. Reaching up, I pulled what felt like a woollen sweater from a hanger, folding it in half, then half again to form a pillow, then I made myself as small as I could, curling up in the foetal position against the wardrobe's hardwood floor.

I woke up to the sound of heavy footsteps passing by the wardrobe towards the en-suite bathroom.

Franco yelled, "Tess, Tess. Where the fuck is she, Nate?"

I tried to call out to him, but my words came out whispered and raspy. My throat felt parched, and try as I might, I couldn't seem to clear it.

"I think I heard something, Franco. Stop your pacing and listen."

I tried again to clear my throat and winced when the wardrobe door opened, flooding my safe, dark hiding place with unwelcome light. I tried lifting my arm so I could shield my eyes from the glare, but my whole body seemed stiff and unwilling.

"Hey, keep still. I got you, Tess." Franco hooked his arms under my back and legs, then lifted me, carrying me over to the bed. I tried to speak again but could only manage a squeak.

"Shh, don't try to speak. You're all cried out and your throat's dry. Nate will bring you a glass of water, and we'll wash up a little to make you feel more alert."

I heard Nate's footsteps as he left the room, leaving me alone with Franco. He lifted me in his arms once again and carried me to the bathroom, grabbing a towel off the rail before gently lowering me down to sit on the side of the bath. He turned on the taps at the sink and half-filled it, dipping a corner of the towel in the lukewarm water.

"I'm just gonna wipe your face, hands and the back of

your neck. You'll need to take off the jacket so we don't get it wet."

Franco was hesitant with his words, as though he expected me to protest, so he added, "You can put it back on as soon as we're done."

Nate came in and handed me a glass of cold water. I gulped it down quickly, spilling a little from the corners of my mouth in my haste to quench my thirst.

After handing the glass back to Nate, I asked, "Why did you wake me? Has something else happened? Have you found them?"

"We have some information regarding where the video was filmed, but we were waiting for you to join us before we patched everyone in via videoconferencing."

I nodded in acknowledgement but closed my eyes before they gave away my feelings about being present for the upcoming discussions. And really, who could blame me for not wanting to hear more about my husband's death?

"Hey! Stay with us, Tess. I know this is gonna be hard for you, but it has to be done. Keeping you and Lily safe is our priority, and we can't do that unless you're fully on board with what's happening around us. I know you don't feel it right now, but you need to stay strong and focused. So let me help you freshen up. You'll feel much better for it."

Franco began unbuttoning Kolya's jacket, and after gently sliding it from my stiff shoulders, he handed it to Nate, adding, "Tess will be putting that back on when we're done," just to reassure me. Though I wanted it back on, I knew I wouldn't be able to carry on wearing it with the polo-neck jumper. It was just too warm.

Without thinking, I lifted the hem of the jumper and pulled it over my head, wincing at the ache in my shoulders before dropping the garment on the floor beside me. Nate turned around and left the bathroom, a gentleman to the core, but Franco remained, glaring at my exposed arms and chest. I looked down to where his eyes were focused and realised he could see some of the love bites Kolya had given me peeking out over the lacy edge of my bra cup. I traced the bite on my left breast delicately. I'd forgotten they were there, but the sight of them filled me with warmth, along with feelings of comfort and satisfaction. My husband had left them there. They were symbols of our last night together. Proof of the love, passion and life we shared. A life that no longer existed for me.

When I finally raised my eyes to Franco's, it was clear he didn't see them that way. In fact, he looked a little angry, although he schooled his features quickly and wiped my eyes with the wet corner of the towel. I noticed a few dark streaks from what was left of my so-called waterproof mascara. Though, to be fair, it would've had to be industrial strength to stay on after all the tears I'd shed. We had wash-cloths in the cupboard under the sink, but I didn't mention them. I let Franco carry on with the towel, watching as he wet another corner with water directly from the cold tap. He leaned over me and lifted my hair before gently wiping my neck. I shivered a little when a drip of water ran down my back.

"Do they hurt?" His fingers traced the bites from the side of my neck down to my shoulders.

I shook my head, so he wet the towel once again with cold water and used it to press gently around my neck, shoulders, and then behind my ears. The cold water seemed to do the trick. I felt so much more awake and a lot less achy.

"My sister did this for me the day after we lost our mom," he said. "I was still a teenager. Angry and full of grief, as well as a half-bottle of Jack. Father Dolan said he'd come see us to discuss the funeral arrangements, and she was worried that if he saw me drunk, he'd report us to the authorities, and I'd end up in foster care. I got mad and yelled at her. I thought she was treating me like a baby, but the cold water helped snap me out of it. Of course, being my sister, she also filled the empty bottle and poured it over my head. But hey, it worked. I looked so damn sober by the time the priest arrived."

Franco wrung out the water from the ends of the towel and draped it over the bath beside me. I grabbed his left hand and held it for a moment.

"Thank you, Franco." I needed to say so much more, but those words seemed to be enough for him.

"You don't need to thank me. I'm here for you whenever you need me, Tess. I just wanted you to be ready for what's about to go down in there. Keeping you safe is more important to me than anything, and right now, we have to be alert and on our guard. You need to get your head together and listen to what they say in there, although it's probably gonna break your heart some more."

Franco took my other hand and pulled me up so I was standing right in front of him. He lowered his head, making his glossy black hair fall into his soulful brown eyes. I let go of his hand and reached up to push it away.

"You need a haircut."

"And you need to put on some clothes."

"The jacket—"

"Is on the bed where Nate left it. I know it's a source of comfort for you, but you might need something else in there." He ran his fingertips up the back of my arms. "Remember what I told you before Sarah's funeral, when you were so worried you wouldn't be able to stand up and speak in front of everyone without crying?" His fingers stopped abruptly, and then he nipped me, hard.

"Ow! Bloody hell, Franco. You could have told me instead of showing me."

"Nah. You needed a hands-on demonstration so you could go in there with fire in your eyes instead of tears. You can do this, Tess. You're strong when you need to be. And if you feel yourself slipping, let me know and I'll pinch you again." He went to nip the back of my arms again, but I pushed his hands away before he could make contact. I picked up my jumper and threw it at him as he laughed his way out of the bathroom.

I pulled the door closed and locked it before crossing to the toilet. I didn't think Franco would be happy with me if I missed what they had to say because I needed to go for a pee. He seemed determined I should be in there instead of hearing what they said from someone else. And although he often infuriated me with his mercurial moods, he was someone I trusted to always have my back.

Standing in front of the mirror as I washed my hands was a bad idea. Though Franco had cleared away the mascara streaks from my cheeks, my red-rimmed eyes had black smudges underneath, so I popped some makeup remover on a cotton wool pad and wiped it all away before washing the rest of my face. Mindful of the minutes I'd wasted, I hurried into the bedroom, putting on a T-shirt and Kolya's grey blazer.

The meeting was being held in the tech room, so I grabbed a cup of tea in the kitchen to take with me. Franco waited outside the room for me, along with Danny's dog, Bess.

She bounded towards me and stopped me in my tracks with her usual trick of winding in and out of my legs. She knew if I had to stop walking, I'd crouch down and fuss her.

There was quite a bit of grey appearing in Bess's jet-black wiry coat, especially around her mouth, and although she was almost nine years old, she was still as fussy and playful as a puppy.

After greeting Bess and giving her a tickle behind her ears, I allowed Franco to guide me into the room, with Bess following closely at my heels.

Kevin waved me over to sit on the chair beside his, which meant I could place my cup on the desk in front of us. Nearly every one of our guards had come to the meeting, though not all sat comfortably like me. Computer and technical equipment took up most of the space, leaving little room for more than a handful of people. Many of its current occupants were leaning against the back wall, including Lainey and Danny. Before I could ask about Lily, Lainey gestured at a screen to the left of Kevin. It took me a moment to realise what I was looking at until he moved so I could get closer. I could see the princess wallpaper in Lily's room, but that was about the only thing I recognised. Sheets were spread over just about every piece of furniture in a tent-like fashion, hiding whoever was underneath from prying eyes.

"It's a castle for Princess Anna and Lily," Danny informed me. "Lily is fast asleep on a makeshift bed, right about here." He pointed to an area next to Lily's wardrobe. "Nan's under there with her at the moment in case she wakes up. Lainey and I will get back to her when we've done in here."

I wanted to ask if she'd mentioned Kolya at all, but I

knew everyone had been waiting for me, so I decided to put my question on hold until the meeting was over.

"Rashid is currently on a flight bound for Albania. It's one of the last known whereabouts of Riass and his men, so he won't be joining us tonight. Jack's driving around the perimeter with Andy, but we can bring them in via video-conferencing before we have Gustav and Roman connected. In the meantime, if everyone's ready, I'll bring down the shutters and activate the rest of the safety features around the perimeter. I'm not saying I think we'll be attacked, but we have this level of security for a reason, and it'll do no harm to test it again tonight."

Though Kevin addressed the entire room, his eyes were on me when he finished speaking, as if asking for my permission. I nodded my consent, grateful for his attempt to offer me a little control in this meeting. The room was full of strong individuals with even stronger personalities, and I didn't have it in me to fight to be heard.

Kevin video called Jack and Andy, who I'd expected to be parked near the gates, but from the glare of the lights through the open Range Rover window, it appeared they were on one of the helipads.

"Jack, Andy, can you hear us?" Kevin asked.

"Loud and clear," Andy confirmed. They must have been viewing the video from a phone or tablet, as we only saw his hand and steering wheel until he positioned the device on the dashboard.

"There were more press at the gate than earlier, so I drove us nearer the house. I don't know what they expected to gain from photographing a moving vehicle, but we caused a commotion when we drove past." Jack leaned forward as he spoke, blocking Andy from our view.

"We're going to activate the shutters and security now,

so shield your eyes, lads," Kevin announced while flipping switches. It only took a second for the hidden bullet and blast-proof shutters to begin covering the doors and windows of my home. We couldn't see the effect from the tech room due to it being windowless. As part of our home security, we also had twenty extra security lights and, if needed, a drone could fly over the property, filming any potential threat. We already had cameras and sensors in operation around the perimeter of the extension—the place I called home—as well as next door in the old manor house where most of the guards lived. In addition to the ones in the residential properties, numerous sensors and cameras were strategically positioned around the grounds of the estate.

We also had a sensor on the roof of the manor house. It could detect incoming aerial threats—such as low-flying aircraft or drones. I remember Kolya, Kevin, and Rashid being like kids in a toy shop the day it was fitted. Kolya had Jonesy operate a drone overhead, then poor Ivan had to fly over and around the grounds six times to see what distance the sensor could successfully function at.

The memory of Kolya's enthusiasm and smiling face on that bright spring day caused my eyes to fill with tears. I'd never see that again.

As if sensing my distress, little Bess jumped onto my knees and whined before licking my chin. She was offering me comfort the only way she could. It seemed like another lifetime since she'd first done that for me. I'd been a cold, scared seventeen-year-old runaway, sleeping rough on the streets of London alongside Danny, her owner. Kolya brought us into his home and gave each of us a life worth living. Neither of us could ever thank him enough.

Jack leaned towards the camera again. "It looks like the

shutters and sensors are all working as they should, but once the meeting's over, if you give us half an hour, me and Andy can go around and check each one before you lift them. I know the roof sensor alerts you every time Ivan comes in to land, but I wouldn't be surprised if it gets tested by the press tomorrow. You know they're going to try and get photographs, especially when they hear James is back in the UK."

"James? I didn't think it was safe for him to get to the airport." The panic must have been clear in my voice because Kevin placed his hand on my arm and gave it a reassuring squeeze.

"Don't worry, Tess. He didn't take any unnecessary risks, and he's been in the air about two hours now."

I breathed a huge sigh of relief, thankful he'd managed to get to the airport safely.

Kevin began tapping at the nearest keyboard before announcing, "I'll bring in the Barinovs, then Gustav."

Manoeuvring Bess onto her back, I began rubbing her tummy. She'd gone into major overdrive with the licking when I'd mentioned James, but Bess could never resist a belly rub, and it stopped my face from being covered in sloppy doggy kisses while I was trying to look at the screens.

I felt a hand on my shoulder and glanced behind me. Ivan crouched down beside me and stroked Bess.

"Roman and Yuri wanted to speak to you earlier, without an audience." Ivan gestured at the guards scattered around the tech room. "But I told them you were too distraught to speak with anyone, even family. They understood, but... Tess, Roman's not accepting Kolya's death. He's seen the footage and has picked it apart to find the answer he needs as a father. He cannot view it... what's the word?"

"Objectively?" Kevin suggested.

"Yes, that is what I wanted to say. He cannot view the video objectively. I just wanted you to be aware. Perhaps deep down, he knows the truth, but he is still insisting Kolya might still be alive."

Ivan's command of the English language was almost perfect, though there were still a few words he struggled with. When I first met Ivan, he spoke with a heavy Russian accent; now his English is laced with a South Yorkshire accent and colloquialisms he's picked up from me.

Nate gave up his chair so that Ivan could sit beside me. If necessary, he could intervene during the conversation with my father-in-law. I hoped I wouldn't need his intervention. I wanted to get this over with quickly so that I could be alone again. Being around so many people felt stifling, despite being so fond of them.

As soon as Roman and Yuri came into view on the monitor, I froze. All the Barinov men were so alike, with their pale blue eyes and strong, handsome features. You could tell immediately they were father and son. I used to joke with Kolya that if I wanted to know what he'd look like in his 70s, I only had to look at Roman. But today, for the first time ever, Roman Barinov looked much older than his years. His grey hair appeared unkempt, and he wore a T-shirt instead of a suit. His eyes were slightly bloodshot, with puffy dark shadows underneath. But then again, it was no wonder he looked so rough. He'd lost two sons in less than eighteen months.

"How are you holding up, Tess?" Yuri asked.

"Not great," I told him truthfully. "I feel so unbelievably tired. I've fallen asleep twice today. It's like I have jet lag."

"You must take advantage of that while you can, *moya doch'*," Roman said. "You will go through stages of excessive sleep and severe insomnia. It is the way of grief, especially when you lose someone you love so dearly."

Moya doch'. My daughter. It's one of Roman's many endearing names for me. He'd never be a father figure, but like it or not, since my marriage to Kolya, he was family to me.

"But in this instance, I feel you should also have a little hope. There is much about today's events that don't add up," he added.

Roman seemed serious about this, and his words made my heart skip a beat. Could he really be alive?

"I see you are wearing one of his jackets." Yuri interrupted my optimistic thoughts. He smiled, though you could clearly see the sadness in his eyes. "Keep it on if it comforts you, Tess. Take both strength and comfort wherever you can find it, especially while your grief is so raw."

Roman's gaze rolled over me, stopping briefly when Bess changed position on my knees.

"She is looking much older now, but I bet she's still as greedy as a pup. Tell me, Tess, have *you* eaten today?"

Smoothly done, Roman. He was trying to take control of my well-being by using the dog as a distraction. I let it slide, allowing him to have his way.

"I haven't felt like it yet, but I'm sure Nan's saved me some stew for after the meeting. I didn't feel hungry earlier, and it would have been hard to swallow food past the lump in my throat."

He nodded at my answer, then he turned his gaze to Ivan before giving him an order. "Make sure she eats something."

"Yes, Uncle."

"How is my granddaughter? Ivan said you told her what happened."

"She didn't understand at first. She thought her dad had just gone to heaven for a visit. I had to explain that when you go to heaven, you can never come back. Then she became clingy and didn't want to let me out of her sight in case I went to heaven, too."

I thought Roman might admonish me for mentioning heaven, when clearly, he believed that Kolya might still be alive. But all he did was nod his head.

"Lily made everyone gather around the kitchen table for a serious discussion about her fears for us. She made us promise to keep safe. For such a small child, she certainly got her point across. Kolya would have been so very proud." Ivan's voice cracked a little at the end, so I stopped stroking Bess and placed my hand over his.

A series of loud beeps indicated another incoming video call. A monitor next to Roman and Yuri's screen flickered to life. There were several men on the screen staring back at us. Among them were Gustav Nilsson and our guards, Mark and Greg.

Gustav was Kolya's European right-hand man. They had been working together for years, and Kolya considered him a good friend. We'd spent holidays with Gustav and his wife, Erica, along with their four children. Their youngest is only a few months older than Lily.

Kevin spoke with Gustav and Roman briefly to ensure that all parties involved could see and hear each other.

"Tess, Ivan, on behalf of everyone here, we want to offer you our sincere condolences. We have already spoken with Roman and Yuri when coordinating our efforts to find Kolya and his team, but once again, Roman, Yuri, we are all truly sorry for your loss. Please note that we also extend our condolences to the friends and family of Jonesy, Lucas, and Darius."

"Thank you, from all of us," I said, glad that he'd also mentioned the loss of our guards. I didn't want their deaths overshadowed by Kolya. Jonesy, Lucas, and Darius deserved so much more than that.

"Kevin, Roman, I know you received the latest information before this meeting started, but I'd just like to catch everyone else up with where we're at now. We all know that the vehicle was attacked en route to the new KOLCAT build site. The call from Lucas came in at exactly twelve fifteen Estonia time—so ten fifteen a.m. over in the UK." Gustav paused for a moment, then added, "Tess, I know you haven't heard the call, so if you'd prefer, we can skip it. It's barely four seconds long, but you can hear gunfire."

"You can play the clip, Gustav. I need to hear what happened." Though my stomach churned just thinking about it, Franco had been pretty insistent I be involved in this meeting, and I trusted him completely.

Gustav nodded, then signalled to someone behind him. Rapid gunfire was the first thing I heard, possibly an AK-47. At least semi-automatic. The fact that I could pick that out from a few seconds of sound clip showed how great my knowledge of weaponry had become. I held my breath when I heard Lucas yelling.

"We've been ambushed en route, currently six miles from—"
"Darius—"

That was it. Kolya had said just one word, angrily shouting out the name of one of his fallen guards; his fury at being attacked pouring out like venom into each syllable. I sincerely hoped he'd emptied a few rounds into his attackers before they killed him. Hell, if I could find the bastards, I'd shoot them myself.

In a way, I was glad to have heard only anger from

Kolya. If I'd heard him cry out in pain it would have been too much to bear.

"Are you okay, Tess?" Kevin asked.

"Yes. I'm just glad I didn't hear... You know."

Gustav cleared his throat and shuffled some paperwork.

"We reached the site of the ambush around ten minutes after it happened. There were no bodies in or around the car, though we could see both blood spray and pooling concentrated on and behind the driver's side. We also noted grey matter in with some of the blood, and we've now confirmed from the video footage that Lucas suffered a shot to the head and several to the body. We're currently taking samples from the vehicle to determine who all the blood came from. Although the front passenger seat was full of bullets, we didn't find anything other than sprays of blood on it, which leads us to believe that Darius had been pulled from the vehicle before Lucas received his fatal head wound.

"I doubt we will ever know what happened to the others during or just after the call Lucas made. We found no other blood around the outside of the vehicle, apart from a trail from the driver's side. Kevin, you confirmed all GPS signals from their phones ceased around the time of the attack, which you said would indicate the use of a scrambler."

"Yes, we lost Kolya's and Jonesy's signals first. So whoever had the interference device will have approached the vehicle from behind. Darius was the last to lose signal, though it was barely a minute after the others."

Gustav nodded in agreement and wrote something down on a piece of A4 paper.

"Roman, do you have the photographs we took of the Land Cruiser?"

Kevin tapped a few keys and brought up some images on another monitor.

Even though most of the guards with us in the tech room had seen the photos before, there were still a few that hadn't. Both Jack and Andy swore, and no one could fail to hear Lainey's sharp intake of breath.

"As you can see, the outside of the Land Cruiser was riddled with dents and holes from at least thirty bullets, although the bullet-resistant material inside the door panels held up well. All four tyres were blown out, but they did have built-in run-flat capabilities, so if Lucas hadn't been hit, they could have still driven away. Every window had multiple impact sites, with cracks spreading throughout the whole pane, though once again, the ballistic plastic inner layers kept the bullets out. The passenger side window appears to have been lowered—possibly to enable Darius to return fire—yet we found no empty bullet casings inside the vehicle. There were no weapons left at the scene, although we know the vehicle carried extensive armoury."

When Gustav brought up the photos from inside the Land Cruiser, I had to look away. It was hard enough hearing the gruesome details, never mind seeing them.

I waited until I knew the photos had changed before I glanced back at the screen. The latest images were of deep grooves in the grass verge. Gustav said they were evidence of tyres spinning. Riass and his men had made a quick getaway.

The next photo was of a map with highlighted areas. Gustav began explaining the significance.

"They must have had three vehicles, possibly SUVs or similar, in which they loaded Kolya and his men. They left the scene via a single-road dirt track hidden inside the forest. Aerial surveillance revealed an old log cabin and barn, surrounded by an acre of land two miles in. Both buildings exploded simultaneously while our helicopter team was flying overhead, and due to the heat, they were unable to land until the buildings had burned enough for the flames to die down. We suspect their vehicles were hidden inside the barn and that Riass and his crew left for Latvia soon after via helicopter, timing the explosion so that we'd focus our search efforts around that area.

"A Latvian coastguard reported a low-flying NH90 military helicopter approaching Latvia's northwest coastline at eleven twenty-five a.m. The man is ex-military, so I would say this information is credible. I am almost certain this was Riass. He probably headed out to sea in a bid to avoid detection, rather than flying over land. We were already monitoring the Estonia/Latvia borders by then. Flying into Latvia at low altitude meant he could avoid having to use air traffic control, so we got lucky with the coastguard. James received the video from Riass approximately two hours after the sighting, and we believe we've found the place where it was filmed. I'm speaking to you from a farmhouse around five miles from there, and have a team covering the area until we can perform a thorough investigation of the site. It's dark now, and we know Riass is not opposed to using explosives. Though time is of the essence, the safety of my team has to be my priority."

Everyone in the tech room murmured their agreement, and deep down, I knew he was right, but I selfishly wanted to say that Kolya should be his priority. I was surprised Roman hadn't said it. When he did begin to speak, he made some extremely valid points.

"I understand, Mr Nilsson, that you are treating this as a

recovery, rather than an extraction mission, but I have a feeling you will not find my son's remains there. I have studied other videos this particular terrorist has appeared in, and the methods he uses to murder his captives are completely different. Riass and his man Bashir like to end their victims' lives on camera in a most violent and graphic way, such as slitting their throat or complete beheading. The only death you can fully confirm is that of Kolya's driver, Lucas. We did not see any visible life-threatening wounds on my son or Jonesy, and we did not see this Darius at all."

My heart lifted a little at Roman's words. Could he be right in thinking Kolya, Jonesy, and Darius were alive?

"I agree. It's not in the usual style of Riass or any ISIS leader, but we've had an expert take a look at the video, and he's ninety-eight per cent sure that Kolya and Jonesy are dead. On close examination, there were no movements at all from any of the bodies on that pile, and we are certain that, even though there were only two seconds of film showing them being beaten, if they were alive, there'd have been some type of movement. I wish I could tell you something different, Roman."

"Mr Nilsson, I can assure you there are drugs out there that are strong enough to fool a doctor into thinking a man is dead. I have often—"

"*Otets*, you have said enough," Yuri interrupted. He carried on speaking to his father in Russian with his back to the camera. Roman answered him, also in Russian, before switching back to English.

"Mr Nilsson, despite the warning from my son not to incriminate myself, I can assure you that *there are* such drugs, and I have seen them used effectively. You are aware of my position in Russia's criminal underworld. You know what people in my business are capable of. I am not a good man, nor is the terrorist who captured my son. Like knows like, after all. This attack had been calculated well in advance for it to be executed with such precision. Riass most certainly had an inside man, yet the traitor was not in a privileged enough position to know that the weapon did not have its guidance system. Therefore, I demand you begin a thorough investigation into all of Kolya's staff with immediate effect. Finding the traitor may not find my son, but it might prevent anything happening to the rest of my family. The safety of Tess and my grandchildren is of the utmost importance."

"Believe me, Roman, I have entertained every possibility. The only employees at KOLCAT who knew the transportation schedule also knew that the guidance system was being flown in separately. The purchaser knew this too, along with Kolya's trusted guards."

"Then I suggest you start with the people my son did not trust and do it quickly. I expect you to keep me informed of any new development as soon as it happens. Also, when you find the Judas who offered up the lives of my son and his men, hand them directly over to me; I will deal with their punishment personally. I look forward to hearing them beg for a quick death."

You could hear a pin drop in the room when Roman finished speaking. Gustav stayed silent, and for a few seconds, I thought *I* would have to break the awkward, disconcerting quiet. Then Jack said, "I'd also like to get my hands on whoever's responsible. I'll make sure they suffer, Mr Barinov. You have my word."

Franco, Kevin and Nate followed with, "Count me in." The rest of the guards in the room and on the monitors also chimed in with what they'd like to do to the person responsible, including Lainey, who sounded unexpectedly bloodthirsty. Ivan stayed quiet until they'd all finished speaking before adding, "I'm bigger than all of you, so naturally, I'll be at the front of the queue."

Chapter Twenty

TESS

The meeting ended rather abruptly after Roman's baleful words. Gustav had no further information for us, and we knew it would likely stay that way until first light. Kevin was busy trying to trace any recent sightings of Riass, as well as any known associates. He thought it might help us work out what or where his next movements might be. Latvia borders Lithuania, Belarus, and Russia, so finding his current location wouldn't be easy.

Lainey and Danny headed back to Lily's room, so I set about making Nan and me a hot chocolate. She came into the kitchen a few minutes later, sporting a noticeable limp and rubbing her left hip.

"I knew I should have sat on the bed instead of getting down on the floor," she muttered.

"Then why didn't you, Nan? I wouldn't be surprised to hear Lainey and Danny had to help you up."

"You're right, they did, but even so, I was still happy to lie there and cuddle Lily. I think it helped."

"Was she sleeping peacefully? I'm worried she might have nightmares. Lord knows I will."

"She was sleeping peacefully, Tess. Lainey and Danny did a good job distracting her and tiring her out with all that tent-making. With how dark it was under the blanket before I switched the torch on, I nearly cuddled up to her doll instead of Lily. It's all the hair that does it. It's the perfect match."

"Kolya hates it. Can you remember when Jonesy put it in the car and kept playing that freaky laugh over and over? He still swears he'll get him back for that... I mean, he used to say it... Christ, Nan, I don't want to use past tense when talking about them. It's just not right."

I put my hand over my mouth to stifle the involuntary sob, but it was impossible to prevent the rest that followed. Nan pulled me into her arms and cried along with me. It was inevitable this would happen. Neither of us was strong enough to do it before. If she'd hugged me earlier, I would have fallen to pieces, and there'd have been no way I could have attended the meeting. Which reminded me...

"Roman thinks that Kolya and Jonesy might still be alive."

"What?" Nan let go of me and took a step back.

I grabbed a couple of pieces of kitchen roll off the side and handed one to Nan. After wiping my eyes and blowing my nose, I began telling her exactly what had happened during the meeting.

When I'd finished speaking, she didn't immediately share her views. Maybe she waited so she could find the right words to use so as not to upset me. It's what I'd have done if our roles were reversed.

"I will admit, there were a few things that puzzled me

about the video, Tess, but at the time I…" Nan sighed, then wiped more tears from her eyes.

I knew what she meant without her saying it. Watching the video broke my heart into tiny pieces.

She turned to pick up her cup of hot chocolate and winced.

"Sit down, Nan, before you fall down. You need to go back to the doctor about your hip. It seems to be a lot worse these last few weeks." She'd been having pain in her hip for a while, and the doctor sent her for an x-ray a couple of weeks ago.

I pulled out a chair and manoeuvred Nan towards it, watching her face contort in pain as she lowered herself down. Once she was settled, I passed her the hot drink.

"I'll be okay after some painkillers. Will you be a love and get me a couple of co-codamol out of the cupboard, please? I think it's the cold weather that's getting to my old bones."

"You might need a hip replacement, Nan. I'll ask Benedict Grayson if he can recommend a surgeon. You may as well go private and have people wait on you for a change. Don't worry about the cost; we'll take care of that. The hospital Kolya took me to when I'd been shot was like a fancy hotel."

"I can't go swanning off after everything that's just happened, Tess. You, Lily, and James need me here, taking care of things."

"You need to stop worrying about everyone else and take care of yourself for a change. We love you, Nan, and seeing you suffering hurts us too. Promise me you'll go and see your doctor for the results of the x-ray, and if he recommends a hip replacement, let me book you in for it to be done as soon as possible."

"Okay, I'll go. But if he *does* recommend a hip replacement, give me a few weeks to process what happened today. I need to be here with you for my sake as well as yours. I need my family around me, and apart from my sister and Jack, you're all I've got left."

"I completely understand," I told her. "Besides, you need to keep an eye on Jack, too. He and Roman are out for blood. He triggered a bit of a Spartacus moment in there."

"I feel like it, too. I don't like thinking that anyone here would double-cross the family. I've known a lot of these guards for years. Jonesy came to work for Kolya about thirteen years ago. Lucas and Kevin joined us after that. It was when Kolya's old security team began looking after James when he went to secondary school. Then Nate, Dave, and Franco arrived. And, of course, there's his team in London. Jonesy introduced Rashid to Kolya. Rashid's children were only toddlers then, and he'd been out of work since he left the army. You brought Danny with you, and then we got Lainey, Andy, Mark and Greg. Then poor Darius. Has anyone spoken to Yannis about what happened?"

"He called earlier after he heard it on the news," Ivan informed us. He walked into the kitchen from the tech room and went straight to the fridge.

"I'm glad I didn't have to speak to him," I told them truthfully. "He's been Kolya's closest friend since they met at university, so I can imagine how upset he'll be. He might feel guilty about Darius, too. It was Yannis who kept on at Kolya to have Darius come and work for us. He wanted to move to England to be closer to his aunt and uncle."

I thought of all the guards' families and asked Ivan if they'd been told what had happened.

"Kevin rang the families this afternoon. It is not a job I would have wanted to undertake."

"Nor me," Nan murmured. She popped the painkillers in her mouth and swallowed them down with a gulp of hot chocolate.

"Have you eaten yet, Tess? Unfortunately, I ate what was left of the stew while you were sleeping, but I can make you a sandwich if you want?"

"Ivan, there was at least half a pan left, and you'd already had pizza," Nan admonished.

"That was hours ago, Nan," Ivan whined. "And you know how hungry I get when I'm stressed or upset."

Ivan was always hungry. Being six foot eight with muscles even the Hulk would be envious of, it was understandable that he'd need more food than the rest of us. But Ivan was also a comfort eater. When he was nervous, stressed or upset, his need to eat went into overdrive.

"We'd better send someone to the supermarket again tomorrow, or this one will end up chewing the cupboards," I joked.

"Very funny," Ivan replied with a huff. "Now, decide what you want me to prepare. I have to text Roman and tell him you've eaten."

"Okay, I'll have a couple of slices of toast, then you can tell *Lord Barinov* I'm not starving myself."

Ivan put two extra slices of bread in the toaster. Typical!

"I don't think Gustav was very happy with my uncle," he remarked. "But I agree with everything he said. Someone had to have betrayed Kolya. And that someone will have to pay for what they've done."

"Ivan, do *you* think Kolya and Jonesy are still alive?" I held my breath while I waited for his answer.

"No. As much as I wish it were otherwise, I do not think they are alive."

Ivan took two plates out of the cupboard and buttered

the toast before bringing it to the table. He sat next to Nan and kissed her on the cheek. "I saw you take the pills. Is your hip bothering you again?"

"I'm trying to persuade her to see the doctor," I told him.

"I will take you," he said while waving a piece of toast in her direction.

We heard a whirring sound as the security shutters began to rise.

"I know we've had practices before, but I wasn't prepared for them this time. I found it quite unnerving when I heard them come down over the window in Lily's room." Nan shivered a little, and I responded in kind. Despite the security shutters being there for our safety, it would have freaked me out, too, if I hadn't been prepared for them.

Jack and Andy came into the kitchen a little while later and headed straight for the kettle.

"It's bloody freezing out there now, and it's getting foggy. I'm glad you're not picking James up in the helicopter tonight, Ivan," Jack said. He kissed Nan on the cheek before placing his hands behind her neck. The unexpected cold made her jump.

"What the…? Jack, keep your icy hands to yourself."

"Just a bit of payback for all the years I've had to put up with your cold feet in bed at night," he replied.

Ivan tapped his finger on the edge of my plate, reminding me to eat my toast.

"Is that why you're not collecting James? Because of the fog?" I asked before taking a bite.

"There's a weather warning out. Severe fog is in for the rest of the night, so it wouldn't have been wise to take the helicopter. We've worked something out to try and shake the press. Franco and Nate will drive the Range Rover to the hotel in Mayfair. Once they get there, Nate's going to switch vehicles before leaving to collect James from Heathrow. Franco will wait thirty minutes, then he'll drive the Range Rover towards Gatwick airport. Hopefully, the press will take the bait and follow Franco. By the time they realise he's not turning into the airport, Nate will have already collected James and his team, and they'll be on their way home."

Andy pulled out a chair and sat next to Ivan. "There aren't many photographers around now. I can't blame them, though. It's brass monkey weather out there. There's still a few cars parked on the grass verge beside the gates but not as many as earlier."

Nan put her hand over her mouth and yawned loudly. "I need more caffeine to keep me awake if I'm going to wait up until James gets home. He must have gone through hell today, having to reassure all those politicians that Riass couldn't use what he'd stolen, when all he wanted to do was grieve for his father."

"It will be hours yet until James comes home. You can't sit up and wait for him with your hip as bad as it's been. Tell her, Jack?" I pleaded.

"Tess, no matter what I do or say, my wife will end up doing whatever she pleases."

"I've got to wait up for him," Nan insisted. "I know he's not a boy anymore, but that doesn't mean he won't need us. Especially at a time like this."

"Then I'll wait up with you too, but I'm not sitting around the kitchen table." Jack took his wife's hand in his, supportive as always.

"Why don't we all get comfy on the sofas and chairs in the lounge?" I suggested. "I'll grab a few blankets and we can settle in for the night."

"That sounds perfect," Nan replied. She tried to hide her pain when she got up from the chair, but we all noticed. Ivan hurried to her side, his face a mixture of concern and determination. Without giving her a chance to protest, he lifted her in his arms and carried her through to the lounge, ignoring her request to set her back on her feet.

After placing her gently on the sofa, Ivan knelt down in front of her and took both her hands in his.

"Nan, you have looked after me since the very first day I came over from Russia to live with Kolya and James. You've cooked and cleaned for me, helped me learn a language I now use daily, and you're always there to advise me when I am troubled. I've had more years with you than I had with my own mother, so let me care for you like a son. It breaks my heart to see you hurting. I can't ask you to put yourself before others; that's not in your nature. But I want you to promise that you'll take better care of yourself from now on, starting with a visit to your doctor about your hip."

Nan teared up, and I followed suit. I knew what his words would mean to her. She cupped Ivan's face in both hands and kissed his forehead.

"Thank you, Ivan. I promise I'll make an appointment with the doctor tomorrow. You are such a good man, and I'd be proud to call you my son. I'm sure your mother looks down on you from above with a heart full of pride."

After witnessing such a touching moment, I settled down in Kolya's favourite chair next to the sound system, though I didn't turn it on. Kolya liked to sing along to songs that suited the mood or how he was feeling. It was a way for him to express himself, and there were quite a few love songs he'd sung to me over the last five years. I remember the first one we slow danced to. It was "With or Without You" by U2. As I went through the words in my head, I wondered if, or how, I could ever learn to live without him.

———

"Tess, are you awake?"

I opened my eyes and tried to focus on my surroundings, which wasn't easy with the lighting turned down low. I was in the lounge along with Nan, Jack and Ivan, who were all fast asleep.

"What time is it?" I asked, rubbing the sleep out of my eyes.

"It's three a.m.," said a voice that sounded so much like Kolya. I looked up in my sleep-filled haze to find him standing there in the doorway. The bright light from the hallway created a halo effect around his whole body.

"Kolya?" I leapt up from the chair, all tiredness forgotten.

"No, I'm sorry, Tess. It's just me."

As the figure moved closer, my eyes finally adjusted.

"James, thank God you're here." Though I wished with all my heart it had been Kolya, I was still so very grateful to have James back home with us. He took me in his arms and held me tight.

"For a moment, I thought you were Kolya. You look so much like him," I mumbled against his chest. I tried to pull away so I could go and make him a drink, knowing how exhausted he must be.

"Don't, Tess. Stay with me. I need this. I've needed it all damn day."

I hugged him back just as tightly, taking as much

comfort from him as he was from me. Nan was right. James had been dealing with the political fallout from Riass's actions, when inside, he must have been feeling as lost and as broken as I had.

I didn't see him cry. I didn't have to. I felt it in the movement of his arms and shoulders when the dam inside him finally broke.

His whole body began to shake, so I ran my hands up and down his back soothingly, trying hard to support his weight for as long as I could. I felt my knees buckle and we sank to the rug, still holding each other. Though I'd thought my heart was already completely broken, I knew right then I'd been wrong. Hearing and feeling the tears of a grown man who'd lost his beloved father cracked the final piece.

"James?" Nan sat up and threw the blanket from her knees.

"Stay right there," I told her. "Let James come to you."

"Give me a minute, Nan. I just have to…"

"Shh, there's no rush. She's not going anywhere, James," I soothed. "Take as much time as you need."

"I told myself I wasn't going to cry in front of you," he said, accepting the box of tissues I offered him. "You need me to be strong for you and Lily, not like this."

"We need you to be real, James. You can be yourself around us, not James Barinov of KOLCAT US. You've had a tough day dealing with the fallout from all this, and I know you probably have more phone calls and a press appearance to make. But give yourself time to process what's happened on a personal level."

"I keep seeing him, Tess. What they did to him… I'm so angry right now I could take whatever weapons KOLCAT has ready and blow the fucker and whoever's supported him to smithereens."

"You aren't the only one, James. Let me put the kettle on, and I'll tell you what happened in the meeting."

Before I left, I whispered, "Nan's having a lot of trouble with her hip, so we need to keep an eye on her."

His puffy, bloodshot eyes shot towards Nan, and his whole demeanour changed. James was just like his father: protective to the core.

I got up from the rug and left the room. I didn't want to be there when they had their moment.

Chapter Twenty-One

TESS

Having gone to bed just after 4 a.m., I'd expected to sleep until Lily woke up at least, but for some reason, I awoke at 7.15 a.m. feeling more alert than usual. My heart was beating way too fast, and I was hit by an awareness that something was amiss. It was more than the fact that my husband and guards were dead, yet I couldn't quite identify what was making me so wary.

I quickly checked on Lily before I went in the shower. Lainey was in the kitchen making breakfast and confirmed that both Danny and my daughter were still fast asleep.

Back in my bedroom, I tried to shake away the uneasiness, selecting an outfit from my wardrobe and then turning on the shower. I thought the warm water and cherry blossom fragrance of my shower gel would relax me, but it did nothing to shake the dark, foreboding feeling. Becoming more than a little anxious, I rang the tech room to ask Kevin if anything had happened. Gustav had been planning to search the video site at first light. Had he found something?

Dave picked up the phone in the tech room and told me that so far, the search team had found nothing. I asked him to have Kevin come and find me as soon as he was awake. I knew he wouldn't just brush off my feelings of apprehension. Kevin has always been a good listener. He's a great friend as well as being our security specialist.

Before I dressed, I took a moment to look in the full-length mirror at the love bites all over my body, knowing they would fade within a week. I'd welcomed that knowledge when all was still right with my world. Kolya had phoned to say good morning and I'd not been happy with him. How I wished I could relive that conversation.

I realised I'd not checked my phone since we arrived back home, and as far as I was aware, it was still in my bag, which had somehow appeared on my bedroom chair. Either Franco or Nate must have brought it through when they came to tell me about the meeting. With all that had happened, I certainly hadn't remembered to bring it in from the car.

My phone's battery was completely dead, which was no great surprise. I'd been video calling with James and Kevin on my way back from Yorkshire, so it hadn't a lot of charge left by the time we arrived home.

After putting my phone on charge, I continued getting dressed, donning stonewash jeans and my favourite blue shirt to cover up the bites on my neck. Hiding them from my inquisitive daughter was a necessity if I wanted to avoid embarrassing questions. Having neither the patience nor the inclination to style my hair, I towel-dried it, then went straight to the kitchen in search of a caffeine boost.

Lainey had eggs boiling on the hob and a rack of toast already out on the table. She offered to put some bacon under the grill for me, but I declined. My appetite was almost non-existent, despite hardly eating anything yesterday.

Danny carried Lily into the kitchen a short while later. She was still in her pyjamas and, as usual, looked decidedly unimpressed with the whole idea of mornings.

"Good morning, Lily. What would you like to eat?" Lainey asked. Lily hid her face against Danny's shoulder and refused to answer.

"Lainey asked you a question, Lily, so she expects an answer," I told her. But still, she said nothing, refusing even to look our way.

"Okay, then, Tess, it's just you, me, and Danny for boiled eggs and soldiers. We can even make little egg people with the shells."

"What a great idea," I replied with enough enthusiasm in my voice to make Lily look our way. "We could even use glue and glitter on them."

"I want to make egg people," she declared as Danny sat her on a chair.

"No, sorry, Lily. Only people who eat an egg can make egg people because that's how you get an empty shell," Lainey said. Danny and I were quick to agree.

"Well, I wanted an egg anyway, and lots of soldiers." I half expected Lily to end that sentence with *duh*, such was the sass in her tone. But I didn't reprimand her. I was just glad she'd taken the bait.

I decided not to tell her that James was here. Her big brother needed his sleep after such a traumatic day. So I set about taking the top off Lily's egg, which seemed slightly too big for the egg cup. Lainey had timed the boiled eggs just right, with enough runny yolk to dip the strips of toasted bread in.

Even though I hadn't been bothered about eating

anything, I really enjoyed our breakfast, and making egg people with the empty shells helped relieve some of the anxiety I'd felt earlier.

Lily sat with her back to the hallway door, so she didn't see James walk into the kitchen behind her. She was busy chatting away about her egg person being Princess Anna but with glittery pink hair, when a voice behind her asked, "Does the egg princess have a brother, like Lily?"

She dropped the glitter glue on the table and whirled around in her chair, almost screaming out his name.

"Hey, pretty girl, did you miss me?"

Lily threw herself into his open arms and gave him a big kiss on the lips before asking, "Did you bring me a present?"

James always brought Lily a gift when he visited, but with everything that had happened, it would have been the last thing on his mind.

"No, I didn't bring you a gift this time because I thought you might like to choose your own. I have to go to London in a few days, so if you show me what you want, I can bring it back for you."

"You do realise asking a four-year-old to choose just one gift is nigh on impossible?" I told him. Lainey and Danny agreed.

"So I'll buy more," James declared as he twirled around the kitchen with Lily in his arms.

Like me, James hadn't been able to eat much yesterday, so I volunteered to make him breakfast. We still had a lot to discuss, and I needed him as alert as he could possibly be, despite all the upset and jet lag.

We'd not spoken about the contents of the video last night, or his grandfather's theory that Kolya could still be alive, but I really wanted to hear his thoughts on all of it—

including Roman's suggestion that one of Kolya's employees had sold him out to Mohammed Riass.

Not wanting to bring all that up in front of Lily, or to erase the genuine smile from James's face, I stuck to making him breakfast and said nothing. I doubt I could have got a word in edgeways even if I'd wanted to. Lily chatted away with James about her new friend at school and about learning to play hopscotch.

"Don't do it," Ivan said, butting in on their conversation when he entered the kitchen. "*She* doesn't play fair," he added, pointing at Lainey.

His short dark hair was wet and stuck up all over, as if he'd just stepped out of the shower and left it. He wore an old blue hoody with black knee-length shorts.

After he'd said good morning to Lily, I asked, "Are you off for a workout?"

Ivan headed straight for the food, as usual. "I'll hit the gym later. I want to speak to Kevin first. I woke up feeling… I don't know, Tess. Sad, of course, but… strange, too. I can't explain it."

"You don't need to," I whispered. "I feel it too."

Lily stopped speaking when James and Lainey glanced our way.

"Are you talking about Daddy again?" she asked. Turning back to James, she added, "He's gone to heaven, and he can't ever come home again. I made everyone promise they won't go to heaven, and because you're my brother, you have to do an extra special promise."

"I promise," James said. He kissed her cheek and carried on cuddling her until she wriggled free of him.

"Mummy, why isn't it school today?"

"It is a school day, Lily, but we thought you might want to stay home and see James." We didn't know when it would be safe to send Lily back to school. Lainey had spoken with her teacher and headmistress about it, and I knew I'd have to contact them at some point to discuss sending Lily some work she could do at home.

"I do want to see James, but I need to go back to school when it's church day because I have to speak to Father Peter," Lily replied.

"Why do you want to speak to Father Peter?" I had an idea it was something to do with Kolya, so I braced myself for her answer.

"Because he works for God and Jesus, so I thought I'd ask him to have a word with them about letting Daddy come home."

"I don't think it works that way, Lily," James told her.

"Well, my daddy says a word in the right ear is often all it takes to get what you want, and I want Daddy to come home with Jonesy and Lucas. And Aunt Tali and Uncle Leksei."

"Then we can call Father Peter and pay him a visit when he's free," I told her. I didn't want to give her false hope, but I couldn't deny her either. I also thought it might do her good to speak to Father Peter about what happened. He was quite a young priest and seemed great with the children at Lily's school.

"I might go for a swim after breakfast. I wonder if anyone else wants—"

"Me! Take *me* swimming with you, James. I can show you how good I am at jumping in," Lily exclaimed. "Mummy, can I wear my mermaid costume?"

"We can put it on under your clothes, but James has to finish his breakfast first." I knew Lily would push her brother to eat his breakfast as quickly as possible, so I tried to distract her to give him some much-needed space.

"Lily, why don't you dress Anna up in her Halloween outfit and show James? We didn't have her with us when he video-called you."

"Can I put my witch outfit on, too?" she asked.

I pretended to think about it for a moment and made it seem like I was going to say no. She was rocking from one foot to the other, eagerly waiting for me to say yes. So I huffed out, "Yes, I suppose so." Before I'd finished speaking, she raced off into the hallway.

"What were you and Ivan talking about?" James asked. I plated up his breakfast and placed it on the table in front of him.

"I had a strange feeling, and I'm sure it wasn't just because I was upset. I felt like… I don't know. It might have something to do with what your grandfather said about someone in the company double-crossing your dad."

"I feel the same as Tess. It makes me wonder if they are planning anything else. For that reason, I think we should up our security measures even further, then maybe I will feel better." Ivan filled his plate and then sat beside to James to eat his breakfast.

"It doesn't seem to have affected your appetite," James remarked.

"You should stop admiring my food and finish your own before I tell my uncle you are refusing to eat." Ivan gestured at James's plate.

"He's an officer in the food police. Roman's orders," I quipped, then added, "He doesn't think Kolya and Jonesy are dead."

"I know. But you saw the video, Tess. The only one we can't really confirm is Darius. As much as I want my dad and the others to be alive, the fact is, without the guidance system, the weapon is useless to Riass. There would be no reason to let them live, unless he planned to torture them for not selling to him in the first place. He'd kill them after he was done with torturing them, anyway. That's what he's known for. So I'd rather they had a quick death than suffer at his hands. I can't bear to think of them in pain with no reprieve."

I nodded in agreement but said no more. It was probably silly of me to hold on to that tiny scrap of hope that Roman was right, and hearing what James had to say about Riass torturing people made my stomach turn.

While James and Ivan took Lily for a swim, I went back to my bedroom and set about tackling all the messages and texts on my phone. Karen and Amina had left their condolences after hearing confirmation about Kolya's death on the news. I called the office and told them about the video. My good friends listened to me cry for nearly twenty minutes, and poor Amina cried right along with me. Karen was so upset when I told her about Jonesy. He'd been pestering her for a date but she kept turning him down, even though I could tell she fancied him.

Amina said the press had contacted them about Kolya's death, and there'd even been a news crew outside the Sheffield office when they'd arrived to open up.

The press knew my involvement in Sarah's Legacy and that KOLCAT was its biggest sponsor, so I hoped any articles they printed wouldn't cast the charity in a poor light. Both Karen and Amina had refused to comment and had advised all staff in every branch of Sarah's Legacy to do the same, but we all knew how the press operated.

Michelle—Jean's nurse for the day—told me they'd had

a reporter ring Jean's doorbell at 5 a.m., which made me so angry. Jean really didn't need that on top of everything else. I told Michelle I'd have my phone on me all day, so if they had anyone else bother them, she should let me know. If it carried on, I'd have to speak to our solicitor, Oliver Ward-Jones, about it.

Oliver had called with condolences from him and his family. He told me to let him know if I needed anything. Benedict Grayson left me a similar message. I knew I should ring him back and thank him, as well as ask him about a surgeon for Nan's hip. I just hoped he wouldn't bring up what Kolya and I did at his Halloween party.

The largest volume of missed calls and texts came from Yannis. I knew he'd be at work, so I sent a message, telling him I was heartbroken but coping with the help of those around me. Not quite thirty seconds after I sent the text, Yannis called me back. I hesitated in answering, only because I knew I'd cry when I spoke to him. But he'd been Kolya's best friend for so long, so I had to answer.

"Hello, Yannis. I'm sorry for not returning your calls and messages yesterday, but I just wasn't up to it."

"You do not need to apologise, Tess. I know how hard it must have been for you. I just wanted to speak to you in person, to let you know I am here if you need me. You only have to say the word and I'll be there. Or you and Lily could come here."

"Thank you, Yannis. But we're keeping our security tight just in case we are targeted, too. It wouldn't be fair to involve you in all this. I'd rather know you were safe than have you around us right now. Plus, the press are hanging about, trying to get a story."

"I don't care about any of that. You and Lily are my priority. James, too. He sent me a message this morning, but he hasn't called me. Will he be coming over to be with you?"

"James is here already; he arrived in the early hours of this morning. I'm sure he'll ring you when he's up to it. He had to call and meet with a lot of important people yesterday regarding the stolen missile launcher, and he just wanted to come home to be with his family."

"I can fully understand that. Do you know how long he'll be staying with you?"

"No, he hasn't said, but I assume he'll be needed back at work to do more damage control, sooner rather than later."

"Of course. Poor James. He's lost both his parents now. I would encourage him to stay with you for as long as possible, Tess. I know you and Nan will look after him, and I think it will do him good to be in familiar surroundings."

"I think you're right, but if James has to go back, there's very little I can do about it, Yannis."

"How's Lily? Have you told her what has happened to her father?"

"Yes, she knows he's dead. Though she still can't grasp what it really means when someone dies. She told us earlier that she wanted to get Father Peter to have a word with God and Jesus, so they'd let Kolya come home. I don't want to keep correcting her, Yannis," I sobbed. "This is all so wrong. I hope Roman finds out where Riass is and tears him to pieces, slowly. He thinks Kolya and Jonesy might not be dead." I grabbed a tissue and wiped my eyes.

"Why wouldn't Roman think he's dead? When I spoke to Ivan, he said that Riass had sent a video that showed the bodies of Kolya, Jonesy, and Lucas."

I distinctly heard a note of panic in his voice. Was he worried that Riass might want to torture Kolya too? The whole idea of it was horrifying. I wished I could forget that James had even mentioned it.

"The video showed a pile of bodies. Lucas was on the

top, and you could clearly see his head wound and the shots to his torso. Jonesy was next, then Kolya. They had their eyes closed and had bruising to their faces, but because of Lucas and the way they were positioned, we couldn't see if or where they'd been shot. But Gustav and James believe they're dead. They didn't move at all when Riass's men began beating them."

More tears rolled down my cheeks at the memory.

"It was just so awful, Yannis. Kevin said I should look away at that part, and I wish I had."

"Will you ask Kevin to send me a copy, Tess? I think I need to see for myself that he's dead. I mean, if there's any chance he could still be alive, we should be out looking for him."

"We already have people trying to find him. As does Roman." I took a moment to compose myself and wipe my eyes before continuing. "Look, Yannis, there's nothing I'd like better than to think both he and Jonesy could still be alive, but Gustav had people analyse the video, and James believes that Riass would have killed Kolya as soon as he found out the missile launcher was missing its guidance system. Without that and the codes, the missiles are worthless."

"Yes, I think James is right. He probably would have killed Kolya when he realised all that effort it took to steal the weapon was for nothing." He sounded both relieved and worried in equal measure, so I had to ask...

"Yannis, I heard the relief in your voice when you agreed James was right in thinking Kolya was already dead. You were worrying about Riass torturing him, weren't you?"

"Relief? I... Tess, I'm not relieved. I just cannot bear the thought of my friend..." Yannis sniffled loudly.

"I know, Yannis. You don't have to say any more."

I was about to tell him I'd call him tomorrow when I realised I'd not mentioned Darius. But then again, neither had Yannis.

"I'm sorry about Darius. I'm not sure exactly what happened to him as he wasn't on the video, but they seem to believe that he was killed first."

"I know. Ivan told me that Kolya yelled his name before the call cut out."

I thought Yannis would have sounded more upset about him. After all, Darius had been one of his bodyguards before he came to work for Kolya. Maybe it was just me overthinking things due to being so upset, or maybe the loss of his best friend overrode everyone else.

That same strange, wary feeling came over me once again. I felt so unnerved that I got up and looked out of the window. I don't know what I was expecting to find; there was nothing to see through the murky, dense fog. Yet I still felt anxious.

Despite knowing that Lily would be safe with James and Ivan, I ended the call with Yannis, slipped unseen out of the kitchen door, and ran out across the patio to the indoor pool.

Chapter Twenty-Two

TESS

Everything was fine when I got to the pool. Two of James's guards, Carl and Tanner, had been waiting outside, and asked me if I was okay. I probably looked as anxious as I felt.

It took a few minutes to persuade Lily to get out of the water, but once she did, I wrapped her in a fluffy pink towel and held her close. Being with her, knowing she was safe and well, calmed my nerves a little, though my stomach was still doing the occasional flip. If they noticed my wariness, neither Ivan nor James mentioned it, which I was grateful for. I wasn't willing to talk about it with Lily around.

Nate and Andy were waiting outside the pool area to escort me back; both were carrying rifles, ramping up my anxiety even further. How bad was the security threat perceived to be to warrant the need for armed guards around our home? It took less than a minute to cross the patio to the indoor pool, for God's sake. I could understand the need for them in the outside world, but not at home in front of my daughter.

I didn't challenge them about it. They were only doing what they thought best, or following a protocol already set out by Kolya. But I didn't like how it made me feel.

After bathing Lily, I wrapped her in a towel and carried her into her room. She'd been swimming quite a lot over the last few days, so once she was dry, I rubbed body balm all over her skin, hoping to prevent another eczema breakout. Sometimes, especially after a lot of swimming, Lily will break out at the back of her knees and in the crook of her arms, so I try to prevent that from happening.

After I'd covered her in the balm, I let her run around naked until it soaked in. Hearing James call out my name, I yelled, "We're in here."

"I wondered where you ladies had got to," he said as he came to sit beside me on the bed.

"I'm not a lady; I'm a girl," Lily admonished.

"And you're a naked girl," he remarked.

Lily rolled her eyes and put a hand on her hip. "I'm not allowed to get dressed until my special cream's dry, or it'll make a mess on my clothes."

James frowned as he scanned Lily's body for signs of a rash. "Sorry, Tess. If I'd noticed her eczema flaring, I wouldn't have kept her in the pool so long."

"Don't worry, she hasn't had a flare for a while, but she was in the pool for hours with me and your dad on Sunday, and I doubt he remembered to put Lily her cream on after her bath. You know what he's like…"

My voice hitched a little when I mentioned Kolya, but I was determined not to cry in front of Lily.

James put his arm around me and pulled me close. I

rested my head on his shoulder, grateful for his presence. Neither of us spoke for a few minutes, our minds occupied with thoughts of Kolya. Lily chatted away, and I smiled and nodded when necessary, but despite trying, I couldn't give my daughter my full attention.

"Uncle Yannis bought me a new doll for when we go and stay with him, but I want to take Anna. She's my favourite doll in the whole world because she looks like me. I didn't tell Uncle Yannis that because Mummy says it's being nungrateful."

"Nungrateful, huh? I think she might have said ungrateful, Lily," James suggested.

"That's what I said. Nungrateful. You're being such a Silly Billy today, James."

Lily laughed and ran to the door when James asked, "What did you say? Time to tickle Lily? Okay, then. Here comes the tickle monster."

Lily squealed and ran out into the hallway, yelling at the top of her voice, "Hide me, quick. James is going to tickle me."

I heard Kevin say, "Better get some clothes on first, Lady Godiva. We have a visitor arriving soon."

"Kevin, I'm not a lady. I'm a little girl. Why doesn't anyone know this?" Lily replied with an exasperated sigh.

"Every time I see her, she's even sassier than the last. I love it. I love her. I didn't know how to feel at first when I knew you were pregnant, Tess. I felt too old to have such a younger sibling. But now... I'm just so grateful to have her in my life. I would have been dealing with this on my own if Dad hadn't married you and had Lily. I know I have Ivan, Nan, Yuri and my grandfather, but it's not the same. She's a part of Dad, like me. We share something. I don't want to have so much distance between us anymore. I don't want to miss out on spending quality time with my family." James sighed, then closed his eyes and shook his head. "I wish I'd studied in England instead of the States. If I'd have known then that I'd lose him…"

"Don't feel guilty, James. Yes, Kolya missed you, but he was so incredibly proud of you and all you achieved. You only did what he did, anyway. He left Russia to study in England and made his life here, too."

"I know, I just… I thought I'd always have him around, you know? Even after losing my mother at such a young age, I never expected to lose him. He always seemed invincible to me."

I slipped my hand in his and gave it a gentle squeeze. "Yannis called me earlier. He said I should persuade you to stay with us for a while. He's worried about you. I don't want to put any pressure on you, James; I know you'll be in high demand over the next few weeks, but I think he's right. You should stay here with us for a while. Lily and I would love to have you with us, and Nan will enjoy coddling you, as always."

"I plan on staying as long as I can, I promise. I have to call Yannis back and thank him for the kind words he used in his message. The last time we met, it didn't go too well, so I'm glad he's been able to put that behind him."

"What do you mean?" I asked.

"We had words the last time I visited him. Not quite an argument, but it wasn't far off."

"Join the club, James. I had words with him on Saturday before we went to the Halloween party. We were fine afterwards, though. The thing with Yannis is, he can be such a pain—criticising your dad for letting work get in the way of family time—behaving disrespectfully, especially towards me. Then he totally redeemed himself at the party. Your dad once said he's like a spoiled child, but he has a good heart and will be there for you if you need him."

James nodded. "He wanted me to partner with him in a new hotel venture. But the Lassiter Hotel Group is in a different league than anything Yannis has—even his five-star properties. They're package holiday hotels that cater to families wanting their two weeks in the sun. Most of our hotels are the high-end boutique style, catering mainly to the wealthy. The rich and famous choose a Lassiter Hotel when they want a place to stay that offers both elegance and high levels of privacy and security. We're performing extremely well in today's market, yet the properties Yannis owns are struggling. The cruise ships aren't as profitable either, and haven't been so for years. I just wasn't willing to add money *and* the Lassiter name to a business venture I couldn't be one hundred per cent sure of. My grandfather would turn in his grave if I went into business with Yannis."

"I can understand you being wary, James. I don't know much about the hotel industry, but I do know all the Lassiter Hotels we've stayed in have been impressive. Don't you find it hard to manage both KOLCAT US and Lassiter's"

"I rarely have much to do with the day-to-day running of the hotels. I have excellent staff who I trust to get the job done. Of course, all executive decisions are sent my way, plus a monthly accounting update. To have gone into business with Yannis would have changed all that. But he wasn't at all happy with my refusal, Tess, so I cut my trip short and left the next day. That was about six months ago, and we haven't spoken since, though we have sent the odd text message."

"I wasn't aware of that. Your dad never said anything."

"I didn't tell him. They've had very few arguments over the years, but I remember Yannis threw a huge strop and didn't speak to my dad for months after he refused to go into business with him. I didn't want that to happen again. They've been friends for so long, and Yannis has been like an uncle to me."

"I suppose all that's happened is water under the bridge now, though, James. When you lose someone, it makes you see things in a different light. It makes you want to bring people closer and tell them how much they mean to you. You never know if it will be the last time you see or speak to them."

"You're right, Tess. Life is way too short for petty arguments. I'll go and call Yannis now. By the way, I've invited George to spend a few days with us. I asked him to watch the video to get his take on it, but I wanted him here in case anyone needs a counselling session. Yesterday's events might be a wake-up call for some of our guards, and talking it out with George might help them. I know I'll be scheduling some time in with him. My sessions with him and Devina after my mum died helped me come to terms with her loss, though I know that learning to deal with my father's death will be much more complex due to how that came about."

I remembered the day Kolya told me about the sessions he and James had with George and Devina, and how he'd tried to get me to speak with them, too. I never did, and I wasn't sure if I could do it now, either.

"He told me how the counselling helped you and him deal with your grief. But honestly, James, I don't think I'm up to talking to anyone about it right now, and I'm not sure Lily really understands enough about death to benefit from speaking with George."

James yawned loudly, then rubbed his eyes.

"Why don't you go back to bed for a few hours?" I suggested. "You look like you could sleep standing up."

"Tess, when I climb into bed tonight, I need to be so exhausted I fall straight into a dreamless sleep. If I close my eyes now, I know what I'll see."

He let go of my hand and slowly stood, stretching his arms above his head, accidentally catching Lily's princess light shade in the process.

"You've always been tall like your dad," I remarked. "I wonder if Lily will have his height or be a short-arse like me."

"I wouldn't worry, Tess. Even as a four-year-old, my sister commands everyone's attention. She doesn't need to have the Barinov height to rule like a queen."

Chapter Twenty-Three

TESS

George Ranley had been working for Kolya for nearly twenty years. He'd hired him and his partner, Devina Morris, on the advice of another high-profile business associate—one who'd also relied heavily on the services of a close protection team.

In most cases, the men and women involved in close protection security detail are ex-military or police, which is certainly true of our guards, and as the job is so stressful, they can perform their duties more capably if they have a mental, as well as physical outlet for that stress.

Both George and Devina offer counselling or therapy sessions to our team at least once a month. Kolya told me it was a requirement for all staff to meet with one of them, even if it's only to say they are fine.

I have never felt the need to speak with either of them before, even when dealing with Sarah's death. I didn't like the idea that someone other than Kolya would know my deepest thoughts, worries and hurt. I thought I'd always be that way—that my ability to cope with shitty situations was my superpower. If that was the case before, it certainly wasn't anymore. Kolya's death was my kryptonite. Without him, I'm broken.

Dave and Franco used the car-swap trick to bring George back from London. He actually lived in Berkshire, but we didn't want to expose him or his home to the press. So George made his way to Lassiter's in Mayfair, and we collected him from there.

Nan handed him a cup of his favourite coffee on arrival, which he accepted gratefully before expressing his horror over what had happened in Estonia. He offered his condolences to all in our household and said that he and Devina would take time out of their schedules to accommodate our needs, as well as any staff members at KOLCAT headquarters.

James and I thanked George for coming out to visit us on such short notice. It was easy to see that the two men had a long history. James had often shared his innermost feelings with him, yet the fondness that was so clearly evident in their hugs and words seemed more like family, rather than client and therapist.

As per his usual visits, George had brought Lily a chocolate lollipop. He gave her his full attention as she chatted away about school and her new friend. With a grandson the same age as Lily and another on the way, I could easily see George being a much-loved grandad. He just had that way about him.

George's wife had a hip replacement last year, so Nan quizzed him about her recovery. Jack mentioned that the doctor suggested Nan have surgery sooner rather than later, or she'd risk problems in her other supporting joints while they took up the strain. She flashed an angry glance his way, and I knew she wouldn't have shared that information with us. James knew it, too, and admonished her for going back on a promise she'd made to him.

Apparently, Nan swore she'd tell James everything the doctor said, as well as agreeing she'd have surgery as soon as possible, if needed. I wasn't going to tell her off for wanting to stay and help us come to terms with what had happened. In her position, I'd want to do that too, but I also couldn't stand to see her hurting. Nan was as much a mother to me as Jean had been. There was nothing I could do to prevent Jean's dementia from taking over her life, but I could encourage Nan to take better care of herself.

Lily asked if we had any cake left over from the weekend. Ivan had polished off what remained of Nan's baking, so they decided to bake a few buns and other treats. As well as putting a smile on Ivan's face, it meant Lily would be occupied while we went to re-watch the video with George. While a part of me never wanted to see it again, I felt that watching it once more might help me see something I'd missed. Something to confirm that Roman was right in thinking Kolya could still be alive.

———

"Nate said you wanted to see me earlier," Kevin said when I sat beside him. "I didn't fall asleep until seven. Then I kept waking up in a panic as though someone had screamed in my ear."

He looked exhausted. The dark shadows under his eyes, along with an ashy tone to his normally healthy-looking skin, gave his face a haunted look. Kevin needed a break, though I knew as soon as I suggested it he'd refuse. Kolya had held Kevin in such high regard. He was awed by his technical expertise and respected him as a person. They were alike in lots of ways. Both were driven in their chosen career; determined to be the very best at what they did. I both adored and respected Kevin, and seeing him looking so drained only added to the hurt inside me.

Ivan came in with tea and biscuits for Kevin, closely followed by little Bess, who sat dutifully at my heel. Of course, once Ivan opened the biscuit tin, Bess darted under his chair, eagerly awaiting the sweet treat he would no doubt share.

I began telling Kevin about my feelings of anxiousness this morning and mentioned that Ivan had felt the same. He said he'd go through our security again after we'd spoken to Gustav.

After James gave George a brief overview of everything we'd learned so far, he instructed Kevin to play the video and read out the full translation of Riass's rant.

I tried to concentrate on every minute detail, but all I felt was rage, then pain. Like someone was tearing at my insides. I'd been clenching my teeth together so hard that my jaw ached, and I hadn't realised I was crying until Kevin passed me a tissue. After wiping my eyes, I glanced over at George and James. James's face was expressionless, as if carved from stone, but George's face displayed a myriad of emotions. Shock, horror, confusion, and the all-too-familiar grief.

"Well, what did you make of it, George?" Kevin asked, because it appeared James was locked inside his thoughts at that moment.

George cleared his throat. "Well, I agree with you, James. The placement of your father's body beneath that of his guards looks as though Riass was making a statement. Like he was showing that he didn't consider Kolya important enough to be on top of the pile: an unworthy foe, if you will. I also note that it's most unlike the rather public executions this terrorist group seems to favour. Or it could be that your father and Jonesy were accidentally killed when they ambushed their vehicle, so they were unable to perform a public execution."

"Maybe he was trying to disguise the fact that Kolya and Jonesy are still alive," I suggested. "That's what Roman seems to think."

Kevin played the audio of the phone call from Kolya and his guards to Mark and Greg. If not for that distraction, I think James and George would have told me not to listen to Roman.

Though I'd not found the answers I sought in the video, hearing the recording of the call again made me realise something.

"Kolya didn't shout out Darius's name because he'd been shot; he did so because he was trying to tell us that Darius was the one to betray them. Yesterday I believed what Mark and Greg had assumed—that Kolya sounded so angry because they'd been ambushed and Darius had taken a bullet. I know you don't think Roman is right in saying Kolya and Jonesy could still be alive, but he's right in saying we can't confirm that Darius is dead, despite what Riass insinuated with the bonfire."

"Play the recording again," George demanded, sitting forward in his seat. James watched George closely. His eyes were half closed, and he frowned as he listened.

"And again, Kevin." James got up from his chair and began pacing the tech room while we once again listened to the brief recording.

"You could be right, Tess. I thought about it last night," Kevin said. "That's why I stayed up until this morning, hoping that Gustav would tell me they'd found something that would prove otherwise. Not that I wished anyone dead, you understand," he added.

"After what has happened, I don't think it would be a breach of therapist/patient confidentiality to say I've had a number of sessions with Kolya over the years, and we've examined his feelings and emotional reactions over many life events." George sighed heavily, as if debating internally how to phrase something. A few seconds of silence passed before he spoke.

"James, I've seen your father broken and grieving over the death of your mother, and I've also seen him angry and frustrated over his attempted assassination when Tess was shot. I've witnessed him cry, rant, yell—expressing himself in numerous ways—so I feel confident in saying I believe the anger we are hearing is directed at Darius. The way he says it, the tone he uses, and the inflection in his voice at the end. I can understand how they'd come to the other conclusion—that Kolya was angry about the attack—but the fact remains that we've no visible evidence that Darius is dead. And if he *is* dead, why wasn't he included in the pile of bodies? Did they find any of his blood in the vehicle? I assume they are testing for it."

"Kevin, pull up all the information we have on Darius and hack his bank accounts. Let's see if he's had any sudden windfalls," James instructed.

George cleared his throat and cast his eyes down at the carpeted floor. "I'll pretend I didn't hear that."

"I know I don't need to ask, George, but I'll do it anyway. Can you assure me that whatever you hear over the next few days is not repeated anywhere else?" James questioned.

"Of course," George replied. "As well as the medical oath, I also signed a confidentiality agreement when I came to work for your father. In the years I've known him, you, and the men who work with you, I'd call it less confidentiality, more loyalty. Your father was my friend, James, along with Jonesy and Lucas. If there's a way to catch whoever betrayed him, please do so. I want to see them brought to justice, along with the terrorists in that video."

After hearing what George had to say, James seemed to relax a little. His relief showed in the barest hint of a smile. "Thank you, George. I'm grateful for your presence here today. If you want to leave now, your usual room in the guards' quarters is ready, but if you're okay with hanging around in here with us, I'd really appreciate your feedback. I'm going to pull up all the information we have on Darius before I speak to Yannis, then we'll arrange a video call with Gustav."

"I would not trust anything that Yannis has to say. He persuaded Kolya to hire Darius. I never liked him, and neither did Franco. But would your father listen?" Ivan grumbled.

"I was never keen on him either," I added. "But he was always so sweet to Lily."

"I can't say I had much to do with him. Dad never brought him to the States. But we can't let how any of us felt about him take away from the issue at hand. Was Darius the one to betray him? Or are we all hearing what we think is Dad's anger towards his guard for... I don't know, not opening fire on Riass quick enough?"

Though I understood what James was saying, I knew I was right in thinking Darius had betrayed Kolya. The anxiousness I'd felt throughout the day had eased since I'd said the words out loud. Kolya was angry with Darius. He'd been about to tell Mark and Greg that Darius had instigated the attack. I'd been so distraught I never thought to question what everyone else told me they thought had happened.

"I want to call Roman," I announced. I didn't just want to speak to him; I needed to hear him tell me what he was going to do when he found Darius. Because I had no doubt he would find him, however long it took. Roman would make that man suffer for causing his son's death, and with the rage that was building inside me, I would gladly stand by and watch.

Yannis didn't answer when James rang him, though he returned the call a few minutes later. James had the call on speakerphone so we could all hear what our friend had to say.

"James, I'm so sorry I missed your call; I'm at a fundraiser on the mainland. How are you doing? How are Tess and Lily?"

"How do you think we are doing, Yannis? Lily and I lost our father, and Tess is grieving her husband. Possibly due to your ex-bodyguard's betrayal?" The anger was clear in both his words and tone. It must have caught Yannis off guard because it took a few seconds for him to answer.

"What do you mean by that, James? My ex-bodyguard's betrayal? Surely you don't mean Darius! Why would he do that? He's a good man and was always a loyal employee. His parents worked for my father for many years, so I've known him since we were boys. I'd have still had him working for me if he hadn't wanted to leave Athilos."

"Tell us again why he wanted to leave, Yannis," I asked.

"Tess? What is this about? I thought Darius was dead."

"Answer the question, Yannis." Just as James had finished speaking, Kevin indicated at a couple of monitors in front of him, showing two bank accounts belonging to Darius, along with his background check. Neither account showed any large monetary deposits.

"Darius lost his father to a heart attack while his mother was dying of pancreatic cancer. Despite my paying for the best care possible, the poor woman suffered terribly. When she died, he decided to leave Greece altogether. He'd lived on my island for most of his life, but he didn't want the memories that were attached to Athilos. The only family he had left were his aunt and uncle, who live in London. They own a takeaway, I believe. I asked your father if he would take Darius on so he could be near them. Kolya knew all this, and I assume he ran a full background check."

Kevin nodded, then pointed at the monitor showing the full details of the background check. I scanned through it, focusing on the paragraph below the pre-employment checks, which summarised the main points. Nothing about it raised any red flags. I began to second-guess the idea that Darius had betrayed Kolya. I felt sorry that he'd lost his father and watched his mother succumb to cancer, and I could understand him wanting to leave Athilos. Island life would have been a lonely life if he didn't spend time with the other guards. He rarely did that when he worked for us. Franco said that apart from the odd game of pool, Darius never socialised with any of our staff. He used to go and see his family in London as much as possible, which I always found quite endearing. But was he really going to visit them, or was he meeting someone else?

When all was said and done, apart from the details on the background check, I doubt any of us knew much about his personal life. But I knew James had upset Yannis, so I tried to explain why we were asking him these questions.

"We are exploring all possibilities, Yannis, but the truth is, we can't say for sure that Darius is dead. During the few seconds of that last phone call, I believe Kolya sounded angry with Darius, as well as with being ambushed. And other people agree."

"Well, I will have to take your word for it, seeing as I don't have access to the video footage or recording."

"Kevin, send all we currently have to Yannis," I instructed. "I'd like to get his take on all this. After all, he knew Darius better than any of us, and he's been friends with Kolya since they were eighteen."

"Yes, and he's seen my dad in anger several times," James added.

I shook my head and whispered, "That's not helpful, James."

"I will review the footage and get back to you as soon as possible. Understandably, your emotions are raw at the moment, so I will excuse your hostility, James. And thank you for trying to diffuse the situation, Tess. You know how important you all are to me, and I hate to think of you suffering. Please know that I am here for each of you, should you need me. You are my family, and I love you all dearly."

I grabbed the phone and took it off hands-free before James could say anything else. "Thank you, Yannis. Your kind words are much appreciated. I'm so sorry to have disturbed you. Call me tomorrow once you've had a chance to look at the video and listen to the call. Goodnight." I hung up quickly, not waiting for his reply.

James held out his hand for his phone, but I kept it close to my chest.

"Promise me you'll switch it off after we've spoken to Roman and Gustav. You need to sleep tonight, James. We all do. Tempers are fraying, and while I know that you and Yannis had a disagreement, this is not the time to start an argument. You never know, by tomorrow he might have more information on Darius that could be useful to us, so I don't want to alienate him."

"She's right, James. Yannis might tell us something that he thinks is irrelevant yet could be quite useful. But you have to remember that once he's seen the video, he'll need some time to process it. He lost his best friend yesterday, and although he's already been told what happened to him, seeing it with his own eyes will hit him hard," Kevin added.

James glanced up at the ceiling. His eyes were glassy; his shoulders jerking slightly as he tried to hide the fact that he was crying. I was about to go over and hug him, but little Bess beat me to it. She jumped up onto a chair so she could lick his hands. He looked down at her and smiled before picking her up to give her a quick cuddle. She was having none of it, choosing instead to lap at his face and ears incessantly, which made him laugh out loud.

Ivan took out his phone and quickly snapped a photo. "I'm sending this to your friend Brad," he said with a chuckle. "I'll tell him she's your new girlfriend."

"You're just jealous because she loves me more than you," James replied as he sat down and tried to fend off the overly enthusiastic yet loveable dog.

"You are wrong, James. Bess adores me. I am her favourite human," Ivan announced while trying to coax her towards him. Bess ignored him and carried on licking a chuckling James. She knew when one of us needed her special method of comfort. Animals are so intuitive.

After about thirty seconds of James and Ivan's playful bickering, I nudged George and said, "Watch this," before grabbing the biscuit tin and giving it a shake. Bess left James immediately, sitting at my feet and presenting me with her left paw. I rewarded her with a custard cream, then snapped the tin shut.

"Well, James, now you've proven how irresistible you are to four-legged females, I suggest we crack on and speak to Roman and Gustav."

James rolled his eyes at me but tapped the edge of his chair to get the greedy little dog's attention.

"Go ahead, Kevin," he instructed before sitting back and waiting for each video call to connect.

Chapter Twenty-Four

Four weeks later

Lily followed me to the utility room to collect our nightclothes and undies from the dryer, and I spent a few minutes showing her how to fold them so they wouldn't crease. She'd brought Anna the doll along "to help" with our chores and repeated my instructions to her.

Lily hadn't been at school since Kolya and our guards were killed and she was missing her friends, as well as her teachers. James and our guards were still concerned about security, so we were staying home until they deemed it safe.

The press had given up stalking our gates last week, which was a relief. Their vitriol against KOLCAT had increased daily until someone leaked the video footage of Riass spouting his vile commentary. Seeing the bodies of Kolya and his guards sparked a little humanity and compassion in all avenues of the media. The tone newsreaders used changed to one of sympathy, and the tabloids featured photos of the families left behind. Of course, they seemed

183

to take delight in focusing on the age difference between Kolya and I, as well as the reason I'd run away from The Willows.

We invited family members of our fallen guards to come and visit with us last week, to collect their loved ones' belongings. Jonesy's aunt and cousin and Lucas's step-brother had accepted our invitation. They'd joined us for a light lunch afterwards and had each spoken to our solicitor, Oliver Ward-Jones, who advised them about the death-in-service payment each of our guards' were promised if they died while working for us. Both Jonesy's and Lucas's nominated beneficiaries would each receive two million pounds once all relevant paperwork was completed. It was taking a little longer than normal because they were killed abroad, and as yet, we had no body for a coroner to confirm that Jonesy was dead, although they'd accepted the video evidence for Lucas.

The British Embassy had been liaising with the families of the deceased, but there was only so much they could do under the circumstances. With my and James's approval, Oliver was overriding the terms and clauses in the contract of employment that Jonesy and Lucas had signed so that the families could receive their entitlements with all the relevant boxes being ticked. Because of the extremely distressing circumstances in which the ones we loved met their deaths, it wasn't appropriate to adhere to contractual agreements, rules, and formalities.

The families were aware we had our own team of people investigating and had asked us to forward any information we uncovered about the whereabouts of Mohammed Riass and his men. We, of course, would only do that after they were all dead.

Jonesy had named his auntie Annie to be the one to

receive any money awarded in the event of his death, and Lucas had wanted his payout to be split between his ex-wife's daughters and his stepbrother. Neither of the men had any surviving parents.

Although there were plenty of tears shed that day, I also found it quite cathartic. We were kindred spirits sharing our feelings and fond memories of the ones we had loved and lost; we also had a few laughs along the way. Jonesy's aunt and cousin had the same sense of humour as our beloved guard, and I could imagine a night out with all of them would have been an absolute riot.

Yannis paid us a visit, along with my friends Karen and Amina. They were a welcome distraction and provided shoulders to cry on. But being stuck at home was getting to all of us, and I was really missing Jean. Video calling her just wasn't the same, and her carer said she seemed to get really agitated afterwards.

James flew back to the States, despite Yannis's objections. But he promised he'd be with us as soon as possible, and true to his word, he'd arrived home during the night with an armful of gifts for Lily.

Going back to work hadn't helped James at all. He was still so angry and upset by the lack of progress in tracing Mohammed Riass and his crew. He'd been up early, sparring with Tanner—one of his close protection team—in a bid to deal with his frustration. Yet he still seemed pretty wound up when I passed him on his way back from the gym.

After Lily and I finished folding our clothes, I transferred the towels from the washing machine into the dryer and set it going.

"Why do we have to put the wet washing in the dryer,

Mummy? Nan says pegging washing out in the sunshine is best."

"It's winter now, Lily, so we don't get many sunny days. When it's cold and damp, the washing won't dry outside."

"I can't wait until it's sunny again. I miss going on my playground and in the outdoor pool. I like to splash you and Nan when you're sunbathing." Lily giggled when I put my hands on my hips and shook my head.

"Cheeky monkey," I said, then picked up the laundry basket and chased her into the kitchen.

Lily ran into James and threw her arms around his legs.

"Whoa, steady on, Lily. You could have fallen." James picked her up and blew a couple of raspberries on her cheeks.

Lily giggled and rubbed her nose against his. "Mummy was chasing me because I like to splash her and Nan when I'm in the pool."

"I thought you were supposed to be helping your mummy clean up today," Nan remarked.

"I have been helping. I've been folding clothes ready to put away."

"Perhaps we should sweep the kitchen for her?" James suggested, tipping Lily upside down so her hair touched the floor. He swished her around a few times as if she were a broom. Lily howled with laughter, and we all followed suit. My daughter's unbridled laughter is such an addictive sound.

Though he'd not been gone long, Lily had really missed James. We all had. Yannis was also thrilled that James was back. He was flying in from London after his morning meeting, so we were all going to have a late lunch together, something Yannis was pretty insistent about.

To my relief, the two had sorted out their differences

and seemed as close as ever. Yannis was looking forward to seeing James again, and he'd made me promise to keep him here until he arrived.

Nan had come by earlier to prep for our meal, but I'd beaten her to it. I'd had a lean topside of beef in the slow cooker overnight, to which I'd added vegetables and red wine. I peeled the potatoes before Nan arrived, so there was nothing for her to do. She wasn't happy about that, but James and I told her she was to refrain from work until she'd had her operation and was fully recovered. That had gone down like a lead balloon, but we thought it might spur her into getting the surgery. Yannis agreed to help us in the fight to get Nan ready for her new hip. As he'd told me on a number of occasions, he could be deviously persuasive when required.

As our lunch had already been prepped, Nan made a list of things to do around the estate, starting with tending to the plants around the patio and pool area. She'd been online and bought some frost-proof covers for the small palm trees. I had no idea which ones were hardy enough to leave alone in winter, so I left that in the hands of our gardening experts. Nan cut the covers into large enough squares to cover each of the plants and palm trees that needed protecting.

Because they were all in raised decorative pots, covering the palms wouldn't take much bending, so Nan persuaded Jack to let her do them on her own, while he and Andy checked on the oak saplings Kolya and Lily had planted on the edge of our property boundary. They'd planted around forty or so, and I wanted Lily to watch them grow and benefit the environment, knowing she and her dad made that happen. Photographs and memories were all we had left of him, but this was a living memory she could treasure and share with her own children.

Though I still hung on to Roman's suggestion that Kolya and Jonesy could still be alive, realistically I knew it was just hope and wishful thinking from a broken-hearted father.

My phone rang while I was checking on our lunch, and in my haste to answer it, I accidentally splashed boiling water from the potatoes on the back of my hand. I cursed loudly, which earned me a telling off from Lily. Within seconds, Ivan had switched on the tap and tugged me towards the sink so I could run my hand under the cold water, but due to the strength and power behind his solid, muscular frame, I ended up falling head-first into his chest.

"Bloody hell, Ivan, give a girl some warning, will you?" I chided while rubbing my head with the back of my other hand. Ivan only grunted in acknowledgement, not letting go of the hand he'd placed under the tap until he was satisfied the cold water had done its job.

"Who was on the phone?" James asked as he placed Lily back on her feet.

I picked up my mobile and noticed a missed call from Yannis. Before I could return it, another call came through, this time from Danny. He was out doing some Christmas shopping with Lainey, and I was hoping they'd managed to pick up a few things from the list I'd given them. Ivan must have glanced at the phone before I answered because he nudged my arm and commanded, "Tell him to bring chocolate from Venchi. I want—"

"Hi, Danny, how's it going?" I asked, cutting Ivan off abruptly. I placed my index finger against my lips, then tilted my head towards Lily. She'd been so picky with her food since Kolya died, and I'd had to forbid chocolate and sweets until her eating habits improved. Ivan bent down to whisper in my ear, telling me he'd text Danny his order.

Venchi was a beautiful little chocolate and gelato shop on the King's Road in Chelsea. I loved the place. Their chocolate gelato was almost orgasmic. Kolya and I had often ordered a tub to be delivered to the hotel whenever we were in London.

"We're still on Oxford Street, so we're only halfway through your list, but Lainey's bought everything she wanted to send to her family, and I've got most of what Nan wanted. We'll wrap ours when we get back to the hotel, then post them tomorrow before we head home."

Lainey and Danny were supposed to be flying to the States to be with her family at Christmas, but they'd cancelled their flights so they could be with us instead. I told them they didn't need to do that, but they wanted to stay in the UK and support me and Lily during our first Christmas without Kolya.

"Those toys you ordered from Hamleys won't be arriving at the store until after four p.m., so we'll collect them tomorrow morning. If there's anything else you need, text it to Lainey's phone."

"Thanks, Danny. I don't think I need anything, but Ivan wants something from Venchi."

Ivan shook his head, then whispered, "Not want, need."

I stifled a laugh, then carried on. "He's sending you a text. I hope you and Lainey enjoy your evening. Take lots of photos of all the Christmas lights for us. See you when you get home."

"Bye, Tess. Give Lily a big kiss from us."

My phone rang again just as the call ended.

"Hi, Yannis. Are you nearly here?"

"Tess, I've been trying to ring you. Is James there?" Yannis asked.

"Yes, he's here, like he was the last time you asked."

"Good. I have all your Christmas gifts with me, and I didn't want to miss him. My business meeting ran slightly over schedule, so our flight time was delayed, but I'll be there shortly."

"Okay, see you soon," I said, then held my phone out to Lily so she could say bye.

James rolled his eyes, then took out his own phone. "Yannis is turning into a right nag in his old age. He rang me last night, then texted me about an hour ago to make sure I'd be here," he said.

"He wanted to make sure you were here so he could give you your Christmas gift before you flew back to the States," I told him.

"But I'll be here on Christmas Day anyway, so he could have left it here for me. It's not like I'm a kid anymore."

"It's not the same though, is it? Yannis isn't close to his family, so you can understand him wanting everyone here when he visits."

"Whose fault is that, though? I've met some of his family, Tess, and they're not the ogres he makes them out to be. He ought to make more of an effort with them if you ask me."

"James, please don't tell me you've had another falling-out with Yannis. We can do without listening to you two argue."

"No, we're good; it's just... I don't know. Maybe I needed longer in the gym to burn off some steam." James ran a hand through his hair, then slumped down on a chair beside Lily.

Nate and Franco came into the kitchen, closely followed by Dave, who was carrying Bess. As soon as he placed her on the floor, she ran to Ivan, looking for food.

Franco slapped James on his shoulder as he passed,

asking, "What's crawled up your a—" he quickly glanced at Lily and added, "butt."

"He is feeling frustrated. He cannot get a woman," Ivan teased.

"Thought that was just you," James replied.

"The gun range is free; why don't you have yourselves a competition? Handguns and rifles, three rounds each. Loser buys everyone pizza. Take Tess with you," Nate suggested.

"Oh no, Lily and I have some clothes to put away before Yannis arrives. But there's nothing stopping James and Ivan from going. You and Franco could take them on. Or Maybe Franco and James versus you and Ivan. What do you think, Nate? Or are you both too chicken?"

Lily began clucking like a chicken, making everyone in the room laugh.

"As long as there are enough guards in here, I don't see why we couldn't make them buy us all pizza tonight. What do you say, Ivan?"

"Only if we go now. Tess is making us wait for Yannis, so I haven't had lunch yet," he grumbled.

"You'd better take a sandwich with you in case you start to feel faint," I joked. But Ivan didn't take it as a joke. After muttering, "Good idea, Tess," he took out two slices of bread and proceeded to butter them.

James texted two of his guards, Tanner and Carl, asking them to come over and take the place of Nate and Franco. Not that we needed them. Our security was tighter than it had ever been.

I made coffee for Tanner and Carl, then took two cups of tea to Kevin and Dave in the tech room, reminding them that Yannis was on his way.

Lily asked if she could put on her coat and help Nan cover the plants, but I said no. I was determined to make

Lily tidy her bedroom while I put her clothes away. There were dressing-up clothes, teddies, and various bits of her fairy tea set scattered around her room. I'd already broken two crayons after accidentally stepping on them.

Lily dragged her doll into her bedroom with Bess following close behind them. The little dog was as good as gold with Lily. She even let her dress her up.

After picking up her toys, we stripped her bed and put on clean bed linen. She helped me with the fitted sheet and pillowcase, but there was no way I'd let her help me with the duvet cover. Not after the last time. She'd somehow ended up inside it, though we had a lot of laughs along the way.

With her bed freshly made and all the toys in her toy box, I sat for a moment while she brought me yet another letter she wanted to send to Santa. Some of it wasn't quite legible, but Dear Santa was clear to see, as well as the word daddy, and also her name at the end.

"I thought I'd tell him how good I was and ask if he'll let everyone come home from heaven for Christmas. Ivan said that Santa might let my daddy help him deliver presents to all the children in the world on Christmas Eve, but I want him here with me, not with any other children. And I've been good and helped you today, Mummy, so that means I won't be on his naughty list."

Though I tried not to let the tears fall, I just couldn't help it. I'd got so good at hiding them from Lily, but it wasn't easy. Especially when she presented me with something so meaningful.

Instead of replying, I picked her up and set her on my knee. She was holding Anna, so I cuddled her, too, and even Bess got in on the act, shoving her head under my arm so she could get even closer. Lily didn't push me to tell her that all would be well and that her daddy would be with us at

Christmas. Deep down, I think she knew that couldn't happen.

On hearing the sound of a helicopter coming in to land, I stood with Lily in my arms, laying her doll on the bed before moving to the window so she could wave at Yannis. My phone rang before I got there, and it took a few seconds to fish it out of my pocket. I thought it would be Yannis, yet it was Kevin's name across my screen. I swiped the green button to answer, but before I could speak, Kevin said, *"Tess, you and Lily need to take cover. I don't know who's in that helicopter, but I'll bet my life it's not Yannis and, oh, fuck, the shutters aren't coming down. What the fuck?"*

"Kevin, what's—" I reached the window as the phone cut off and saw a larger-than-average helicopter landing beside ours. It was matt-black in colour and looked as if it could be ex-military. Even before its wheels had touched down, five armed men dressed head to toe in black leapt out onto the helipad, their rifles raised as they ran towards our home.

I crouched down under the window, holding on to Lily while tugging the curtains closed. A feeling of dread slid through me, leaving me cold and shaky. Was this Riass and his men? Were they here to take us captive or to kill us? I could hear shouting about guns and ammo from the other rooms, and I was grateful that Kevin had the foresight to grant Carl and Tanner access to our hidden weapons.

"Mummy, I'm scared. Those people have guns," Lily cried.

I kissed her forehead, then smoothed a few wayward curls away from her pale face. "Shh, it's okay. They won't come near you. I'll keep you safe, I promise. But I need you to do something for me, Lily. It's a bit like hide-and-seek. I'm going to lay you down inside one of your big drawers and put some pillows beside you, so if someone opens the drawer, they won't see you. And I need you to be really quiet and still for me, sweetheart. You can't make a noise until you hear someone you know calling your name, okay?" I shuffled us away from underneath the window as I spoke, aware that every second wasted would count against us making it out of there alive. Her ice-blue eyes were full of fear and unshed tears, but my brave girl nodded and pressed her lips together.

Once I could stand up safely away from the window, I opened up the drawer that held Lily's nightclothes, throwing the contents on the floor before placing her inside. Grabbing the pillow from her bed and a decorative throw cushion, I wedged them in beside her. And for extra, I hoped, unneeded protection, I pulled a Kevlar vest from under her bed and double-layered it behind the drawer front.

"Remember, Lily, keep quiet and still, even if you hear gunshots." I switched my phone on silent and gave it to her. She knew my password and how to make a call.

"If you don't hear anyone for a long time after the gunshots end—longer than it takes to sing the fairy song in your head twenty times, then you can call Lainey and Danny and tell them where you are, okay?" She nodded again and gripped my phone firmly. "I love you lots, Lily-pot," I whispered as the drawer closed, shielding her from view.

I heard a loud smash, then Nan crying out in pain, followed by a burst of gunfire.

No. Not Nan. Please don't hurt Nan.

She'd been outside on the patio, tending to the plants. Exposed and with no means of defence.

Please, God, keep her alive, I prayed. She means the world to me.

I was shaking so hard it took two attempts on the finger-print scanner for the drawer containing the hidden weapons to open, but once it did, I took no time at all in loading the full magazine clip into the rifle. After pocketing another full clip, I dropped to the floor.

To keep Lily as safe as possible from stray bullets, I crawled away from the drawers and crouched between her desk and toy box. From this position, I'd be a few feet from the back of the door if it opened.

In my haste to move away from my daughter's hiding place, I'd forgotten to grab myself a Kevlar vest, but I daren't attempt to go back and get one. Fear and nausea had me rooted to the spot.

There was another round of gunshots, this time from inside the house, causing Bess to bark frantically. I pulled her to my side and tried to soothe her, telling her she was a good girl when she finally stopped barking.

The gunshots increased rapidly—our guards no doubt returning fire on our unwelcome guests. Bullets, thuds and crashes created a terrifying cacophony of deathly sounds around my home—a place where my daughter and I should have been safe.

Nate and Kevin's room was on the other side of the extension—along with the tech room—and the kitchen was directly in the middle of the building, with a hallway leading to our lounge and bedrooms. I'd left Carl and Tanner in the kitchen drinking coffee. Kevin and Dave had been in the tech room, so there were only five of us in the house who'd be armed. If the shutters had come down, it would have triggered an alarm in the guards' quarters and shooting range, where James, Ivan, Franco and Nate were. They would have been with us in minutes. But Kevin said he couldn't get the shutters to come down, so I knew the alarm might not have worked either. Unless Jack and Andy had noticed the helicopter and came to help, we would all have to fight. Including me.

Someone cried out in pain above the gunfire, and I hoped with everything I had it wasn't one of ours.

I glanced towards the window; the continuous loud rat-a-tat sound of automatic weapons being fired outside drawing my attention from what was happening in my home. But as the curtains were closed, I couldn't see what, or who, the bullets had hit. The sound of a door crashing into a wall made Bess growl, but a slight tug on her ear had her quiet again.

Heavy footsteps making their way towards the bedrooms made my heart beat harder, faster, and loud enough for anyone to hear. I felt dizzy and nauseous, my palms clammy. After wiping them on my jeans, I held up my rifle with shaking hands—my finger poised and ready over the trigger —trying hard to keep a steady aim on the closed bedroom door.

I tried to remember all the weapons training I'd done with Franco and Jonesy. They taught me how to handle a weapon, where to aim, and how to shoot my target. But being in my daughter's bedroom instead of our firing range made those past lessons seem almost obsolete. The enemy was no longer just a dark silhouette on a poster; this enemy was a living, breathing threat to my family.

As I readied myself for the door to open, a number of scenarios flashed through my mind. What if it was one of our guys approaching? What if I accidentally shot Kevin or Dave? Surely they would call out and let me know it was them.

The sight of the door handle lowering brought me back to the here and now. I held my breath as I stared down the sights of the rifle; the weight of it suddenly seemed too heavy for me to hold. The door hinges squeaked as it opened, bringing forth a low growl from the little dog beside me, yet I doubt whoever was behind the door could hear it due to all the noise from the rest of the property.

"Shh." Though I knew the sound wouldn't calm Bess, I could offer her little else. To take my eyes off the door and my hands off the rifle could mean my death, and I needed to protect my daughter's life above all else.

The door opened wider, and I focused my aim on where I thought the gunman's midsection would be. Franco's words from my training sessions echoed around my head, drowning out the rapid thudding between my ears. *"Always aim for the midsection and double tap. You're more likely to hit something and take your enemy out, even if it doesn't end up a kill shot."*

A tall figure dressed head to toe in black stepped slowly into the bedroom, and with their eyes focused on Lily's bed, lowered their weapon.

Anna. They'd spotted Lily's doll. Did they think it was a sleeping child?

The gunman began backing out of the room slowly, but before I could breathe a sigh of relief, Bess ran out from beside me and leapt towards him. It took a split second for him to raise his rifle and shoot.

"No," I screamed, and saw the shock register in his brown eyes as I opened fire, pulling the trigger repeatedly while raising my rifle higher, watching his body jump and recoil when each bullet hit. I didn't stop shooting until I put a bullet between his eyes. He was probably dead before that, but I wasn't willing to take any chances in case he'd been wearing a vest. When his lifeless body hit the wall and slumped to the floor, I finally lowered my weapon.

I brought myself to a standing position on shaking legs,

my ears still ringing from the sound of each shot I'd fired. I swallowed hard and shook my head, trying my best to disturb the after-effects so I could regain my hearing.

When I glanced down at Bess, I cried out in horror and pain, sinking to my knees beside the sickening sight of her lifeless body. She was missing the top of her head—blood and shattered fragments of skull lay all around her, along with other stuff I didn't want to think about. She'd tried to protect me and had lost her life in doing so. If only she'd gone for a walk around the estate with Jack and Andy.

I reached out and touched her back leg, whispering how sorry I was, and that I'd look after Danny for her, knowing how devastated he'd be by her loss. She'd seen him through good times and bad and was loved by everyone.

Hearing a noise out in the hallway, I raised my rifle once again. It took a few seconds to register that the sound of gunfire had ceased but, until I knew who was out there, I had to assume this was another gunman.

"Tess. You okay in there?" Franco's voice sounded gruff, his tone wary. I scrambled to my feet without letting go of my weapon, not trusting that the threat was fully eliminated.

"Franco," I shouted, "is it safe?"

"It's safe, honey. I'll come get you."

"TESS!"

"TESS!"

James and Ivan's voices were frantic with worry and fear, though I preferred Franco's gruffness. I didn't need to hear fear in those I relied upon to be fearless.

Franco stepped over the body of the gunman and, after stowing his Beretta in the back of his jeans, held up his hands in a placating manner. "It's just us, Tess. You can put down the rifle. You're safe now."

Ivan and James followed Franco into the room and

stared down at my hands, confusion replacing their panicked expressions. I nodded but still held on to the weapon. In my mind, I knew I should do as Franco said, but my hands didn't want to let go.

"Tess, where's Lily?" James questioned, though he, too, held up his hands.

Ivan glanced around the room and spotted Bess. "Oh, no, what did they do to you, little girl?" he choked as he dropped to his knees beside her.

"She tried to protect me, Ivan, and he killed her, so I kept on shooting until I knew he wouldn't get up again," I told him, lowering my weapon. I stepped into his open arms and let the warmth of his embrace melt away some of the cold, agitating fear.

Even though he was kneeling, because of his six-foot-eight-inch height, the top of Ivan's head was level with my ears. "You did well, *milaya moya*. You kept Lily safe, yes?" he whispered.

"I hid her in a drawer," I told him.

"I'll get her," James said, taking a few steps towards them. Before he could get there, Franco and Ivan yelled, "NO!"

"We need to move this fucker first and cover Bess up," Franco said. "And it'd be best to put a blanket over Lily's head while we carry her through to our quarters. She shouldn't have to see her home like this."

Ivan dragged the duvet from Lily's bed and placed it carefully over Bess. I managed to stop Anna from falling on the floor and carried her over to the drawers, propping both the doll and rifle against the wall.

After waiting a few seconds for James and Franco to move the gunman's body out of the doorway, I opened the drawer in which Lily hid, pulling out the vest, pillow, and cushion from beside her. She squinted at the light after being tucked away in the dark, and I could tell she'd been crying. Her cheeks and lashes were wet with tears and her nose was running, yet even though she'd been so distraught, my brave little girl still held on to my phone. When she opened her eyes and saw me and Ivan, she grabbed my hand and whispered, "Have the bad men gone now, Mummy?"

I lifted her out of the drawer and held her close. "Yes, they've gone now, sweetheart. I told you I'd keep you safe, and you did really well and stayed quiet for me. You are so brave, Lily, and I'm incredibly proud of you."

"And I'm proud of both of you," Ivan declared as he wrapped his arms around us. "But when we heard... I was so worried."

A thought suddenly occurred to me. "What about Nan? Ivan, I heard her—"

"She fell while trying to run away. They didn't hurt her, but we think she broke her hip when she hit the ground. Jack and Andy are with her now. Tanner was hit in the thigh, and Dave is missing the top of his ear, but they'll be fine, Tess. They're taking Nan to the foyer of the guards' quarters and will call an ambulance. We can deal with the clean-up in this building later."

"Hey, there you are, Lily. You were hiding so well I didn't see you," James said when he came back into the room. Ivan dropped his arms from around us and let James take over.

"Did you see the bad men, James?" Lily asked.

He placed a kiss on the top of her head, then held us tightly. "I did, Lily. But they're gone now. There's no need to be scared."

James tried to take her from me, but I wouldn't let her

go to him. He looked upset, yet I didn't have it in me to care. No matter what they said, I still didn't feel safe, and I needed to hold my daughter. I needed to hear her heart beating and feel her breath upon my face. She could have been taken or killed if we hadn't been prepared. I survived the loss of my husband, but I couldn't live without Lily.

Franco approached us with a blanket, and I took it from him gratefully. "We're gonna head out across the patio and into the manor house. They've already taken Nan over there, and she wants to see you before they come for her. Andy's given her a shot of morphine, so she's coping with the pain."

"How long until the ambulance gets here?" I asked.

"ETA about ten minutes, so we don't have long." Franco placed his hand on Lily's head. "Hey, baby girl. Your mommy's gonna put this magic invisibility blanket over your head, but you can't peek out from under there or the magic won't work, okay?"

"Will it stop the bad men with the guns from seeing me?"

"The bad men are gone, Lily," Franco assured her. "I just wanted to see if we can surprise Nate. He said he doesn't believe in magic. He doesn't believe in the Loch Ness Monster, either."

I felt Lily frown against my shoulder. "Nate is silly," she murmured.

"He sure is. So how about we play this invisibility trick on him, like in the wizard movie you like to watch?"

"Okay," she whispered. But I felt her body tense when Franco covered her with the blanket.

I made my way out of Lily's bedroom, stepping carefully over the heavy wet bloodstains on the carpet. I wasn't sure where they'd taken the man I'd killed, and I didn't want to ask. There was no way I'd let my daughter sleep in that room again. I wanted to get us as far away from there as possible.

The scene that greeted me in the kitchen made me stop in my tracks. The table lay on its side and was peppered with bullet holes. All the glass-fronted cabinets were smashed; shards of glass and broken crockery lay across the worktops and along the floor. My gaze followed a spray of bullet holes in the wall, tiles, and bread bin. The slow cooker lay on its side; the joint of beef it contained now lost amongst the broken debris. There were sprays of blood on the walls and cupboards, along with a few pools on the floor, although thankfully, no bodies. Tears blurred my vision, but due to carrying Lily and holding the blanket over her head, I couldn't wipe my eyes.

"I've got you, Tess," Franco said. He used his sleeve to wipe away my tears, then placed his hand on my upper back, guiding me away from the scene of chaos and devastation that used to be my home.

Chapter Twenty-Five

TESS

We marched under the covered patio to the guards' quarters as quickly as possible. A mix of blood and bullet casings were scattered all around, and the wind had blown Nan's carefully cut-out frost-proof material onto the covered outdoor pool. She must have been so frightened while she lay there with all that gunfire going on around her. But knowing Nan, she would have been more worried about me and Lily than she was about herself.

Nate had driven down to the gates so he could escort the ambulance through when it arrived. Dave and Tanner were being tended to by Kevin in the kitchen, though I was reassured once again that they would be fine.

Walking through the guards' quarters in the old manor house was a much better experience than walking through the extension where Lily and I lived. The property showed no evidence of the chaos and terror the gunmen had brought to our home. There were no bullet holes in the walls; the furniture was right where it should be, and there wasn't a trace of blood anywhere, which made me think they were only after me, Lily or James. Possibly all three of us. But why? What would they gain from taking one or all of us at this point? They had to know by now that we would never hand over the guidance system, and none of us had the codes. Especially me and Lily. We had nothing to do with KOLCAT. It wasn't lost on me that the gunman was backing out of Lily's room without scanning it for threats, because if he had, he'd have noticed me pointing my rifle directly at him. I saw him lower his weapon when he spotted Anna. If Lily *had* been the target, he would have taken a shot or explored that room further.

Due to the size of the manor house, it took a couple of minutes to get from the back of the property to the foyer, where Nan lay on the floor awaiting the ambulance. During the whole time it had taken us to get there, James had been barking orders at people over his phone. I'd been lost in my thoughts, replaying everything that had happened in Lily's room. I hadn't a clue he'd been speaking with Gustav until we got to Nan.

She was leaning back against the bottom of the staircase with Jack and Andy beside her. They'd covered her with a duvet to keep her warm, and if not for Nan being on the floor with her features pinched in pain, I would have said she was sleeping. After discarding the blanket I'd been covering Lily with, I sat on the floor beside her, carefully adjusting our positions so that we both faced her.

"Look who's here, Nan. I told you they were fine. Not a scratch on them." Jack stroked his wife's cheek as he spoke. He sounded calm, but his watery eyes and forced smile told a different story.

Nan opened her eyes and glanced our way, holding her hand out to Lily. "I was so worried about you. They said you were fine, but I had to see for myself." Her words were slurred and her eyes took a few moments to focus.

"Bad men came so Mummy put me in a drawer. I had to stay quiet and still until they'd gone away," Lily told her.

"I heard you cry out, but I couldn't come to you," I sobbed. "I'm so sorry, Nan."

"Don't you apologise, Tess. A mother's priority should always be her children. You did the right thing, so stop your tears. We've shed enough of those these last few weeks, and I'll be damned if I'll let you cry any more. Promise me you'll stay strong, love. I didn't want to leave you while your emotions are still so raw, but fate had other plans."

"You must have been so scared out there on your own with all that going on around you." I wiped my eyes and sniffed loudly, trying hard to keep it together for Nan.

"I tried to run back to the house but slipped on a piece of the fabric I was covering the plants with. Two of the gunmen came up to me, and I thought, this is it; I'm done for. And yet... you'll probably think it's the morphine talking, but I think one of them was going to help me up. Then Carl and Tanner came out and—"

"Eliminated two," Jack said. Nodding towards Lily, he added, "Little ears and all that."

"So that left three of them," I concluded.

"No. There were eight of them, plus the pilot," James said from behind me.

"Eight?" I gasped. "I only saw five before I dropped below the window. Are they all…"

"The one who was going to help me ran back to the helicopter after being shot in the arm. Franco and Nate came running out of here as I heard the helicopter lift off, and then Jack and Andy appeared."

"I can't understand how the shutters didn't come down. They were fine when we tested them," Andy said.

"Kevin's looking into it. We'll—" James paused to answer his phone. "It's Yannis. I told Kevin to call and tell him to turn back." He swiped to answer.

"James, what the hell is happening? Kevin said there'd been an incident and I should turn back, but he won't tell me why."

"Please, Yannis, just do as he says. I'll be in touch—"

"The ambulance is coming up the drive," Andy announced.

"Ambulance? Who needs an ambulance?" Yannis yelled so loudly down the phone that we could all hear him.

"You'd better tell him, James. We won't keep him away now. Get him to land on the grass in front of the manor and come through the front entrance. We can send him and his guards to the games room until the ambulance leaves." I moved Lily off my lap, then leaned forward to place a gentle kiss on Nan's forehead. "We'll come and see you in the hospital as soon as you feel up to it, and Lily will make you the best *get-well-soon* card ever, won't you, sweetheart?" Lily nodded but began to cry.

"Hey, don't cry. I'll be okay, Lily, I promise." Nan's reassurance didn't help one bit, and Lily's tears didn't subside until Ivan let the ambulance men in.

We stepped back and watched while the efficient paramedics assessed Nan and prepared her for the journey to hospital. Yannis arrived while they were transferring her to the ambulance, and the poor man was as distraught as we were. But then again, he'd known Nan for years and thought the world of her. If it hadn't been for Lily holding his hand, I think he'd have cried.

Jack was allowed to ride in the back of the ambulance as they made their way to the John Radcliffe in Oxford. The teaching hospital had an excellent reputation, and while she wouldn't have the perks of private healthcare, I knew Nan would receive excellent treatment, regardless.

As soon as the ambulance drove away, I made my way down to the kitchen to see Dave and Tanner. James had already called Kolya's friend, Benedict Grayson, informing him of their injuries and asking if he'd treat them. He'd agreed, although he did state that he'd only operate on Tanner. Dave would need to see a plastic surgeon.

Yannis followed us down to the kitchen, asking us why they'd had to land in front of the old manor instead of the helipad. I told James to explain what had happened and left him to do so out in the hallway. I didn't want Lily to hear what he had to say; she'd gone through enough already. Assured by Franco that the guards' wounds were covered, I kept her close beside me.

Dave sat on the floor with his back against the wall, holding a bucket between his knees. His eyes were closed, and his head was bandaged all the way around with thick padding over his right ear. I dropped to my knees and placed my hand over his. As soon as I did so, his eyes opened.

"I'm not going to ask how you're feeling, Dave. I'm assuming you'll say *'like shit'.*"

"I've had better days, love; I'm not going to lie." He squeezed my hand, then added, "I'm glad you and Lily are okay. To think of how many times you bitched at us and the boss about having hidden weapons in her room…"

"Yep, good job you all ignored me, as usual."

"He'd have been proud of you today, Tess. You did good." Dave closed his eyes again and pulled the bucket to his chest.

"Are you going to be sick?" I asked, beckoning Andy over.

"I was all right until Kevin gave me that pain juice," he replied.

"Morphine can make you feel nauseous, especially if you're a wimp like him," Andy joked as he crouched in front of Dave. "Now then, soft lad. How many fingers am I holding up?"

Lily leaned forward. "Dave, he's holding three fingers up," she whispered loudly.

Dave chuckled. "Thanks for helping me, Lilypot."

I lifted Dave's hand to my lips and kissed the back of it. "Thank you for everything you did to keep us safe in there; I'll never forget it. I'm just sorry you were hurt in the process. We'll leave you in Andy's capable hands and go and see Tanner, but we'll come and say goodbye before Ivan takes you both to the hospital."

Dave kept hold of my hand. "Promise me you'll trust your gut, Tess. When it comes to your or Lily's safety, just… trust your gut."

I squeezed his hand in acknowledgement, then made my way over to Tanner. He sat in just his boxers and a T-shirt on a chair by the kitchen table, his left leg raised on the seat of another. He had thick dressings taped to both the front and back of his outer thigh.

"It went through and through," Carl remarked. He smiled, adding, "There's no resistance when it goes through fat."

"Fuck you, Carl. There ain't no fat anywhe—" Carl elbowed Tanner and pointed at Lily, who was peering out from behind my legs. "Oops, sorry for cussing, Lily."

"Why haven't you got any trousers on, Tanner, and what have you done to your leg?" she asked.

Tanner's eyes shot to mine, silently asking what he should say. Before I could answer, Carl replied, "He took them off to wash them, then fell over and hurt his leg. That can happen when you're kinda tubby and have poor balance." Carl winked at us, and Tanner shook his head. I tried not to laugh at his exasperated expression.

Both men were handsome, tall, and muscular. Carl sported a leaner, athletic frame whereas Tanner was body-builder huge. Both were from the US and had been guarding James since he was fourteen. Tanner was Creole through and through, having beautiful coffee-coloured skin with black curly hair and big brown eyes. Carl, on the other hand, was a blond-haired, blue-eyed Ryan Gosling looka-like. They ribbed each other constantly, with Tanner saying Carl was too skinny and Carl saying Tanner was getting fat, but I knew Carl's current jibes were just to keep Tanner's spirits up. Jonesy used to laugh at them whenever they started on each other. He used to call them Laurel and Hardy and would sometimes play the theme tune on his phone when they entered a room.

God, I missed Jonesy. He would have been the one in charge of everything and, along with Kolya, would have already had a plan of action. I wasn't even sure who was running things at present.

Tanner moved position on the chair and winced. Bright red blood began seeping through the dressing on his thigh.

"I'm sorry you were hurt, Tanner, and I know it's no consolation, but the surgeon who'll be taking care of you is the one who patched me up after I'd been... you know," I said, gesturing towards his thigh. "And you've seen how neat my scar is."

"Don't worry about it, Tess. Tanner's not good-looking

enough for a woman to want to go near him with his pants off, anyway."

Lily pushed out from behind me, wagging her finger at Carl. "You shouldn't be mean to Tanner, especially when he's got a poorly leg."

"You tell him, Lily," Tanner encouraged with a smile.

"If you're mean to people, then Santa puts you on his naughty list—like the bad men that came with the guns. They made Nan fall, and they hurt Dave's head."

Both Tanner's and Carl's eyes flashed to mine. "Franco told us you hid her?" Carl said, though it was more of a question than a statement.

"I thought it was Yannis in the helicopter. We went to the window to wave at him and saw…"

Tanner cursed again but didn't apologise this time. He looked distraught.

"We're all here; that's the main thing, Tanner. But once again, I'm so sorry you were hurt, and I want both of you to know how grateful we are for all you did today. You are my heroes, and if there's anything you need, just let me know."

Feeling a hand on my shoulder, I turned to see who it was. Franco pulled me into his arms and held me tightly. Reaching out to Lily, he tugged her towards us, resting his hand on her head while she hugged our legs.

"I need to hold you," he murmured into my hair. "The adrenaline's worn off and I'm coming down hard. You've always been a fighter, Tess, right from the get-go, so deep down I knew you'd take care of business. But I was so fucking scared that something would go wrong. That your gun would jam or, I don't know… a whole heap of things went through my mind. All I do know is, the world would be a dark place for me without you in it."

"Right back at you, Franco," I whispered. "It was your

skills that kept me and Lily safe. All those hours spent prac-
tising down at the gun range with you and Jonesy. I even
heard your voice in my head while I waited for the door to
open. Although, to be fair, I don't think Lily was his target.
He was backing out of the bedroom when Bess ran at him.
He seemed genuinely shocked to see me with a gun, and he
never fired back. Not that I gave him a chance. I tried filling
his chest and added one between his eyes for good measure.
I don't know whether I should feel bad about that—if I
should be walking around full of guilt or remorse. I feel
neither. I took a man's life, Franco. But I'd do it again to
keep my daughter safe."

"Is she okay?" Yannis asked from behind Franco.

Loosening his hold on me, Franco replied, "She's
standing right here. Why don't you ask her?" Franco bent
down and scooped Lily up in his arms. "Do you think you
could help me, baby girl? I need to get a blanket and some
pillows for Dave and Tanner. Ivan will fly them to the
hospital soon, and they'll need to be comfortable on their
journey. I know you're real good at helping and looking
after people."

"I'll help you, Franco," Lily replied. "I could put on my
doctor's outfit and bring my stessascope."

"I don't think you need your outfit or your stethoscope,
honey. One of your pretty smiles will make them feel a
whole lot better," he said as he carried her off to the utility
room where Nan kept the spare towels and bed linen.

"Tess, are you okay? I can't believe what happened."
Yannis grasped both my arms and held me while he looked
me over.

"Yes, I'm fine now. But Dave and Tanner were hurt.
Bess is dead, and Nan was lucky not to get caught out there
in the crossfire. I'm just so bloody grateful that Kolya

insisted we have all those hidden weapons. I used to get upset about the ones in Lily's room, even though she wouldn't be able to gain access to them. But they saved our lives today."

"I wasn't aware you kept all those weapons in the house. Kolya never said anything," Yannis mumbled.

I couldn't get a read on his odd expression. Was it shock, anger, confusion?

"Only a handful of our guards were aware until the day after he was killed. Kevin and I agreed that had to change in case they came at us in our home. And it's a good job we did, or Riass could have killed us all."

"I can't believe that James left you all alone. You assured me he was with you," Yannis spat.

"I was armed, Yannis, and I wasn't alone. There were four guards in the house with me."

"He should have been with you, Tess. Protecting you. A woman should never have needed to arm herself." Those last few words came with a look of sheer distaste. Well, fuck him!

"No, I shouldn't have '*needed*' to arm myself, but the fact I had the means and skill to do so could have saved Lily's life today, and it might do so again in the future. So fuck you and your stereotypical, male chauvinistic ideas. I don't need James here to keep me safe. He's here because he's my and Lily's family, and his presence is comforting for all concerned. But you've no need to worry, Yannis. If it came down to it, I know James would protect me with whatever means he could. Just like I would protect him. And those means of protection would come no less deadly because I'm a woman."

I turned to leave, but Yannis put his hand on my shoulder to stop me. "I have offended you, Tess, and that was truly not my intention. It is something that seems to happen more often as my friendship and attachment to you grows. I see your strength, your resilience, and the love you have for your family and those close to you. You and Lily are very dear to me, and your safety and well-being are paramount. Kolya was my best friend. More like a brother, in fact. The only thing I can do for him now is to make sure the ones he loved are protected. Work commitments mean I can't always be here to carry out that duty, so what happened here today feels like I've failed my friend and his beloved family. That is a hard pill to swallow right now. So, forgive me, please, and allow me to help in any way I can."

My anger toward Yannis abated slightly. There was guilt written all over his face. It had been creeping in since he'd seen Nan being placed in the ambulance.

"Yannis, I can't let you suffer this misplaced guilt you seem to be harbouring. Causing us to feel unnecessary negative emotions is just another way for Riass to strike out at us, and I won't allow that man to have any power over me or those I care about. So snap out of it and help me decide where to go from here, because I really don't want to go home right now."

Yannis grabbed my hand and placed it on his chest. "You can come back to Greece with me. Back to Athilos. You are familiar with the island, and my home has the same security system as yours, so you know you and Lily will be safe."

"That security system didn't work so well for us today, did it?"

"Then we need to figure out why, so I can be sure my home is secure enough for you and my precious goddaughter. I will also assign you a team of guards while you stay here and sort this out," he said, gesturing around the room.

"That won't be necessary, Yannis. I might pull Mark and Greg away from the search for Riass and reassign one of them to James until Tanner has recovered. The other can stay here and help Kevin and Andy. Franco, Nate, Lainey and Danny can stay with me and Lily, but I won't be going anywhere until I've seen Nan again. Despite wanting to be as far away from here as possible, we can stay the night right here in the manor house. The shooting range in the cellar can lock from the inside and is as secure as any panic room."

"Then I and my men will stay here, too. I doubt Riass will attack again tonight, but if he does, he will encounter a team of angry Greeks." Yannis smiled, then winked, adding, "And you don't have to be an expert in Greek mythology to know you don't fuck with those."

Chapter Twenty-Six

TESS

Though Ivan had wanted to get Dave and Tanner to the hospital as quickly as possible, he also wanted to stay home with me and Lily. With two guards down, he worried that we'd be inadequately protected. After a full five minutes of reassurance from Yannis, James and I, he finally relented, flying the injured men and Andy—who'd had army medic training—to the rooftop of the private hospital in London, where Benedict Grayson would be ready and waiting.

Kevin called Lainey and apprised her of the situation, so she and Danny were going to fly back from London with Andy and Ivan. He didn't mention Bess, thank goodness. Ivan said he'd tell Danny everything on the flight home, and none of us envied him that particular job. Nate wrapped Bess in her blanket so Danny didn't have to see her fatal wound. He'd been doing so well over the last few years, and I hoped Bess's death wouldn't set him back. She'd been his four-legged saviour when he'd been living on the streets and had kept him going whenever things got tough. Just like she'd been doing for me since Kolya's death.

Lily fell asleep in my arms after Ivan left, so Franco brought in two large sofa cushions to lay her on. It was safer for us all to stay together in the kitchen. There was a downstairs bathroom just outside, so we had everything we needed.

Kevin had gone back to the tech room to bring a couple of laptops over to the manor. He was going to work on those until Ivan and the others came back. Yannis and one of his guards followed him in so they could see for themselves the devastation in my home. When he came back to the manor, Yannis seemed lost for words. He sat at the table, shaking his head.

"I'm so sorry, Tess," he murmured.

"Why? It wasn't you who attacked us."

He glanced my way, then shook his head again. "I need to get you away from here. I know you wish to see Nan, but I think she'd want you out of Oxford. We could fly to Greece this evening so that you and Lily can wake up in the morning with nothing to do but relax and forget about what happened here. You could stay with me as long as you need to. Move over permanently, if you want."

"No, Yannis. I'm staying in the UK until I've seen how Nan, Dave, and Tanner are, then I'll decide what to do. I could move into the hotel for a while, or to Glengarran. I just need to get my head straight and process everything that happened today."

"You can do that with me, on the island. Or you can moor your yacht in the bay and stay there. I know you have so many happy memories of you, Kolya and Lily sailing around all those beautiful places, so staying there might bring you both a little peace. And I could have some of my men keep watch over the yacht and the bay."

"I think that's a great idea," James said. He'd sat between me and Kevin at the large oak dining table and was watching him remotely connect the laptops to the tech room server.

"I'd fly you both to the States with me, but I need to be sure it's safe first. Nan said the gunmen didn't seem to want to hurt her, and I overheard you telling Franco that the one you killed was backing away from Lily's room. If he'd been after you or my sister, he would have been in there turning the place over until he found you. They were either amateur wannabe mercenaries, or their target was someone else. Namely, me."

"But you can't be sure about that, James, and I'd rather not take my chances where Tess and Lily are concerned. The same goes for you. I will require daily updates via text and a phone call to say you are home safe in the evening, like your father used to whenever you stayed with me on Athilos." James opened his mouth to object, but Yannis carried on. "I know I may seem like a nagging old uncle, but I'll rest easier when I know you are safe in your home and that your day has ended without incident."

"Oh, fuck!" Kevin exclaimed. He spun one of the laptops around and pointed to something on the monitor. Nate and Franco came over and stood behind us.

"What is it?" James asked as we all leaned closer to Kevin.

"Those letters, symbols and numbers are the codes that identify who initiated the lockdown process, and also who cancelled it. You can see that the first one is from me on the main computer in the tech room: *KVN>2-tecsys**, and right below that is *KLA>1-celpne**. That's the code for Kolya's phone's home security app. Someone used the boss's phone to access and override our security system. That's why I couldn't get it to comply. We'd configured it that way so that Kolya had the authority to interrupt or suspend my request, which enabled him to take control in the event of a safety breach. I set you up with the same system on yours, Yannis."

Yannis nodded, then frowned. "Does this also mean that my home won't be protected? Tess and Lily will be visiting me in the next couple of days, so I need to know I can keep them safe."

"If you have your phone to hand and you've not told anyone your access code, then no, your security system won't be compromised."

"But how did they get into his phone? My dad used fingerprint scanning to open his phone and... Oh, fuck. They must have removed his finger." James tipped his head back and placed his hands over his face. My heart sank, my stomach churning as I pictured the scene.

"Not necessarily, James. Someone can lift a fingerprint from a glass or another smooth surface," Kevin remarked. "It's not easy, but it isn't impossible with the right equipment. Kolya used a series of numbers to gain access to the remote security app on his phone, but he set that up, and even I wouldn't know what those numbers were."

"I do," I announced. "He used the dates of both James and Lily's childhood milestones and would change them on the fifteenth of every month."

"Milestones?" James queried.

"Yes. Like the day you said your first word or rode your bike without stabilisers. This month was the date that Lily cut her first tooth. I wouldn't be able to tell you the exact date, but Kolya knew it. He'd been away at the plant in

Germany, and I'd sent him a photo. To be honest, you could barely see it, but he'd saved the photo and marked the date in his diary."

"I hadn't realised he'd done all that," James said in a quiet voice. "He always seemed to be working when I was growing up, but he was around more after my mum died. I just hadn't realised he was so sentimental."

"I doubt the boss would have told Riass what the numbers were. He would rather have died than put you in danger, so it's highly probable that someone saw him key in the number. He used to use the app to remote access the security cameras, so someone must have been watching him," Kevin concluded.

"Yeah, and we all know who that was. Fucking Darius, the traitorous bastard," James spat, glaring across at Yannis.

"Now hang on. You have no proof that Darius was involved in this attack, or even if he's still alive," Yannis countered.

"Darius didn't know about the hidden weapons, either. The boss insisted that only those who spent a significant amount of time over there had full access to them. We changed that after he'd been killed, giving everyone, even James's guards, full access to the weapons in each room," Nate clarified.

"How come I never heard about this? I've stayed with you since then. Did you not trust me enough to protect you, Tess?" Yannis sounded hurt, but it wasn't about trust.

I shrugged my shoulders and sighed. "I've spent time at the range with you, and let's face it, Yannis; you're not a great shot. Jonesy even nicknamed you Bent Barrel. And what did you once tell me? Oh, yes, *'I'm a lover, not a fighter.'* I can understand and appreciate that because we are all

HELEN BRIGHT

different. The baggage that comes with being married to or working for Kolya isn't for everyone. Between us, we killed seven men today," I said, gesturing around the room. "Granted, it was self-defence, but we can't even report their unprovoked attack to the police due to us using those same hidden weapons that you weren't given access to. By not doing so, we were protecting you, so if everything went tits up, you could swear you had no knowledge of them."

"Speaking of the shooters," Franco cut in, "we need to dispose of the bodies, but I don't want to leave you here without enough guards."

"How are you going to do it?" James asked.

"Douse them in petrol and burn them. We can smash up any leftover teeth and throw the bones in the new wood chipper that Jack showed me," Carl replied enthusiastically from across the table.

The room went quiet as everyone turned to face Carl.

"I think the *way* you said that horrifies me more than *what* you said," I told him. Everyone around the table agreed.

"What? I have box sets of CSI and true crime dramas. So sue me." Carl shrugged his shoulders, ignoring our raised eyebrows.

"Remind me not to piss him off," Franco murmured.

"I can't believe how unaffected you appear to be about all this. Does talking about the disposing of bodies not sicken you, Tess? It certainly sickens me," Yannis declared.

To say I was shocked was an understatement. How could anyone think I was nothing but repulsed by what we had to do? But I had to sanction it. I had the lives of the men who'd protected me to think of, as well as the fact that I had also shot and killed someone.

"I'm going to ignore that you said that, Yannis. But in

future, I suggest you think twice before you share your misguided assumptions about how I feel," I warned. "Being on my shit list is not a good place to be right now. I still have Roman and Yuri to deal with yet, and believe me, you'll think me an angel once you've heard what they have to say."

"Roman will demand that you and Lily fly to Moscow to be with them; you know that, don't you?" Kevin said, stating the obvious.

"I know. But I don't think it's a bad idea right now," I admitted. This drew a gasp from most of the men around me.

James banged his fist on the table, making me jump. "No. Dad wouldn't want you staying with them. I love my grandfather, but I don't trust him one bit. Once he has you and Lily in Moscow, he'll never let you leave. I've no doubt he'd keep you safe and protected from Riass, but who would protect you from him?"

"I agree with James," Franco said. "If Roman gets you and his granddaughter over there, he'll do everything in his power to keep you. You know what his position is within the hierarchy of the Russian mob, Tess. He's the boss of bosses. The head honcho. He has judges, police and politicians in his pocket. If he decides you're staying in Moscow, honey, then believe me, you're staying."

I put my face in my hands and groaned loudly. "I know all that; I just... I feel like I'm being pulled in all different directions, and none of them are safe. I want to stay in the UK to be near Nan and Jean and my work at Sarah's Legacy, but if someone's still after us, my presence alone could put them in danger. I'd love to live at Glengarran, but we'd need to update security measures if we're staying there full-time. It's a listed building, so some of the extra security we installed here would be out of the question. And the extra guards patrolling the area whenever we stay there is just not practical on a permanent basis."

"Leave it with me, Tess. I can look into other feasible security measures." Kevin tapped his index finger against the side of the laptop in front of him. "I have the footage of the attack from each of the cameras. Do you want to take a look before I send it to Roman?"

Just thinking about it made my skin prickle with fear and apprehension, and I wasn't sure it would do me any good to see what happened in Lily's room.

"I don't want to go over what I did. I'll probably see enough of that when I close my eyes tonight."

Kevin squeezed my shoulder. "I think that's inevitable after something like this, Tess. I'll knock that off the screen for now and add an extra feed from the other outside cameras. Once you've seen enough footage, you could put the kettle on and give Jack a ring to see how Nan's doing, while we take a look at what the cameras and mic picked up in Lily's bedroom."

As he tapped away at the keypad, I took a deep breath and braced myself for what was to come.

Watching the large black helicopter coming in to land from what I assumed was the roof camera was a whole different experience, and if it weren't for the fact I could see some familiar sights surrounding it as it landed, I could have been fooled into thinking it wasn't my home. Kevin turned down the sound, but even on low, you could tell the helicopter had a lot more power than the one Yannis used.

Looking at the black-clad rifle-carrying figures pouring out of the helicopter sent my thoughts hurtling in all different directions, but the one question at the forefront was: *which one of them did I kill?* The black balaclavas they wore covered everything but their eyes, and though it made them appear more menacing, I couldn't help but feel relieved about it. It meant that the man I shot remained a nameless, faceless entity. An inhuman enemy. Not even a dark stain upon my conscience. A no one.

All eight of our attackers had hit the ground running, and it was obvious they meant to gain access to the inside of the extension and not the guards' quarters. They wore thick bulletproof vests with cross-body ammo belts and carried what appeared to be AR-15 rifles.

The camera switched to the patio and poolside, bringing Nan into view. She stood there looking confused for a couple of seconds, and though I knew this was a video and it had happened over an hour ago, I wanted to yell for her to run.

When Nan finally came to her senses, she dropped the plant covering and tried to run towards the doorway into the extension. She'd taken no more than three steps before she slipped on a piece of the fleecy fabric and came crashing to the floor, her shoulder and hip taking most of the impact. I heard her cry out in pain, the sound a cold reminder of what I'd heard from Lily's bedroom. Two of the men went up to her, but only one pointed their rifle her way. I knew she hadn't been shot, but I still held my breath until the one pointing his rifle moved away. The other man knelt beside her and offered her his hand. Nan was right: he was going to help her.

Carl and Tanner came running out of the kitchen door wearing Kevlar vests and immediately took down two of the gunmen before taking cover behind the wall of our poolside shower. The other gunmen fired back continuously as they moved nearer to the kitchen door, each bullet chipping away at the tiled wall covering James's guards, along with the kitchen windows. Carl and Tanner yelled at Nan to stay down before returning fire, clipping the one at the side of Nan in his upper arm and causing him to drop his weapon. He picked it up with his other hand, firing back haphazardly.

There was so much gunfire coming from all around that it was hard to tell who'd shot Tanner. He cried out and fell backwards against Carl, but it didn't prevent either of them from returning a rapid-fire assault.

Dave stepped out from behind the kitchen door and hit two of the shooters, one in the chest and the other through the neck. I watched in horror as a bullet skimmed the side of Dave's head and took off the top part of his ear. "No," I cried as I watched him fall backwards. He hit the door with an audible thud and slid down to the floor. Kevin paused the playback for a moment, and Franco grabbed my shoulders from behind, speaking soothing words in my ear.

"Shh, he's okay, Tess. He's a tough guy."

"But he was hit in the head. You saw it. Look at all the blood, Franco." It was all over the door and… "Oh, God. How did he survive it?"

"It grazed his scalp, and there's always a lot of blood with a head injury. It must have knocked him senseless for a couple of minutes because he can't remember anyone getting past him. I think the gunmen thought he was dead because they stepped over him without a second thought." Kevin pressed play once again, and we watched as two of the remaining gunmen did just that.

"If these guys were professional mercenaries, they would have popped him again to make sure he was dead," Nate remarked.

The man that Dave hit in the chest rolled to his side and stood up slowly. The bulletproof vest had done its job and saved his life. He began making his way towards the kitchen door when he was hit in the back of the head by Carl. I probably should have been grossed out by the gruesome sight before me, but all I could think at that moment was, *"That's for Dave, you evil fucker."*

Kevin switched cameras to the ones inside the kitchen, which showed him crouching behind the upturned kitchen table with his rifle at the ready; the thick oak surface providing him half-decent cover. He shot the lead gunman in the chest and pelvis, but the guy kept on firing back as he went down—spraying bullets around the room that was once the hub of our happy home. The second gunman almost clipped Kevin as he made his way through the kitchen. Yet another shooter, who aimed at the glass cabinets containing our crystal glasses and fancy tableware, followed him. Kevin was in such a vulnerable position, and it's a testament to his skill that he could finish off the first shooter and take out the third. But somehow, during those precious few seconds, the second gunman to enter the kitchen had made his way through to the hallway.

And that right there was my limit. I couldn't watch any more of it. I couldn't view the playback of the most frightening moments of my life.

"I'm done, fellas. I know what comes next."

Kevin paused the playback and squeezed my hand. "I'm sorry I couldn't stop him getting through, Tess. I should have been more prepared and put in a whole new security system as soon as we heard about the attack in Estonia."

"No, Kevin. You don't get to blame yourself. I won't let you. As I've said before, if we allow ourselves to be mired down in guilt and negativity, it's another winning strike for Riass, and I won't let him have that." I pushed my chair out from the table and stood on legs that felt as though they'd barely hold me up.

Trying not to let the men around me see my weakness—knowing they'd worry even more—I gave myself a few seconds before I turned to leave, asking, "Now, how many of you want tea or coffee?"

Chapter Twenty-Seven

TESS

Waking up to sunlight glaring out from above the top of the heavy drapes was a sight that warmed my very soul. It meant the storm had finally passed, and I could go back to the yacht without getting seasick from being tossed around on the turbulent waves. It had been hard to tolerate, even on a yacht the size of the Princess Annis.

Not that staying with Yannis in his luxurious Greek villa was such a hardship, but I wanted to be somewhere I could just be me. A woman in mourning for the husband she loved and the home she had to leave behind in such dire circumstances. Having Lily meant I had to smile through the pain of loss and grief—for her sake, if nothing else—but I also needed to shut myself away for a little while and let myself wallow in it, too. Lying in the bed I shared many a passionate night in with the husband I still yearned for, helped in a way that talking about my feelings never could.

Yet, being in Yannis's home without Kolya felt… well, it just felt wrong. Their friendship went back a long way, and Kolya had spent many holidays on Athilos with his late wife and James. There were more photos of Kolya, Catherine, James, and Yannis on display around the villa than there had been before. Seeing Kolya so happy with another woman made me feel cheated. He'd been my first in everything; in love, sex, marriage, and probably the only man I'd ever give my heart to.

Yannis didn't have any photos of me with Kolya, but there were plenty of me and Lily, and a few of Yannis with both of us. I'd found that quite odd, but Franco went a little further and said it was disturbing. Ivan and Nate agreed, but what could I do about it? It wasn't my home. When Ivan had mentioned it, Yannis brushed it off. He said he was waiting for the ones Adrianna took the last time we visited. She told him she'd taken quite a few of Lily, too. If they were anything like the shots Adrianna captured last year, I knew I'd be keeping a few myself. Even at nineteen years old, she was such a talented photographer.

I rolled over and picked up my phone from the bedside table. It was 7 a.m., so I'd managed around four hours of sleep, which was pretty good for me. In the seven nights since the attack on our home, I'd barely slept for more than three hours straight.

On the night of the attack, we'd all slept in the kitchen on mattresses the guards had brought down from upstairs in the manor. It was the safest place for us to be. The gun range in the cellar could have been used as a panic room if we were attacked again, though we all thought the likelihood of that was pretty remote. Their previous strike hadn't gone so well, and in all probability, they'd need a little time to regroup. Still, it was better to err on the side of caution.

Lily and I had slept between James and Ivan, and throughout the night, the rest of the guards had taken turns keeping watch over the property.

As expected, Danny had been utterly distraught when he learned what happened to Bess. He buried her near the saplings that Kolya and Lily had planted. I knew how much fun Bess had chasing squirrels around the wood, so I thought her final resting place was fitting.

I'd worried about Danny having a setback in his recovery due to Bess being killed, but after going through the extension to collect her body, his distress had turned into raging anger. He'd volunteered to dispose of the bodies, along with Carl and Franco, and insisted he was the one to douse them in petrol and light the match.

Kevin had photographed the faces of our attackers—well, the ones who hadn't been shot in the head, at least—then ran them through a software programme he'd developed, trying to find a match. Only one showed a hit, bringing up the details of a Syrian male who'd been processed as a refugee in a camp near the Turkish border.

It wasn't unheard of for men like Riass to recruit refugees. He offered them a better life than they were forced to live in most of the camps. People who had little hope were as easily groomed as the girls across both South and West Yorkshire and Rochdale had been. Don't get me wrong; I wasn't excusing the man. He attacked my home, so he deserved everything he got. But was it merely a coincidence that the man who'd shot me while trying to assassinate Kolya five years ago had also been Syrian? Back then, Kolya hadn't even heard of Riass, so it seemed unlikely that the two were linked. Nevertheless, it was something that couldn't be ignored, and it brought up a question that none of us wanted to think about, namely: what if Riass wasn't behind the attack on our home?

Lainey was horrified by what had happened and felt even worse because she hadn't been there to protect us.

After she'd helped Danny bury Bess, she came back to the manor and sat with me and Lily. She put on a brave face for Lily, telling her all about the Christmas lights in London, but it wasn't long before our beautiful, tough Lainey broke down and cried, her tears falling on my daughter's hair while she rocked her gently.

She'd brought Lily's doll over from her bedroom, along with our toothbrushes and a suitcase full of my and Lily's clothes, which I'd been grateful for. It meant I didn't have to battle my way through our wrecked home. Yannis had ordered his guards to help clear out my broken kitchen, so it would be less work for Andy and Kevin after we left.

Roman and Yuri had hit the roof when we finally made them aware of what had happened, and after watching the camera playback that Kevin sent them, I could almost feel their anger and distress, despite the distance between us. Roman had insisted that Lily and I fly to Moscow as soon as it was safe and was intent on sending some of his guards over to join us. I didn't want strangers looking out for us, though. I needed people I knew and trusted. But to appease him, James said he'd accept a guard until Tanner was fit enough to return to work.

I advised Roman I'd be pulling Mark and Greg from the search for Riass so they could cover for Dave and inspect the yacht before we arrived. He told me it wasn't the best time of year to be sailing in Europe, and he'd been right, of course, but Yannis assured Roman we'd be safe on the island with him.

Yuri sent a jet to Heathrow to collect us the next day, not wanting us to risk using a KOLCAT jet until they could be sure it wouldn't be targeted. I told them I wasn't going to leave without seeing Nan and Dave, but everyone agreed the logistics involved with keeping me safe made that an unreasonable request. I knew they were right, but not being able to see her in person—to hold her hand and tell her how much I loved her—was the straw that broke the camel's back. It was like what happened with Jean all over again.

When she'd had her heart attack, Sarah and I hadn't been allowed to visit her. They removed us from the only home we'd ever felt safe in, and we hadn't been able to see for ourselves that she was being cared for and had everything she needed.

After the day I'd had, it was just too much.

I'd shouted at nearly everyone in that room like an errant teenager, telling them that my opinions should matter because I was the boss now, and when Roman insisted once again that Kolya was still alive, I took my frustration out on him. I yelled at him and swore; told him he was playing with my emotions and needed to wake up to the fact that Kolya was dead. Both Franco and Ivan tried to caution me, whispering that I had to remember I was pissing off an extremely dangerous man, but I just didn't care. I'd had enough of the highs and lows of hope and despair, and reminded him I wasn't someone to play with. I was a fighter in my own right, as I'd proven earlier when I claimed that man's life without a second thought.

To everyone's surprise, Roman said nothing until I stopped my rant. Then he asked, "Do you feel better now, Tess?"

"I won't feel better until I know that Nan, Dave, and Tanner are going to be okay and I can finally get out of here," I told him. "I don't particularly care if people think I should be a submissive little woman who'll sit here saying yes, sir, no, sir, three bags full, sir, whenever they try to lay the law down. That has never been who I am, and I'm not willing to change for anyone."

"I'm glad to hear it. I doubt the submissive little woman you speak of would have killed a man to protect my beloved granddaughter, would she?" Both Ivan and Franco let out a deep breath when Roman smiled, then added, "My dear, you are a Barinov through and through. I am proud of you for standing up for yourself, and it pleases me that despite all you've gone through, you still have so much love and compassion for others. But might I suggest a compromise?"

I shrugged my shoulders. It was childish, I know, but even though my anger had lessened, frustration still held me in its tight grip.

"Could you send a guard to the hospital to see Nan and get them to video call you from there? You could speak to Nan that way and see for yourself that she is doing well. I would also like to check on her progress. She has taken care of my son and his family for so many years, and my heart breaks to know that she suffered today. Yuri and I will send flowers and let her know that we are thinking of her. I doubt the injured men would appreciate flowers, but make them aware I am forever in their debt."

I nodded and blinked away tears. The unexpected sincerity in Roman's voice had been my undoing. I reached out and touched the screen with my fingertips and smiled a little when he did the same.

"I'm sorry for what I said about Kolya," I'd told him. "It's just... I keep hoping you're right, that you'll call me one day and say you've found him and you're bringing him home to me. But every time you and Gustav investigate a new lead, it turns out to be false, and the hope I cling to shatters, leaving misery and anger in its wake. I can't live like that, Roman. It's not healthy."

"I understand, my dear, more than you know. I felt that way

for so long after we lost Aleksei and Talia. Every day I waited for news that my son would be found alive. That they'd been picked up by a passing fisherman and hadn't been in touch due to amnesia or something. But, of course, that never happened. I didn't even get to bury my son. He was lost to the sea, and there was nothing I could do to change that. It made me feel powerless—like I did when we found out my wife's cancer was terminal. So when I could not see any visible fatal injuries on Kolya, I refused to believe that he was dead. If I do so, I cede any power I have to keep my son alive to that *ublyudok terrorist*."

After wiping my teary eyes on the back of my sleeve, I said, "I can't imagine how it feels to lose a child. I know that without Lily, I'd just give up. When I hid her in that drawer, I told her to wait until she heard someone she recognised before she made a noise. I was prepared to die to keep her safe because keeping her alive and well is everything to me. I suppose that's how you feel about Kolya; that your search and hope are keeping him alive. I hope more than anything that you're right. He's my one, you know. I thought we had forever."

Roman nodded. "How about I make you a deal, Tess? I will continue with the search for my son but will not give you any details, even if it appears promising. In fact, I won't speak to you about Kolya being alive until I hand him over to you in person. How does that sound?"

"Sounds like a good deal to me," I told him. "Thank you, Roman, for being so understanding." Then I did something I'd never done before. "I love you," I said, and a beaming smile lit up his whole face.

"I love you too, *moya doch'*."

I probably shouldn't feel so special when a man as notorious as Roman Barinov calls me daughter, but I still can't help the warm feeling I get from hearing those words. Maybe it's the orphan in me. Who knows?

My own daughter stirred in bed beside me, her arms stretching out as she yawned.

"Good morning, Lily," I whispered. She rolled towards me without opening her eyes.

"I'm tired," she said, and yawned again.

"We need to get up, Lilypot. Uncle Yannis has to go to work today, so he wants us to join him for breakfast."

"I don't want any breakfast. I want to stay in bed," she protested.

"That's a shame. I thought we could go Christmas shopping today."

Lily opened one eye. "For toys?"

"Maybe."

She seemed to think about it for all of five seconds, then pushed the covers down using her feet.

"There aren't any shops here, though, Mummy, so we'll have to tell Ivan to take us to London. Then we'll see the Christmas lights, too."

"Ivan can't take us to London in the helicopter, sweety. It's too far."

"Then where will we go?" she questioned.

"We could go to one of the neighbouring islands or to Athens."

"But I want to go to London, then we can go ho—" Lily's voice caught on that last word, and she paused for a moment. "We can live with all the guards, Mummy. We could sleep with Ivan in his bed. It's really big and bouncy, and he lets me do backflips on it." She put her hands over her eyes as if to hide when she realised what she'd said.

"You'd better not be doing backflips on any bed, Lily. You know that's not allowed."

"If we can stay in the guards' house, I promise I won't do any more. Pretty please, Mummy."

"Why do you want to stay in the guards' house?" I asked.

"Because I don't want to live in our home in case the bad men come back, but Nan and Jack's cottage is there, and lots of the people I love live in the guards' house. Santa knows where it is, too, because he left me some presents under the tree in the big room. Do you remember, Mummy?"

"I do. But Santa will know where to leave presents for you even if you aren't at home. Is that why you didn't want us to stay with Uncle Yannis for Christmas?"

Lily nodded. "I don't think Santa knows where Uncle Yannis lives, and there aren't any other children on the island. Adrianna sometimes comes, but she's a grown-up now."

"I think you'll find that Santa knows where every little boy and girl lives. He used to leave presents here for Uncle Yannis when *he* was a little boy."

Lily pulled a face, scrunching up her cute little nose. "But Uncle Yannis is old. Santa might not even remember how to get here."

"Uncle Yannis isn't old. He's the same age as your daddy."

Lily thought for a moment, then opened her eyes wide. "We have to go back to the guards' house for Daddy, too. He won't be able to find us here."

I closed my eyes and tried to compose myself. "Lily, sweetheart…"

A knock on the bedroom door saved me from having to explain to my daughter yet again that her daddy wouldn't be coming home from heaven.

"Are you decent?" Danny shouted.

"Come on in," I answered.

Danny strolled into the bedroom, closely followed by Lainey.

"Good morning, you two. The weather's beautiful today, so Lainey and I thought we'd go for a run early, in case you wanted to head back to the yacht after breakfast."

I could see the hopeful look in their eyes. They didn't like being here. None of our guards did. Yannis wasn't as welcoming as Kolya had been. My husband had treated our close protection team like extended family members. Not that he didn't give them orders or anything—they did work for him, after all—but the guards were always welcome to eat with us, especially at breakfast and lunchtime. If Kolya had been away for a while, they used to give us time on our own as a family, but other than that, they were regular fixtures at our kitchen table.

"I'm looking forward to getting back to the yacht myself, but I think we need to make a contingency plan in case the weather turns again." Just thinking about it made my stomach churn.

"Did Kevin say when the additional security measures will be in place at Glengarran?" Lainey asked.

"Not until February, or possibly later, depending on the weather in the highlands." Winters can be hard that far north, though Glengarran after a good snowfall is picture perfect.

"I want us to go back to where you live so we can be ready for Santa coming. We can all have a sleepover in the kitchen again, can't we, Danny? I don't think Santa would mind if we did that because the tree goes up in the other room where the telly is, so we won't disturb him when he leaves everyone their presents." Lily was chatting away merrily to Danny as he picked her up from the bed and twirled her around the room.

"She doesn't want to stay here for Christmas, but we can't go back home. Not yet, anyway. Roman wants us to go to Moscow, though James and Ivan think that's a bad idea. I know James will join us, wherever we are, but I understand his reasons for staying away from there. When Riass stole the weapon, it put KOLCAT under serious scrutiny from governments all over the world. They know that James has close family in Russia, but it will still make Homeland Security a little apprehensive if he goes there."

Lainey nodded in understanding. She had no words to help with my dilemma. She knew how frustrated James was when he had to stay in the UK instead of joining us on the island. He was supposed to fly back to the States, but KOLCAT lost a major order the day after our home was attacked, and he'd been asked to attend a meeting in White-hall with the Secretary of State for Defence. He still had to fly out to the States so he could wrap up some business before joining us for Christmas.

As soon as Lainey and Danny left for their run, Lily and I washed and dressed quickly and made our way downstairs to where Yannis awaited us in his lavish dining room. The six sliding doors were all open and showcased a large veranda that overlooked the blue-green waters of the Ionian Sea.

"Good morning, my darlings. When I awoke and saw the sun shining down over Athilos, I thought my view couldn't be more beautiful. Then I see you two, and I realise how wrong I had been. You, my dears, are the epitome of beauty." Yannis placed his coffee cup on the table and stood to greet us, kissing my cheek before hoisting Lily into his arms and doing the same.

"Uncle Yannis, my mummy said that when you were a little boy, Santa used to bring you presents."

Yannis smiled and set Lily on his knee. "She's right. He brought me lots of presents. In fact, if I've been very good, he still brings me gifts."

Lily seemed shocked by his response. "Do you have to write him a list?"

"No. When you're a grown-up, you don't need to make a list," he replied.

"Did you make a list when you were a little boy in the olden days?" Lily queried.

I tried to hold in my laughter, but I hadn't a hope in hell of doing so.

"Hey, I'm not that old," Yannis admonished. He began tickling Lily in punishment.

Ivan entered the dining room and grunted what sounded like a good morning. Lily yelled out his name and wriggled off Yannis's lap to get to him. He scooped her up in one of his big, brawny tattooed arms and planted a kiss on her lips. Then he set her down on the chair beside me before taking the seat next to her, much to Yannis's dismay.

"You were supposed to wake me and Franco up before you came down," he said, then followed it with an angry grunt.

Ivan still looked tired. His dark-brown hair, which had a slight wave to it, was sticking out at the sides, and his facial hair had grown so much fuller over the past few weeks. His personal grooming had fallen by the wayside since Kolya died, but then again, mine had fared no better. My eyebrows desperately needed sorting out, although I had shaved my legs after Lily complained they were spiky.

Franco strolled into the dining room with a frown on his

face. I held up my hand and said, "Don't," before *he* told me off, too.

Yannis glared at Ivan and Franco. He'd already expressed his displeasure at having any of my close protection guards joining us in what he considered our *private time* when we'd arrived here last week. Ivan said he wasn't a guard, he was family, and Franco had completely ignored him. When Yannis had raised his voice and repeated himself, Franco merely said, "I answer only to Tess, and I go wherever she and Lily go."

Yannis told us he had more than enough guards patrolling the grounds. He said he could accept Lainey as she was Lily's nanny—something that made me laugh out loud, considering she was ex-army and could probably outperform most of his guards with her eyes closed—but he didn't see the need to have Ivan, Franco, Nate, and Danny join us. I told him I wasn't willing to go anywhere without them and reminded him that Kolya always insisted he bring our close protection team when we'd stayed with him before.

Thea, Yannis's new cook, and Maya, his housekeeper, brought out a selection of fruit, honey, sweet pastries, and a rack of toast. Yannis poured Lily and me fresh orange juice while we tucked into the goodies on offer. Everyone thanked Thea and Maya, who each made a fuss of Lily before they went back to the kitchen to bring me a pot of tea. God bless them.

I don't care where I am in the world, it's either two cups of tea to start my day or avoid me at all costs.

"I was thinking, as the weather is looking so promising, perhaps you and I could have dinner out on the veranda this evening. I'll be on the mainland until six, so I probably won't be back until after seven. By the time I've had a shower and dressed for dinner, Lily will be ready for us to kiss her goodnight, won't you, darling?" Yannis hinted, frowning at Lily as she copied Ivan by pouring honey on her toast. Ivan winked at her as he took a big bite, so she placed a honey-smeared kiss on his bicep, some of it catching the sleeve of his black T-shirt. Ivan didn't care at all, he just wiped it up with his fingers and then stuck them in his mouth, claiming, "Yours tastes better than mine," before pretending to steal her toast.

"I'm sorry, Yannis. I was thinking of heading back to the yacht today. We've taken up enough space in your home as it is, and I've been looking forward to spending some time there. Kolya and I had so many happy memories of our time spent sailing around the Mediterranean and Caribbean."

A whole range of emotions seemed to flash over Yannis's features. Shock, anger, frustration. In the end, he took a deep breath and nodded.

"I understand, Tess. Perhaps we can have dinner together tomorrow night when you come back to the villa."

"I don't know if I will come back to the villa, Yannis. Lily wants to go back to the UK for Christmas and—"

Yannis slammed his fist on the table. "No! I forbid it. You will stay here with me." He stood and pushed his chair back so abruptly that it fell onto the floor with a loud clatter. Franco and Ivan did the same, mirroring his combative stance.

I stayed seated, as if the threatening, overbearing behaviour of the men in the room had little effect on me.

"Yannis, I'm sure I don't have to remind you that no one has the power to forbid me from doing anything." I turned to Lily, who was looking at everyone, totally bemused. "Come on, Lily, let's go and pack."

"No, please. You've got me all wrong, Tess. I just can't bear to think of you going back there. Not after..." Yannis gestured to Ivan and Franco. "You know you cannot guarantee their safety back there."

He glanced back at me with a look of pure sorrow; a contradictory expression from the fury of earlier. "Tess, let me take care of you and Lily until we can put an end to this threat. As I've said before, I can do no more for my friend than keep the ones he loved most in the world safe and well. Please don't take that one thing away from me."

Yannis mentioning Kolya sucked the wind right out of my sails. Yes, I was still angry at him for trying to lord it over me, but his reasons behind that were well-intended. And yet, I didn't want to excuse his behaviour, either.

"I can understand where your concern is coming from, Yannis, but in future, I'd advise that you err on the side of caution when choosing the words you use. I don't appreciate being dictated to by you or anyone, and I don't care if this is how you've been brought up to treat the women in your life. You will speak to me as an equal and with a healthy dose of respect, or you won't speak to me at all." I hadn't once raised my voice, but I made sure my daughter was listening to every word I said.

I refuse to let Lily see me cower down to anyone. We're surrounded by men every day, and it would set a poor example if I gave in and let them run and dictate every aspect of my life. That's not to say I won't listen to fair suggestions when they're delivered in the correct manner, though. I'm not an idiot.

"I hope you can accept my sincere apologies. I do have a habit of putting my foot in my mouth where you are concerned, Tess." Yannis gestured towards the veranda. "May I speak with you in private?"

Before I could answer, Lily remarked, "Uncle Yannis, you really shouldn't put your foot in your mouth. Especially if you have stinky sock feet like Danny." Lily crossed her eyes, wafting her hand up and down in front of her nose with dramatic effect.

My daughter broke the intense atmosphere surrounding the adults in the dining room in her typically funny way. Even Franco managed a smile, though he quickly schooled his features and focused his penetrating stare back on Yannis. Ivan tugged on one of Lily's curls before sitting down again, continuing to eat as if nothing had happened.

Yannis ignored Franco's stare and walked around the table to Lily. Crouching down between our chairs, he said, "Lily, you brighten my day and constantly make me smile." He tried to kiss her cheek, but she moved her head away quickly.

"I can't let you kiss me, Uncle Yannis. You might give me foot germs," she mumbled behind her hand. Ivan made an exaggerated gagging noise that made Lily and Franco laugh.

Yannis laughed along with them, but I could tell he wasn't happy. I felt a little sorry for him, in a way. He'd offered us his home as a safe haven and, more often than not, we'd clashed over even the silliest of things. But then again, we always had. It was like a little dance we did. He'd say something that annoyed me, I'd have a go at him, he'd placate me and make up some silly excuse, and then I'd forgive him. When we had Kolya to referee our little arguments, it didn't seem so bad; now I found it exhausting. But nearly every day, Yannis would do or say something totally endearing.

Yannis stood and held out his hand. "Come and have a

quick chat with me, Tess." I placed my hand in his and glanced over at Franco before he could follow.

"It's okay, Franco. I'll just be a minute. Eat your breakfast before Ivan steals it."

Yannis steered me towards the veranda. The sun shone brightly over its exquisitely tiled floor, which featured an image of Poseidon rising from the sea, holding his trident high above curling blue waves. Yannis gestured towards the pale grey cushioned rattan seating that overlooked the path to the sea. Like a gentleman, he waited until I was seated before he sat beside me.

He took my left hand in his and seemed to hesitate for a moment before he said, "I was going to ask you about this tonight after we'd eaten, but maybe it's better to do it now. Please don't feel as if you have to do this for me, though; I'd hate to add to your grief in any way." Yannis sighed and squeezed my hand before carrying on. "I've been going through my photographs and videos, and I found a few of me and Kolya that were filmed during our university years. I admit to shedding a tear when I played them, so I put them away again. But I thought if we went through them together, it might make it easier. If you don't feel as though you can do it, then that's okay. I could look at them again when things aren't so raw."

I couldn't help the smile that spread across my face. "Do I want to see videos of Kolya as a teenager? Hell yes! I've seen the odd photo of Kolya at that age, and of him as a child, but to see a video of him and hear how his voice sounded would be brilliant, Yannis."

Kolya looked a lot like James when he was younger. But to hear him speak and see how he acted around his friends at that age... I couldn't wait to watch that.

"I have a lot of video footage of him when James was a

child, but Catherine's on most of them, so I didn't think it appropriate to show you those, but I thought James might like to see them."

"I think he'd love to see them, Yannis. After all, they have both his parents on."

Yannis smiled. "I remember when they were potty training him. If we were outside, James had a habit of pulling down his underpants and peeing everywhere. Kolya would tell him to keep still and point it at one spot, but he rarely did."

I laughed and told him, "You need to remind him about that and dig out those videos when he finally brings a girl-friend to see you."

His eyes lit up with a hint of mischief. "I like the way you think, Tess."

"So, these videos of you and him in your uni days... What did you get up to in them? You have me curious now."

"Come back to the villa and have dinner with me tonight—or tomorrow—and I'll show you. You might need to down a few drinks to cope with how devastatingly hand-some I was back in the day, and I'll understand if you're tempted to throw your underwear at me."

Back in the day? Yannis seemed to get more handsome with age, and he knew it. He had light-brown eyes framed by thick black lashes. His olive-toned skin, jet-black hair, and strong masculine features spoke of his Greek heritage. He was around five foot ten but often appeared taller due to how he carried himself. I'd never once seen Yannis slouch. Even when he was relaxing with friends at home, his posture seemed almost regal.

"What do you say, Tess? Will you stay here a little longer and have dinner with me?"

I sat back in the chair and cast a glance at the Princess Annis that was anchored in the bay. I desperately wanted to go back to the yacht, but I also didn't want to upset Yannis. He needed me to help him come to terms with his loss, and I couldn't be sure, but I thought helping Yannis might also help with my grief, too.

"Okay, I'll stay and have dinner with you tonight, but I can't promise about tomorrow," I warned.

He put his arm around me and pulled me close. "I know you and Lily are struggling with being away from England, especially with Christmas fast approaching. Going back to Oxford isn't the wisest decision after what happened there last week, but we could always stay at the hotel in London. The penthouse suite at Lassiter's has excellent security, and with enough guards flanking us, we could take Lily for a drive around London to see the lights and watch the fireworks over the London Eye on New Year's Eve. I'm looking forward to experiencing a traditional family Christmas this year. Nan and Jack could join us, and you could pay a visit to your beloved Jean."

"I thought about that and discussed it with Kevin, but if anyone were to target us again, it could put the hotel residents in danger."

"Remember, Tess, you'll have my security team there, too." Yannis ran his fingers up and down my arm as if to soothe me, or him. I couldn't be sure. He turned a little so he was facing me.

"You know, my dear, while we are over there, you could also look at a few properties. You don't have to live in Oxford anymore. Kolya would understand if you looked elsewhere. I know it's probably not something you wish to talk about, but I'm assuming he left you sufficiently provided for in his will. However, if that is not the case, I'd be more than happy to buy you and Lily a home wherever you choose to live. I love you both so very much, and I want to see you thrive and enjoy life again. I know it will take time, and there'll be many more tears before your heart begins to heal. Promise you'll think about it, at least."

I nodded, and Yannis smiled. "Would you mind doing me a favour today?" he asked.

"Of course," I replied.

"Adrianna has some photographs for us. There are a number of Lily, and I'm sure there will be quite a few of you and Kolya. Would you bring them back to the villa for me? She'll be arriving on the island in an hour or so, now that the sea is calm."

"Would you like me to invite her over to have dinner with us this evening? I'm sure she'd love to spend time with you." I raised both eyebrows suggestively.

"Oh, not you, too. Kolya mentioned that Adrianna had a crush on me. I don't want to encourage the girl, Tess."

"She's not a girl anymore, Yannis. She's a young woman. A beautiful one at that. I married Kolya when I was seventeen and had Lily at eighteen, so at nineteen, I'd say Adrianna is plenty old enough for you."

"It's not the same, Tess. I remember her as a baby. I've watched her grow up. I like to think I have some morals, though many would argue I had none. So please don't invite her to dinner."

"Don't worry, I won't. But it would be nice if she wasn't alone on the island, so I'll see if she wants to hang out with me and Lily for a while."

Yannis shrugged his shoulders. "Well, my darling, I'm afraid it's time for me to leave, though I'd much rather spend the day with you and my honey-covered goddaughter."

He held my hand as we walked back into the dining room and didn't let go until he reached my chair, which he graciously pulled out for me. Then he kissed me and Lily on the cheek before saying he'd see us both later.

Franco stared directly at me and raised one eyebrow.

"What?" I poured myself a second cup of tea and met his intense stare with one of my own.

"I don't like to see you being played," Franco replied.

"I'm not being played, Franco. Yannis is a good man, but he's used to getting his own way and isn't often challenged by strong women. If he knows what's good for him, he'll learn how to deal with it, because I'm not the only female here who's a force to be reckoned with. Little Miss Lilypot is as stubborn and strong-willed as they come."

Lily held up her arms and flexed her biceps. "I am strong, Mummy, but my muscles aren't as big as Ivan's."

In response to Lily's words, Ivan lifted his arms to reveal his bulging biceps. Lily laughed out loud before poking them. Then glancing at Franco she demanded, "Show me your muscles, Franco."

He did as she asked, tensing his arm muscles to reveal those solid, tattooed biceps, which, while not as Hulk-like as Ivan's, were impressive, nonetheless.

"I think there's way too much testosterone around this table. I vote we walk down to the beach for a paddle in the sea, then we'll call and see Adrianna."

"Yay!" Lily wriggled her shoulders and punched the air. "Are you going to swim in the sea with me?" she asked.

"I don't think it will be warm enough, Lily. You have to remember that even though the sun is shining, it's still winter," I told her.

Lily pulled a face. She looked so glum, and I could tell

that Ivan was about to cave and offer to go swimming with her. I shook my head in warning.

"We may as well go back to London where it's real wintertime than stay here in a pretend one where the sun's shining. That's like God doing a big fib in the sky," she mumbled. Then she spun around to face me and asked, "Can we get Anna from the yacht? You did make a promise that when it stopped being so windy, we could go back and fetch her. Can we, Mummy? Please…"

We'd flown in from the yacht when the wind had just begun to pick up, and I had limited what we brought due to not wanting Ivan to make too many trips. He'd brought me, Lily, Franco and Nate on the first flight and then Lainey and Danny with our luggage on the next. Poor Mark had offered to stay on the yacht to oversee security there. Greg had flown back to England to help Kevin and Andy at home in Oxford, so there'd been just Mark and the staff suffering through the storm on the yacht.

Our home had been cleaned up since the attack and work on the new kitchen would begin just after Christmas. I'd asked James to choose the style he wanted, as well as the new colour scheme for when the decorating began. As far as I was concerned, it was his home now, and the only reason I'd set foot in there again would be to pay him a visit.

"We can bring Anna back later if you're good," I told Lily before taking a bite out of a croissant.

My daughter rolled her eyes and replied, "Of course I'm going to be good. It would be silly to be naughty when it's this close to Christmas."

Chapter Twenty-Eight

TESS

Lainey and Danny took one of Yannis's motor-powered dinghies and headed back to the yacht. I think Danny was struggling, to be honest. He was restless and irritable. He missed his brave little Bess and was dealing with so much anger over how she died, and he wasn't the only one. But my anger was laced with guilt, too. Danny said I was wrong to feel that way, yet Bess had died while defending me. How could I not feel guilty about that?

Nate watched over us from the rocks beside the cove. He wasn't the only one watching us. A sullen-looking guard named Tassos was keeping a close eye on our movements through binoculars from the edge of Yannis's sun terrace. Both Nate and Tassos were armed, along with all of Yannis's other guards. They stood out amongst the cloudless blue sky and sandy-coloured rocks, spoiling an otherwise serene vista. Yannis was taking my and Lily's security extremely seriously after the attack on our home. He'd never had as many armed guards patrolling his property when we came here with Kolya.

The small cove made for quite a suntrap, causing the sand to feel warm underfoot, and the crystal-clear Ionian Sea didn't feel so cold once the first few waves had lapped at my toes.

Ivan had Lily tipped upside down, threatening to dunk her head-first into the sea. She was screaming with laughter, and I was reminded of a time when Ivan had done the same to me by the pool at home. Bess had licked my face while I was held upside down, loving the excitement of a new game. I'd not had Lily then, and I was still fairly new to Kolya's world and what I believed was a marriage of convenience. I couldn't have been more wrong. My marriage was full of love, trust, and respect. Through Kolya, I gained a family, and without them I wouldn't have survived all our recent trauma and grief.

The muted tones of "Iris" by the Goo Goo Dolls rang out from the pocket of my cropped jeans, alerting me to an incoming call. In my haste to answer, I almost dropped my phone in the sea, but thankfully Franco caught it before it hit the water. He'd remained mostly silent as we strolled along the beach, apart from when he'd touched my shoulders and asked if I was wearing sunscreen.

I hadn't checked to see who was calling before I answered and was surprised to hear James say hello. He told me he'd cancelled his trip back to the States because he had a few more business issues to sort out in Europe, so he'd flown out to see us, bringing with him the toys I'd ordered Lily for Christmas. He was calling from Heathrow—the unmistakable sound of taxiing aircraft made it hard to hear him until he boarded KOLCAT's luxurious Gulfstream G650ER. We decided not to tell Lily he was on his way, thinking how nice it would be for him to surprise her, and I didn't tell James about the videos that Yannis had found. I knew it would hit him hard emotionally when he saw them and hoped that Yannis would make him copies so James could show his own children when the time came.

While Lily busied herself collecting pretty seashells, I updated Ivan and Franco about James's flight, then texted Nate and Mark the details. Ivan said he'd fly out to Kefalonia to pick him up from the airport when he was due to arrive. It takes a little under three and a half hours to fly from London to Kefalonia, so we had plenty of time to visit Adrianna.

The difference in the weather since the storm had broken was unbelievable, and I felt my shoulders beginning to burn. I took a bottle of sunscreen out of my bag and had Ivan apply it to Lily, while Franco made sure my shoulders and back were covered. I'd worn a pretty blue cami top, which Kolya had always said was his favourite, along with a matching blue cardigan I'd popped in my bag as soon as we'd hit the beach. Lily wore a lilac-coloured dress with a wide-brimmed straw hat to keep the glare of the sun away from her face. She had sunglasses in my bag, but she wasn't keen on wearing them. I was glad of mine. They'd been my saviour on so many days since grief became the ruling power in the kingdom of my emotions.

Ivan's sunglasses were practical, in that he could wear them in his capacity as a pilot as well as his regular day-to-day activities. The aviator style really suited him, especially the ones he wore with the grey-tinted lenses.

Franco wore his sunglasses like those particular accessories had been made with him in mind. The brown-black lenses and black frames gave him a dark, almost threatening vibe and, yeah, I'll admit that along with the whole tall, muscular, handsome Italian-looking package that was Anthony Franconni, the sunglasses also gave him a sexy, mysterious edge. Of all the men I was surrounded by on a daily basis, Franco and Ivan got the most looks from the women we encountered. And I couldn't blame them one little bit, although Kolya was still the only man I'd ever truly desired in that way. In my eyes, Kolya had always been the one that stood out amongst all the rest. To me, he'd been perfect.

I looked at the photos of him on my phone every night before falling asleep and wished more than anything that he was still lying beside me.

Though my bag contained everything we might need for a trip to the beach, I'd only brought one small towel, so we sat on the rocks with Nate for a while until our feet were dry enough to brush the sand away and put on our shoes. Ivan just had to tickle Lily's feet while brushing the sand away, causing a bout of uncontrollable laughter, which was something I was grateful for. It meant she was less focused on the rifle Nate was holding. Franco was also carrying, but the Sig was tucked into the holster that rested against the waistband of his dark-blue jeans. The black T-shirt he wore was just loose enough to hide it. Of course, anyone with a military or close protection background would know he was concealing a weapon.

Once we had our shoes on, we made our way down the rocky path to Adrianna's home on the other side of the island. The little cottage used to belong to Galena, her grandmother, who'd been the housekeeper at the villa since before Yannis was born. He'd let Galena stay on at the cottage after she retired and had been heartbroken when she passed away earlier this year. Adrianna had asked if she could still come and spend time at her grandmother's place at weekends and during her college breaks, and Yannis had agreed. Everyone knew Adrianna was head over heels for Yannis, but he wasn't interested at all.

After walking barely five minutes towards Adrianna's home, Lily managed to get two stones in her shoes. We stopped to empty them, then Ivan hoisted her up onto his shoulders, carrying her the rest of the way, which only took us another six minutes when we weren't slowed down by my dawdling daughter.

You couldn't see Yannis's villa from Adrianna's cottage. The pretty white building with its vibrant blue door and window shutters was at the bottom end of an incline on the other side of the small island. The boat that had dropped Adrianna off was still moored by the jetty. I'd caught the boat before when we were travelling to Athena's—a tavern on the neighbouring island of Nisi. Stavros Nikesi, along with his son, who was also named Stavros, ran the boat between Kefalonia, Nisi, and Athilos. It didn't stop at Athilos every day—only when supplying the villa with fresh produce, or if you'd let Stavros know you needed to take a trip. Yannis used his helicopter if he had to go anywhere, so it was usually only his staff who travelled with Stavros.

A quick glance behind us revealed one of Yannis's guards standing at the top of the incline, holding a rifle. No matter how I tried to be okay with seeing armed men I was unfamiliar with, it still freaked me the hell out, and I couldn't wait to disappear into Adrianna's home.

She came out to greet us as we approached the small walled patio at the back of the property. Lily hadn't spotted her at first. She was too busy waving at Stavros, who she could easily see from her position atop Ivan's shoulders. As soon as Adrianna shouted hello, Lily's focus switched to the pretty Greek nineteen-year-old, who seemed to become even more beautiful every time I saw her.

"Adrianna," Lily yelled, and ran towards her as soon as Ivan lowered her to the ground.

When Lily reached her, Adrianna lifted her up and twirled her around, telling her how much she'd grown since she last saw her. Adrianna's command of the English language was almost perfect, her Greek accent giving her words a friendly, almost melodious ring.

When Ivan, Franco and I reached Adrianna, she lowered Lily to her feet and tugged me into her arms, whispering, "I'm so sorry for your loss. When I heard what had happened on the news, I couldn't believe it. I called Yannis and begged him to tell me it wasn't true. I have hope we will hear more good news when you find the terrorist group."

I gave her that practised smile I wore when I was trying to be brave for others and responded with, "Kolya's father would love to hear you say that."

For a moment, Adrianna looked slightly confused but then smiled and ushered everyone towards a table and four chairs under a sheltered area of the patio, away from the glaring rays of the sun. As we approached, Lily spotted a tiny gecko and yelled *"lizard"* so loud it made Adrianna jump.

While Adrianna went to fix us all a lemonade, I answered all of Lily's lizard-related questions.

1. Can I keep it?

2. Is it a boy or a girl?

3. Why can't I keep it?

4. Do you think it's hungry?

5. What does it eat?

6. Did you really mean it when you said I couldn't keep it?

7. Can I hold it?

8. Do you think it loves me already?

9. Can it swim?

10. Can I just keep it while we stay with Uncle Yannis so it doesn't get lonely?

Adrianna brought out a pitcher and five glasses on an old wooden tray and set them on the table. "You might want to wait for the ice to cool the lemonade a little before you pour it. I brought it with me today, so it hasn't had time to chill."

"I'm sure it will be lovely, regardless," I told her. "I can't believe the difference in the weather. The storm took us all by surprise."

"I know. I worried about the windows because I hadn't fastened the shutters before I left here last week. I had to go back home for my mother's birthday or I would have stayed here until a couple of days before Christmas. All the flights from Kefalonia to the mainland on Christmas Eve have sold out, so I need to leave the day before. Stavros says he'll pick me up, which means I won't have to ask Yannis for help."

"Don't you get lonely here all by yourself?" I asked. It seemed odd for a nineteen-year-old with the world at her feet to want to spend so much time on her own.

"I love it here. It's so peaceful, Tess. I can concentrate on my work, and it makes me feel close to my grandmother. I miss her so much. Being in her home, around her little ornaments and treasures or, how you might say, knick-knacks, makes me smile."

"I can understand that," I told her. I liked being around Kolya's things. Whether that be his clothes or books or music, it all helped provide me with a memory of him.

"Doesn't Yannis keep an eye on you while you're here?" Franco asked. "Does he check in with you to make sure you're safe on your own at night?"

"Oh, yes. Well, if he knows I'm here, he does," she replied.

I frowned, trying to work out what she meant by that. It was Yannis's own private island, so surely he would know who was or wasn't on it.

"Doesn't the boat guy tell him who he ferries to and from the island?" Franco looked a little unnerved. I knew what he was thinking. Could someone be here who was a threat to me and Lily without Yannis's knowledge? Ivan had overheard the conversation from where he crouched beside Lily while she tried to convince him that he really did need a pet lizard.

"Stavros is used to bringing me and my family over to Athilos. I know he calls through to the villa before he brings anyone other than regular staff. Yannis doesn't allow tourists, so Stavros only ferries people who work for him, or men who are here to fix something at the villa or one of the other staff properties," Adrianna replied dismissively. But I could tell it didn't appease Franco, who'd begun tapping his foot on the tiled patio floor as he cast a watchful eye over our surroundings.

I took a sip of my lemonade and placed a comforting hand on Franco's thigh. He covered my hand with his for a few seconds, returning the gesture, then excused himself so he could make a call, probably to Nate, who would then call Mark, who would more than likely alert Kevin, who wouldn't be able to do a bloody thing from his base back in Oxford. I could see how it could be a security issue, but Yannis had armed guards patrolling the island like they were expecting the next Terminator.

Adrianna went back inside for a moment and came out with a folder full of photos. The ones of Lily around the pool at Yannis's villa were my favourites—until I got to the ones of me and Kolya. I normally hate seeing myself in photos, especially with my bare, freckly shoulders. But she'd captured some great shots of us both, and I cried happy tears when I came across one where Kolya was so thoroughly focused on me that everything in the background seemed unnecessary. The way he looked at me—how the back of his fingers touched my cheek—brought back so many memories of the intimacy we shared. In another, he'd fixed those ice-blue eyes on my lips, no doubt making me desperate for his kiss and more.

"May I have these?" I asked as I scrambled to find a tissue in my bag to dry the tears rolling down my cheeks.

"Of course you can, Tess. These are all for you. Let me know if there are any you'd like me to enlarge for you."

"Thank you," I replied, then quickly closed the folder to regain my composure.

"I can show you a few of Kolya from his visits with Yannis before he met you. They're on my laptop, but I could print some off for you," Adrianna offered.

"Thanks, I'd love to see them." I got up from the spindly wooden patio chair and followed Adrianna to the bright blue door. Before I could enter the cottage, Franco put his arm out to stop me.

"Sorry, Adrianna, I need to check inside before I can allow Tess to enter." He held up his hand before she could assure him it was safe. "Not that I don't trust you, but we're being extra careful because of what happened. And I'm sure such a beautiful, kind-hearted young woman like you wouldn't want me to risk losing my job by not following protocol." He gave her one of his sexy-and-I-know-it smiles.

Adrianna seemed momentarily shocked and angry at Franco's insistence that he check her grandmother's old home, but I watched her anger melt away when he called her beautiful.

She stepped aside and gestured towards the small kitchen, "Be my guest."

I waited beside the door while Adrianna took Franco on a tour around the interior, which only took a few minutes. When they emerged, Franco was asking about her future plans after she finished her studies. While she chatted away, he gave me a nod, letting me know all was okay. I had no doubt it would be, but if his relaxed demeanour was anything to go by, it had certainly given him peace of mind.

When he passed by me at the doorway, I grabbed his T-shirt and begged, "Please don't let her convince Ivan to keep the lizard, or gecko, or whatever it is. And tell him he's not to buy her one, either, no matter how sad she pretends to be." I nodded towards Lily and Ivan, who were busy trying to get the poor reptile to climb onto their hands.

"I'll try my best," Franco advised, then made his way over to the determined pair.

The inside of Galena's old cottage was so much cooler than it had been outside. The sudden drop in temperature made me shiver, so I put on my cardigan. There were family photographs on every wall, and the furniture—although old and well-used—gave the cottage an almost French, shabby-chic appearance that so many designers strive for.

"Adrianna, it's so beautiful," I declared. "No wonder you want to stay here so often."

She removed a laptop from a rucksack propped against the kitchen table and switched it on.

"I have all my photographs stored with dates and keywords, so it might take a few minutes to find some with Kolya on."

I nodded absentmindedly while tracing my fingers over a photograph of Galena in her younger years. The Galena I knew had kept her grey hair in a tight bun, and her face had been lined with age. Yet in the proudly displayed photograph, though sepia in colour, Galena would have been in her late teens/early twenties, with long black hair cascading over her shoulders in waves. Her granddaughter certainly favoured Galena in the looks department.

"Here are a few of Kolya and Yannis on the main veranda," Adrianna informed me, turning her laptop so I could take a look.

Kolya had a short, neat beard and was dressed in a long-sleeved white shirt and grey slacks. He held a glass of amber-coloured liquid, most likely a Scotch, and had his head thrown back in laughter. Yannis was gesturing towards the beach and was also laughing. They appeared to be sharing a joke, not posing for a photograph. I tapped the arrow in the scroll bar and found another few photos, which were obviously from the same evening, and it struck me as odd that Yannis would have Adrianna over to take random photos such as these. They weren't posing for the camera, just two friends enjoying a drink outside on a warm summer's evening.

As I continued looking through the rest of the photos, I asked, "Does Yannis often have you over to take photos when his friends are around?"

Adrianna hesitated before answering, so I glanced over my shoulder at her, awaiting her reply.

She cast her eyes down, avoiding my gaze, then answered in a low voice, "He doesn't know I take them."

Turning to face her, I clarified, "So Yannis isn't aware that you sneak up to his villa and photograph him and his friends?"

She shook her head, then added, "It's not always when his friends are over. I just like to see him sometimes. Especially when he takes an early evening stroll on the beach or he's sat relaxing on his veranda. I love to photograph all his different expressions. It's like I can get inside his head and read his thoughts. I have a place I can go to on the rocks on the right-hand side of the villa where no one can see me, and I sit there and watch him, taking the occasional photograph until the sun dips below the horizon. It makes for a beautiful photograph, don't you think?"

I stared at her, open-mouthed. I'd just heard her admit to full-on stalking Yannis, and I wasn't sure how to deal with that.

"You know that what you are doing is wrong, Adrianna, don't you? I mean, there's an actual word for it, and it's not one I ever thought I'd use regarding you and your relationship with Yannis. You're basically stalking him. He could have you arrested."

"No, it's not like that, Tess, I swear. Yannis is good to me. He pays for my tuition and makes sure I have enough money to pay my rent. He lets me come and stay here in my grandmother's cottage and, did you know he took me out to the best restaurant in Athens on my birthday? I've been in love with him since...forever. When he found out about my love of photography, he gave me all of his father's old cameras and photography equipment. He even helped set up a darkroom in the smallest bedroom in the cottage for me to develop my own photos, and he encouraged me to follow my dreams. He's so handsome and kind, and so very manly, yet he doesn't see me as anything but a child. I've tried wearing more revealing clothes and makeup to make me look older, but he doesn't seem to notice. Franco just said I was a beautiful young woman, so why can't Yannis see me that way?"

Adrianna looked like she was going to cry, and though I

knew I should address the stalking, I couldn't bear to see her so distressed.

"Look, maybe you need to take a break from Yannis and Athilos and focus on something else for a while. Isn't there anyone at university you are interested in? Franco's right: you are a beautiful young woman. You're also smart and talented"—I held back on saying *and also a little unhinged*, though the thought was there—"and I'm sure there are a few guys at university who are interested in you."

"But I don't want anyone else. The guys at university seem so immature when I compare them to Yannis. Maybe I'm like you, destined for an older man. I remember when you first came to the island with Kolya. You were what? Seventeen? Eighteen?"

"Kolya and I met and fell in love under extraordinary circumstances. He hadn't known me as a young child. He hadn't grown up with my parents or been looked after by my grandmother. Which is actually a good thing, seeing as my grandmother is a proper psycho who's serving yet another prison sentence for being an evil drug-dealing bitch."

Adrianna appeared shocked by the description of my grandmother, which was, in fact, wholly accurate.

"What should I do, Tess? I don't even want to think about being with anyone else. But I know I can't go on as I am. I feel so unhappy when I'm away from the island. I know Yannis hasn't been happy lately, either. You can see it in the photos." She pulled up another, more recent file.

"Adrianna, terrorists killed his best friend and possibly one of his old guards. Only a psycho would be happy about that," I retorted.

Adrianna frowned. "His old guard? I wasn't aware that one of the other men worked for Yannis."

"Darius used to be his guard," I said. "Even I recall seeing him guarding Yannis."

"Darius did, yes, but he's already been found. I meant one of the other guards. Like I said earlier, I hope you have more good news when you find the terrorist group. It was so good to see Darius sharing a bottle of wine with Yannis, but it was also unexpected. I'd not heard anything on the news about him being found, and I almost gave away my hiding place when I considered crossing the rocks to see him."

I felt my stomach plummet towards my feet and held on to the table to steady myself. I lost focus for a moment, and I swear my heart skipped a few beats.

Adrianna placed her hand on my arm. "Are you all right, Tess? I'm sorry; it was inconsiderate of me to talk about Darius being found while you are still grieving the loss of your husband."

I shook her hand away and folded my arms around my torso, as if giving myself a hug. I couldn't hide the quiver in my voice as I asked, "When did you see Darius?" following that with, "Did you photograph him?"

"He was here around a fortnight ago." She opened up the most recent file. "And these are the photographs I took that evening. It was getting dark, so I had to change the settings on these photos to alter the detrimental effects of the lighting surrounding the veranda. I used a digital camera, as well as an old one. I developed a few of the negatives from the old camera in the darkroom."

Adrianna moved away from the laptop so I could click on the arrows to view each photo. My hands were shaking so much as I hit the keypad that I accidentally jumped a few photos ahead. But I'd seen enough. Yannis and Darius seemed to be studying an A2-sized piece of paper in the first few photographs, though I couldn't tell what was on it.

They both wore serious, pensive expressions, which steadily changed into smirks, then laughter. Were they planning something? Was Darius still on the island, watching and waiting for me to drop my guard so he could finish me off like he did my husband? Or had he already attempted that?

The realisation that Darius could have been one of the men who attacked my home made me cry out with fury and revulsion. But that wasn't just aimed at Darius. No. It was clear to see from his continuous insistence that Darius had been killed in Estonia, that Yannis, a man who was supposed to be a family friend, was behind the attack on my home.

"Franco," I yelled at the top of my voice, unable to hide the pain and distress that was tearing through my heart and mind.

Franco came running into the cottage, closely followed by a clearly panicked Ivan with Lily in his arms.

"What is it?" Franco demanded.

I pointed to the photos on the laptop. "They were taken a fortnight ago," I told him. "Adrianna has been stalking Yannis, taking photos of him without his knowledge or permission. It's him, Franco. Darius. He was here on the island. Yannis lied! He knew Darius wasn't dead. They were planning something. Look."

I tried to click back through the photos, but I couldn't get my fingers to function. They felt so cold they were almost numb. Franco removed his sunglasses and took over the laptop, clicking through the images in the file. I remembered Adrianna saying she had more photos in the darkroom.

"Bring me the others you took that night," I commanded, trying to gain some control of this dangerous yet devastating situation.

"Tess, what's wrong? You look like you've seen a ghost." Adrianna was backing away from us nervously. She glanced at the outer door as though she was about to bolt, but Ivan blocked her path.

"Just do as she asks, Adrianna," Ivan said, his tone soothing rather than demanding.

Franco looked up from the laptop. "Go with her, Ivan, and don't let her use her phone. We don't want her telling Yannis that we're onto him."

Ivan passed Lily over to me, then followed Adrianna through the cottage.

"What's the matter, Mummy? Why are you upset?"

I shook my head and swallowed down a sob. "I've seen something that has made me very sad and really angry, all at the same time. So I need you to be a good girl and do exactly as I say, okay?"

Lily nodded. "I don't have to have a lizard if you don't want me to."

I smiled at my daughter, despite my sadness.

Adrianna came into the room with Ivan close behind her. He was carrying three large photographs, which he handed to Franco. "It's definitely him," he said.

The photos were in black and white, though the images were clear, and if not for what they signified, they would have been great ones to frame and display.

Franco studied them carefully before closing his eyes and pinching the bridge of his nose. "We need to get you and Lily away from here as soon as possible. Adrianna, too. If he finds out she…" Franco stopped and thought for a moment. Turning to Adrianna, he asked, "How far back do these files go? We need to check the last six months, and do you have any from five and a half to six years ago?"

"Why?" Adrianna folded her arms across her chest and glared at Franco.

"Because Tess's home was attacked by a team of armed men eight days ago, and I believe that Yannis and Darius were behind that attack. So we can assume they were also allied with the terrorist group who attacked Kolya and his men in Estonia, and possibly the failed assassination attempt when Tess was shot."

Adrianna shook her head. "You're so wrong. I know these men. Neither of them would do something like that. Yannis is good-hearted and—"

"You're wrong, honey, and these photos prove it. Now I'm going to ask you again, and please be aware that my patience level has sunk to an all-time low, so don't jerk me around." Franco focused a threatening glare directly at her. "Do you have photographs on file of Yannis five or six years ago that he didn't know you were taking?"

Adrianna nodded while nervously approaching her laptop. "I began taking photos of Yannis when I was twelve. I used to wait for my grandmother to finish work and walk back with her. One night she was working later than usual because they were having a party at the villa, so she was organising the rest of the staff. Yannis never minded me hanging around, but his ex-wife was a bitch and made it clear I wasn't welcome. That night was the last time I saw her on the island. Yannis divorced her soon after," Adrianna added with a smile.

"Anyway, I walked along the rocks around the right-hand side of the villa, hoping to photograph the smaller cove at dusk. I thought I looked the business with the fancy camera and its zoom lens. Wanting to take what I thought would be an arty photo, I climbed higher onto the rocks to capture a wider shot that showed the pinks in the sky. But when I turned around, I realised I could see directly onto the main veranda off the dining room, which meant that Yannis, his bitchy wife, and all his guests, would be able to see me. I remember crouching down so quickly that the camera Yannis had given me banged against the rocks. I thought I might have broken it, so I tested all the camera settings and extended the lens to the fullest, which zoomed me in so close to Yannis that it seemed as if I could almost touch him."

Adrianna closed the current file and scrolled down until she reached the first file, which was simply entitled *Party*.

"Here are those first photos," she said. "I know they aren't much to look at. I've learned a lot since then, but this is what started it for me. I was fascinated, not just by him, but by his lifestyle, too. Some of his guests were celebrities and politicians from the mainland. Of course, you probably won't recognise them."

She was right: I didn't know who any of them were. Franco took a seat at the table and brought the laptop directly in front of him. He began opening up each file and clicking through the photos. The first few files had so many photos in, and not every shot was clear, especially when Adrianna had photographed Yannis through the French doors leading to the veranda, where we'd had our breakfast earlier that morning. It wasn't until Franco was seven files in that I recognised anyone other than Yannis himself, but the impact of that recognition brought me to my knees with a wailing cry.

Ivan reached me within seconds and pulled Lily and me into a tight embrace. "I have you, Tess. It's okay. No one can hurt you now. Not with me around."

Franco was cursing loudly and Lily began to cry.

Adrianna placed her hand on my shoulder. "Tess, what's wrong? What—"

"Quiet," Franco snapped as he took out his phone and dialled. "Nate, I need you to get into a position where you can cover our asses from here to the helipad. We'll be ready to fly back to the yacht in ten minutes. Look as casual as possible and say nothing to Yannis's guards. We need to get Tess and Lily away from the island as soon as possible. We'll also be taking Adrianna."

"No," Adrianna yelled. "I'm not going anywhere with you, and I want you all to leave, right now."

Franco ignored her. "You'll need to call Danny to come back with the dinghy and pick you up. Tell him to bring Mark and make sure they're fully armed. Once we're in the air, you can hightail it back to the yacht."

I couldn't hear exactly what Nate said due to Lily's sobs, but Franco replied, "Darius was here with Yannis two weeks ago. Long story, which I can't get into right now, but we have photographic evidence to back that up. And fuck, Nate... Yannis met with the shooter who took Tess down. He had him here, on the island."

This time I did hear Nate's reply, and it wasn't something you'd want to repeat in polite company.

Franco tilted his head to his shoulder to support his phone, and with both hands free, he opened up a browser on the laptop and accessed his email address, sending Kevin the files containing both Yannis and the shooter, and Yannis and Darius.

"Tess will be fine," Franco said when he closed the laptop and looked my way. "Seeing the shooter was obviously a shock. But you know how strong our girl is, Nate. She won't let anything keep her down for long. We'll be at the chopper in ten." He listened to whatever Nate said, then replied, "Roger that," before hanging up.

There were a few seconds of silence before anyone spoke, and everyone in the room seemed to freeze. Lily had stopped crying, thankfully, but the whole atmosphere seemed charged. As if you knew this was the calm before a never-ending storm. A dangerous storm. Yannis had armed guards watching us, and he'd been pretty insistent that we stayed on the island. Why? What did he have planned for us, really?

Franco's voice interrupted my thoughts. "We have to go. I told Nate ten minutes. Ivan, you can carry Lily. The rest of us need to get there as quickly as possible without arousing suspicion." He pointed at Adrianna. "You, grab your passport and the most sentimental item you have in here that's small enough to fit in Tess's bag."

"I'm not going anywhere. You can't make me. All this with Yannis is just a misunderstanding. He would never hurt me or anyone else."

"Adrianna, please. I know you heard everything Franco told Nate over the phone. You are not stupid. You know that any man who is willing to kill his best friend is not the type of man to act reasonably when he learns you have incriminating photos of him stored on your laptop. So do as Franco says. It's for your own good," Ivan pleaded. He picked Lily up and took her outside. "I will wait out here, so be quick," he added.

"I'll delete the photos," Adrianna said, making a grab for the laptop. I took hold of her arm and pulled her back.

"He will kill you, you know. Just because you've known him a long time, it doesn't make you immune to his evil. Kolya had been his best friend for almost twenty-seven years, yet Yannis had him killed. James is his godson, and he's known him since he was born, but he still sent armed men to my home to shoot him. The Yannis you think you know, the one we all thought we knew, is a lie. He's evil incarnate, and if you don't agree to come with us, we'll never be able to keep you safe from him."

Perhaps Adrianna could hear the fear and sincerity in my voice, or maybe she realised the truth in what I was saying. Either way, she nodded and picked up the bag for her laptop.

"My passport and money are in here. I'll need to pack some clothes and—"

Franco took the bag from her and placed the laptop inside. "Leave your clothes. We'll get you anything you need once you're safe. We'll take the laptop with us, and I'll require your phone, too."

Adrianna reluctantly handed her phone over to Franco, who placed it inside the bag.

"She needs the toilet," Ivan announced as he walked back into the cottage with Lily. She wasn't the only one, and there was no way I'd risk going back to the villa just so I could pee.

"So do I," I said. "Come on, Lily." Ivan lowered my daughter to her feet so she could grab my hand as we made our way along the narrow hallway.

The one-story building had a large bathroom, which also contained a washing machine and a tall chest of drawers with a tiled top. Lily did her business and I quickly followed. While I sat peeing, she questioned why someone would have a washing machine in a bathroom. Although I was extremely worried about facing Yannis's guards, I encouraged her questions, hoping she couldn't hear the nervousness in my voice when I answered.

I could hear Ivan speaking Russian loudly, no doubt on

the phone to Roman or Yuri. I was relieved to know he'd called them. It was going to be bad enough speaking to James about it.

Once I'd flushed the toilet and it was time to wash our hands, Lily noticed how badly mine were shaking. When she asked me why they shook, I told her it was because I felt cold in Adrianna's home. It wasn't a total lie. It was so much cooler in the property than outside, but Lily accepted what I told her and admitted that she was cold, too. I thought she might have forgotten how upset we'd both been, but I couldn't have been more wrong. Before I could open the door, she flung her arms around my leg and hugged me hard—her straw hat falling on the floor as she did so. I crouched down to her level and gave her a big kiss, telling her, "I love you lots, Lilypot," before picking up the hat and placing it back on her head.

"You won't leave me, will you, Mummy? I know everyone is angry because of something on Adrianna's computer, and it made you sad, too. And the last time something on a computer made you sad, you told me that Daddy had gone to heaven and he couldn't come home. I don't want you to go to heaven, Mummy. I want you to be with me every day. We don't have to go back to England, and I won't even care if Santa doesn't know where to find me. I just want to keep you. Forever. I want to say a prayer and tell Jesus he can't have you. He's got enough people in heaven with him, anyway."

Lily squeezed my leg even tighter and didn't let go until Ivan came to find us.

"What is happening here? You are having a hug without Ivan, eh? That is just not acceptable. We should make it rule number one: Ivan should be included in all hugs. It is a good rule, I feel." He bent at the knee to peel her away from my leg, but she refused to let go.

I was conscious of the time that Franco had confirmed with Nate, and I knew we'd lost precious minutes going to the bathroom. We couldn't afford to lose any more if Lily had a meltdown, so I swallowed back my tears and said, "I think we should have a race up to the helicopter. I'm sure Ivan will win because he has long legs and can run really fast, even up that big hill. I might let him carry me while he's running so that I won't get tired, then he can put me down just before we get there so I can be the winner. Let's go and see if Franco and Adrianna want to race us, too."

"That's not fair. I've only got little legs, so I won't be as fast as Ivan," Lily complained. "I bet Franco will carry me. He can run super-fast."

"Sorry, Lilypot. Franco has to carry Adrianna's laptop, so he can't carry you. Adrianna might carry you. I've heard she's really slow, but you never know," I said, shrugging my shoulders while giving Lily a look that said she had no chance.

"Why can't Ivan carry me instead? You're not a little girl, Mummy; you're a grown-up," Lily stated. She'd let go of my leg and waved a hand in my direction. "And grown-ups can run their own races. Anyway, Ivan said I'm his favourite person in all the world, so it should be *me* he carries, not you."

"I'll carry you, *moya milaya*. We should sneak out now and get a head start." Ivan held his arms out for Lily, who leapt into them with a smug smile.

"You will keep up with us, won't you, Mummy? I mean, I know me and Ivan are going to win, but I want you to be right behind us where I can see you."

"I'll keep up with you, Lilypot. I promise."

Ivan bent low enough to give me a reassuring hug and a kiss on the cheek. Before he pulled away, he whispered in my ear, "I called Yuri and gave him a quick rundown. Franco tried getting in touch with James but he couldn't reach him, so he asked Kevin to keep trying."

"Thank you," I said, then followed with, "I think it's time we started that race." Ivan nodded and tapped my shoulder before making his way back down the hallway.

I was about to follow when I heard my phone ring, so I stopped for a moment to fish it out of my bag. It was James. I hesitated for a moment before answering, not wanting to hear the anger and hurt in his voice when I told him what we'd discovered.

I tried to make my voice sound as though I was in control, when in reality, I was in bits. "James, there's something I need to tell you, but I don't have much time, so you have to listen to what I'm saying before you let your anger take over, okay?"

"I already know, Tess. Kevin just told me. He's emailed the photos that Franco sent him. I... I just can't believe it. I mean, I have the evidence in front of me, but... What the fuck, Tess? He was his best friend, and my mother's, too. He'd known her even longer than my dad because their families used to spend time together. How could he do that to my dad? And to me, someone who loved him like an uncle? Because I'm one hundred per cent certain now that the men who attacked us last week were looking for me. I mean, if you think about it, he kept asking if I was there, didn't he? He gave some bullshit excuse about Christmas gifts, but he was pretty insistent I should be there. And we were expecting his helicopter coming in to land, so we wouldn't implement the full security measures until we saw it wasn't him. By that time, the app on my dad's phone had overridden the lockdown Kevin tried to initiate. The phone that Darius had taken from my dad when he..." James

tried to choke back an angry sob, but I heard it plainly. *"I'll fucking kill him, Tess. As soon as we get you and Lily out of there, I'll find that rat bastard and blow his fucking brains out myself, I swear."*

"Only if I don't see him first," I replied. "James, I have to get going. Yannis has armed guards watching us like hawks, and we have to get to the helicopter and off the island without him suspecting anything. So I'm going to hang up now and I'll call you as soon as we're back on the yacht with an update. We're going to have to make our way to the airport so you can fly us as far away from here as possible."

"I hate that I'm not there with you, Tess. If anything happens to either of you because I let you go with him…"

"Don't even go there, James. He had us all fooled, not just you. Now, I need you to stay calm, and whatever you do, don't let him know we're onto him, no matter how tempting it is. Because Yannis will call me as soon as his goons tell him we're leaving Athilos, and if I don't answer, he'll try to call you. For all our sakes, especially Lily's, do not pick up that phone."

"I won't," James said. *"Keep safe, Tess. Kiss Lily for me and tell her that her big brother loves her to the moon and back."*

"Will do," I replied, then promptly hung up.

I heard Adrianna cry out in alarm from somewhere outside, so I hurried into the kitchen and found Franco standing in front of her at the outer doorway, blocking her from my view. His voice took on a low, threatening tone that I'd never heard him use before.

"I'm warning you, pull another stunt like that and you'll regret it. You see, normally, I'd never hurt a female, but for the woman I love and that little girl out there, I'm willing to make an exception. And if you attempt to alert one of

Yannis's guards, I'll take this gun and put you down quicker than you can blink."

"That's enough, Franco," I commanded. He stepped away from Adrianna and lowered his weapon. Though his words had given me questions, it wasn't the time to ask them.

I looked over at Adrianna, who had tears running down her face. "No one is going to hurt you, I promise."

"She tried to run down to the boat dock while I was messaging Nate to tell him we'd get there later than planned. I grabbed her and brought her back inside before anyone could see her, but if she pulls another stunt like that when we reach the chopper, they're likely to shoot before asking questions. Getting you and Lily safely off the island is more important to me than any morals I should possess. I'm not gonna apologise for threatening her, Tess. Not when I meant every single fucking word of what I just said."

Franco was breathing heavily, his brows drawn together as he waited for me to acknowledge that I accepted what I'd heard. That he loved me and Lily. Loved me more than just the platonic way in which I loved him. Loved me enough that he'd kill to protect me and my daughter.

"I won't say anything. I still think you're wrong, but I won't do anything that could hurt Lily." Adrianna wiped the tears from her eyes before meeting my gaze. "I just want to know when you will let me go. I mean, it's like you're kidnapping me."

"Okay. New plan. We'll leave you here and let you take your chances with Yannis and all his guards with their M16 rifles. When he finds out I'm on a plane heading away from Greece, he's going to want to know why, and I'll send him all the evidence we uncovered here today. I don't think he'll be as forgiving as you're insisting, given all the stalking, photographing without permission and, of course, there's also the other men and women you photographed him with. I highly doubt all those people are considered pillars of their communities."

Adrianna's eyes widened, but it was almost as if she looked right through me for a few seconds. Then she shook her head as if clearing her thoughts. "You are right about some of the people in the photographs. There are a few who have questionable ethics and business practices, so even though I have my doubts, I will go with you, Tess. And you don't have to worry about me saying anything to Yannis's guards, either. I'll go along with whatever plan you have and worry about the consequences later."

"Let's get going. We've wasted enough time already," Franco snapped. Adrianna nodded and took one last look around her grandmother's old kitchen before picking up her camera bag and stepping outside.

Chapter Twenty-Nine

TESS

We made our way quickly up the hill, running some of the way as if we were racing with Ivan and Lily. Her laughter, along with our loud cries of "Oh no, she's beating us," stopped the guards from becoming suspicious of our speedy getaway, but when we made our way towards the helipad instead of Yannis's home, one of his armed men approached us. He asked us in somewhat broken English what we were doing.

"We're going back to the yacht so I can pick up some more clothes, and I've invited Adrianna to have lunch with us," I told him.

The guard seemed confused and said, "Yannis say you stay here, where we watch."

"Yes, I'm aware of that, and I thank you for looking out for us. But Yannis has invited me to dine with him this evening, and I'd like to dress more formally for a change. I have dresses on the yacht that would be more appropriate than the casual clothing I brought with me," I replied. Again, the guard seemed confused.

When Adrianna stepped forward and began translating what I'd just said, I held my breath, glancing between Ivan and Franco nervously. None of us had a clue what she was saying to the guard—she could have been selling us out as far as we knew. But Adrianna seemed calm and smiled when she finished speaking.

For a moment, the guard stared right at me. He looked like he was torn, unsure whether to insist we stay on the island or to let us go. Then Adrianna said something else to him and he took two steps back, waving us on with his left hand. Ivan opened up the rear doors to the helicopter and helped Adrianna and Lily inside, buckling them up before stepping back to let me hop up and take my seat.

Trying to keep up with the pretence that we'd be coming back to the island, I glanced at the guard and said, "See you later."

"Okay," he replied, looking anywhere but at me.

Once Franco had taken his seat across from me and his door was closed, I asked Adrianna what her last few words to the guard had been.

"I told him you had begun your period and needed to collect your tampons, which are on the yacht."

I let out a nervous giggle as Franco looked her way and smiled. "Good job, Adrianna. You keep that up and we can all breathe easy in another few hours."

I caught sight of Nate as we took flight. He stood guard on the rocks and watched us leave. His hands were on his rifle, ready to defend us if necessary, so he couldn't return Lily's wave. My stomach churned with the fear that somehow Yannis's guards would cotton on to what we were doing and wouldn't let him leave.

"Mummy, why won't Nate wave to me, and what are tampons?" Lily asked.

"Nate might not have been able to see you through all the sand that the rotor blades kicked up, and...a tampon is something that ladies need, so you don't have to worry about that yet."

"Oh, okay," Lily said. She yawned loudly and slipped her hand into Adrianna's. "When we get to the yacht, I'll show you my doll. Her name is Anna, and she's got the same hair as me. You can play with her if you want. She's big enough to wear my clothes, and sometimes I pretend she's my friend, and we are at school. I miss my real friends...and my school." She yawned again, then asked, "Will *you* be my friend, Adrianna?"

"I'd love to be your friend, Lily, and I can't wait to meet Anna," she replied.

The helicopter—a Eurocopter—wasn't as big or as luxurious as the ones we had at home. It was much noisier in the back, too. The passenger area had three seats on the back wall, where Adrianna, Lily, and I were sitting, with two seats on the opposite side where Franco sat. Due to our limited room, his long legs bracketed mine. He'd put on a headset so he could communicate with Ivan. Franco's fingers moved deftly over the screen of his phone, pausing as he looked across at me.

"Nate says the guards were on the phone as soon as we were airborne, so I'd expect a call from Yannis."

Not even two seconds after he'd finished speaking, my phone rang. The sound startled me, even though I was expecting his call. Franco removed the headset so he could listen in. "Take a breath, Tess," he said, then unbuckled his seat belt so he could place his hands on my knees. I swiped to answer, then put the phone on hands-free.

"Hi, Yannis, what's up?"

"Tess, my guards tell me you are on your way to the Princess

Annis. I thought we agreed you were staying on the island." Yannis sounded upset, but I knew that was mostly an act.

"I wanted to wear something a little more formal for our dinner tonight," I told him. "Because of the storm, I only brought the basics with me, and it seems so long since I wore a nice dress and high heels."

"Hello, Uncle Yannis," Lily bellowed.

"Hello, my darling. I hear you are flying back to the yacht."

"Yep. Mummy was upset, and now Adrianna's going to be my friend and play with my doll."

"Why was Mummy upset, Lily?" Yannis questioned, a note of suspicion in his playful tone.

I glared at Lily and shook my head in warning, but my daughter ignored me.

"Because she's a lady and needs tampons, but it's not something I have to worry about because I'm not a lady yet."

I took the phone off hands-free and said, "Wow! Thanks for spilling the beans, Lily. How embarrassed do I feel? Well, now you know everything, Yannis. Intimate details and all."

Yannis chuckled. *"My goddaughter is hilarious. I simply adore the both of you."*

Franco squeezed my knees and smiled, mouthing, "He bought it?"

I nodded, then schooled my voice once again, trying my best to sound happy to be speaking to the man who murdered my husband and his bodyguards.

"We're just about to land, so I'll see you later."

"See you later, Tess."

I ended the call and threw the phone in my bag. Tilting my head back against the seat, I took another deep breath and shuddered.

"Hey, look at me, Tess. You did good. He bought it. That gives us time to get a plan in motion without his men listening in." Franco tapped his hands against my knees before pointing out of the window. "Look, Danny and Mark have just picked up Nate, so you can stop worrying about him, too."

Franco was right. I had been worrying about Nate, as well as all our other guards.

Whenever we moored off Athilos, we either had supplies brought to the yacht by Stavros, or we took the helicopter to Nisi or Kefalonia. We never up-anchored unless we were leaving. There was no telling what Yannis would do if his guards told him our yacht was on the move.

When we landed on the yacht's helipad, I felt an over-whelming sense of relief, which unfortunately didn't last long. My hands felt sluggish as I unclipped my seat belt, and weariness swept away some of the anxiety that had plagued me since I laid eyes on those incriminating photos. The tiredness felt unnatural. Too sudden in its appearance to be anything other than worrisome.

Franco opened the door and hunched down to avoid the rotor blades as he stepped onto the helipad. He was greeted by Lainey, who leaned into the back of the helicopter, grabbed my hands and said, "I'm so sorry we left the island without you."

I wanted to reply, but I couldn't seem to find the words at first. Then I squeezed her hand and summoned a smile. "I should have stuck to my guns and left with you, Lainey."

"You okay, Tess?" Franco questioned. I nodded, but it was clearly a lie. Lainey stepped back so I could disembark, but my legs felt so fatigued I could barely even stand.

"Franco," I said, in a voice so low it was almost a whisper, "why do I feel so tired?"

He slipped one hand under my legs and the other behind my back. "I've got you, baby. You're safe now." Then he lifted me out of the helicopter with ease.

I watched Lainey climb in and pick up Lily before laying my head against Franco's chest. "For how long, though, Franco?" I murmured.

"While ever I'm beside you, Tess. And you know I'll never leave you, so I guess we can say forever."

Franco carried me away from the helipad, which was situated on the bow of the yacht, and brought me towards the open doors of the main sitting room where Philippe, the steward on the Princess Annis, awaited my arrival.

"Good afternoon, Mrs Barinov. Can I get you anything?"

"Some fruit juice or any other sweet drink, as quick as you can, Philippe. I think she might be experiencing delayed shock," Franco said as he placed me on the long leather sofa.

Lainey came strolling in holding Lily's hand, Adrianna hot on her heels.

My daughter ran towards us and launched herself onto the sofa beside me, losing her straw hat when she landed. "Aren't you very well, Mummy?" she asked as she placed her hand on my forehead.

"Your mommy's fine, Lilypot. She just needs to stay out of the sun for a while, that's all. Why don't you and Lainey take Adrianna to your room so you can show her your doll? If you're lucky, she might even take some photographs of you," Franco told her.

"What a great idea," Lainey declared in a fake happy voice. "Come on, girls, let's go find Anna." Then she squeezed my shoulder and added, "I'll keep her occupied while you figure out our next steps."

Lily jumped up and down on the cream leather sofa with her shoes on, and although she knew she wasn't supposed to do that, I didn't have it in me to chastise her. Thankfully, Lainey did, and after giving me a big kiss and saying sorry, she jumped down onto the lush beige carpet and ran towards the elevator. Yes, the Princess Annis had a fancy elevator for its three floors, which was quite extravagant, I know. But Kolya said he'd always admired the spec of the vessel from when Yannis had first taken delivery of it.

Yannis... The Princess Annis was his yacht before Kolya bought it for me. With that realisation came the need to escape. Escape from everything that reminded me of that despicable man, but I could hardly move a muscle. I felt dirty, like even the sofa's soft leather and the luxurious wool carpet underneath my feet were tainting my skin with the evil filth that was Yannis Markos.

"Calm your breathing down, Tess, or you'll hyperventilate," Franco ordered. He grasped my hands and demanded, "Look at me. Look directly at me and nowhere else. Focus on my face. We're gonna get through this, Tess. Finding out about that bastard has been an immense fucking shock, but we are miles away from him right now, and he doesn't even know we're onto him, so that gives us an advantage."

"Killing that *ublyudok* would give us a much better advantage," Ivan interrupted as he walked into the sitting room. He slung his sunglasses onto the coffee table and rubbed his eyes. "Do you know what he's done now? Nate said two of his guards have just followed the dinghy in a speedboat. It's moored between here and the island."

Philippe came back with a tall glass of pineapple juice and a plate of biscuits, which he handed to Franco. "I have instructed Loretta to bring tea, coffee, and a selection of other beverages, along with cake and sandwiches. Chef is in the kitchen if you require anything else."

"Thank you, Philippe," Franco replied. He placed the glass in my hand and helped guide it to my lips. "You see, Tess. You have all these people looking out for you. Everything's gonna be fine now. What's that saying? Forewarned is forearmed. Knowledge is power, baby. And with James on his way, that gives us a tactical advantage that Yannis will never see coming."

I took a few big gulps of juice, then closed my eyes. It wasn't just that I was tired. All the thoughts and images in my head were becoming too painful to cope with. Images of Kolya and me with Yannis before I even knew I was pregnant with Lily. Of Yannis holding Lily for the first time; my tiny, helpless little baby in his murderous hands. All the holidays we'd shared with him on Athilos, as well as those times he'd stayed with us in our home, not knowing the evil he was capable of. I replayed conversations with him, looking for any indication that he intended to rip my family apart. We'd had quite a few arguments over the years, but I'd brushed off his irritating behaviour because Kolya always said, *"That's just Yannis being Yannis"*... A man whose spoiled brattishness carried on well into adulthood. I couldn't help feeling that this was all my fault somehow. Like I should have seen this coming.

"Keep those eyes open, Tess. Here, drink some more juice. I need you to stay alert for me, honey," Franco prompted.

It took a few more sips before I felt the tiredness lift, and when I followed it with a cup of tea, it almost dispelled the feeling I was somehow responsible. Almost. But I knew that whatever happened next, I'd always have that nagging doubt in my mind that I should have known better than to trust my husband's friend.

After popping a couple of paracetamols and half a biscuit that Franco insisted on, I felt more than ready to join in with the conversation going on around me. I'm not sure when everyone in the dinghy had arrived back, but Danny, Mark, and Nate were walking the perimeter of the yacht with their weapons in hand. The fact that they were away from the island helped me focus on what needed to happen next.

Ivan was on the phone with Roman, jabbering away in Russian. I could pick out the odd word here and there, as well as all the swearing. He looked my way and held my gaze, saying something else in Russian, then he jerked his head a little, silently asking if I wanted to speak to Roman. I nodded and held out my hand for the phone. He put it on hands-free and then passed it over.

"Tess, how are you feeling? Ivan said you were in delayed shock. You must not worry about anything, moya doch'. I will see Markos dead before the day is done."

"I'm sorry, Roman. This is all my fault. I should have known we couldn't trust him. When I think back over the last few years and how much time we spent with him, I should have picked up on how devious he could be."

"I will not have you blaming yourself. None of this is your fault. Do you hear me, Tess? You could not know any of what that traitor had planned."

"But I should have sensed it, Roman. I never used to trust anyone as blindly as I trusted him. Kolya would excuse his behaviour and because I wanted to fit in with him and his friends, I just went with it. In my old life, I would have stuck to my guns when someone pissed me off and kept well away from them. I don't know what has happened to me over the last few years, but I really don't like it. Trusting so blindly will not keep me and my daughter safe. I argued with him this morning, do you know that? He forbade me from leaving the island, so I gave him what for—like the old me would have. But then he mentioned having videos of him and Kolya when they were younger that he'd planned to show me, and how keeping me and Lily safe was the only thing he could do for his friend. And I fell for it, Roman. I pushed all that anger and apprehension to the back of my mind and let him control me, just like everyone else seems to want to do. In one way, I can't blame them. I mean, who could trust my judgement with my recent track record?"

"That's enough! I will not have you blaming yourself. I've heard enough of that from my grandson. He is on his way to the nearest airport, so you must tell me how you plan to meet him there. I have men flying to the airport from Cyprus, so you will have extra protection. Those same men will make sure that Yannis Markos suffers before he takes his last breath."

I shuddered at the coldness in Roman's voice. I knew his words weren't just idle threats.

"I don't have a plan, Roman. If we leave in the yacht, his guards will alert him. And he'll know we aren't planning on coming back because we never island hop if we're staying with him."

"So let Ivan fly you. You can tell Markos you need to go shopping or sightseeing."

Lily came dashing into the room with Anna, almost tripping over the doll's legs in her haste to speak to her grandfather.

"GRANDAD!" Lily yelled as she pulled the phone out of my hands.

"There she is, *moya zolotse*. How are you, my little treasure? Do you miss your deda?"

"I do miss you, and Anna misses you, too. Look, she's wearing my dress."

Lily had swapped her lilac dress with the yellow one that we'd dressed Anna in before we left, and Anna now wore the lilac one that Lily had been wearing earlier. Of course, with Roman not being on a video call, he couldn't see what Lily tried to show him, but I watched Franco do a double take, then smile. From the back, you could hardly tell Lily and her doll apart.

"That's it!" I exclaimed with nervous excitement. "That's how we get away. Yannis won't suspect I'll be leaving for good if he still thinks Lily's here," I continued while running my hands through the copper curls on Anna's head.

I saw Lainey's eyes widen as she realised what I was about to say. "I'll stay behind with Anna. He thinks I'm Lily's nanny, so it makes sense if I'm with her."

I shook my head. "No, Lainey. I can't leave you here. You need to come with us."

Lainey held up her hand to silence me. "Now, I know you aren't going to give me some bullcrap excuse about keeping me safe because I'm a woman, 'cause you wouldn't dream of undermining my strength, training and service record, would you?"

She couldn't have been more wrong. I would never undermine Lainey's strength and worth. But I would admit to feeling a little more protective of her than the male guards. As with Ivan, she was special to Lily. They were stand-in parental figures if anything should happen to me.

"No, Lainey. I wanted you with us for all those reasons, and because you're my role model. You are everything I once thought I could be. A strong woman who knows her own mind and controls her own destiny."

Lainey smiled. "Good save, Tess. Thank you."

I watched Franco make his way to the sitting room doors and beckon for Nate, Mark, and Danny to come inside. Once everyone was present, I made Lily keep quiet for a moment and began telling them my plan.

"We know that Yannis has guards watching us from both Athilos and the speedboat they've anchored nearby, so we need to give them something to report back that tells them our departure's only temporary. Yannis knows I wouldn't leave Lily here if I didn't plan on coming back, so by showing him that Lily's staying," I said, pointing towards Anna, "we won't arouse his suspicion until the yacht's on the move, which won't be until our helicopter nears Kefalonia."

"I'll be staying behind on the yacht," Lainey added. "Yannis thinks I'm Lily's nanny, so when his guards report back that I have Lily in my arms while waving goodbye to her mommy when the helicopter leaves, he'll buy into the ruse that Tess will be returning."

"I'd like to stay with Lainey, if that's okay with you, Tess," Danny said, hooking an arm around Lainey's shoulders. "He knows we always babysat Lily together whenever he went out with you and Kolya, and I'll have my gun if his guards decide to make a move. You always have Franco and Ivan by your side, so it won't make anyone suspicious if they go with you."

"They've seen me doing armed patrols on the island as well as back here, so it makes sense that I stay," Nate said before taking a sandwich from the plate. "Mark can fly the chopper to Kefalonia so that Ivan and Franco can sit with you, Lily, and Adrianna in the back. That means you'll each have a guard, which will make me feel a whole lot better about letting you go without me."

"I'll fly us there, no problem," Mark continued, "we just have to get Lily in the back of the helicopter without any of them seeing her, which is pretty hard to do, considering they're using binoculars to spy on us, even though they can see quite clearly from the boat."

"Then we hide her, somehow." Danny's eyes went to my bag. "Do you have a beach bag or maybe an overnight bag she could fit in?" he asked.

"No, this is the only bag I have on here. Everything else is back in the villa." I couldn't think of anything on the yacht I could carry her out in without arousing suspicion. Yannis would most certainly call when we left the yacht, and I thought it best to tell him I was going shopping for personal items. Lily mentioning tampons was something I could use as a reason why I needed to shop. I doubt any man would argue with that.

"Hey, Ivan. Have you any jackets or hoodies here on the yacht?" Franco asked.

"Yes. I didn't expect the storm to last as long as it did, so I left most of my luggage here. Why? Are you cold? I think my hoodies will be too big for you, my friend. You'd be better asking Nate or Mark."

"I agree. They would be too big. But they'll give me enough room to hide our little Lilypot in there with me," Franco replied, adding a wink for my open-mouthed daughter.

"Yay! Adrianna, we're going to play hide-and-seek," Lily yelled. She ran towards Ivan with his phone still in her hand. He took it from her and asked his uncle, "Did you hear all that?"

"I did. I just need to know when you plan on leaving. James will land at the airport on Kefalonia in an hour and fifteen minutes. How long will it take you to fly there?"

"Around twenty-five minutes, maybe less. I'll call James and reconfirm his arrival time. Do you have an estimated time of arrival for the men you are sending from Cyprus?"

"They are due to land ten minutes after James. They will get you to the plane safely, then they'll find Yannis Markos and ensure he is no longer a threat." Roman sighed heavily. He sounded so weary when he said, "James tells me you will all be flying back to England, but I wish you would reconsider coming to Moscow for Christmas. I can keep everyone safe here, Ivan. You know this."

Ivan looked my way and shook his head as he said, "I'll speak to Tess and James about it." Then he said goodbye and hung up the phone.

"I don't want to go to England," Adrianna said. "Can't I stay here on the boat with everyone? They can drop me off when they arrive in Kefalonia. I can stay with a friend until it's safe to leave." She looked like she was going to cry, but then again, she was in love with Yannis, and Kolya's father had just confirmed that he was going to have him killed. I wanted to let her go, but I worried she would tell the authorities what she knew.

Ivan placed his big hands on her shoulders, then pulled her in for a hug. "I know you are choosing not to believe the worst of him still. I can understand that. You've had feelings for Yannis for many years, and hearing what my uncle has planned for him cannot be easy. But you have to understand the terrible things he did to my cousin, and what he tried to do to Tess and James. I want you to come with me for a moment, Adrianna. I will get Kevin to send through some videos and sound clips that will make you see things a little differently."

"I'm scared, Ivan," she admitted before breaking down in tears.

"So am I, Adrianna. But you must know I will do whatever I can to keep you safe. Franco, too. None of us wants you to come to any harm, especially from the man you are in love with. Now, come with me while I collect one of my jackets for Franco, and I will show you why we have to leave Greece."

Chapter Thirty

TESS

With Lily tucked safely inside Ivan's bomber jacket that Franco wore, we made our way to the helicopter. The jacket was jet black, and the sun cast a slight sheen to it. Up close, you could tell that there were odd lumps and bumps in the front of it, despite how well we'd tried to disguise the fact that my daughter's arms and legs were hugging Franco's torso as tightly as she could. So, with his back to the guards that Yannis had spying on us from the speedboat, I made a show of handing Franco my bag and a jacket of Lainey's, which he held in front of him. It hid most of the lumps and bumps, as well as his right arm and hand supporting Lily's bottom and lower back.

Lainey had Anna in her arms with a blanket wrapped around the doll's legs. I kissed Anna's cheek while the guards were watching—a minute or so before Franco made an appearance—then I placed the straw hat on her head so she wore everything Lily had been wearing on the island.

Kolya used to find the doll's exact likeness to our

daughter disturbing. Little did he know it would help save our lives one day.

As we'd discussed, Ivan led the way to the back of the helicopter, effectively blocking out even more of their view. When we got there, he stood aside to let me in. I made sure I blocked the window when Franco climbed in after me and took his seat, then Adrianna followed Franco as closely as possible before Ivan climbed in and closed the door. Mark had placed a bag inside the passenger area with a Kevlar vest for each of us, but we couldn't put them on until we knew we were no longer being watched.

We all waved at Nate, Danny, Lainey and the doll as our helicopter rose and took flight, keeping up the pretence that we were waving at my daughter. Placing the straw hat on Anna's head meant that Lainey had to hold it down so it wouldn't get blown off by the draft from the rotor blades, which was a way to hide the doll's face from Yannis's guards. Once we were out of sight, Nate, Lainey, and Danny were going to the seating area at the top of the yacht with Anna. From there, Lainey and Danny planned on reading one of Lily's books to Anna, so they could pretend that she'd fallen asleep. Danny was going to wrap the sleeping Anna in the blanket so they could make their way inside, in the hope that with nothing to see, the guards in the speedboat would leave. By that time, we'd be nearing Kefalonia, so the yacht could leave the bay without putting us in danger. Lainey, Danny and Nate wouldn't be there in time to meet James's jet, so they'd booked a flight to Larnaca airport in Cyprus, and they'd board a flight to Gatwick from there.

I just hoped that everything we'd planned would come off without a hitch, and that Yannis wouldn't take his anger out on Lainey, Danny, and Nate. I would never forgive myself if they were hurt.

Once we were out of view of Yannis's guards, Franco unzipped Ivan's jacket and exposed a giggling Lily to everyone's view.

"That was really funny," she mumbled against Franco's T-shirt as he hugged her tightly and kissed the top of her head.

"You were so good, Lilypot. You did exactly as I asked and kept as still as could be," he praised. We all joined in, heaping more praise and compliments with regards to Lily's good behaviour, and due to all that exuberant flattery, combined with the noise of the helicopter, I almost didn't hear the opening bars of "Iris" coming from my phone.

I didn't need to look at the screen to know who was calling. We expected he'd make contact as soon as his guards let him know I was in the air. I stared at the phone, not trusting myself to keep up the pretence that everything was fine if I answered.

"Do you want to do something else fun that's a bit like hiding?" Franco asked my excitable daughter.

"Ooh, is it like a game?" Lily questioned.

"Yes, it's a great game, but it's also a hard game, Lily, and I don't think you could win this one because you're a chatty little girl, so maybe I should play it with Ivan and Adrianna instead."

"But that's not fair," Lily complained. "And I'm not always chatty, am I, Ivan?"

"Not when you're asleep," Ivan replied. "What's the game called, Franco?"

"It's called *who speaks first, loses.* You have to keep quiet while someone else is on the phone, so if you speak, you lose. The winner gets special permission from Santa to open a gift on Christmas Eve before they go to bed."

Lily gasped, and her eyes widened. Franco had uttered the magic words, *Santa* and *Christmas*. There was no way she wouldn't try to win this game.

My phone stopped ringing, but not even ten seconds later, it rang again.

"Tess has another call, so whoever wants to play this game, give me a high five and keep a lock on your lips. It might help if you put your hands on your ears, Lily." Franco held up his hand away from Lily so she couldn't be the first to high-five him. She bounced around on his knee in frustration while Ivan and Adrianna got their high fives in first. Then she hit his hand with hers and made a show of twisting an invisible lock on her lips before putting her hands over her ears. Franco looked my way and gave a nod of his head to let me know it was safe to answer.

Satisfied that Lily would keep quiet and not give her presence away to Yannis, I finally took the call, though he never even let me say hello before he began questioning me.

"Tess, where are you going? And why didn't you let me know you were leaving the yacht? I shouldn't have to find out from my guards that you have abandoned your daughter to fly God only knows where."

All the good intentions of keeping my emotions out of the call went out of the window with his accusation.

"Abandoned? You'd better tell me which twat of a guard said I'd abandoned her?" I ordered. "Because when—"

"Calm down, Tess. Perhaps it was a poor choice of words, but it was a shock to know that you had left without telling me."

"I'm not your fucking prisoner, Yannis. I can go wherever I want, whenever I want. I don't have to report to you or anyone else if I want to go shopping."

"Please don't be angry with me, Tess. I am in charge of your

safety while you are here. I could have picked up whatever you needed before I fly back to Athilos." Yannis put on that hurt *"you've got me all wrong"* voice he'd been using to manipulate me for the past week, masking the lying, evil snake he truly was.

Ivan reached across and grabbed my hand to stop me from shaking. He could see I was struggling to keep my cool. His touch helped me stay focused on the matter at hand—trying to keep quiet about the fact that Lily and I would be leaving with James in less than twenty minutes.

"I don't need you to do my shopping, Yannis. There are certain things I want to buy for myself. Personal items. And I needed a break, too. So Adrianna and I will spend a few hours in Kefalonia, shopping, drinking, and generally having a good time. A lot of places are closed with it being out of season, but she says she knows some little boutiques that will be open."

"What a coincidence. I'm flying into Kefalonia to check the building work at one of my hotels. I could take you both out for a late lunch."

"You're flying into Kefalonia now? You told me you'd be on the mainland today." I couldn't keep the horror out of my voice. Ivan ran his fingers through his hair and shook his head.

"I was, but I was made aware of a problem in one of the beach-front hotels we own on the island. We can't afford a delay this close to the Christmas break, or the extension and pool will never be finished in time for when the new season starts in April. I said I'd go and sort it out so I could be nearer to home in case you needed me."

I swallowed hard and tried to sound as though my stomach wasn't tied up in knots over this new information.

"Adrianna and I ate on the yacht, and I wouldn't dream of keeping you from your work, Yannis."

"Then we'll just have a few drinks in the hotel, my darling. I will

wait for you at the airport and take you there with me. I already have a car waiting, but since you have guards with you, I can ask someone from the hotel to send a minibus so we can all fit in."

"No. There's no need to wait. Franco's arranged car hire for us. Just let me know the address, and when we've done with our shopping, I can meet you there. I'm looking forward to spending time with Adrianna. I rarely spend time with my friends anymore. It will make a nice change and will give me something to talk about during dinner this evening." It was hard to stay so calm and non-aggressive while fear and anger were riding my emotions as hard as they were, but I think I managed to pull it off.

Lily began wriggling on Franco's knee, clearly getting fed up with staying silent. He caught my attention and made a slashing motion against his throat, telling me to end the conversation as soon as possible.

"I have to go. Text me the address of your hotel and I'll let you know when I'm on my way. Bye." I hung up before he could say anything else but still held on to my phone, half expecting him to call me back, so I was surprised when he didn't.

"Did he say when he would arrive at the airport?" Franco asked. I shook my head and stared out of the window with regret. I should have asked him that, amongst all the other things we needed to know to keep us safe, but I was trying so hard not to tell him I knew everything he'd done to destroy my family.

"Ha, I won, Franco. You talked first," Lily yelled. She turned around and treated everyone to a smug smile.

"Yeah, but you didn't win against Ivan and Adrianna, did you? They haven't spoken at all yet."

Lily covered her face with her hands. "I don't like this game, Franco. Can we play something else?"

"We sure can, honey. As soon as we land, we can play a great game that will get us all on the plane in super-quick time. Now, let's put your special vest on, then you can sit next to Ivan so he can fasten your seat belt for when we land."

"Okay," she mumbled as she climbed down from his lap. "But the next game has to be easier than the not-talking one, Franco, or I'll never get to open a present on Christmas Eve."

Franco unzipped the bag and handed Lily's specially made Kevlar vest to Ivan, who put it over my daughter's head and tightened the side straps. The rest of us unbuckled our seat belts and each grabbed a vest.

"Are you okay, Tess?" Adrianna asked from her seat next to Franco as he helped her tighten her vest. She'd been quiet since Ivan had shown her the video of Riass spouting all of his terrorist shit while the bodies of my husband and guards were piled up like they were nothing. Like they'd never been loved or had loved in return. Ivan said she cried when she watched it, but what got to her the most was when she saw the attack on my home. Watching me hide my daughter while waiting for the gunman to attack, then seeing him shoot Bess, made her understand why we were so concerned for our safety and, in turn, her safety. Whether she still had misgivings about Yannis's involvement, I really couldn't say.

"Ask me that when we're about to land in England, Adrianna, because if I say I'm okay before that, it will be the biggest lie I've ever told."

My phone pinged with a text from Yannis. "He's sent me the address of the hotel," I announced. Handing my phone to Adrianna, I asked, "Do you know how far from the airport that is?"

"Probably about fifteen to twenty minutes by car. There's much less traffic at this time of year. It would take longer in the summer months."

"Ask him what time he'll arrive at the hotel," Ivan said. "That will give us an idea of when he will land. I'll message Nate and let him know about the change in our situation. With Yannis being here, they won't be able to leave the bay until we are at the airport."

I texted Yannis back, asking him what time he'd arrive at the hotel and how long he thought it would take to sort out the problems he'd mentioned. I also told him we'd only have one drink with him because I wanted to get back to Lily.

I received another text, but it wasn't from Yannis. James had messaged to say his plane was making its approach to the airport and would be landing within the next ten minutes. I relayed the message to Ivan and Franco.

Ivan put on a headset and passed the details on to Mark, who confirmed our ETA was around fifteen minutes away. My hands shook as I sent a text back to James, warning him that Yannis was flying into Kefalonia airport.

"Has Yannis replied yet?" Franco asked.

I shook my head and stared down at my phone, willing it to ping and display a message from Yannis. I prayed he'd already landed and was making his way to the hotel. But the phone was silent, and the only thing it showed me was the time, temperature outside, and a photo of Kolya and Lily that was my screensaver.

I glanced out of the window, hoping the glorious view would distract me enough to calm the raging storm of anger and betrayal tearing through my mind. Sunlight touched the blue-green sea below, creating a magical, sparkling diamond effect on the tips of the rippling waves.

But not even the beauty of the Ionian Sea, nor the pretty, picturesque blue and white homes—so typical of the Greek islands—could give me the peace I so desperately needed.

Franco held out his right hand and I passed him the phone. He transferred it to his pocket, then held out his hand again and placed it over my left, which was currently pressing against my knee. I was trying to stop my foot from tapping the floor—an annoying, involuntary reaction I have when troubled with nerves, worry or fear. It would be safe to say that the last two hours had delivered all three in abundance.

"Hey, you need to keep it together, Tess. We can't have what happened when we landed on the yacht happen here. You're gonna need to move as quickly and as safely as possible. I know it's hard to even think straight right now, but that little girl over there is depending on her mommy stepping up to the plate and acting like the boss I know she can be," Franco said.

Boss... That's what all the guards called Kolya. Thinking about that brought tears to my eyes. I didn't want to be a boss. A safe, simple life with Lily would suit me better. A life where we didn't need to worry about someone kidnapping or taking potshots at us because of KOLCAT, or some betraying bastard we used to call a friend.

"I'm no boss, Franco. I'm just a frightened mum who wants all this to stop. I don't want to live this kind of life anymore. I don't want Lily to grow up in it, thinking it's normal and something she has to endure."

"Who says a boss has to live this kind of life? Anyone can be a boss, Tess. The way I see it, a boss is just someone who's in charge of their life or home or work. YOU get to make the decisions. YOU have a say in how things are gonna be from now on. And if you say you want out of this kind of life, then you get your daughter someplace where you can start again and be who YOU wanna be, without being dictated to by anyone. Because a boss wouldn't let that happen. When I first met you, and for a little while after, you were definitely a boss. You didn't take no shit from nobody."

Lily caught Franco's swear words and was about to reprimand him until Ivan adjusted her seat belt and distracted her.

"When you first met me, I was a teenage runaway who'd just been shot. Not exactly boss material, Franco."

"You don't think that made you a boss? Why the hell not? You'd survived a pretty shitty life up until then by being the boss of you and your mom. You made the brave decision to leave the children's home so those scumbags couldn't get hold of you. You also survived on the streets of that goddamn unforgiving city until you saw a lone gunman try and take Kolya out, whereby you made a split-second decision to save the man's life. You weren't only a boss, Tess, you were a fuckin' superhero boss."

"Swearing again! Why are you being so naughty, Franco? Don't you know how near it is to Christmas? You won't get any presents from Santa if you keep saying words like that, will he, Ivan?" Lily looked up at Ivan expectantly.

"No, Santa certainly won't visit him if he keeps swearing, and it won't be long now until he's here," Ivan said while glancing at me and Franco. "Perhaps Franco could check your mummy's phone to see if the Santa tracker is showing where he might be."

Franco took my phone out of his pocket and shook his head. "There's nothing on there yet," he said. We both knew that Ivan was talking about Yannis. I'd expected him to have messaged me back, and the fact that he hadn't didn't bode well for us.

Ivan slipped the headset back on. "I'm going to check in with Mark to see if we can arrange runway transportation from the helipads to the plane. It will cut down on the time it will take to get you both on board, and the less exposed we all are to anyone hanging around waiting, the better."

I wasn't going to bank on us having transport to the aircraft, not with less than ten minutes to go until we landed. It wouldn't have mattered if there wasn't a chance of Yannis being there. We could have easily spared a few minutes to walk from the helipads to meet James. But without knowing if Yannis would be at the airport, it would be better not to take that risk.

We were lucky that the KOLCAT jet James regularly used carried enough fuel for a flight time of up to fourteen hours without refuelling. It was always filled to capacity at Heathrow and back in the US. If he had to refuel, it would add at least another forty-five minutes to our time in Kefalonia. Often, if you called ahead, you could have them waiting on standby, which could cut your refuelling time down to around thirty minutes. But some fuel carriers think they have all the time in the world to do their job—unless the airport is operating under strict take-off slots after several delays. Thankfully, the KOLCAT jet wouldn't be at their mercy.

Adrianna stared out of the window while wringing her hands together nervously. I felt sorry for her, in a way. She didn't want to be anywhere near us, but the alternative for her could be so much worse. When Yannis found out she'd been photographing him for all those years, he might react violently towards her.

It wasn't only the evidence we'd gathered about his

involvement with Kolya that Adrianna had to worry about. As she herself had admitted, Yannis had also met with some prominent shady characters from Greek society too, and who knew what they'd do to her?

"Five more minutes, Tess," Ivan said. I looked across at my daughter and watched as her eyes closed slowly and her head fell forward. She jerked back up with a start, her eyes opening wide, but it wasn't long before they closed again.

Franco put his arm around me and whispered in my ear. "She'll be asleep by the time we land, but that won't be a bad thing. If we don't get transport, we'll make sure it's safe and then run to the plane. It will be much easier if she's fast asleep in Ivan's arms. I'll have your back, and Mark will watch over Adrianna. We can do this, Tess. We have to. I won't let that bastard hurt you or Lily."

He unbuckled his seat belt and took out his gun, checking he had bullets in the magazine before slotting it safely back into his belt holster. I'd watched him do this twice before we left the yacht, and I wondered if it was an ex-soldier thing or whether it was something he was doing because he was nervous. I decided it had to be an ex-soldier thing because I couldn't bear it being anything else. Franco was my calm in the storm, the one I trusted to keep his head while everything around us went to shit.

The familiar sight of our destination greeted me when I glanced out of the window. The small airport is situated on the south-west of Kefalonia, and it's the one Kolya preferred to fly to and from whenever we visited Yannis. It was usually so busy, especially during the summer, but now it appeared as though it had closed down for the season, like the rest of the Greek islands. I knew after we'd left, I'd never return under any circumstances. I could feel it in my gut that even the mention of the place, along with Athilos, would bring me nothing but nightmares. I'd had enough of those already.

As Mark lowered the helicopter down to our landing spot, I caught sight of KOLCAT's G650ER that would take us away from the danger Yannis represented. It wasn't far away at all, so we wouldn't need any runway transportation. The helipad was almost right next to the quiet, out-of-the-way area where the private planes were, so I hoped that Yannis had arrived before James had landed.

I sent James a text to let him know where we were. Mark said he'd inform our team on the yacht as soon as we were at the airport, but I also messaged them and insisted they kept me updated during each step of their journey home.

"That's Yannis's helicopter," Adrianna cried out in alarm. My breath caught in my throat as fear gripped me hard.

Ivan relayed Adrianna's sighting through the headset so that Mark could take further precautions if needed.

Franco looked out of the window to where she was pointing. "There doesn't appear to be anyone in there, from what I can tell, so just do as we planned and get to the jet as quickly as possible. We won't let anything happen to you; I swear."

As soon as the skids touched the tarmac, Ivan unbuckled his and Lily's seat belts and cradled my sleeping daughter against his chest while we waited for Mark to check it was safe for us to leave. The ever-decreasing whining and whir of the rotor blades after he applied the brakes seemed like a foreboding auditory countdown until we heard him exit the helicopter.

Ivan's phone rang, so he swapped my daughter to his other arm and pulled it out of his pocket. "Uncle," he answered, then listened as Roman told him something that made him smile. After he hung up, he proclaimed, "We have help. Roman says his men have just landed and Kevin has also disabled all the security cameras."

The cabin door opened and Mark announced, "There's no one in that helicopter, which is a relief because the airport can't provide us with transport. Still, it should only take us a couple of minutes to get to the plane if we run. From what I can see, we're supposed to keep right and go through a covered portico alongside the airport terminal, but for speed, I suggest going straight along the tarmac. It's mid-December, so it's not like it's busy, and we're hardly venturing onto the main runway. The section where the private planes pull in is always quiet, even during the height of summer, but for some reason it's like a ghost town out there today. We need to pass a couple of airport maintenance and service vehicles en route, but they don't appear to be occupied, and by the time any airport staff realise what we're doing, we'll have already reached the plane."

"Do you have your gun?" Franco asked.

"Locked and loaded," Mark replied. "Not that I'm saying you'll need it, Tess, but Danny said to give you this. There's a full magazine in there, and he said if the bastard confronts you, tell him one of those bullets is from Bess."

He passed me Danny's pistol: a Beretta Px4 Storm Compact. I wasn't the biggest fan of handguns, but Danny knew this one gave me less trouble during our regular competitions. Though significantly reduced in this model, it did still have a slight recoil, yet somehow I found it easier to focus with this Beretta when time was of the essence.

I accepted the semi-automatic gun with shaking hands, and Franco—my mentor in all things weapon-related—watched as I checked the safety and then placed the gun inside the open front pocket of my shoulder bag.

"Everybody ready to go?" Mark questioned. When everyone in the cabin murmured their affirmations, he stepped aside with the door open wide.

Franco disembarked first and quickly scanned our surroundings. Once he'd determined all was safe, he was followed swiftly by Adrianna, then me, and finally, Ivan, who adjusted Lily in his arms before taking off across the tarmac. Adrianna followed Ivan, seeming to trust him more than anyone else. Mark followed Adrianna, and I ran after him, trying my best to stay focused on the people in front of me and not the man who could be watching from anywhere.

After just a minute or so of us sprinting towards the KOLCAT jet, I saw James and Carl running towards us, and my heart warmed when I noticed Tanner standing in the doorway of the plane.

Ivan didn't stop when he and James neared each other; the safety of my daughter being his immediate concern. I couldn't hear what James shouted to Carl over the sound of the G650's engines, but he hesitated briefly before running alongside Adrianna back to the plane.

James reached me less than ten seconds later. I threw my arms around him and hung on for dear life as I panted breathlessly into his shoulder.

"Thank God you're both safe, Tess. I kept looking at the photographs Kevin sent, and then Yannis called to ask why I'd just landed here. I'm sorry, but I couldn't stop myself. I told him, Tess. I told Yannis we knew what he'd done and had evidence to prove it."

I backed away from James and shook my head, knowing what he'd done could have tipped the scales further against us. "I told you not to do that, James. Why didn't you bloody listen?" I yelled.

"This is not the time or place for a touching family reunion," Franco shouted angrily.

Mark tapped me on the shoulder. "We need to get you both on the plane, Tess. Now." He took my hand and pulled me into a run. The bag I carried slipped from my shoulder into the crook of my arm, swinging wildly as we ran, but I couldn't stop to adjust it.

The steps to the aircraft were just a couple of meters away when I heard a burst of gunfire from somewhere behind me. I tried to turn—my instincts to make sure that James and Franco were safe overriding the need for self-preservation. But Mark wouldn't let go of my hand, tugging me forward until we reached the steps, where he spun me around so he could cover me as we ascended. Another three shots rang out, and I stumbled onto the unforgiving aluminium steps—the weight of Mark's body slamming down hard against mine, making the metal dig further into my knees.

I waited a couple of seconds for Mark to get up, but all he did was groan, then I heard Ivan yell my name and swear profusely, the steps beginning to shake with the strain as he thundered his way towards us. Within a couple of seconds, Mark was lifted off me.

"He's been hit in the arm, but I think the vest took the other bullets," Ivan yelled to someone above us. When I raised my head, I saw Carl dragging Mark out of Ivan's arms.

I turned my head and screamed when I saw James and Franco lying on the ground under the wing. James was trying to wriggle out from under Franco's body. His chest was under Franco's back, and for one terrifying moment, I thought my guard was dead. But then he raised his hand and fired his gun at Yannis and three others, who were taking cover behind a stationary service vehicle barely four metres from the nose of the plane. I lost sight of the bastards as they crouched down low, and I knew that James and Franco wouldn't have a hope in hell of getting a shot in from their current position. Yannis and his guards popped their heads up once more and each took a shot at James and Franco, a bullet from one of those guns hitting Franco in his lower leg. I cried out again and Franco briefly glanced my way, yelling for me to get to safety, but I was momentarily frozen. Mark and Franco had been shot; James and Franco were fully exposed in their current position, and Yannis and his men were so warped that they were risking stray bullets near an aircraft's fuel storage.

Carl pushed past Ivan and leapt over me before lifting his rifle and opening fire on the shooters behind the vehicle, shouting back to Ivan, "Go, go, go."

Ivan tried to grab my arm and pull me up the steps, but I shook him off and dug my hand into the front pocket of my bag. No way would I leave James and Franco at further risk, and if one of those bullets hit the fuel tank on the wing, we might not be able to get Lily off the plane in time before the whole thing went up in flames.

"We need to get you on board, Tess," Ivan said as he grasped the back of my bullet-proof vest, hauling me upright and then over his shoulder so he could carry me up the steps. But I already had Danny's gun in my hand, and when we reached the top step, I had a clear shot at the man who was currently edging around the vehicle to avoid Carl's rapid-fire assault.

So I took the shot.

Yannis dropped his gun and fell back with both hands clutching his neck, attempting to stop the blood from pumping out of his throat. I'd aimed for his head, but the result would be the same. It was a fatal shot, no matter how much medical attention Yannis sought. He glanced up at me before his hands slipped from his throat. He knew I'd been the one to end his life. I thought it would have satisfied the twisted need for vengeance that had been building since I'd discovered what he'd done, but that wasn't what happened at all. Seeing Yannis drowning in his own blood was both sickening and upsetting.

The guard beside him went to help his boss but was shot in the chest by Carl, who already had his sights trained on the other two guards. They set off running back towards the helipad but were gunned down by a group of men who approached our aircraft from the opposite direction.

Ivan had stopped moving when I took my shot, and when he saw the strangers gun down Yannis's men, he let out a sigh of relief. "Roman's team from Cyprus have arrived. The one on the left is Dimitri," he said with obvious relief while lowering me to my feet. "Go inside. I'll take care of everything."

Though it was good to know the strangers were on our side, I couldn't set foot on that plane until I knew James and Franco were following me.

"No, Ivan. I need to get to them," I shouted above all the noise. "Franco was hit in the calf, so he won't be able to walk."

"Then I'll carry him if I need to. But you have to get on board and stay there. We are far enough away from the terminal for passengers not to see you, but I don't know about any of the airport staff. Having such a distinctive hair colour means you are easily identifiable, so go and be with your daughter. If she's awake, she will need her mother right now."

He left me standing in the doorway with Tanner close

beside me, then made his way down the steps, waving his hands and shouting, "THEY'RE WITH US. ROMAN SENT THEM." Carl and Franco lowered their weapons, and Tanner and I watched as James slid out from under Franco and helped him sit up.

"I should have been down there with him," Tanner said with a nod towards James. "Me and Carl. He shouldn't have sent him back with the girl. We should have had our full team with us. If we'd have known before take-off, we could—"

"It's only been a week since you were shot, Tanner. No way would it have been right to have you out there, and Carl was following orders." I looked down at the gun in my hands and shook my head. "If James hadn't told Yannis that he knew what he'd done and had evidence to substantiate it, he might not have attacked us."

Tanner shook his head in denial. "Yannis said he was in the airport's private lounge waiting for you when he spotted us. He called James immediately, demanding to know why he was meeting you. I think he already knew you were leaving," he said, trying to defend his boss.

"He could have told Yannis he was flying in for a surprise visit," I insisted, even though I knew Yannis might not have bought it.

"Give him a break, Tess. He's gone through hell since his pop was killed, and when they attacked your home, James knew he was the target. When a random stranger tries to kill you, it hits you hard, but when you find out someone you loved as family wants you dead, that's the kind of mind fuck that can break you. He kept going through the photos Kevin sent and had tears rolling down his face the whole time. All he said was, *I sent them to him. I thought he'd keep them safe, but he could have killed them, and it would have been my fault,'* even though we all told him that was bullshit. Yannis fooled us all, not just James. I know he shouldn't have said anything, but he was hanging by a thread until he knew you'd landed, and when Yannis gave him attitude, he just fucking lost it. Especially when he told him why he did it, and why he wanted you and Lily alive."

"He told him?" I asked in a voice laced with stomach-churning curiosity and an unhealthy dose of fear. Fear of what the truth would do to my already fragile psyche. Tanner nodded, then gave my shoulder a reassuring squeeze.

I glanced back down at James, who, along with Carl, was helping Franco get to the steps. Ivan was talking with the men who'd been sent to assist us and was gesturing towards the bodies of Yannis and the guards who'd tried to help him. There was so much blood surrounding them, and most of it belonged to the man who'd killed my husband.

I slid the safety into place on Danny's gun and put it back in my bag. Franco had reached the bottom step, so I ran down to greet my brave, determined guard, swapping with Carl to take the weight on his right side. James followed behind us.

"I've got you, Franco," I told him as we took the first step.

"I should spank your ass for not doing as I told you. Why didn't you just get on the plane?" he moaned. Sweat was pouring from his brow, and it looked as though he was about to pass out.

"I wasn't going to leave you, Franco. You and James needed me. Besides, I had Danny's gun and I... I had a clear shot at Yannis, so I took it. I hit him in the throat, Franco. I watched him choke on his own blood." I burst into tears, sobbing hard by the time we hit the fourth step. Franco turned slightly and pulled me into his arms.

"Don't cry, Tess. You did what you had to do. What a boss would do. Didn't I tell you that's what you were? You saved our lives. You and Carl stopped those bullets from having our names on them. We're safe now, baby. Me and James get to live another day because you were too much of a boss to obey orders."

His words didn't soothe me. If anything, they made me cry even more.

"Honey, I'd love to give you comfort, but my calf and ribs are fucking killing me." All the colour seemed to drain from Franco's face as he grasped the handrail beside him. I turned to ask James for help and noticed he was no longer behind us. Carl stepped up and took my place, almost carrying Franco onto the plane.

At some point during my crying bout, James had left us to greet the men who were with Ivan. One of the men—Dimitri, I think—looked up at me and gave me a salute. Not knowing what else to do, I gave him a single wave in return. It seemed kind of surreal to worry about how to greet a hitman, especially while we were in a public place with four dead bodies around us. Ivan shook his head, no doubt annoyed that I'd not yet ventured inside the plane, and James wouldn't even look at me. So I finally did as everyone wanted and went to check on our injured guards.

Chapter Thirty-One

TESS

Blood covered the right side of the luxuriously comfortable cream leather seat where Kolya used to sit. Jonathon—one of our regular flight attendants—was trying to administer basic first aid and had tied a strip of torn white sheet above the place where Mark had been shot, midway between his elbow and shoulder. He pressed a towel against the bleeding wound site to stem the flow of blood, but it still seeped through. Mark's seat was semi-reclined and his eyes were closed, though the grimace on his face revealed he was in too much pain to be resting. I glanced around the plane, searching for my daughter and Adrianna, who were nowhere to be seen.

"Lily was asleep, so Ivan put her in bed. She's with the girl and Marianne, and it's better she stays there. This would only upset her," Jonathon said, gesturing at the injured men.

I nodded in agreement. It *would* be too much for Lily to see, especially after what had happened back home, so I hoped that Marianne—another of our flight attendants—

would be able to keep her occupied in there when she woke up. I desperately wanted to see her and hold her, but I also wanted to check on Mark's and Franco's wounds.

"There's no exit wound, and I can't be sure it hasn't gone through bone," Jonathon confirmed as I knelt beside Mark. "We have morphine, but I'm not qualified to administer it."

"If you bring it here, I'll administer it myself," Mark groaned.

"I'm so sorry, Mark. Were you hit anywhere else? You went down pretty hard," I enquired, placing my hand on his knee.

He opened his eyes and gave me a semi-smile. "The vest did its job, but my ribs took the impact. Carl said you took that bastard out with one shot. I'm proud of you, Mrs B."

"You kept me covered while the bullets were flying. I'll never forget that, Mark."

"Just doing my job, love," he replied as he winced and sucked in a breath. "I could really do with that morphine or whatever you've got that'll take the edge off."

"Here you go, man," Tanner said as he rubbed Mark's uninjured arm with a sterile wipe and administered the injection.

Jonathon frowned. "Where was the warning about feeling a slight prick before you stuck him?"

Tanner laughed. "That would have been a lie. There's nothing slight about my prick." He swapped the bloodied towel on Mark's arm for a clean one. "How's that feel, buddy?"

The tense grimace on Mark's face began to soften. "Better than before."

"Good to know. I have another couple here for you. How are your ribs?"

"It hurts to breathe, but it doesn't feel like there's anything major going on." Mark's voice became a little slurred, which was probably due to the morphine, but Tanner did some basic checks on him, just in case.

I squeezed Mark's hand and kissed his cheek. "If you feel like anything changes, then let someone know as soon as possible. Don't try to be brave, Mark. I'm going to speak to my father-in-law about getting us some medical help. It will take too long to get back to England."

Mark nodded in response but kept his eyes closed.

I made my way over to Franco, who lay on the sofa in the TV area. Carl was pressing white cotton padding and gauze against the side of his calf.

"It's gone straight through the muscle and possibly tendon, but there doesn't appear to be any bone damage. It's gonna hurt like a mother while you heal, Franco," Carl said. "From one to ten, how's your pain?"

"Ribs six, calf nine," Franco replied.

He gestured for me to sit beside him, but there was no room, and I didn't want to hurt him, so I knelt down next to him and kissed his forehead.

"I'll get Tanner to bring you something for the pain," Carl said while wadding up more material to press against the wound. "You gotta stop bleeding, man. You're making a real fucking mess here."

"I've got something right here that's good for my pain," Franco replied. He took hold of my hand and asked, "How are you doing, honey?"

"I'm worried about you and Mark, but I'm waiting to see what's going on before I call Roman and tell him we need to get you and Mark to a doctor. There are four dead bodies out there, Franco. We can't just get rid of them like we did at home."

Tanner gave Franco a shot of morphine and pulled a sachet out of the extensive first aid kit. "I'm gonna pour some of this into the wound to help stop the bleeding." Picking up the sachet of haemostat, he told us, "I had to phone Andy to ask about this stuff. He said I couldn't give it to Mark because it's possible he has bone fragments in there, but you should be fine. I can't have you bleeding to death on my watch."

Glancing across at Mark, I asked, "Can you do person-to-person blood transfusions? I mean, I don't know if that's a possibility, but if it is, I'm good for it."

"If anyone needs a transfusion, that's gonna have to be done in a hospital. Me and Carl are only trained in basic first aid. Andy and Lainey would know what we can do with the medical equipment the boss keeps on board, but they aren't here," Tanner replied.

I squeezed Franco's hand. "I have the same blood type as you. Just think, Franco. You could have had some of me inside you. The blood of a boss," I joked.

"I'd like it a whole lot better if I had some of me inside you, baby," he said with a lazy smile.

I tutted at what I assumed was just a throwaway lewd comment, but after his earlier declaration, I wondered if he really meant it.

"I guess the morphine's working," Tanner chuckled. "Though once I pour this in your wound, I guarantee that sex will be the last thing on your mind."

Carl removed the cotton padding and leaned back while Tanner poured a grainy-looking substance inside the gaping wound in Franco's calf. Franco grimaced, then swore before his features softened once again.

James and Ivan boarded the plane, along with Dimitri. They headed my way, so I stood to greet them.

"Mrs Barinov, my name is Dimitri. Your father-in-law has asked me to take care of your current situation. I see that you have two wounded men who need medical attention, so we will clean up as quickly as possible. We will require the use of your helicopter and yacht. Ivan has spoken to his comrades on board the vessel, and they have agreed to wait there and assist us. We have the coordinates of its current location, so there is nothing you need to do other than hand me your gun. Ivan tells me that you killed the man who betrayed your husband, and with a single shot to the throat. This will work well for what we have in mind." Dimitri held out his hand for the weapon, and though I took it out of my bag, I hesitated when handing it over.

"It's not my gun, it's Danny's, and it will have our prints on it."

Dimitri closed his hand over mine, taking the gun from me. "It will be thoroughly cleaned, and the serial numbers will be removed. Trust me, Mrs Barinov, there will be nothing left on this gun to tie you or your guards to any crime."

I nodded my thanks and looked at Ivan for reassurance. "Roman is planning for us to fly to an acquaintance of his who can provide no-questions-asked medical assistance. He'll call me when he has it sorted. He would also like to speak to you, Tess, when you have a moment," he said.

"Is Lily still asleep?" James asked while staring at the floor. "Ivan told my grandfather that she slept through everything."

"She's in the bedroom with Adrianna and Marianne. I haven't checked on her in case I woke her up. I don't want her coming out here and seeing Mark and Franco like this, so I'd like her to stay in there as long as possible."

James nodded. "I'll go and sit with her so Marianne can

come out here and assist Jonathon. What do you think we should do about Adrianna? The threat to her life has gone now that Yannis is dead, but do you think she can be trusted not to tell the authorities what happened?"

"Is this something you need our assistance with?" Dimitri asked.

James, Ivan and I gave a resounding "No!" We all had an idea of what would happen to Adrianna if Roman's men decided she was a threat.

"I do not wish to scare her, but there are photographs of other prominent people on her laptop. We can assure her that those photographs will not see the light of day if she keeps quiet about all this," Ivan suggested.

James and I agreed that's what we should do. As he'd known Adrianna since she was a small child, James volunteered to speak to her about it, thinking it would sound better coming from someone she thought of as a friend rather than people she'd accused of kidnapping her.

James shook Dimitri's hand, then made his way towards the bedroom, which was situated at the back of the plane. I caught up with him before he reached the door.

"Please don't tell her it was me who killed him," I pleaded. "Despite everything, she loved him, and I don't want her to hate me."

Without turning around, he replied, "She'll probably hate us, anyway. However I try to sugar-coat it, we're still threatening her, Tess. There's no getting away from that."

He was right, of course, but there was little else we could do about it. I watched him walk through the bedroom door and sneaked a quick glance at my sleeping daughter. Adrianna sat beside her, stroking her hair. The window in the bedroom faced the opposite side of the doors to the aircraft, so she wouldn't have seen Yannis and his men die, but the tears streaming down her cheeks told me she knew they'd been killed.

Seeing her so distressed gave me a strange sense of guilt. I say strange because it wasn't how I expected or even thought I should feel. It was almost as if all the thoughts swirling around my head had voices. There were loud ones saying that the kill was justified, that Yannis needed to die because he'd taken the love of my life away from me and would have killed James and Franco if I hadn't stopped him. He'd also aimed for me, too, and if it wasn't for Mark, Lily would have been an orphan today. But there were also whispering voices that told me I'd just killed a friend. A man who'd treated Lily like a little princess and made me laugh more times than I cared to mention. Someone who'd only recently supported me at the Graysons' Halloween party, and all those years ago at Sarah's funeral.

An image of Yannis in his Halloween makeup flashed through my mind. I'd named him one of my soul demons without giving much thought to the meaning. But in hindsight, it turned out to be quite a fitting name for him. Yannis had not only taken the life and soul of the man I loved, but in doing so, he'd ruined mine. No act of vengeance would bring my husband back. There would never be any real justice for Kolya, Jonesy and Lucas, no matter how many people Roman or I killed.

Chapter Thirty-Two

TESS

Adrianna left the bedroom five minutes after James went in. I noticed she wasn't crying anymore. Marianne approached her and asked if she needed anything. Adrianna shook her head, her eyes scanning the interior of the plane as she took in the sight of our injured guards.

Dimitri had left the plane with Ivan, but the latter returned soon after. He announced we'd be flying to Sicily, where Roman's contact would be waiting to transport our injured guards to a private medical facility.

Adrianna approached me cautiously, and I wondered if it was because I frightened her. I had blood on my hands in more ways than one, though playing nursemaid to Mark and Franco suited me better than being a stone-cold killer. Had she guessed it was me who fired the lethal shot? Or did she just suspect I'd been the one to end the life of the man she'd idolised?

She knelt down next to my seat beside Mark and said, "I'm sorry I didn't trust you sooner. I just found it so hard to believe what you were telling me when all I knew from

Yannis was kindness. But this"—she gestured around the plane—"I would never have believed he was capable of it."

"You weren't the only one fooled, Adrianna. My husband had been his best friend since he was eighteen and look what happened to him."

I laid my head back on the seat and sighed. We'd be taking off as soon as Ivan had the all-clear from Dimitri, so we needed to know whether she'd be coming with us. Looking her in the eyes, I asked, "What are you going to do now?"

"I'm going to go home and stay with my parents. James said he'll be keeping my laptop so he can access the other photos and figure out if Yannis had met with anyone else involved in the attack on his father. He said it might help identify where they've left his body. James also told me he wouldn't let anyone else know I'd been photographing them on Athilos, which I'm grateful for. He asked me not to tell anyone what happened here today, and I won't, Tess, I swear," Adrianna insisted as she grabbed my bloodstained hands.

"I know you won't, and I'm grateful for your silence," I told her reassuringly.

A thought occurred to me. "Yannis said he paid for your college tuition. Obviously, that won't be happening anymore, so I'll pay for your tuition, books, and accommodation. I also have some regular photography work for you, if you wouldn't mind travelling to England. I'll cover your travel expenses and pay well over the going rate if it's something you'd be interested in?"

Adrianna's eyes opened wide. "Of course I'm interested. Thank you for considering me. And thank you for offering to pay for my tuition and everything, but James said he'd like to take care of all that for me." She lowered her voice a little. "You should go to him, Tess. He was crying when I left him. I've never seen a grown man cry before. I tried to comfort him, but he wouldn't let me. He told me Yannis tried to shoot him today and if not for Franco, he'd be dead. I'm glad I didn't have to witness that."

I unbuckled my seat belt and hugged Adrianna before walking her to the door of the plane. The service vehicle had gone, and so had the bodies behind it. There wasn't even any blood on the tarmac, although the whole area looked wet. They must have hosed it down, erasing all the evidence of the deadly shoot-out.

I watched Adrianna walk down the steps and make her way over to the VIP lounge in the terminal building. She turned back to wave as she neared the entryway, then hurried inside.

Tanner came up behind me and rested his hands on my shoulders. "Are you confident she won't say anything?"

"I don't know," I answered truthfully. "But what is there to see, even if she did tell anyone?"

Tanner glanced down at the runway. "The Russians were thorough, I'll give them that."

"Excuse me, Tanner, Mrs Barinov. They've given us a take-off slot, so if you could retire to your seats, the captain will commence with our departure," Jonathon informed us.

Tanner and I went to check on Mark and Franco before I made my way down to the bedroom. Ivan looked up from the screen of his phone and reminded me that Roman wanted to speak to me. Then he took his seat and went back to texting whoever it was he'd been messaging.

Ivan was usually content to let others take charge, but he'd been an absolute rock for me recently. And his help and support with all that had happened over the past few hours had been invaluable. We had each suffered an unbearable loss when Kolya was murdered, but as I glanced around at everyone, I realised how lucky James, Lily, and I were to have all those people to protect us.

Marianne stopped me before I could enter the bedroom. "Mrs Barinov, would you like to wash your hands before you go in there?"

I looked down at the blood coating the back of my fingers and nodded. Although the bedroom had an en-suite bathroom attached, I crossed to the sink in the galley and washed away the blood of the heroes who'd saved us.

James put his finger to his lips as I entered the bedroom, so I closed the door as quietly as I could.

"We're about to take off if you want to go and grab a seat. I'll stay here with Lily," I told him.

He shook his head. "I'd rather stay in here, so you can go back out if you want. I won't leave her on her own."

Even if Adrianna hadn't told me he'd been crying, the red eyes and damp tear tracks down his cheeks would have certainly given him away.

Lily lay in the middle of the bed with James sitting beside her, leaning back against the padded, navy-blue headboard. I lay down beside her on the right side of the bed and put my arm around her. Brushing my fingers against his left hand, I asked, "Tell me about the phone call, James."

The plane began to move, making its way towards the runway, and for a minute or two, I thought James was ignoring me. But as the plane picked up speed and the sound of the engines reached their roaring crescendo, he said, "He knew, Tess. He already knew I was here to collect you and Lily."

"What do you mean? How could he have known? No one would have told him, James. I mean, I realise Darius was nothing but a Judas, but I know none of our other guards would ever betray us. And no one on the yacht was privy to our discussions. Not even Philippe. A lot of the staff on there used to work for your grandfather, and they wouldn't dare risk Roman's wrath."

"I don't know, Tess. Maybe he guessed when he saw our plane. He called me when he saw us land. It's hard to miss an aircraft with KOLCAT written on it. I played along at first, though maybe my voice gave me away. I'd been looking at the photographs of Yannis and Darius that Adrianna took. I wanted to see something in them that would make Yannis innocent—like maybe the date she took them was wrong or that it was just someone who looked like Darius. I didn't want it to be true, Tess, even though the evidence proved otherwise." James tilted his head back and closed his eyes before any tears could escape.

"I can understand why you did that. You weren't the only one who wanted it not to be true," I admitted.

"I could hear it in his voice. It had an edge to it, Tess. A dangerous, mocking edge. I told him I was here because I missed my sister and had things to discuss with you. Yannis laughed and told me he didn't believe me. He said that you and I were piss-poor liars, and though he knew you'd have a hard time keeping your emotions out of it, he'd expected better from me. That's when I lost it. I told him that my dad had expected him to honour the friendship they shared. I said I'd expected him to be as loyal to us as we were to him. Yannis laughed again and said my dad didn't know what loyalty meant, and that if he had, he'd have bought the shipyard from him. He carried on listing things that had happened throughout the years—nonsense things, Tess. He went on and on, listing petty stuff in a rant that culminated with the fact that my dad was a thousand times more successful than Yannis could ever be. I asked him about the attack in Oxford, and he admitted that Ivan, Franco and I had been the targets. Me because I'd refused to go into business with him and—get this—I was no longer the sole heir, so I was of no use to him, and Ivan and Franco because of how close they are to you."

I closed my eyes and gave thanks to whatever god was listening that James, Ivan and Franco had been down in the shooting range that day.

"James, did Yannis say what he had planned for me and Lily?"

"His words were, *'Tess being a grieving billionaire widow makes up for the fact she's nothing more than a common, foul-mouthed little bitch. Marrying her would have been the means to a very wealthy end for me.'* I said you had his number and that you'd never have married him."

"Too bloody right," I muttered angrily.

"He said that Lily was the golden child, just like I had been when he'd first attempted to have my dad assassinated. The day you were shot, Tess."

A cold chill ran through me, and I shuddered.

"Did he say what he meant by that?" I asked.

"He was my godfather. Before you came along, my dad had it written into his will that if anything happened to him, Yannis would have the ultimate say in what happened to KOLCAT until I was of age, with the advice of senior management, of course. My inheritance would go into a trust until I was twenty-one. I was almost twenty when he tried to have my dad assassinated, if you recall."

I nodded, picturing the small party we had for him. Then I remembered, "You and Brad went to stay with Yannis after your birthday."

"We did. I feel physically sick when I think about how he acted when we went over there. I discussed the assassination attempt with him. I was so worried about my dad, and he tried to reassure me, telling me I had nothing to worry about and that my dad would be more careful from now on, when all along it was him, Tess. He'd tried to murder my dad so he could control me and, therefore, my inheritance. And I spent my holiday with him like I always did."

"So that's why he'd kept Lily safe?" I surmised. "The shooter wasn't looking for Lily that day in Oxford."

"Yeah, I think so. The conversation didn't get that far, but I'm assuming he'd have tried again to get rid of me, then you, when you refused to marry him. He'd have had Lily and some of her inheritance all to himself then."

I shook my head. "Whatever he and Kolya had planned, I know for a fact that if anything had happened to me and you, Roman would have made sure that Lily ended up in Moscow with him and Yuri. Yannis would have been nothing but a mere irritation to him," I stated. James agreed.

"Despite hearing him say those things, and seeing the photos of him meeting with Darius, I still can't get my head around it, Tess. I mean, he was family to me. We spent holidays with him, and he came to my school for sports days, concerts, and plays. I used to draw him pictures and he'd put them in his office. He attended all my birthday parties when I was a child, and we spent quite a few Christmases with him, too. But in the end, all that shared history meant nothing to him. I loved him, yet he wanted me dead." James covered his tear-filled eyes with his hands. "I couldn't bear to look at him, Tess. When the men my grandfather sent came to move his body, I couldn't look because, even after knowing all he'd done, a part of me still couldn't bear to see him dead."

"You aren't the only one, James," I confessed, glad that it wasn't just me who'd been feeling that way. "Even though I know he deserved it for what he'd done to Kolya, I don't think I could have killed Yannis if you and Franco were safely on board. But he and his men kept on shooting, so I had to stop him."

"I thought he'd killed Franco," James admitted. "He pushed me down when they started shooting at us. I felt his body jerk when the bullets hit his chest, and if it wasn't for the vest he was wearing, Franco would be dead, and it would be my fault. He's out there hurting right now because he was protecting me. I was so worried about you and Lily after speaking to Yannis, I barged out of here without putting on a Kevlar vest. I may as well have been wearing a target on my back."

"If you were, it wouldn't have been Yannis that hit you," I muttered, unable to resist adding a touch of gallows humour to the grim conversation. "He wasn't called Bent Barrel for nothing. He probably shot Franco in the calf when he was aiming for the plane."

James laughed through his tears. "You're probably right. My dad and Jonesy used to give him hell for it, didn't they? His guards were good, though, Tess. Ivan said Mark's injury looks bad. My grandfather has someone in Sicily who owes him a debt, so he's arranged for us to fly there. They'll have an ambulance on standby at the airport."

I took out my phone and contemplated calling Roman.

"If you're going to call him, give me a minute, please. He'll probably want to speak to me again, and I don't want him to know I've been crying. He wouldn't understand, you know? Roman Barinov sees emotional attachments to anyone other than blood family as a weakness. But Yannis *was* family to me, Tess."

I nodded and put down the phone.

"How are we supposed to get past all this?" James asked. "How do people learn to trust again after they've experienced such a monumental betrayal?"

I shrugged my shoulders and sighed. "I don't know, James. But I think it would be best to keep our circle small and not let anyone new in for a while."

James brought my hand to his lips, placing a kiss near my knuckles, just like his father used to.

"You are so brave, Tess. You helped save me and Franco today, even though it should have been *me* who was keeping *you* safe. Yannis underestimated you, and your worth. You are so much more than just the widow of Kolya Barinov."

I smirked while thinking of Yannis's insulting description. "Yannis figured that out right before he died. I'm not just a common, foul-mouthed little bitch; I'm a common, foul-mouthed little bitch with a good aim, and I'll fight to the death if someone comes after my family."

Chapter Thirty-Three

TESS

Lily woke up during my phone call to her grandfather, and after speaking to him, she spent the rest of the flight watching TV in the bedroom with James and Ivan.

I spent half the flight tending to our injured guards, wishing I knew more than basic first aid. Franco was doing better than I thought now that the bleeding was no longer a problem and his pain was under control. But Mark was in a bad way, and I prayed he wouldn't take a turn for the worse in the time it took us to arrive at our destination, which, thankfully, wouldn't be long.

We arrived at Catania airport in Sicily an hour and twenty minutes after take-off. A glance out of the window as we came in to land revealed the most spectacular scenery. The sea was a mix of the deepest blue merging into a stunning turquoise and crystal-clear aqua in some of the pretty coves. Vast stretches of tree-filled countryside surrounded towns of sandstone-coloured buildings, all nestled within the hills and valleys of this breathtaking island. But the one thing that no one could miss was the grey cloud hanging over the active volcano, although I found that Mount Etna worried me a lot less than putting my faith and our safety in the hands of a stranger.

Roman told me he had an acquaintance in Sicily who owed him a debt. He said he'd kept Gianni Russo's family safe many years ago, and now it was time for him to return the favour. According to Roman, Gianni would be waiting for us at the airport and could provide no-questions-asked medical care for our injured guards. However, I hadn't expected an ambulance and two charcoal-grey stretch limousines to arrive alongside our plane as soon as it came to a stop.

It was cooler in Sicily than it had been in Greece, and the sky was overcast with grey clouds. I cursed myself for not thinking ahead and bringing Lily a warmer coat. With everything that had happened, it was ridiculous of me to worry about something so trivial, but I couldn't switch off the mother in me, no matter how dark life seemed to get.

James carried Lily down the aircraft steps and I followed close behind. It was clear to see exactly who Gianni Russo was. Four men—who were so obviously his guards—flanked the tall, attractive man with salt-and-pepper hair and deep-brown eyes. Though his guards appeared relaxed with their laid-back Italian swagger, they had that familiar, wary edge that our own close protection team had. Russo wore an expensive-looking silver-grey suit, yet his guards dressed casually, wearing cotton or leather bomber jackets with jeans or chinos.

Russo was Mafia, of that I had no doubt. I'd already gathered that from speaking with Roman. Though he hadn't outright confirmed it, the fact that we were meeting an old acquaintance of his in Sicily who owed him a debt big enough that he'd take care of our injured men, as well as providing us with a safe place to stay, kind of gave it away. But just looking at the man told me he was mafioso. The way he held himself, his whole demeanour. Roman did it, too. It was almost as if they were royalty, although that might not be the right word. They sit at the top of the structured hierarchy within their organisation, but they are more than a king to those who serve under them. In fact, I would probably say that Roman's word is gospel amongst those in the Barinov Bratva. They treat him like a god. But then, he does decide the fates of those who go against him, and he has an arrogance that comes from someone with immense power. Gianni Russo had those same traits, and though I knew Roman wouldn't send us to anyone who would hurt us, I reserved judgement on whether I could trust the man.

James balanced Lily on one arm and held out his hand. "Signor Russo, I am James Barinov. This is my baby sister, Lily, and her mother, Tess Barinov."

"I'm not a baby, James; I'm four, so that means I'm a little girl," Lily admonished.

Gianni Russo laughed as he shook James's hand. He spoke very good English, albeit with a slight American accent. "I am very pleased to meet you, Lily. I have a granddaughter who is also four years old. Perhaps you can play with her during your stay in Sicily."

Lily nodded and asked, "What's her name?"

"Her name is Sofia, and her brother's name is Giovanni, but he is eight and prefers his Xbox to his sister, so she will be happy to have another little girl to play with." After gently cupping Lily's cheek, he turned to me and smiled. "Your daughter is beautiful, and not shy at all. She will go far in this world."

"Thank you for agreeing to help us at such short notice," I said as I shook his hand. "We have two guards with gunshot wounds—Mark Rush and Anthony Franconni."

Signor Russo's deep-brown eyes narrowed slightly. "I knew an Anthony Franconni once, back in New Jersey. Your guy Franconni... Where is he from?"

I knew Franco was from New Jersey—and that he was named after his father—but I didn't know Russo well enough to share that with him. For all I knew, Gianni Russo could have hated the Anthony Franconni that he was talking about. Besides, Franconni could be a common name in New Jersey. So I ignored his question and gestured behind me to the steps of the plane, where Ivan, Carl and Tanner were helping Mark and the man in question descend onto the tarmac.

"We did what we could with the limited supplies we had on the plane, but they've both lost a lot of blood, so they'll need to be treated without delay. We're willing to pay for the best medical care available," I told him. As an afterthought, I added, "I'll do whatever it takes to ensure the health, safety, and privacy of those who are important to me."

Signor Russo stared at me for a few seconds, expecting me to answer his question. I held his gaze and lifted my chin slightly, trying my best to give the impression of being someone who wouldn't buckle under pressure. At first, he seemed a little irritated, but then a slow smile appeared on his handsome face, and he nodded in approval. Russo clearly respected the loyalty and protectiveness I showed for my guards.

"Please be assured, your men will receive only the best medical care. I have a doctor awaiting their arrival at the nearest hospital."

"Thank you, Signor Russo. I'd like to be informed as

soon as possible about every aspect of their treatment and care."

"Of course, Mrs Barinov. If you give me your telephone number, I will pass it on to the doctor I have on standby at the hospital. But for now, let me take you to one of my villas so you can relax. I understand you've had a very traumatic day."

"Signor Russo, the last six weeks have been hell on earth for us, and your kindness and hospitality are very much appreciated."

"Of course. My condolences to you all. I understand that you and Roman have people searching for the man responsible for the death of his son. When they catch him, I'm sure he will pay for his crimes against your family."

Mark and Franco were now in the ambulance, so I went to check on them before we left. The short journey from the aircraft had left them looking much paler and weaker than before, so I didn't hang around. I reassured them they were in excellent hands and that I'd visit them as soon as possible. Carl volunteered to accompany them, and though it meant we had only Ivan and a recovering Tanner for protection, I felt better knowing our injured guards had someone they knew looking out for them.

Before leaving the plane, Ivan, Tanner, James and I had all taken guns and ammo from its hidden armoury. Carl was currently carrying two Sigs in ankle holsters, just in case. Signor Russo's offer of help might very well be genuine, but then again, we all thought that of Yannis, and look how that turned out.

I debated on whether to tell Franco about Signor Russo's interest in him, but the paramedics had given him and Mark something for the pain and were hooking them up to IV drips and blood pressure machines, and I didn't want to get in their way.

Before I left, I beckoned Carl over. "Call me as soon as you have an update."

"I will. I'm gonna need to know where we're staying. Nate said Lainey and Danny had packed up all the clothes that everyone left on the yacht, and they'll bring them to Sicily. They're going to fly over tonight, so you, Lily, and James can have a full team with you ASAP, but maybe you could arrange for the crew to sail the yacht here." Carl leaned in closer and whispered, "We don't know these people, Tess. I tried to talk to James about it, but the guy's not firing on all cylinders right now. Finding out that Yannis had his father killed really fucked with his head. I mean, who is that guy?" He gestured towards Signor Russo. "Is he some Mafia don big shot?"

I shrugged my shoulders. "I assume so. I mean, the head of one of the biggest crime families in Russia called in a favour from him, which he said was a debt owed."

Carl stared at me for a moment, his expression one of expectation. He clearly thought I'd tell him I wasn't okay with it. But he'd been wrong.

"Carl, my husband was recently betrayed by a man he trusted and considered a friend. One of his guards set him and another two guards up to be killed by terrorists, and most likely tortured them beforehand. My home was attacked, and I was forced to defend it by killing a man in my four-year-old daughter's bedroom—the same room in which I'd hidden said daughter and watched my friend's dog get the top of her head blown off. I then flee to the home of the very man who instigated the whole fucking thing to stay on his island under his protection, and barely two hours ago,

I shot that man and watched him drown in his own blood. Compared to all that, being whisked away to an Italian villa by a Mafia boss while my injured guards receive medical treatment sounds like a relaxing spa holiday to me."

Carl held up his hands in front of him. "Okay, okay, I get what you're saying, but just listen to me, Tess. You need to stay on your guard until we know more about this guy and who he associates with. Now, I know you're a smart cookie, but, honey, like you just said, you've had a tough fucking time of it lately, and a predator like him, he'll see that and use it to his advantage. Never give an inch, is all I'm saying. He might owe Roman Barinov a debt, but you, James, and Lily are leverage to some people. Always remember that. And if you feel like something ain't right when you get to this villa, text me the location and keep your hand near your gun." He pulled me in for a hug and placed a kiss on the top of my head. Nodding towards the ambulance, he said, "They're ready to go. Text me as soon as you get where you're going."

"I promise."

As I made my way back towards the waiting limousines, I tried to formulate a plan of action. Even if Signor Russo turned out to be a trustworthy ally, we couldn't stay in Sicily forever. We'd have to remain on the island until our guards were well enough to travel, then we could fly back to the UK. I didn't want to go back to Oxford, but I was desperate to see Nan and Jean. The only place I could think of going to was Glengarran, and though Kevin had promised to make it safe enough to become our full-time residence, he'd already told me it wouldn't be feasible during the winter months.

Earlier that morning, before my entire world went to shit once again, Yannis had suggested I buy a home somewhere else, and I must admit, the idea had appealed to me.

Tanner, James, and Lily were seated in the backseat of the limo, which left Signor Russo, Ivan and I sitting opposite. During the twenty-minute journey to the villa, Signor Russo pointed out various places of interest and restaurants he recommended. He told us to mention we were guests of his if we ate out somewhere to ensure we had the best table and service.

I couldn't help asking, "What do the people here refer to you as? I mean, if we're to mention your name, do we say Signor Russo or…"

He smiled. "You can say Signor Russo. If you are with me, you might hear some people say Don Russo, and some of the old men who knew my father and brother call me Don Gianni, but things are much more relaxed than they used to be. It's not like the movies, Mrs Barinov. Not for many years now. Don't think it's gone away. It's too deeply embedded in our Sicilian blood to do that. But we all find new ways—legitimate ways—to elevate our position in society that demands as much, if not more, respect from those around us. Although your father-in-law doesn't seem to let that bother him." He raised one eyebrow in a friendly challenge.

"I don't have any knowledge of Roman's business dealings, though I know what he is and what he's in charge of. The man is my father-in-law and, as such, has always shown me kindness and respect. Prior to meeting my husband and having Lily, I had no family of my own, just a foster mum and sister. I've known and seen true evil from people who've prayed to their god and done good deeds in their communities, so I believe there's good and bad in most people. The man I…" I glanced over at Lily—who was watching cartoons on Ivan's phone—before I continued speaking. "The man I eliminated today had been my husband's friend since they were at university. He'd been like an uncle to my daughter and James, and we trusted him to keep us safe, but all along...it was him. He tried to have my husband assassinated five years ago, but I got in the way of the bullet and saved his life. Of course, we didn't know that then, or he would have been out of the picture a long time ago. But then his guard came to work for us and, together with the terrorists, they murdered my husband and our beloved guards. A week ago, he organised a team of armed men to attack my home in a bid to take out James, Ivan, and my guard, Franco. Luckily, we'd been prepared and eliminated all but one of our attackers, who escaped via the waiting helicopter."

I rubbed the fingers of one hand against my forehead before carrying on.

"They shot Tanner in the leg; a bullet skimmed the side of Dave's head—and I still don't know how he didn't have more serious injuries. Nan, who is more like a mum to me than our housekeeper, fell and broke her hip during all this and, throughout everything, that two-faced, betraying scumbag pretended to care about our safety. He offered help and a place to stay, and like lambs to the slaughter, we went. It was only by chance that we found out who was behind everything. He'd caused all the fear and hurt and tears. The friend. The legitimate businessman. So forgive me, Signor Russo, if I don't distance myself from Roman because he doesn't hide his involvement in Russia's criminal underworld. There's no pretence or holier-than-thou masquerading with my father-in-law, so at least I know what I'm getting with him."

I hated the fact that I'd repeated what had happened to

us again. It was as if doing so not only made others understand the danger we'd survived, but it brought it home to
me, too.

Russo nodded while studying me intently. "Roman was
right about you. He said you were made for this life of
ours."

I huffed out a semi-laugh. "So he keeps telling me, but I
don't know if I agree with him."

"Really?" James questioned. "I don't often side with my
grandfather, Tess, but I have to say, with the way you dealt
with everything today and the strength and resilience you've
shown…"

I could have disputed what James said. Could have told
him that shock had taken over my limbs earlier and I'd had
to be carried out of the helicopter, and maybe I should have
mentioned the tears I'd cried and the worry and fear I was
still feeling. But we had a stranger in the car with us, and a
very powerful stranger at that. There was no way I'd let
myself show fear and appear weak in front of a man like
Gianni Russo.

I turned the conversation around by asking for the
address of the villa so I could send it to Carl and Lainey.
The Villa Rosa was only twenty minutes by car from the
airport and set in the most spectacular countryside location.

Tall pines and various green shrubs surrounded the
gated entrance and perimeter of the villa, giving it a
secluded feel. But as you drove up the long, winding driveway, you were met with cypress trees and oleanders. Nearer
to the substantial, stone-built property, Signor Russo pointed
out the abundance of orange, lemon, and clementine trees,
some of which looked ready to be picked, even though we
were in mid-December.

We entered the property through two ornate wooden

doors into a large hallway with white walls, arched recesses and a high ceiling. The floor was tiled in a simple white, black and brown Moorish design throughout the downstairs. I remarked how warm it was inside the property and was surprised to learn that the old converted farmhouse had underfloor heating.

"Through here is the dining room, kitchen, and utility room." Signor Russo smiled when he had to raise his voice to be heard over Lily's incessant jabbering that she'd seen the best pool in the entire world. "And here is the room where I am sure you will spend most of your time."

The sitting room was huge. A large stone fireplace was the focal feature of the back wall, and the room had been split into three sections, just by how the chairs and sofas were placed. The main area surrounded the fireplace, but the second section was just four sofas facing each other. The third area included a few chairs near a small indoor bar. But none of that was what caught your eye about the room at all. No, the thing that drew you was the same thing that captured all your attention in the dining room and kitchen. As soon as you walked in, you immediately faced a wall of old-fashioned, small-panelled picture windows with a solid wood panel at the bottom. They spanned the whole external wall and showcased the twenty-five-metre heated swimming pool and the beautiful fruit trees and gardens.

Signor Russo said something in Italian to one of his men, then handed him a key. He walked towards the windows and began unlocking them, which was when I realised they were actually bi-fold doors that opened onto a sun terrace with steps down to the pool area. There were cushioned sun loungers and parasols placed strategically around the pool's edge, and lights that I knew would make the area look magical when darkness fell.

"It's beautiful, Signor Russo. I really didn't expect this."
I realised how that might sound—as though I didn't think
he'd have something so nice for us—so I quickly added, "I
mean, I thought we'd be hidden away somewhere. Because
that's what we've had to do since my husband and his
guards were ambushed."

James nodded in agreement. "The terrorist who killed
my father used to belong to ISIS. I don't have to tell you
how far and wide their reach is, Signor Russo. I must admit,
this place looks like heaven on earth, but won't we be a little
too exposed here?"

Russo shook his head, beckoning us back inside the
house with two fingers. Ivan shushed Lily when she
complained about having to leave the pool area. She'd
wanted to stay and dip her toes in the water because, apparently, everyone should know that's how you test a pool to see
if it's good.

"There are four guard stations around the property, and
I've had them manned since you landed here in Sicily. We
have cameras and sensors located around the perimeter and
throughout the grounds. The display screens are through
here, in the office." We followed him back to the hallway,
then into a room near the front door. Though it had a PC,
laptop, and several monitors, it was much smaller than our
tech room back in Oxford.

"I will have Matteo, the son of one of my men, handle
that side of security for you if you wish. He's just finished
college. A very smart young man and loyal like his father,
but with brains like his mother, thankfully. Two of my men
will stay here with you inside the villa until the rest of your
guards arrive." He gestured to the man at his left. "The
kitchen is fully stocked, and Luca will cook for you today.
His sauces are delicious, but his English is not so good."

Tipping his head over towards the man on his right, he said, "This is Paolo. He is ambidextrous, so he can shoot as well with his left hand as he can with his right, and his English is exceptional. He will converse with Luca for you if needed."

I smiled and said hello to the men, and James shook their hands. Neither man smiled back at me, although they both had one for Lily and tickled her under the chin.

"You must also remember that this is Sicily, and if anyone is in the area who should not be here, even if it's just a lost tourist, my people will know about it within minutes. Believe me when I say that we've had threats from ISIS before. We had ghost ships carrying ISIS soldiers landing on the beaches from North Africa, but that was dealt with swiftly by my people. Any other time, governments will condemn organisations like mine, but they are happy for us to take over and keep their communities safe when they have neither the balls nor the resources to do so." He glanced at Lily—who was gazing lovingly at the pool—before he continued. "I will leave you to rest, but if you need anything, please reach out to me at any hour."

Signor Russo shook our hands and exchanged a few words with Luca and Paolo. He stayed long enough to swap numbers with us, then left with the rest of his men in one of the limos, promising Lily he would bring his granddaughter over for a play date.

Luca went into the kitchen while Paolo kept up a steady pace around the perimeter of the pool.

After taking Lily to the downstairs toilet in the hallway, we made our way back to the sitting room, where James, Tanner, and Ivan were making themselves comfortable. Lily began pestering us to dip our feet in the pool, so I went back to the downstairs toilet and brought out a spare towel from the rack to dry our feet. When I came back to the room, Lily had made everyone follow her outside.

"I hope Luca is making plenty of food. It's been so long since I've eaten that my stomach thinks my throat's been cut," Ivan remarked as he lay down on a sun lounger and rubbed his rumbling belly.

"I could do with a good twenty-ounce steak right about now, and maybe a rack of ribs," Tanner said.

"There's a barbecue and pizza oven on the terrace near the steps up to the kitchen. My uncle is a butcher. He can supply you with whatever meat you want. The boss always keeps the freezer well stocked for guests, but I think meat is best when it is fresh, no?" We all looked up at Paolo and nodded.

"Thank you, Paulo; we will take you up on that. Tanner will tell you what he needs because he's our go-to barbecue king, but if there's anything you recommend, let us know so we can add it to the list," James said.

Like Greece, Sicily's currency is the euro, so at least we had money, although we'd need more soon.

Paolo made a call to his uncle and let the men guarding the property know we'd be having a delivery later. Then he carried on walking around the pool, giving Lily the occasional wave.

James, Ivan and Tanner spoke in hushed voices behind me and Lily, no doubt discussing everything that happened earlier. She hadn't once asked any questions about why we weren't going back to stay with Yannis, which was a relief. I really didn't want to talk about him in a way that Lily would expect me to. She loved him, and it would break her heart if she found out what he'd done. I didn't want her to know betrayal like that while she was still a child. I knew I'd have to find a way to broach the subject of Yannis's death with her, but I hoped that wouldn't be for a long time, and she could never find out that it was me who killed him. Not until she was old enough to understand the visceral need a woman has to protect her family and those she loves.

My heart hurt for my daughter. One by one, the people she adored and places she felt safe were being taken away from her, and it was mostly down to Yannis. I glanced back at the men speaking in hushed tones behind me and knew that they were most likely planning our next steps without me, and as much as I trusted them, I couldn't have that.

"Guys, save it. I don't want you planning anything that affects me and Lily without discussing it with me first," I snapped.

Lily stopped splashing her feet in the pool and glanced up at me. "Are you okay, Mummy? You sounded mad. Are you mad at them?"

"No, Lilypot, I'm not mad at all. I just…" I looked back over my shoulder at the three men who were staring at me with their eyebrows raised.

I shook my head and continued speaking. "I need time to process everything before we have yet another sudden upheaval." Glancing down at Lily, I added, "We both do."

Ivan took off his shoes and socks and came to sit beside me. Rolling up his jeans, he said, "We weren't making plans about our future without you, Tess, I promise. You know I wouldn't do that."

I did know that deep down. Out of everyone I had in my life, I knew Ivan would always have my back. Lainey, Danny, and Franco, too, though they weren't here right now. I didn't have any siblings, which was a good thing when you think about it. I mean, my mum couldn't even look after one child, never mind another. But if I ever had the chance to pick a big brother, the one I'd choose would be Ivan. He's also my best friend and the person I trust more than anyone in this world to take care of Lily if anything should happen to me.

I leaned into Ivan's side and let him pull me into a hug. Tears welled in my eyes, but I didn't let them fall. Instead, I breathed in the powerful, masculine scent of my protector for a few seconds, enjoying the smell of the expensive cologne I'd bought him for his birthday from a boutique in Paris.

Kolya had whisked me away for dinner and a shopping spree in April, and I knew when I first smelled the cologne it was meant for Ivan. He'd worn it every day since and had even repurchased it. Nan loved it too, and had ordered some for Jack, though it didn't smell the same on him.

Some people can just own a scent. They make it theirs. Their body takes possession of each individual component inside the bottle and says, "this is me". I used to sleep with Kolya's suit jackets every night because they smelled just like him. I thought it was just because of his usual cologne, so when the scent began to fade as the weeks went by after his death, I picked up the bottle and gave the jackets a good spritzing, but it was never the same. He'd not worn them, so his body hadn't had the chance to do its thing and make the fragrance personal to him. Despite already knowing he was dead, I'd cried buckets when I realised I wouldn't get that back. That living, breathing scent of him.

Even though the pool was heated, the cool breeze and overcast sky made the water much colder than I'd antici-pated, but at least it shook me out of my melancholy when Lily cupped her hand into the water and splashed me and Ivan. Before we could retaliate, Luca yelled something from the upper sun terrace in front of the kitchen.

"Your food is ready," Paolo translated.

"Thank God for that," Ivan said as he got up from the side of the pool. He helped Lily and me stand, then picked her up. Instead of drying her feet, he strode towards the steps that would take him to the upper sun terrace in front of the kitchen.

"Ivan, wait, you haven't dried her feet," I remarked while running along quickly to catch up with them. The gun in my bag thudded against my side with every step I took, but I didn't feel confident enough in my strange yet beautiful surroundings to store the weapon elsewhere.

He looked at me as if I'd grown another head. "Tess, I am desperately hungry. I haven't eaten anything substantial since this morning. Tanner is already up there, and you know how much he eats. It won't harm us if our feet have to air dry, and it's better to have wet feet than to starve to death."

I rolled my eyes at his overdramatic statement. But where Ivan and food were concerned, you couldn't achieve anything good on an empty stomach. He placed Lily in the chair beside James, then took the seat next to her. After grabbing two freshly baked rolls from the basket in front of him, he sliced one in half for Lily and began buttering it.

Luca had cooked a pasta dish with what Paolo said was sardines. I wasn't all that keen on it, but surprisingly, Lily enjoyed it. I ate some of the freshly baked bread and the tossed salad with the tasty dressing.

It seemed so surreal to be sitting on a sun terrace in Sicily, enjoying a meal and wine on a Mafia boss's property. Especially after shooting a family friend who'd betrayed us. But nevertheless, that's what was happening, and I couldn't help but feel like my life was turning into one long, dangerously crazy fairground ride. One where the brakes had broken and it just couldn't stop.

Chapter Thirty-Four

TESS

I awoke to the sound of footsteps hurrying past our bedroom door. Lily was fast asleep in bed beside me, her mouth slightly open as she took in steady, even breaths. I rolled over as gently as I could so as not to disturb her and picked up my phone from the bedside table. A quick press on the home button showed me it was 3.35 a.m., so I'd only been asleep for around forty minutes.

I heard voices echoing through the hallway, but they were speaking so low I couldn't tell who it was or what they were saying.

We weren't expecting anyone else to join us. Lainey, Danny, and Nate had arrived around midnight and had brought most of our luggage from the yacht. Roman's men still had possession of it, but they assured me it would be in the waters around Sicily within the next couple of days.

I heard more footsteps outside our room, and then Ivan called out to James in a whisper loud enough for me to hear.

"What the hell is happening now?" I mumbled to myself.

More movement out in the corridor was enough to shake me out of my bleary-eyed funk.

I crept out of bed as quietly as I could and opened the door of the antique rosewood wardrobe where I'd tucked a gun under the spare blankets on the top shelf. I was only wearing pyjama shorts and a T-shirt, and the room felt much cooler now that I was out of bed.

I slipped on my fluffy fleece robe, and after tying it at the waist, I picked up my gun, making sure it was locked and loaded with a bullet in the chamber before opening the bedroom door.

The underfloor heating was hardly noticeable as I made my way as quietly as possible towards the curved staircase. The tiles were pretty and in keeping with the rest of the decorative byzantine features, but you can't beat the warmth of a carpet underfoot when you've just got out of bed.

The Villa Rosa had eight bedrooms in total: five upstairs and three downstairs. There was also a separate annexe with two bedrooms, two bathrooms and a kitchenette. Along with me and Lily, nearly everyone had claimed one of the spacious and tastefully decorated upstairs bedrooms, each of which had two queen-sized beds and an en-suite bathroom.

Tanner and Carl had both taken a downstairs bedroom, though when Lainey, Danny and Nate had returned, they'd worked out a rota with Ivan so that there were always three of them on guard at all hours.

As expected, Franco and Mark were still at the hospital. Both had undergone surgery earlier and were being monitored overnight. Franco was expecting to be allowed home within twenty-four hours, but Mark would be staying where he was for another couple of days, at least. I'd spoken to both men before I went to bed, so I knew it wouldn't be them who'd arrived at such a late or, to be precise, early hour.

I reached the stairs, and with my back pressed against the textured white wall, I glanced over the bannister rail to the hallway below.

A tall, burly, dark-haired man stood with his back against the door and, at first, I thought it might be another of Signor Russo's men. But a second lingering look took in other features that I recognised. The tattoos creeping past the white collar and cuffs of his shirt, each symbol a story of the man's prison and Bratva journey that continued down onto the fingers holding the Ceska pistol—the gun my husband had given him hell about.

"Feliks?"

Before the first syllable had left my mouth, he had me in the sights of his Ceska. He called out my name and then something in Russian, while only very slowly lowering his weapon, but I didn't understand what he'd said.

Ivan came running into the hallway. "Tess, what the...? It's okay. You can put down the gun, *milaya moya*. It's just Feliks. He brought along an unexpected visitor."

"I know it's Feliks," I replied as I walked down the stairs. I slid the safety into place on my gun and removed the clip, sliding both items into the pocket of my robe. I was on first-name terms with Feliks, but we'd never shared more than polite conversation. He was part of Roman's personal guard detail, so I'd only ever seen him when we'd visited my father-in-law. But I was so happy to see someone I knew and trusted that when I reached the bottom of the stairs, I threw my arms around him.

"I'm so glad you are here," I told him. "I'm sorry I pointed my gun at you. I heard people rushing around and

347

then voices down here. After the day we've had, I didn't want to come out unprepared in case...."

At first, Feliks seemed slightly bewildered by the physical contact, but then he relaxed and pulled me into a tight embrace. "It is okay, Tess. All is well. You must never apologise for protecting yourself."

"That's women for you, Feliks. One minute they are pointing a gun at you, the next they demand a hug or diamonds, or both," said a voice I never in a million years expected to hear outside of Moscow.

I let go of Feliks and spun around quickly, coming face-to-face with my father-in-law.

"Roman!"

For the second time that night, I stood on my tiptoes and threw my arms around a man's neck, but this time I never wanted to let go. Roman stroked his hand down the back of my head and twirled a few of my curls between his fingers while I told him how much Lily and I had missed him. I babbled on and on in the hallway about the terrible day we'd had, and how I'd never forget the sight of Yannis clutching at his throat. I hadn't realised I'd been crying until Feliks tapped me on the shoulder and passed me a handkerchief.

Thinking about what James had said on the plane, I tried to regain my composure. "I'm so sorry, Roman. I didn't want to cry again. Now your shirt's all wet and you probably think I'm weak and—"

"*Moya doch'*, I will never think you are weak. You came out here tonight armed and ready to fight, even though you went through a traumatic experience today and must be exhausted." He cupped my cheeks in the palms of his hands and kissed my forehead. "I am honoured that you trusted me enough to help carry the burden of your tears. Sharing them with me means they will not stay on your shoulders and weigh you down. A man should always take away his woman's fears and sadness. My son is not here to do that for you, so I will act on his behalf. But I would do that for you anyway, Tess. You are as much a daughter to me as Yuri is a son."

I nodded my acceptance as more tears fell. Ivan placed his hands on my shoulders, gently massaging out the knots.

"Tess, why don't you go to the bathroom and take a moment to compose yourself? Splash some cold water on your face and take a few deep breaths. Roman can wait in the sitting room while I bring you a brandy in hot water. You need to switch off your thoughts and relax for a while. You haven't been in bed long; that's why I didn't come in and wake you to tell you that Roman was here. But I bet you didn't sleep at all, did you?" he asked.

"I had about forty minutes, I think."

"Do as Ivan says, *milaya moya*, then come and sit by me and James in front of the fire. I only have a matter of hours before I need to be back in Moscow."

"You're not staying?" I questioned, the hurt so clear in the high pitch of my voice. "But you have to stay, Roman. We need you."

"Tess, he shouldn't even be here now. You know that." Ivan shook his head. "Roman took a big risk coming here tonight, but he knew what today had done to you and James, and he wanted to offer you support in person. Yet every minute he spends outside Russia is dangerous—not just from international government agencies, but also from other rival *business* organisations. So you need to make the most of his presence here tonight. Now, go and blow your nose and splash some water on your face. I'll have that hot brandy ready for when you return."

I patted Ivan and Roman on the arm before heading to the bathroom. I didn't trust myself to speak without crying, so I hoped the gesture conveyed my appreciation of them.

After using the toilet, I blew my nose and splashed some water on my face, as Ivan had suggested, but it did little to disguise the blotchy skin and red eyes that my crying bout had caused. So I took a spare hand towel from the rack and ran the cold tap for a few more seconds until the water was as cold as it could possibly get, then I wet a few inches of the towel with it before pressing it over my eyes for a minute. It didn't do much for the redness, but my eyes didn't feel as tired, sore, and puffy. I took a few deep breaths before I opened the door again, trying hard to control the tidal wave of emotions that Roman's presence had released.

Before I joined Roman, Ivan, and James, I went to speak with Feliks, who had since acquired a chair and was sitting between the bottom of the stairs and the front door. He stood as soon as he saw me approach.

"Feliks, I doubt Lily will wake up because she was still up playing until late, but if you think you hear her, will you let me know? She's not used to being here yet, so I don't want her to wake up and think she's all alone."

"Do not worry, Tess. Ivan and Roman have already checked on her. They left the light on beside the bed and the door semi-open so I can hear her," he said. "I will come and get you if I hear even the slightest noise. Though I have to say, I am tempted to make that noise so I can see *moya printsessa*," he said with a mischievous grin.

I smiled and shook my head. "If you knew the trouble I'd had getting her to stop talking and go to sleep tonight, you wouldn't be saying that."

Yuri once said that Roman had more bodyguards than

Putin, and though I found that hard to believe, he rarely went anywhere in Moscow without at least six or seven.

Feliks, Oleg and Dima were Roman's main three guards. They're also the only ones who can speak English, or choose to, anyway.

Feliks and Oleg are both in their early forties, and from what Kolya had told me, had been in Roman's employ since they were teenagers. Lily adores them. They spoil her completely, bringing her sweets and other gifts whenever we visit. They call her their little printsessa, which she loves.

Dima is completely different. He's not as friendly towards us, though neither is he ignorant. He prefers to keep things more professional, I suppose. He doesn't have tattoos and that Mafia bad-guy appearance like Feliks and Oleg, but that doesn't make him any less menacing. Dima is ex-Spetsnaz: a Russian special forces, survivalist, fighting machine. He's also the one who usually coordinates all Roman's personal security, but after what happened to Kolya, Roman had him hunting down Riass and his men.

Dima appears to be in his early thirties, and though there's no denying he's jaw-droppingly gorgeous, gazing into his beautiful hazel eyes leaves you feeling cold and... I don't know. Hunted, almost. He certainly has that predatory look about him. If anyone could hunt down Riass—out of all the people we had out there trying to find him—it would probably be Dima.

Ivan handed me the cup of warm brandy as soon as I entered the sitting room. Roman and James were sitting together on a sofa in front of the roaring fire. A couple of logs had been added since I'd gone up to bed, and the room was so much warmer than it had been. The beautiful view over the pool and gardens was hidden behind tapestry-style drapes in rich autumnal colours. I presumed Roman had requested the drapes be closed to hide his presence. Like Ivan had stated, he'd taken a big risk travelling to Sicily. I knew our people were trustworthy, but I still wasn't sure about Russo's men.

James glanced up at me and gave me a sad smile. He was wearing the same shirt and jeans from earlier, but they were both slightly creased, and I wondered if he'd slept in them. After combing his fingers through his messy dark hair, he finished off whatever was in his glass, then tilted his head back against the cushion and closed his eyes.

James had had enough to drink before he'd gone to bed, so I hoped he wouldn't have any more or he'd have the hangover from hell. He was also quite an argumentative drunk, though by the looks of it, he'd already gone past that stage.

"Come, Tess, sit with me and James. There is much we have to discuss, and I have so little time to spend with you before I leave. I need to be on the plane by eight a.m., but I would like to have breakfast with my granddaughter before I go."

"She will love that, Roman," I told him as I sat down beside him. "But she won't understand why you have to leave."

"Do not worry. I will think of something to tell her that she will accept without question."

We sat back in silence, and I took a small sip of brandy, enjoying the warm, mellow feel as it slipped down my throat. After taking another sip, I set the cup on the table, then took the gun and magazine clip out of the pocket of my robe. I placed them both beside the cup, then snuggled into Roman's side. He whispered something in Russian, put his arm around me and sighed.

Neither James nor Roman said anything about the gun.

Nor did Ivan, though he did look a little sad. I knew he'd rather I had nothing to do with guns, but without all my training and experience, some of us might not be here right now.

I wouldn't normally act so familiarly with my father-in-law. Yes, we'd hug and kiss each other on the cheek whenever we arrived in Moscow or as we were leaving, but I'd never once sat and cuddled up to him. Yet nothing about it felt wrong or out of place to me. If anything, it gave me a great sense of relief.

I trusted Roman to keep Lily safe, just like I'd trusted my husband. And I needed that trust and belief so badly. I needed it to cancel out the worry and fear that one day I wouldn't be enough to keep the bad guys at bay.

Roman Barinov radiated power, and though I knew that power came from a place of darkness and fear, I also knew he'd do his best to keep all that away from Lily. And as the saying goes, better the devil you know than the devil you don't.

"Ivan, would you mind bringing my grandson a strong coffee and possibly a sandwich? I have something I would like to discuss with you all, and I have a feeling he will soon be asleep."

"Not my fault you turn up in the middle of the night without warning," James mumbled.

"You know why I did so, James. No one can know when or if I ever leave Russia. It's too risky," Roman reasoned.

"Not even your own fucking grandson? Really? Give me a break," James replied angrily.

"James," Ivan cautioned.

"Yes, listen to your cousin, James. Just because you are drunk, it does not give you the right to disrespect me," Roman declared.

I pulled out from under his arm and turned on the sofa to face them, shocked by the anger and hurt plainly evident in James's tortured expression. He pointed a finger at his grandfather.

"I'll show you some respect when you do the same for me. You treat me like a child—like you get to dictate everything about my life because my dad's no longer around. Well, I've got news for you, Roman. My dad hasn't been doing that for years, not even with KOLCAT. And I get that, because of who you are, you have to be secretive about"—James pushed up from the sofa and threw his hands in the air—"all that fucking Mafia shit, and quite frankly, I don't want to know about any of that. But, for fuck's sake, I'm your grandson. Don't you trust me? Is that it?"

Roman was about to answer, but James was on a roll and cut him off before he could even get a word out.

"Do you realise what keeping secrets nearly did to this family today? We ended up in a shoot-out at a fucking airport. Franco took a bullet while saving my life, and Mark was hit while protecting Tess. If she hadn't taken that shot, then who knows how many of us you'd have had to bury? That deceitful bastard lied to our faces for years, and if it wasn't for Adrianna, we would have never known. He was planning to end my life before today. Did you know that, Roman? I should have died that day at the house, along with Ivan and Franco. He even had his fucking guard working undercover for him. By the way, I want that bastard found and fucking tortured for as long as possible before he dies. That man deserves to suffer the worst death possible, and I want to be the one who kills him, so don't get any ideas."

"Very well. When he is found, I will send for you. You

can be the one to end him, if that's what you want. But you have to be sure it's something you can live with, because once you've taken a life, there's no going back. It will change you, James. You need to be prepared for that," Roman said. His voice sounded deceptively calm, but I noticed his hand shaking when he reached out to take the glass of neat brandy Ivan handed him.

"I have changed. We all have. Since my dad was…" James grabbed hold of his hair and made a strangled cry through gritted teeth. "When will it end?"

My heart broke a little further to see James suffering so much. I got up from the sofa to comfort him, but Ivan beat me to it. James tried to push him away, though Ivan was having none of it. He wrapped his big burly arms around him in a bear hug and wouldn't let him go. James didn't cry, but he was shaking. I followed Ivan's lead and stood behind James, hugging him as tightly as I could. I chanced a look at Roman, half expecting him to join in, but all he did was stare into the bottom of his brandy glass.

How could he comfort me and not James? He was his grandson, his own flesh and blood.

"Come on, let's get you that coffee and something to eat. I think there might be some of that nice bread left that Luca made. Do you want anything, Roman?" I asked.

"Give me a few minutes, and I'll follow you to the kitchen," he replied before knocking back the rest of his brandy.

I glanced up at Ivan, who held my gaze for a moment. He gave a quick nod before letting go of James. With unspoken words, he'd let me know he'd stay with Roman and try to smooth things out with him.

To be honest, James had taken us both by surprise. I'd never known him speak to anyone that way before, never mind his grandfather. And what was the deal with James calling him Roman? If I were Roman, I'd be angry about that too.

The kitchen was much cooler than the sitting room, having no fire to keep up the warmth, though the heating through the tiles helped a little in the smaller room. The coffee was instant, but I didn't think that mattered to James. I avoided mentioning the argument with his grandfather because I didn't want him to become defensive, but I hoped they could both get past it in the few hours that Roman had left with us.

I'd picked up my gun and its magazine clip before I left the sitting room and, being too heavy and bulky to carry around in my robe, they now sat beside the kettle and sugar pot.

"I wish you didn't feel the need to carry that around," James said.

"I only picked it up because I heard Ivan wake you and knew something was going on down here. After… you know"—I waved my hand in circles—"I just needed to be sure nothing bad was happening," I told him truthfully.

"That's exactly what I was trying to say in there. If he'd told us he was coming, I wouldn't have hit the bottle so hard —something I only did so I could guarantee I'd fall asleep —and you wouldn't have freaked and come out armed and ready for action. When I told him all that before you came down, he just patted me on the shoulder and laughed. Like it was nothing. I'm not having that, Tess. He sorted out a place for us to stay and sent us here, and we had to trust him with that, so surely he can trust us in return?"

My heart sank when I looked up and noticed Roman standing in the doorway.

"I do trust you, James. But this is something that was

decided just a few hours ago between me and Gianni. He has his people out looking for anyone suspicious, not just from Riass, but from the agencies who know you are here, too. Do not think for one minute that the CIA and MI5 do not have the itinerary of every flight that you and the KOLCAT jet make. If Gianni had eyes on anyone in the area, I wouldn't have left the plane tonight. I wasn't trying to keep secrets from you; I was trying not to disappoint you, but it seems I have done so anyway."

Roman came to the table and sat beside James. I handed him a coffee made with a touch of milk and half a sugar, just the way he likes it, then I took out the rest of the homemade bread. Ivan set butter and cheese beside the bread and pulled out a chair for me.

While Roman told us about the plan he'd made with Signor Russo, I began slicing the bread.

Now, there's a reason why Nan and Kolya never let me slice an uncut loaf of bread, and that reason was obvious when the first slice came out like a thick wedge. Roman took the knife from me and proceeded to cut perfect slices from the opposite end of the loaf, while Ivan buttered the wedge I'd cut and ate that. I hadn't much of an appetite, but it pleased me to see Roman and James tucking into their sandwiches without arguing.

I asked Roman what he wanted to talk to us about, but he said it could wait until we'd eaten, which made me a little anxious. Thankfully, as all the men ate quickly, I didn't have to wait very long.

"Dimitri—the man you met at the airport—had already pre-arranged for there to be no airport staff around from just after James had landed until you were almost ready to take off again."

357

"How did he manage that?" I asked. "I thought he'd only just got there."

Roman's half-smile became more of a smirk. "Dimitri has ways and means of getting things done. I do not ask, nor does he volunteer the information. I just reward him substantially for a job well done.

"We could not be sure that Yannis did not have people on his payroll, and we thought it best that we bring him to the airport once you had left. I thought you could call him and say I had suddenly taken ill, so you were flying out to Russia to visit me and wanted his support, or at least to see him before you left. When he took the bait, Dimitri was going to kidnap him and bring him to Moscow so I could interrogate him for information on my son's captors before I took his life. But fate had other ideas about how Yannis Markos would meet his end." Roman rubbed the back of my hand and looked at me with both pride and adoration before he carried on speaking.

"As you know, my men flew the bodies of Yannis and his guards back to the yacht." He took a sip of his coffee, then continued. "They met with some of your people and discussed the islands and tides with the crew. The yacht sailed into Kefalonia so that your guards could leave, and also to allow for some of the crew to go ashore for the night. Then they went back out to sea to where the yacht was still visible from the harbour. As soon as it was dark, my men put the bodies of Yannis and his guards in the two motorised dinghies, then made their way to a secluded cove in an uninhabited part of the coastline. The bodies, along with the guns that each of the dead men carried, have been placed underwater in a rocky area, where there is no chance of them being dragged out to sea when the tide goes out. My men shot bullets at random around the nearby rocks to make it appear more of a shootout than a targeted setup. Those bullets were all from the guns used to kill Yannis Markos and his guards, and he will have enough bagged cocaine on him to arouse suspicion that this could have been a drug drop gone wrong."

Roman said all this so calmly, as though he was reading out tomorrow's weather forecast, not a staged murder scene.

"I have photographs if you care to see them," he added as he pulled his phone from his pocket. James went to take a look.

"No!" I cried out in absolute horror. My chair scraped against the tiled floor as I pushed away from the table. I'd seen enough death today; I couldn't bear to witness that macabre scene.

Ivan gripped my arm and pulled me against him. He barked out something in Russian to his uncle, then said, "You can do whatever you want, James, but she's been traumatised enough."

Roman called out to Ivan, but he ignored him and walked me back through to the sitting room.

"Are you cold?" he asked. I shook my head, but he grabbed a soft chenille throw from one of the sofas and wrapped it around me anyway. "Then let's go outside for a while and leave them to it. We knew something had to happen to their bodies, but we don't have to see it."

Ivan pulled back the curtain and opened the glazed doors wide enough for us to slip outside into the cold, dark night. We made our way down to the sun loungers in silence. Being barefoot, I was grateful for the pretty poolside lighting that showed the way down the stone steps, enabling me to tread carefully.

Ivan pushed two of the loungers together and lay down beside me. He took out his phone and swiped through his contacts until he reached Kolya's brother, Yuri. He glanced back up the steps and around the pool at the guards while he waited for Yuri to answer. At first, he spoke to him in Russian, but then he grabbed my hand and switched over to English so I could understand.

"Tess is outside with me, but James is in the villa with your father. I'm worried about him, Yuri. He was drunk before your father arrived, and we all know that James does not handle his alcohol well. I didn't want to leave them alone together, but Roman was about to show something... Tess couldn't have dealt with that, and I doubt it will do James any good. But he's angry right now, and he's looking to channel that anger. I don't want your father taking advantage of that," Ivan said in hushed tones.

I couldn't hear Yuri's reply, but whatever it was, Ivan was in full agreement. He also said they could discuss the other matter when he arrived. What the other matter was, I had no idea, but I allowed myself a smile when I knew that Yuri would be visiting us.

As soon as Ivan ended the call, I asked, "When is he coming?"

"A day or two before Christmas, but he'll probably stay until New Year's Eve. He'll let us know later in the week." Ivan turned to look at me. "That's brought a smile to your face."

"I always enjoy spending time with Yuri. He's a good man," I said.

"He's the best of men, Tess. Despite what he is, what he's had to become because of his birthright, his heart is still good. He has sacrificed so much in his life. I hope the next one is kinder to him."

"Why are you so worried that Roman will take advantage of James?" I questioned. "He's his grandfather, Ivan. He loves him."

"I don't doubt that. But he's also a cruel and manipulative man who will use a person's weakness to his own advantage. What Roman has always wanted is his family by his side—his blood family. His sons, grandchildren, and you, it seems. All part of the Barinov Bratva."

"Kolya never wanted that," I murmured.

"There was a reason he distanced himself and his family from Roman. He wanted to keep you all as far away from Bratva life as possible. He seemed to soften towards his father after Aleksei... Maybe because of his own grief or his father's age, who knows? But he would never let his son be influenced by Roman. This I know!"

Ivan slapped his hand down hard on the small drinks table beside the lounger, causing it to flip over onto its side.

"I know you're angry, Ivan. But I'm happy to see Roman. And I'm glad he sent his men to the airport. If this works—you know, the staged scene with Yannis—then at least we don't have to worry about me and Carl going to prison for shooting him and his guards. I'd sooner die myself than be taken away from Lily."

"Don't let me hear you talk like that, Tess. You must always do everything you can to live, no matter what. Some women don't get that choice. My mother didn't. Kolya's mother, too. And you don't have to worry about Roman's plan not working. He has a habit of getting away with leaving people facedown in water," Ivan said bitterly.

I sat up and faced him. "I'm so sorry, Ivan. I didn't mean to be insensitive. I know how hard both your mum and Kolya's fought against breast cancer. You were so young when she passed away. You must have been devastated."

Ivan nodded.

Something occurred to me then. Ivan had just said that Roman had a habit of leaving people facedown in water, and I remembered Kolya telling me he thought Roman had Ivan's father killed and dumped in the Moskva River.

"Kolya once told me he suspected Roman had something to do with your dad being murdered. I'm sorry if this brings all that back for you," I said with utmost sincerity.

Ivan shook his head. "My father wasn't a good man. He was a terrible husband who had been violent with my mother on more than one occasion. I was so relieved when they divorced, although the process was messy and lasted for quite a while. My grandfather had considerable wealth and took care of his daughters financially. My father wanted the lion's share of my mother's money, though her lawyers ensured he got nowhere near as much as he requested. He'd had very little to do with me, but when my mother passed away, he tried to get custody and failed.

"I went to live with Kolya's mother and father, but then my aunt died and my grandfather not long afterwards, and my father tried to get custody of me again. He knew I stood to inherit a sizeable portion of my grandfather's estate. He hired lawyers and went to the press about how he was trying to get me away from my *Bratva uncle*, so I could live a better life instead of one full of crime and death.

"A few days later, photographs of him taking drugs and visiting prostitutes were delivered to the press. Anonymously, of course. Then he went missing. Some of his colleagues said it was unusual for him, while others—no doubt paid by Roman—said he would often go missing after going on a drug-and-alcohol-fuelled binge. He was found a few days later, floating facedown in the river. I don't mourn him, Tess. I just... I'm wary, that's all. As I've said, I know my father wasn't a good man, but neither is the man who had him killed. I know he treats you well right now. He adores you, anyone can see that. You have no family, so you eagerly accept his and make it your own. You gave him a grandchild, which puts you on a very high pedestal. You saved his son's life, and now the lives of both his grandchildren. No wonder there is such awe in his eyes when he looks at you. But the thing is, that pedestal is unsafe now that Kolya's not here. Time, along with what he deems is unsuitable behaviour, will stop him thinking of you as a Barinov. You have a quick and often wicked temper, which he has indulged in the past few weeks due to your grieving, but how long will that last? I remember how sweet he was with Talia at first, and look how he was with her in the end."

"I get what you're saying, Ivan, but we seem to be relying on Roman and his contacts right now. I want to go back to the UK, but Kevin says it isn't safe at the moment. If the country's security services could get their heads out of their arses and stop worrying about being brought up on human rights charges by radicalised wannabes claiming they're innocent, they could raid the rest of those suspected cells with known links to Riass, and we could all go to Glengarran."

Ivan was quiet for a moment, and I thought he might try to talk me into going back to Oxford, but instead, his words were a little cryptic.

"What if I could offer you another option?" he whispered. "A chance for you and Lily to leave this life behind and make a new start? I know I could make it happen, but would you be willing to do that, Tess?"

"Just me and Lily? That's a pipe dream, Ivan. I have responsibilities in the UK. People I love. I couldn't leave Nan and Jean, Sarah's Legacy, and you and James, of course. I can't just up and run away anymore. I have a family now, and they need me."

"You'd still see me, Tess, just not as often. And trust me. You wouldn't be without family."

Before I could question him about it, the doors to the villa opened, and Roman shouted, "Ivan, Tess, come back inside and sit by the fire. You'll catch a cold out there."

Ivan pushed himself up from the sun lounger and held out his hand. He pulled me upright and carefully adjusted the blanket around my shoulders before we made our way inside. As he did so, he whispered, "Say nothing to Roman about what I've just suggested, or I'll be the next one lying facedown in water."

James sat on the sofa with his head tilted back and his mouth open. He was snoring loudly, and it took Ivan a few tries to wake him. He kept insisting he was fine and wanted to stay up with his grandfather, but in the end, he knew he wouldn't last until Roman left. He hugged Roman, then me, then Ivan, leaning heavily on us as he did so, and then he made his way to the stairs, grabbing onto the furniture as he went. The coffee and sandwich had done little to quell the effects of all the alcohol he'd imbibed, as evidenced by his increasingly unsteady gait. Ivan followed him, not trusting he'd be able to manage the stairs by himself.

"He'll have a hell of a hangover in the morning," I said to Roman as we watched them leave.

"You would think so, especially after seeing him like that. But my Yuri... I've seen him far worse, and yet he wakes up the next morning as if he'd never touched a drop." Roman shrugged his shoulders but continued to stare out into the hallway, as though he wanted to follow his grandson.

"Why don't you go and check on him?" I suggested.

Roman shook his head, then gestured toward the sofa for me to sit. "Ivan will see that he gets to his bed safely, and now I have you all to myself for a change. Tell me, my darling Tess, is there anything that you and Lily need to make you feel more settled here?"

I looked around the tastefully decorated yet comfortable room and shook my head. "I'll need a Christmas tree and decorations, but I'll get Kevin to send ours over. I want Lily to have as many familiar things as possible surrounding her this year. We can't stay here forever, obviously, but we also don't want to go back home after what happened there. Lily wants to be in England, but she's scared. So I think it's best if I start looking for a new home and I'd like that to be in the North of England. Possibly Yorkshire, so I can be near Jean and the main office of Sarah's Legacy."

Roman sighed and gave me a sad smile. "I can understand why you feel you have to do this, and while I am hoping that my son is still alive, I realise that as time moves on, this will be unlikely, if it ever even was. I just… how can I say this without sounding harsh?" He paused for a moment, then said, "By leaving your home, it feels as though you are moving on from my son and the life you shared."

I shook my head and closed my eyes, determined not to cry again.

"I am moving on, Roman, but not from Kolya. I'll never move on from him. What I want is to move me and Lily away from bad memories—from the fear of being attacked in our home. But forgetting all that, let's think about some of the memories that home will always hold. Memories of

Yannis's visits and his sly, pathetic guard waltzing around the place in the guise of protecting us. It will never be the same for me now. No matter how many good times I had there, it will still be the place where all that happened. The place where I watched that terrorist display my husband's and guards' bodies like rubbish on a heap. There's no chance I'm going back there to stay for more than a day, Roman. None at all."

"I can understand that. You are a wonderful mother, Tess. I do not like to think of Lily being frightened. When I saw what happened that day when those mercenaries came I—"

"She'll never forget that, Roman, and who can blame her? James wants to keep the place for himself, but he's going to keep the old manor section as his home—like it used to be when his mum was alive—and the guards will stay in the extension. Maybe in time, Lily will want us to stay overnight there with James, but I'm not sure she can do that yet."

Roman's phone alerted him to an incoming message. He glanced down and then announced, "Gianni is on his way here. We can leave Lily asleep for another thirty minutes or so, unless he says it's unsafe for me to be here."

"You trust him that much?" I asked.

"I wouldn't have sent the most important people in my world to him if I didn't," he replied. "We have a long history, Tess. Back when I wasn't such a wanted man, I spent time setting up some businesses in New York. The Italians ran the docks and most of the boroughs and neigh-bourhoods, especially around New Jersey; the Irish muscled in wherever they could, and the gangs from the Bronx had their own thing happening. But we came in with enough money, guns, and *products* to take over from just about everyone. Of course, what we didn't have were contacts at the ready and a way to distribute those products, so it made sense to enter into a business arrangement with whoever held the most power, which was by far the Russo family.

"Vincente Russo was the boss back then. He was a good businessman. Ruthless when needed, yet he knew a good deal when he saw one. Some of the other families were unhappy about working with Russians, but he convinced them it was in their best interests financially. And it was. Apart from the odd disagreement here and there, we co-existed somewhat peacefully with most of the New York bosses, and the Russo-Barinov partnership was extremely profitable. I always preferred Gianni to his brother. He was a family man. Loyal to his wife and good to his men. Vincente thought himself a playboy. He had many mistresses and had a temper that grew quicker as his drinking grew heavier.

"The Russo organisation had invested in plenty of legitimate businesses over the years, so they were able to stay under the FBI's radar when they made their big sweep of all the New York crime families in the early eighties. The authorities knew who and what they were, of course, but they couldn't get enough on them to take them down.

"Some of the other families questioned why the Russo organisation were the only ones not having their lives ripped apart by the Feds. They accused the brothers of feeding the FBI information about the other families so they could get rid of them and take over New Jersey and the other boroughs completely. Then in 1984, there was an assassination attempt on Vincente while he and his family were out celebrating his wife's birthday. His son was killed at the scene and Vincente took a bullet to the chest and died before he reached the hospital. His wife and daughter were unharmed. Within minutes of that happening, Gianni was also targeted while he did a deal by the docks, but he was saved by one of his capos.

"At this point, Gianni did not know who he could trust. After all, though many people knew where Vincente would be dining, no one outside the Russo organisation knew where Gianni would be. He couldn't rely on the other Italian crime families after they'd accused them of giving information to the FBI, so he contacted the only other person he trusted could help take his wife and children—along with Vincente's wife and daughter—to a place of safety. I was only too happy to offer my assistance. I had my man in New York collect them and fly them to Cyprus, where I picked them up and took them to a villa I owned. They stayed there under guard for three months until Gianni found out who in their organisation betrayed them and ordered the hits on him and his brother.

"When it was safe to do so, I escorted Gianni's and Vincente's wives and children over to Sicily to stay with their relatives. I also provided extra guards for Gianni so he could remain in New York and bring stability to the Russo organisation. The stronghold the Italian crime families had over New Jersey and New York imploded. They all seemed to be at war with one another. It was the worst thing they could have done, but it wasn't so bad for us.

"The FBI were all over it, and for Gianni, it wasn't worth the risk to remain in the US. That's not to say he doesn't still have business there. He just runs it from a place where the air is much cleaner, and an abundance of citrus fruits hang heavy on the trees."

"You sound as though you envy me, my old friend," Signor Russo interrupted. I'd been so engrossed in Roman's tale from the past, I'd not heard him enter the villa.

"I certainly envy the weather you have here. It was snowing when I left Moscow," Roman replied.

Signor Russo strolled into the room, heading straight for the bar, where he poured himself a cognac. He still wore the same suit from earlier, though he'd added a navy cashmere sweater.

"I can add to your story, Roman. I'm sure that your daughter-in-law will be interested in hearing this specific detail," he teased as he sat on the sofa across from me.

Roman looked at him curiously, waving his hand in a gesture that said, *"go ahead"*.

"The night my brother and nephew were killed, I was down at the docks with Tony, one of our Jersey capos, and two of his soldiers, Gio and Paulie. I'd bought in Benny and Joey V to drive the delivery truck back to a hidden location. We loaded them up and sent them on their way with a shipment that was normally brought in on a Friday or Sunday night. Due to the FBI sniffing around—as well as my brother not trusting that anyone wouldn't rat us out—we'd swapped the days and times of our regular shipments and drops in our less-than-legal operations." Signor Russo raised his eyebrows a couple of times and his face broke into a smile that made him appear so much younger.

"Tony said something didn't feel right, so we were a little more cautious. But everything went as smoothly as it usually did, right up until we were getting back to the car.

"They appeared out of nowhere. Two black SUVs came right at us. I hadn't enough time to draw my weapon when the first round of bullets came at us. Gio, who was about to get in the door on the driver's side, was hit in the arm and belly. I dropped to the ground, attempting to crawl towards the passenger door, but the second SUV came screeching my way. Tony, Paulie, and I opened fire on them, and a few shots hit home, blowing out a couple of windows. But they had semi-automatic rifles, and when they began firing back, I knew we were done for. I raised my gun and carried on shooting, thinking that if I was going to die tonight, I'd take a few of those bastards with me. Dirt and gravel hit me in the face as each shot pierced the ground around me, and I thought the next thing to hit me would be a bullet. But I was wrong. Tony dove on me, covering as much of my body with his as he could. I tried to shrug him off but he told me to stay down. I yelled out to him, *'Tony, no!'* but it was already too late to get any kind of sense into him. I felt his body jerk with every slug that hit him. I still feel it some-times, even now, and I also hear the sickening sound each bullet made as it sank into his flesh through the leather jacket he always wore. Thut-thut-thut. Thirty-four years later, and I still wake up in a cold sweat thinking about that night."

Signor Russo took a swig of his cognac before contin-uing with his story.

"The SUVs began pulling away, but I could still hear gunfire. Turns out that the men from the boat had joined in the fight but it was too late for two of my guys, and it would have been for me if not for my good friend and capo, Tony Franconni."

Signor Russo paused for a moment while the name registered in my tired brain, then he nodded and said, "I went to the hospital to see your injured guard, Anthony Franconni. We had a long talk, he and I. He knew who I was, and let's just say he wasn't all that pleased to see me."

"I will speak to the injured men tomorrow, Tess," Roman interrupted. "They saved the lives of my family, so I owe them a debt. I will also pay for all their medical care."

Before I could inform him that I'd be taking care of all

that, Signor Russo insisted, "In the case of Anthony Fran-conni, that will not be necessary. I will see that he has every-thing he needs, amongst other things. It's the least I can do for Tony's boy. You see, the police were already on their way to the docks by the time the men from the boat came to our aid, and there wasn't time to move the bodies of our men. Gio survived the attack, but he was in a bad way for a long time. As Roman says, he flew my family and Vincente's wife and daughter over to Cyprus, where he could keep them safe. But we didn't have the means to get all the men who worked for us and their families hidden away.

"The Feds began investigating us more thoroughly. They knew they had just cause by now, what with Vincente and his son being assassinated, as well as two of his employees found dead at the docks and another in hospital. They went through not just my and my brother's accounts and most of our assets, but also the accounts of Gio, Tony, and Paulie.

"Now, normally, we would send regular payments to the families of our dead and injured men, but as I've said, the funds we could access were limited during that time. I was able to send enough to pay for Tony's and Paulie's funerals and to get the families through the next few months, but we could do little else but offer small handouts until we got access to our accounts again, which took over two years.

"The FBI did a real number on Tony's family. As well as seizing their bank accounts, they raided their home in broad daylight and didn't seem to care that the press was photographing all of it. In the end, they had to leave their house and move into an apartment. Their old place was fairly big and had been in a nice neighbourhood, but they couldn't afford the mortgage without Tony's income, and they could hardly declare the small reparation we sent them.

"I remember building a wooden fort with Tony in his backyard. It had a Tarzan swing and a slide, and it took us almost twelve hours to put it together, even with the instructions. He was a good father to his kids. His wife, Maria, worked two jobs to give them a good life after he was killed, and I vowed to change everything for them as soon as we got back to being operational without the Feds on our backs. The thing was, when that time finally came, Maria wouldn't accept my help. I was in Sicily by then, but like Roman, I had a representative in New York to run the Russo organisation for me. He went to see Maria on my order and tried to convince her to take the money I offered, even if she just saved it to pay for her kids' college education, but she still wouldn't accept it. She said she didn't want her kids' lives tainted by or beholden to the Mafia in any way. I tried to call and tell her that wouldn't be the case, but she refused to speak to me. I found Tony's daughter a few years ago. She's married now and lives in a nice neighbourhood. She swore like a sailor when I said I owed her a debt and tried to offer financial help. Couldn't kick me off her porch fast enough and wouldn't tell me where her brother was. So for all these years, I've had to live with the knowledge that I never helped the family of the man who gave up his life so I could live mine."

Signor Russo closed his eyes and took a deep breath in. After letting it out slowly, he added, "When I heard you say your guard's name, I did wonder if it could be Tony's son. You weren't very forthcoming when I asked for information, and I couldn't rest until I found out for sure if fate had finally given me a way to thank my brave capo for what he did that night."

Roman got up from beside me and walked across to his friend. He opened his mouth as though he was about to say something, but no words passed his lips. Instead, he patted Gianni Russo on the shoulder and left the room.

Though the story Signor Russo told about Franco's father was sad enough to bring tears to my eyes, witnessing the touching moment between the two ageing Mafia bosses certainly brought a lump to my throat. I don't think I'd ever seen Roman show that much compassion for anyone who wasn't family. And even with family, those moments were undoubtedly on the rare side.

I coughed a little and made a "hmmm" sound to try and clear my throat, then said, "I'm sorry you've been living with so much guilt for all these years, but Franco is a very proud man, and he might not accept any financial help from you. It's written in each of our guards' contracts that we pay for medical procedures and follow-up care while we employ them."

Signor Russo smiled. "You are right, Mrs Barinov. He is a proud man, just like his father. He slung a few insults my way, though many of them were undeserved. I think his mother's words are written too deep in here and here," he said, tapping his index finger on top of his head, then on his chest above his heart, "so he won't listen to anyone else. But even proud men have their weaknesses."

"Weakness? Franco? Never!"

I was about to rip into Signor Russo for harassing Franco when he'd just come out of surgery, but he pointed right at me and said, "It's you, Mrs Barinov. You are his weakness. You and your daughter."

I shook my head, about to deny his claim, but he cut me off with, "The nurse came in and adjusted his pain medication. She told him he might start to feel drowsy. So before he fell asleep, I asked him to let me know one thing I could do for him, and then I swore I would leave him alone for tonight. The medication hit him pretty quickly; you could see it happen. I placed my hand over his in reassurance, letting him know I was still there. I expected him to be asleep in seconds, so I was surprised when he grasped my hand tightly. *Just keep Tess and Lily safe for me; that's all I need from you,*' he said, then he let go of my hand and closed his eyes."

Signor Russo placed his glass on the side table, then leaned forward, resting his hands on his knees, thumbs together. His smile turned to more of a smirk, and I didn't like where this was going.

"Signor Russo, as well as being employed as my body-guard, Franco is a very dear friend to me. I'm not surprised he asked you to keep me and Lily safe, especially after what he did for us. It's the kind of shared experience you can never forget."

That caught his attention. With an eyebrow raised, he asked, "What did he do for you?"

"He helped deliver Lily. There had been a terrorist attack in London the day I went into labour. The streets were cut off around the hospital, so they couldn't get staff out or patients in. Ivan and Franco helped me through all of it, though it was only Franco down at what Rashid called *the business end,*" I said, pointing downwards. "My husband arrived just minutes before Lily did, and he was so grateful for what Franco had done for us. So you see, Signor Russo, you're not the only one who feels they owe him something. He means a lot to me. All our guards do. I told you earlier that I had no family until I met my husband, so the guards and the rest of his staff became my family. I love them all. That's why I wouldn't get on that plane today until I'd shot the man who was trying to kill Franco and James. Everyone was shouting at me to get to safety, but I couldn't leave them exposed like that. It's what we do for the people we love. For family. We protect them, don't we? It's what Franco's father did for you and what Franco's asking you to do for him. That's not a weakness, Signor Russo. It's loyalty. A quality that men like you should value."

Signor Russo stared at me. A studious expression had replaced the condescending smirk.

"I think you and I are going to be friends, Mrs Barinov," he said as he nodded slowly. "Tony's boy has done well for himself. You are fierce yet devoted to the ones you care for. Both are good traits, but when you open your heart to so many, the second can often leave you blind to what's going on around you."

"Like with Yannis? Oh, believe me, I've learned my lesson the hard way where caring for snakes like him are concerned," I retorted, still annoyed that he'd mentioned Franco again.

"Not just him," Russo clarified. "Think about everyone else in your circle of friends and acquaintances, including guards and whoever you see as family. A threat could come from anywhere, mia cara, and anyone can be bought; remember that."

"I can assure you, the close protection team who currently guard us are as loyal as they come," I declared. "I have no doubts about any of them."

"That's good to hear, Mrs Barinov. It will make my debt to Roman easier to deliver on. But I want you to promise me; the second you feel in your gut that something isn't right, you call me."

"What if my gut is wrong?" I replied.

Signor Russo smiled. "I see in you what Roman sees.

You fit well into this life of ours, so trust me. If you feel it in your gut, it won't be wrong. Often, your eyes see something that your heart or head could twist to suit its own needs, but your gut," he said, tapping his belly, "will tell you the truth, even if you don't want to hear it."

The sad thing was, Signor Russo was right. I let myself be swayed by Kolya into giving Yannis and Darius the benefit of the doubt, even when my gut told me there was often something not quite right about their recent behaviour.

But I hadn't always felt that way about Yannis, and I'd never once considered he was involved in Kolya's death. So it seemed my gut instincts couldn't always be relied upon.

An irrational thought I'd examined before sprang to mind. One that, had I not been so fraught with anxiety, grief and exhaustion, wouldn't have brought such a sickening wave of baseless self-judgement.

By not acting on my gut instincts, was I partly responsible for Kolya, Lucas, and Jonesy's death?

Next in The Runaway Series

vinci-books.com/therunawayssalvation

A promise kept. A truth revealed. A danger unleashed.

Tess finds refuge in Sicily, where Signor Russo's protection offers a sense of safety. Will tragedy consume her, or can she still find happiness?

Turn the page for a free preview…

The Runaway's Salvation: Chapter One

TESS

The nightmares began the night after Roman left us. At first, I blamed the stress from everything we'd gone through, combined with a lack of sleep from Roman's clandestine after-midnight visit. But sadly, they'd carried on throughout the next few weeks—my yelling and screaming sending waves of terror throughout the entire household.

The first night had been awful Lily had been grumpy all day due to Roman waking her up extra early so he could see her before he left. He'd told her he had to make a special trip to Sicily to collect a part for Santa's sleigh and would deliver it to the North Pole, so he thought he'd visit her along the way. I could tell that Lily didn't believe him, but she was too tired to argue. Still, the extra-early morning left her tired and grouchy with everyone, and she threw a tantrum of epic proportions when a badly hungover James refused to go in the pool with her. I tried to get her to take a nap with me, but she just wouldn't give in to it. So, by the time we went to bed that night, we were both about ready to collapse.

I must have only been asleep a couple of hours when I awoke to find Ivan, James, and Lainey in the room with me and Lily. James had Lily in his arms, trying to stop her crying, while Ivan had my arms pinned to the bed. He'd been yelling my name, trying to wake me, and even through the haze of troubled sleep, I could clearly see the worry in his and Lainey's eyes.

It took twenty minutes of reassuring Lily that I was okay and that I'd only had a bad dream before she finally went back to sleep. Knowing that I'd frightened her made me feel terrible, even more so than the dream did, although that was bad enough.

Lainey had stayed in my room with Lily while I went downstairs with Ivan and James. Danny was already in the kitchen making me a hot chocolate, and Franco came in on his crutches a few minutes later. He'd been discharged from the hospital in the afternoon and should have been resting, but apparently my screams had been loud enough to wake him, even though he was staying downstairs in the annexe. Carl and Tanner were working security and had to convince our new Italian guards that everything was okay.

Danny made me tell everyone about my nightmare, even though I didn't want to. He said that talking about it might help prevent it from happening again. I wish he'd been right.

I'm not quite sure how the first nightmare began, but I recall being at sea in the dark of night. I could feel the sway of the yacht under my bare feet as I padded across the deck, and a slight breeze flipped my ponytail around as we sailed towards a cove lit by moonlight. Kolya was behind me; he stood so close I could smell his cologne and feel his breath on my neck. I smiled and reached out behind me to grab his hand, but when I did so, he laughed. Only…the laugh wasn't Kolya's. It belonged to Yannis. I let go of his hand and ran across the deck, leaping out onto rocks, where I could see bodies lying facedown in a shallow pool. The rocks hurt my bare feet as I made my way over to the macabre scene, but I didn't let the pain stop me. Needing to check it was definitely Yannis, I grabbed his hair and lifted his head, but those lifeless eyes and the deathly pale face belonged to Kolya. It was at this point in my nightmare that I woke up screaming.

Everyone around me on the night of that first night-mare offered me a valid reason for the terrifying event. Ivan blamed Roman for telling us so casually how his men had staged Yannis and his guards' bodies, which made sense given the direction of the dream. James blamed it on the fact that Yannis had been an evil bastard who'd caused his father's death, a sentiment that everyone else around the table was on board with. Franco said it was because I'd been expecting a phone call from the police in Greece about Yannis's sudden demise, but that hadn't happened.

The news had broken in Greece by early afternoon, and I'd been stressing over what I'd say to the police if they contacted me. After all, I'd been staying with him the day before they found him dead. James and I had discussed it and decided I should say that Yannis had asked me to loan him three million euros, and he'd been angry with me when I refused him, so I'd arranged for James to come and collect us and left without Yannis knowing what we were doing.

So again, what Franco said had an element of truth to it. I had been worrying about the police phoning and about what I would say to them, despite going over everything with James.

The only one who didn't bother with reasons or excuses that night was Danny. He told me outright he thought it likely I had PTSD. James asked if he meant it was from shooting Yannis. Danny shrugged his shoulders and said, "Take your pick. Could be from that, or it might be from finding out that Yannis had orchestrated it all. Or it could be from the attack on her home when she had to hide Lily away and shoot an armed man who'd just killed my dog in front of her. Could also be from losing her husband and guards to a terrorist who sent a video showing his men kicking the hell out of their lifeless bodies. It could be any number of things that have happened to Tess over her lifetime or a culmination of all of them. All I'm saying is we shouldn't ignore this because no good could ever come of that."

Franco and Ivan agreed, suggesting I speak to George or Devina about some counselling, sooner rather than later. I promised I would do that as soon as the police had contacted me about Yannis—if the nightmares persisted. Everyone seemed surprised by the fact that I'd be willing to talk to someone. Kolya and Franco had tried to get me to speak to one of the counsellors after I'd been shot, but I'd always refused.

I'd never been comfortable talking about my feelings before. I thought it would make me vulnerable, but I knew I couldn't continue the way I had been. If the grief wasn't crippling enough, with everything else that had happened, I could feel myself...unravelling, if that makes sense.

And that feeling still remained.

With every new day, more threads came loose. My grief would tug them hard, and then a turbulent mix of anxiety, fear, and despair had them twisting around and around. Pretty soon, I knew the threads that made up the tapestry of my life would be scattered around in unmanageable, messy piles. I wondered just how long it would take until I unravelled completely, and there was nothing left of the old me.

Mark spent three days in the hospital before he was allowed to come back to the villa. He still looked pale and weak but was in good spirits, telling us how he'd been looked after by the most beautiful nurse he'd ever seen. He opted to stay in Sicily to recuperate, though I think that had as much to do with his devotion to Fia, his nurse, as his loyalty to us. I must admit, the healthcare provided by the hospital was second to none, and Franco's daily physio-therapy sessions meant he only needed to use his crutches and leg brace occasionally.

Kevin and Andy flew over from England the week before Christmas and brought our pre-lit Christmas tree and all our decorations. Having our other guards here calmed something inside me. They were my family, and I missed them so much. If they could have brought Dave, Nan, Jack, and Jean, that would have made it even better, but sadly, that wasn't going to happen.

Dave and Nan were still recuperating back home, and though I spoke to them regularly via video chat, it wasn't the same as being with them in person.

The distance creeping between Nan and me seemed greater than the miles that separated us. I couldn't put my finger on what had first created it, and despite our regular video calls, I felt it more keenly with each passing day. I asked Ivan if he thought it was because I'd killed Yannis. He said it wasn't that at all.

It horrified Nan and Jack to learn that Yannis was behind Kolya's death and the attack on our home, and they were glad that he was no longer a threat. But you know when you just know something? Well, I knew that Nan and Jack were disappointed in me somehow, and I wished more than anything that someone else had pulled the trigger on Yannis Markos.

Kevin decided to stay with us over Christmas, which Nate was thrilled about. They'd been apart so much because of their different duties, and I could tell it was taking a toll on their relationship.

Tanner and Carl had to share a room to accommodate Andy and Mark, then Yuri arrived, so we had a full house over the holiday period. With so much hustle and bustle, you'd have thought my mind would have been far too occupied for all the dark thoughts and nightmares, but that couldn't have been further from the truth.

With every smile or happy thought, I felt a sharp stab of guilt pierce my heart. Yet I knew I had to try, not just for Lily, but for everyone else in the villa who was putting on their own fake smile. It was all a show. Our own fictional version of a happy Christmas without Kolya, Jonesy, and Lucas. Charles Dickens, eat your heart out!

On my phone's playlist, I had "Someone You Love"—a song by Lewis Capaldi—playing on repeat. The words resonated deeply with me. It was as if he'd written them about my own personal feelings. I'd been tough and kept an emotional distance from everyone other than Jean and Sarah—until I met Kolya. Then I let my guard down, but his death pulled the rug on all the comfort and happiness I'd enjoyed since we'd come together. I'd got used to being someone Kolya loved. But now his love was lost to me forever, and I almost wish I'd never let down my guard at all, so I wouldn't feel the crippling pain of loss. But then I wouldn't have Lily or Ivan, Franco, and James, and everyone else who'd brought meaning to my life over the past six years.

I became slightly obsessed with looking through all the

photos I ever took of Kolya, right from when we first met until the last ones I had of him. It made me feel sick to my stomach to see those of him and Yannis together before the Graysons' Halloween party, so I went through all my photos and deleted every single one I had of Yannis Markos, and carefully cropped him out of the ones that contained Kolya. I'd arranged for the make-up artists to have Kolya and Yannis made up exactly the same, and apart from their eye colour and height, they'd looked uncannily alike. My soul demons. Maybe that's why my nightmares changed?

I'd been having the same one nightly—the one where it was Kolya, not Yannis, who was lying dead in the shallow pool of water. Sometimes I'd wake up yelling *no*, or I'd shout out something incoherent. But a few days before Christmas, the nightmares took on a more horrifying edge.

The new nightmares began with us at the airport in Kefalonia. Mark had been shot, and Ivan was carrying me up the steps of the aircraft. I could see Franco and James on the ground, and I knew that Yannis and his men would end up killing them if we didn't intervene. Just as I did on that fateful day, as soon as I was able, I took the shot. But instead of the bullet hitting Yannis in the throat, it hit him right in the centre of his chest, and suddenly everything about Yannis's appearance changed. Blood spread rapidly across his white shirt, obscuring the word SOUL as it did so. He looked up at me, his face now painted in the Halloween soul-demon skull design, yet his eyes were my husband's mesmerising ice blue. It might only have been a bad dream, but watching Kolya die right in front of me, knowing I'd fired the shot that ended his life, made every-thing in my world seem so much darker. Since Kolya's death, we'd all felt like we'd been living in the shadows, but now everywhere I turned felt as dark and cold as a mid-winter night.

I think I frightened everyone on the first night of that particular nightmare. My reaction to it lasted longer than everyone in the villa considered normal. I'd screamed bloody murder, threw up twice, and couldn't stop shaking for over an hour. I was so upset that I wouldn't go back to sleep that night. Franco volunteered to stay up on the sofa with me, and Ivan slept with Lily, so she wasn't on her own.

James blabbed to Roman about my nightmare episodes, and he, in turn, spoke to Signor Russo, who organised for a doctor to come and visit. I wasn't too happy about it, but I was polite with the doctor and must admit he was kind and listened without judgement to all my woes, though I couldn't tell him everything, of course. I just told him that my husband and his guards had been killed by terrorists and our family had also been under attack since, so obviously, this caused me to feel anxious and low, and the nightmares were a new and unwelcome symptom. Doctor Bianchi offered to prescribe me medication to lift my mood, but first, he wanted to run a few blood tests. He noticed how pale I was, which I must admit was more so than usual, and I had lost weight recently—though that was understandable since my appetite had diminished over the past few weeks. He gave me a form, and Nate, Carl, and Franco took me to the hospital to get the blood test done later that day.

Doctor Bianchi came back two days later with my test results. I was anaemic, so he gave me a prescription and said I might want to wait a couple of weeks to see if my low mood and anxiety improved when my iron levels built back up. He said my sleep pattern should improve, too, so I took him at his word and decided to ride it out. He prescribed me three nights' worth of sleeping pills, and though they helped me sleep, they also left me feeling like the walking dead the next day, and I had to leave Lily with Lainey and Danny while I took a nap mid-afternoon.

I woke up from that nap screaming and crying after having the dream where I'd shot Kolya again, so I wasn't too keen on taking any more of the sleeping pills.

When Franco wasn't doing his physical therapy, he was by my side, helping to keep Lily occupied and making sure I could cope with whatever life in Sicily threw at me. Franco's ability to speak Italian was an enormous help, especially with the extra guards that Signor Russo provided whenever we went anywhere.

Kolya's brother Yuri arrived five days before Christmas. Lily was thrilled to have him with us, especially since he brought a ridiculous amount of presents, all neatly wrapped and ready to place under our tree that we'd only just finished decorating. He and Ivan were as thick as thieves, and more than once I'd almost stumbled upon them discussing something they obviously didn't want me or anyone else to overhear. I don't know what they were talking about specifically, but I heard them mention Aleksei and the name Simeon quite a few times.

Ivan and Yuri stayed up drinking on his first night in Sicily, so they were still awake when I had my nightmare. Yuri had known about them, but he was shocked by how long it took for me to shake off the terrifying dream. The panic and fear gripped me hard and wouldn't let go, no matter where I was or who was holding me in their strong arms and telling me I was safe. It all felt so real to me, and I couldn't seem to make anyone understand that—apart from Danny, that is. Ivan looked helpless; James seemed angry about it, and Yuri… I didn't have a clue what Yuri thought because he was slightly drunk and whispering something in

Russian as he held me in his arms and rocked me like a baby. Franco glared daggers at Yuri and seemed kind of disappointed in me, which set me off crying and made everything ten times worse.

After that terrifying episode, Yuri decided someone should sleep beside me every night until the nightmares passed. So that's just what we did. Lily slept on her own in one bed, while Lainey, Ivan, and Yuri took turns at sleeping beside me, although in the end, it was mostly Yuri who stayed with me.

James had little patience with me since we'd arrived in Sicily, but to be honest, I wasn't the only one he'd been snapping at. He was glued to his laptop and phone all day —working on various KOLCAT UK and US contracts— but he was drinking heavily every night, and we were all worried about him.

The Runaway's Salvation: Chapter Two

TESS

Christmas Day was never going to be easy for any of us, but as adults we owed it to Lily to make it as magical as we could. She had the same idea about us, too, because although she smiled and tried to show excitement, it was clear to see she was missing her father more than anything. Kevin filmed Lily opening her presents so we could send the video to Roman. It was normally Kolya's job, so seeing someone else do it highlighted the fact that he wasn't here anymore.

James kept trying to get Lily to play with her new toys and have fun, but you could tell that her heart wasn't in it. She was also feeling quite tired, having woken up in the early hours with me screaming for her father—not something she could easily forget.

James had had his first drink at 10 a.m., and by the time we sat down to eat later that afternoon, he was becoming a little unsteady on his feet.

Lily and I sat between Yuri and Ivan, with Franco, Lainey, and Danny beside him, then Nate, Kevin, Tanner,

Carl, and James, followed by Mark and Andy. Yuri's regular guards from Moscow—who were staying in a cottage behind the tennis courts—were guarding the property until early evening, when Andy, Nate, Carl, and Tanner would take the next shift. I'd hoped that having everyone together like this would help Lily and I get through the day, but sadly, things didn't quite go according to plan.

With it being Christmas, Lainey had insisted we say a prayer before we ate, thanking God for the plentiful food and asking him to bless the ones we loved, both here and in heaven. Before she could finish, Lily folded her arms across her chest and said, "I'm not talking to God. I've fallen out with him because he takes daddies to heaven and doesn't bring them back at Christmas, even when you've been behaving and doing everything Mummy says."

"Good on you, kiddo," James slurred. "You shouldn't have to pray to someone so cruel. He takes mothers, too, you know. He took mine and Ivan's. And Daddy and Uncle Yuri's. So make the most of your mummy while you can, Lily, 'cause no doubt he'll take her, too. He won't allow our family to be happy. We're all fucking cursed."

James knocked back the last dregs of whisky from the bottom of his glass, ignoring the angry yelling from everyone around the table. Lily's eyes filled with tears, and her bottom lip wobbled as I gathered her in my arms, assuring her I wasn't going anywhere, and that James was only saying mean things and swearing because he was drunk. But Lily knew that James's mum had died when he was a child, and that Kolya's mother had passed away when he was sixteen, so she knew there was some truth to the hurtful things her brother had said.

Yuri rose from his spot at the head of the table and walked around to where James sat. Without saying a word, he fisted his hands in the front of James's shirt and hauled him up out of the chair.

"Nephew or not, if you weren't so drunk, I'd make you pay in blood and bruises for the hurt you caused your sister and her mother just now. Do you hear me?"

"Loud and fucking clear," James said as he tried to shake off Yuri's grip. "Now let me go so I can eat my Christmas dinner. I wouldn't want to miss the only decent thing about today."

"You won't be eating in here, James, unless you want to eat off the floor like a dog," Yuri replied.

He glanced back at Ivan, who had his arms around me and Lily. "Take his plate into the sitting room, along with a glass of water. I won't let him continue to upset Lily and Tess, nor anyone else around this table."

I shook my head. "No, we should all be together. He didn't mean it, Yuri. He's had too much to drink, and today has been a tough one for all of us." I couldn't keep the hurt and anger out of my voice, despite my placatory words.

James's bloodshot eyes fixed on mine, and I thought he might carry on throwing hurtful words our way. Then his expression changed to one of *"What the fuck just happened here?"* and he staggered back, away from the table and Yuri.

"I'm sorry, Lily, Tess. I don't know what...I'm just so sorry. I can't do this. Not today. I can't... I have to go."

James turned to leave but stumbled into the doorframe. Yuri was there to catch him, and he was joined by Nate a few seconds later. Both men hooked his arms over their shoulders and escorted James out of the kitchen.

I half expected Tanner and Carl to follow, but when I looked their way as if to question them, Carl shook his head and said, "He won't listen to us, Tess. We've tried talking to him about his drinking, and the reasons why he feels the need to do it, but he just won't listen. He even threatened to fire Tanner yesterday when he suggested he speak to George about it."

"I don't care what he has going on in his head; it doesn't excuse what he just said to Lily." Franco slammed his cutlery down and got up from his chair steadily. He seemed to struggle with his leg a little, but he was trying not to use his crutches. After allowing himself a few seconds to rest, he made his way over to me and Lily.

Ivan let his arms fall away from us and sighed heavily. "I agree that what James did is unforgivable, but he's hurting, Franco. It's not just from grief and loss; he's harbouring a lot of guilt, too. Every time he sees you struggle to get around, the guilt tears through him. He knows you only got that wound through protecting him. And you, Tess"—Ivan cupped my cheek and tilted my face until his eyes held mine —"what you had to do that day and the consequences you are troubled by because of it—the nightmares especially— he cannot bear to see you suffer so."

"He shouldn't feel bad for me," I insisted. "I'll be okay. I just need a little time, that's all. I think everyone does, including James. I'll talk to him later when he's sobered up. In the meantime, we have all this lovely food waiting for us. Let's not waste it."

Though everyone ate their food on what was normally such a special day, there was little to celebrate around the table. The meal was just as tasty as it always was, yet there were few who cleared their plates, and no one had seconds of anything, not even Ivan—a sharp contrast to all our previous Christmas dinners, where everyone ate Nan's festive feast until they could barely move.

Ivan was quite a heavy sleeper, especially after drinking vodka with Yuri.

And he snored.

Loudly!

I didn't have a nightmare the first night he stayed with me because he snored so loud that I couldn't even sleep. It wouldn't have been so bad if he wasn't a snuggler. He pulled me into his side so we lay like spoons, then he flopped over onto his back with his arm still underneath me and snored out a weird sort of sawing sound. Whenever I tried moving away from him, he pulled me back and carried on snoring. Ivan wasn't too bad if he only had a couple of drinks, but any more than that, and it was pointless trying to sleep beside him at all. Lily woke up twice and asked if someone was landing the helicopter when Ivan slept in our room.

Lainey slept beside me for a night, but I didn't want to keep her away from Danny's bed over the Christmas holidays. I felt bad enough that she'd cancelled her trip back home to see her family. Franco also volunteered to sleep beside me, but getting up and down the stairs wasn't easy for him, and I worried that I'd accidentally knock his wound if I was tossing and turning during the night.

So Yuri spent the rest of his time in Sicily sleeping beside me, and true to his word, he woke me the first moment he thought I was having what he called a night terror.

Yuri used to wake up earlier than Lily and me, but on the morning after our dreadful Christmas Day, I beat him to it. For just a few sleepy, blissful moments, I thought the man beside me was my husband. The resemblance was so striking in the early morning light that it took my breath away.

The Barinov men looked so alike. All were extremely handsome, with strong cheekbones and masculine jawlines and the same brown hair, although Yuri's was greyer at the sides than Kolya's and Aleksei's had been. And they'd all inherited Roman's piercing, ice-blue eyes. As had James and Lily.

Yuri opened his eyes and caught me looking at him. Perhaps I should have looked away and apologised for staring, but right at that moment, I didn't have it in me. It was as if speaking the words would break the spell, and for just a few minutes longer, I wanted to hang on to the pretence that this was the Barinov who'd told me he loved me every single day since we'd first made love.

Yuri must have realised what was going through my mind because he reached over to my side of the bed and pulled me up against him, so we lay chest to chest. Then he wrapped his arms around me and held me close, stroking his hand down my back and placing soft kisses on my forehead. He was about the same height and build as Kolya, and it felt good to cuddle up to him like that. Yuri always slept shirtless, with long flannel or jersey pyjama bottoms, and the warmth from his bare chest felt comforting. We only stayed that way for a matter of minutes, but for the first time in what seemed like forever, my mind knew a little peace.

Too bad that couldn't last.

Grab your copy...
vinci-books.com/therunawayssalvation